FRENCH CREEK

French Creek

Peter Rennebohm

NORTH STAR PRESS OF ST. CLOUD, INC.

This is a work of fiction. Names, characters, places, and incidents are the product of the author's imagination or are used fictitiously. Any resemblance to persons living or dead or actual events is purely coincidental.

Cover art by: Mark Evans

ISBN: 0-87839-211-4

First Edition
October 2004

Printed in Canada by Friesens

Published by
North Star Press of St. Cloud, Inc.
P.O. Box 451
St. Cloud, Minnesota 56302
nspress@cloudnet.com

Dedicated To

PATRICIA ANN HAWLEY RENNEBOHM

My mother introduced me to the wonders of books at an early age. A bibliophile her entire life, particularly partial to mysteries and adventure stories, she was an edacious reader. I am certain she inherited her love of books from her mother, my grandmother—Marguerite Hawley.

As a young boy, I was fortunate enough to be able to accompany her on weekly trips to a branch of the Minneapolis Public Library, where I'd head for a small area set aside for animal/adventure books. Alone, sitting on a squeaky planked floor amid zillions of dust mites buzzing in shafts of sunlight, I inhaled that distinctive, musty-dusty, libraryish smell, and excitedly puzzled over my weekly allotment of stories.

Television was in its infancy, which was probably a blessing. Thanks to my mother, I relied on an active imagination fed by authors whose words were magical. In time, I developed an insatiable desire to read anything and everything I could, including the wonderful stories of Beverly Cleary, Jack London, and Marjorie Kinnan Rawlings.

Mother loved to read, and I can only hope that if she were alive today, she'd enjoy this story. She opened the door for me, and I'll be eternally grateful for her influence.

ACKNOWLEDGEMENTS

The creative process that goes into the writing of a book is not something accomplished without help and critical comment from a good many friends, relatives, and professional associates. I'd like to take this opportunity to mention a few who have been extremely supportive and encouraging, and thank them for their help.

My wife, Shari, who never let me get too far ahead of myself. Her early post-it notes scattered within the rough early drafts were harsh, but necessary and true. In typical fashion, I chose to ignore her comments for as long as possible, until it became patently clear that in almost every instance—she was right.

I have been fortunate to have a few people close to me that I trust—that I respect as readers and critics; these include my "first" readers, Tom Carlson, my sister Dale Mayer, and Becky Planer. They, along with my publisher, Corinne Dwyer of North Star Press, immediately responded with enthusiasm over this story, and encouraged me to seek publication. Many thanks to all four for their shared excitement.

Alice Peppler, my first copy editor, had the misfortune to see the very rough first draft in 2002 but said it, "had promise—keep working on it." I did, for over two years.

And to all the others who have supported me during this entire writing process, including daughters Emily and Jennifer, good friend and fellow-novelist Michael O'Rourke, John and Nancy Peyton, Gene Phelps, Harvey Stanbrough, Jimmy Olsen, John Rosengren, and Tony Bouza—thank all of you from the bottom of my heart.

Peter Rennebohm

"No man is an island, unto himself.
Each is a part of the main, a piece of the whole."
—John Donne

❖ 1 ❖

French Creek, Minnesota
February 11, 1993

JOHN WAS DRIVING TOO FAST. He knew it and didn't care. Angry that he had wasted so much time, he slammed the Explorer into four-wheel drive and gunned the engine. The front tires fought for traction, kicking up snow and loose gravel.

This is insane! No other cars, no houses, no signs—nothing! The steep hills and endless curves slowed his progress. *I've been driving in circles on these goat paths forever. Damn place doesn't exist . . . except in someone's imagination. I should give up and go home.* He decided he'd drive over one more hill. If he didn't find what he was looking for, he'd call it a day.

John noticed that all the fields he passed were barren—overgrown with noxious weeds, lying fallow and neglected. They all looked like they hadn't been worked in years. The few farms he passed appeared to be abandoned. He gripped the steering wheel with both hands. Anger and frustration grew with each passing mile. He glanced down at his knuckles and noticed they were white. Blue veins stood out in stark contrast, winding across and over his pale skin. *Looks like the roads I've been driving*, John observed. *What the hell am I doing? If I wind up stuck in a ditch I'm really going to be pissed!*

He crested one last hill and slammed on the brakes. The Explorer skidded down the hill and fishtailed from one side of the road to the other. John fought to retain control of the truck. Finally it slid to a stop. He sighed gratefully, then stared through the cold, frost-cracked windshield. A rush of air passed his lips. Spread out in front of him, over acres and acres of rolling countryside, was the largest junkyard he had ever seen.

Endless rows of rust-brown, broken-down cars and trucks of every possible size and description receded into the distance as far as he could see. John's previously dour mood brightened. With a sense of relief he realized that the object of his endless search actually existed. The French Creek Salvage Yard. John's initial impression was one of wonder at the symmetry of the broken down wrecks as they were laid out in the yard. In perfect order, the rusted hulks were positioned in neat rows that seemed to John like unending stretches of over-ripe corn. Instead of stalks of corn, each row was lined with dead, decayed chunks of iron.

He sat in the truck and stared in awe. Except for the junkyard, the countryside was beautiful. *This appears to all be fertile farm land around here that hasn't been worked in years. I don't get it. With all the picturesque hills and valleys, there should be thriving, productive farms around here. Maybe the ground's contaminated somehow.* John wondered about these things but not for long. He had little daylight left to complete his mission. He stepped on the gas and continued down the hill.

In a moment, John drove through the main gate of the salvage yard and stopped in front of the office, just beneath a small, weathered sign dimly lit by a single bulb over the door. FRENCH CREEK SALVAGE YARD. It was barely legible. The building was wood

2

sided and badly in need of a coat of paint. One other truck was parked in front of the building. A second sign read, NOTICE! VISITORS NOT ALLOWED ON PREMISES WITHOUT STOPPING IN OFFICE FIRST.

John now understood why he'd had so much trouble finding the place. With no signs alongside any of the roads he traveled, it seemed the owners had little interest in doing business with the general public. That was okay, he reasoned. Some businesses did great just on word of mouth. But he had just wasted two hours looking for the place, and he had no idea if they had what he wanted. Still, with that many acres of old vehicles, his chances looked pretty good. He glanced at his watch—3:45 P.M. He thought he still had plenty of time. His business shouldn't take more than thirty minutes, and he'd be headed back home.

It was a typical early February day in Minnesota, cold and cloudy. The wind blew from the northwest with just a hint of snow in the air—just another in a long line of dreary, dismal days that seemed endless to the residents of the gopher state. John stepped from his truck and pulled on his green down jacket. The lack of sunshine had a way of depressing everyone, and John was feeling the effects.

He had spent the day making sales calls on customers he visited only infrequently. The drive west was simply an excuse to locate what he had been told was the largest junkyard in the county. John was on a mission: to find a particular vintage steering wheel for an old pickup he had been restoring all winter. Already feeling guilty for having wasted so much time, John was anxious to find the wheel and head back to Minneapolis. *Hell, I could easily have fixed the old one with a roll of tape and some epoxy.* He stepped from his truck and zipped up the jacket.

He automatically locked the truck. Glancing around, he noticed that the wind had eased somewhat, and the sky looked like it might be clearing a bit in the west. John approached the door to the office, but hesitated before entering. For some unknown reason, he had a sudden urge to forget the steering wheel, turn around, and go home. Standing on the worn, wooden stoop somehow created a strong feeling of intruding where he didn't belong. He was not a welcome visitor, but didn't know why.

He opened the door and stepped inside. A blast of heat carried the strong odor of mold or decay and caused him to wrinkle his nose. One quick glance revealed a filthy, dusty interior. Many years' build up of accumulated oil and grease covered the wooden floor. The walls held signs warning visitors not to touch or remove anything and not to wander away from the main office.

Two windows bracketed the door and afforded a dusty, distorted view of the small parking lot and the road beyond. The main room, quite large in its original form, was made smaller by thousands of old car parts stacked floor to ceiling. Little free space left remained in the room. An adjacent hallway held more of the same grease-laden clutter.

John approached what he guessed was the parts counter. Sitting on a stool behind the counter, reading a paper, was a man who looked about fifty years old. Stringy gray-black hair protruded from under a green John Deere cap. The name "Ray" was printed over the pocket on the front of his greasy blue work shirt, and a red, crescent-shaped scar curled along his right cheek. The man hadn't shaved in some days and looked as dirty as the dark, oily floor.

"Hi, how ya doing?" John asked.

Ray glanced up and straightened on the stool. He had the sort of puffed-up look many smaller-statured men acquired to look bigger than they were. "You lost, or lookin' for something particular?"

John's first reaction was one of distaste. He didn't like the guy—something in his tone or maybe the look in the coal black eyes barely visible beneath his cap. "Actually, I'm looking for a steering wheel for a 1970 Ford F150. I heard that if anyone would have it, you might."

Ray smiled a sly, slippery grin that seemed to slowly spread like thick oil across the lower half of his face. He exposed a mouth full of yellowed, nicotine-stained teeth. "Who told you that?"

John first felt, then smelled the man's breath as it drifted across the counter. A combination of onions and garlic assaulted him. He took a step back. "Some guy back in Minneapolis heard about this place."

The man sat back, and John moved again to the counter. Without thinking, he bent and rested one arm on the counter, then looked down and promptly retracted his arm. The counter was caked with grime. He couldn't begin to tell what color it had been when new.

"Hey, Dale, come here a minute!" Ray shouted in the direction of a back room, then turned back to John. "You care what kind of shape it's in?"

"Well, the one I've got is cracked, so I want one that isn't."

Another man entered the room. He resembled Ray but looked a bit younger and not quite as alert. Dale was just as grubby looking, though, and as he came closer, John noticed the man had a cocked left eye—it looked off to one side for a bit, and then back over John's shoulder, like it had a mind of its own. Much like one of Minnesota's most popular fish—the walleye. *Quite the pair, these two*, thought John. *One's got a wicked scar, the other a wandering eye. Ugly on ugly.* There was a difference though. Dale looked a little slow; Ray just looked owlly.

Dale wore an identical dirty blue shirt to Ray's but with his own name printed on the front.

"Yeah, whatcha' need, Ray?" Dale said.

"We got any steering wheels for a '70 Ford pickup that ain't cracked?"

"Don't think so, but I'll go look." Dale left the room.

"Why do you need it?" Ray asked, directing his attention back to John.

"I've been fixing up an old truck this winter, and the steering wheel's broken. I wanted to find another one. I've been looking all over the Twin Cities, but no one has one."

Ray appeared to have lost interest in the conversation. He glanced over John's shoulder, fixing his gaze on the front window. "That a new Explorer?"

John was startled by the sudden change of subject. He turned to look out the window, but, from where he stood, he couldn't see his truck at all. Apparently Ray could. John said, "Yeah. Just picked it up last week. How'd you know I was driving an Explorer?"

Ray paused before responding. "Oh, uh . . . I saw you coming down the hill. Pretty spendy, ain't it?"

"I guess, but I travel quite a bit, and the four-wheel drive sure comes in handy this time of year."

At that moment, Dale returned to the office. "Nope, don't got any that ain't cracked."

"What about out in the yard?" Ray asked.

"Yeah, probably. Be back quite a ways over the hill though."

"Guess you'll have to go out and pull one yourself," Ray said to John.

John hesitated before responding. He was disappointed. He thought he'd be done by now on his way home. He hadn't planned on having to wait while they located a wheel, and he certainly hadn't expected to have to pull it himself. Junkyards usually didn't work that way. He glanced at his watch. His frustration returned, and he felt his face redden—now more determined that he had come too far to give up.

John wasn't fixated on old trucks—wasn't a gear head by any stretch. On the contrary, as with most things in his life, John had purchased the old truck on impulse. He had always wanted to own an old pickup, so he bought one. His knowledge under the hood had its limitations, so he concentrated on cosmetic changes—

painting, seat covers, trim, and the interior of the cab. John enjoyed a challenge, and working on the old truck helped fill his weekends. The broken steering wheel represented the last piece he needed to complete the project. "If I find one, how do I take it off?"

"Thought you said you pulled one off already," Ray said.

John grew more irritable. He was embarrassed by his lack of mechanical skills but was not about to admit to this shortcoming. "No, never got around to it. It's still on my truck. Can I borrow whatever tools I need?"

Ray pointed to one of the many signs adorning the shop and read out loud. "We don't lend tools. We rent them."

"How much?" John asked.

"Ten bucks an hour for a box-end wrench, plus deposit."

John thought this excessive. "What am I removing, anyway?"

Ray smiled, his rotten mouth a gaping hole. "You don't know much about trucks, do ya? Take off the big nut holding it to the steering column."

John felt his face redden, but decided to ask, "Don't you have anyone here who can go with me?"

"If I send Dale, I got to charge you for his time—forty bucks an hour. It's up to you." He turned back to his newspaper.

Without selling a single part, John felt Ray was out to fleece his customers by charging exorbitant rates for tool rentals. Word of mouth probably didn't bring in much business. He hated to give in to the man, but he had already spent so much of his day simply getting to where he now was that he hated to give up. Once the steering wheel was secured, his work on the truck would be completed, the project finished. He wanted that satisfaction.

He felt fairly confident that he could deal with a box-end wrench. With a new resolve and commitment to finish what he set out to do, he made up his mind. "I'll just go out to my truck and get some boots and gloves. I'll be right back." He stepped toward the door, then stopped and looked back. "How much of a deposit do you need, anyway?"

Ray pointed to another sign: $100.00 DEPOSIT ON ALL RENTALS.

"A hundred dollars for a wrench? Are you kidding?"

"Nope. Take it or leave it."

"I don't have a hundred dollars," John said.

Ray's upper lip curled. "We take any major credit card."

John marched back to the counter and withdrew his wallet. He pulled out his American Express card and tossed it on the counter.

Ray picked it up and flipped it back. "Don't want that one," he said.

"Why not?"

"They charge too much."

John picked up the unwanted plastic and pulled out his VISA card. With intentional sarcasm he asked, "I trust this one will do?"

Ray took it and put it beneath the counter. "That'll work just fine."

I should make him run the card and return it. Too upset to pursue the conversation any further, however, he strode across the greasy floor, opened the door, and stepped outside into the cold air. As he walked back to his truck, he glanced over his shoulder at the setting sun and tried to gauge how much time he had before darkness set in. He didn't have much time left and knew he must hurry.

John unlocked the Explorer and wondered about Ray's attitude. As a salesman, John always did his utmost to convey an eager, willing spirit with his customers. It wasn't always easy. *I've never been that rude to anyone!* For the second time that cold day, John considered giving up and going home.

Instead, he slipped on his nylon over-pants along with his boots, tugged a stocking cap over his ears, and put on a warm pair of leather gloves. Dressed for the bone-chilling cold, he again locked his truck. He'd learned long ago to carry emergency supplies, just in case he got caught out in one of the frequent, winter storms that slashed through the state or he ran out of gas. In addition to a blanket, shovel, candy bars and two candles, he always carried warm boots, a down jacket, stocking cap, gloves, and a pair of nylon over-pants.

John noticed three additional signs attached to the wire fence. One Notice warned: Gates are locked at 6:00 p.m. Sharp! Another said, No Trespassing. And a third read, Beware of Dogs! All three were much larger than the small, poorly lit sign over the door. Suddenly, out of the stillness, as if on cue, John heard dogs barking in the distance. He shuddered at the thought of running into them. He went back inside.

Ray was nowhere to be seen. "Hello?" John called.

He heard a voice in the back room, then the sound of a phone being replaced in its cradle. Ray came out front, and John asked, "Say, I'm not going to run into those dogs am I?"

Ray curled his upper lip. "No, you'll be okay. We don't let them out until we lock up for the night."

"Well, that's encouraging," John replied. "Now, how and where do I find a 1970 Ford?"

"Thought you said you owned one."

"I do."

"Well, it'll look just like yours!" Ray said.

His smug demeanor was not lost on John, who by this time was speechless. Wanting to leave immediately but knowing he would not, instead, John smiled and in as humble a tone as he could muster, asked, "Well, can you give me a general idea where to look?"

Apparently Ray had had his fun for the day. He responded slowly and carefully, as if speaking to a small child. "They'll be back over the hill. South of the office. Some distance away, I'd say.

If you can open the driver's door, look for the sticker on the inside. It'll have the VIN number and model year on it."

"Okay, thanks." John felt confident he could locate the VIN numbers.

Ray handed John the wrench, and in a voice more strident than necessary, said, "Stay out of the areas marked Keep Out!"

John just asked, "Which way?"

Ray pointed at a door behind him. "Through there."

John followed the gesture, and as he walked toward the door, he noticed another sign: NO SMOKING OUTSIDE! John almost laughed as he considered what possible hazards could befall him having a smoke in the middle of a seventy-year old junkyard in February in deep snow. He left the office. The door slammed shut behind him, and the sound echoed over and through the thousands of derelict vehicles spread before him.

John trudged up the snow-covered road. Before long he had to zigzag between the many rows. He wanted to cover as much ground as possible in the brief time available. He watched for any evidence that the wrecks were the same model year of his truck.

With the strangely adversarial shop behind him, John considered how he came to be in the junkyard. He had heard about the French Creek Salvage yard a few days earlier and decided to check it out. Unable to locate his steering wheel at any of the Twin Cities' yards he visited, he cancelled all his appointments in town for the day. It had been some time since he'd last visited customers west of Minneapolis, and in his mind, that gave him the excuse he needed to search for the elusive steering wheel. He'd spent the weekend putting the final touches on the old Ford, and all that remained was to replace the wheel.

When he first had brought the truck home the previous October and parked it in the garage, his wife questioned the wisdom of his purchase. "What do you know about fixing up an old truck?" Debbie had inquired pointedly.

PETER RENNEBOHM

"Not much, but I can certainly take care of all the superficial stuff," he replied, "and learning *how* to fix it up is the fun part."

Debbie, of course, had felt that there were other, more important, items needed in their home—like a new washing machine. But once she witnessed John's excitement and pleasure in his new "hobby," she didn't argue further. By then she was all too familiar with John's sudden impulses and how quickly his projects became passions. She couldn't resist the opportunity to remind him of the washer, however. "How much did it cost?"

John hesitated, reluctant to admit that he spent much for the old clunk, but he hated lying to Debbie and finally admitted the truth. "$700.00."

"What? John! We need that new washer!" Debbie said.

"I know, but once I fix the truck up, it'll be worth a thousand bucks."

She eyed him critically. "Yeah, but will you sell it then?"

"I don't know. Probably," he said, fibbing just a little. He knew Debbie wasn't buying his story, but at least his answer kept her at bay for a while.

John smiled at the memory of that brief conversation. *Debbie knows me too well.* At least he had found a good deal on a washing machine after that conversation. He knew that meant he could keep the truck for a while.

As he climbed through the drifts between the wrecks, the task before him looked impossible. He was in a graveyard, except the bodies scattered around him were above ground. The scene reminded him of a crack that Mac, his father-in-law, had made the previous summer. They were playing golf at the time when another, older gentleman had inquired, "How ya doing, Mac?"

Mac had replied, "Pretty damn good! At least I'm still on the right side of the grass!"

John chuckled and continued on. Finally he began to feel better about his decision to proceed. The memory of Ray's

11

unfriendly demeanor slowly faded as he slogged through the deep snow.

He didn't know which way to go. It would soon be dark, and it was getting colder. His mood began to change, as if drawn down by the winter-setting sun and the deepening cold. The dogs continued barking somewhere off to the west. He stopped to get his bearings. The office was still behind him, now a long distance away. John stood and pivoted on top of a small hill. Hundreds and hundreds of ancient, broken down, rusted cars and trucks of every possible vintage presented a maze that seemed impossible to penetrate. Finding the right truck among the thousands of wrecks now seemed hopeless.

There were rows of delivery trucks with faded writing on the sides: Anson's Dairy, Slim's Tree Service, AA1 Towing, Mike's Appliance, and many more. The quantity of vehicles was staggering, and all had been parked according to their age.

Something tugged at his mind. He stopped and looked around.

He took one step and paused. Directly in front on him sat the Anson's Dairy truck. The hair on his arms stood up. His heart skipped, and then resumed its normal rhythm. *Weird!* When he couldn't think of any good reason for his reaction, he kept going, anxious to be finished with his self-appointed task.

He soon discovered the junkyard placement system. Close by the office rested the more recent models, and for some strange reason, the farther away John walked, the older the vehicles got. *It should be just the opposite,* he told himself. The old ones parked first—close to the office, and the newer ones farther afield as they came in. He couldn't envision that they rotated them each year as parts were removed. The newer vehicles obviously had more value, but it seemed to John like a waste of effort to keep moving everything around all the time. And if they didn't do that to the massive junkyard, why this arrangement?

Many of the trucks were stacked on top of each other, as if the lower one had been stripped of anything useful and another put in its place—literally. Because of the drifted snow John struggled to find the make and model he needed. He didn't have his reading glasses, and with the failing light, discerning the numbers and dates on the plates proved difficult. He noticed a metal Ford emblem on one of the trucks that appeared to be in good shape and examined it more closely. He pulled out his pocketknife, removed the emblem, and stuck it in his back pocket. The oval metal emblem would be perfect for the hood of his truck. *I won't tell old Ray about this little item . . . he owes me something for all this work and for being such a smartass.*

As he advanced deeper into the rows of vintage trucks, he noted that they all started to look similar. The original paint had faded, and they shared a common brownish, rust tone—almost black. Oxidation etched the metal over countless years and left each vehicle with a generic look of aged sameness.

Once again, John noted with interest the printing on each—Cenex Farm on one, Mill City Flowers on another. He wondered about the history of each. Many had addresses that indicated they originally came from the Twin Cities. He recognized the names of local companies that had gone out of business years ago. He wondered how they all wound up in this place. Trucks from the Cities should have been dumped in junkyards closer to town. He pulled the collar of his coat tighter to his neck and slapped his hands together for warmth. John decided that there was a lot about the junk business he knew little about and continued searching.

He grew frustrated and impatient to be on his way. *I probably wouldn't know another 1970 Ford F100 if it jumped up and bit me in the ass! Even if I can pry a door open, it's almost too dark to read the VIN. I'm freezing my balls off, digging through snow drifts in a creepy field full of dead cars, looking for a goddamned*

13

steering wheel! To hell with the signs! I'm having a smoke! John lit up, inhaled deeply, and immediately felt better. He continued his journey over the hill, blowing smoke from his nostrils as he walked.

As he came up over the first rise, John realized that he was nowhere near the area of older pick-ups. He would have to walk another two hundred yards to reach the correct model years. Off to one side, he could hear a machine of some sort traveling back and forth between the rows. Before long, a huge forklift truck approached from the west. It carried a rusted car. John noticed that the driver looked like Dale, the weird guy with the stray eyeball.

As he passed in front of John, Dale didn't even turn his head. John waved as Dale passed, but the gesture was not returned. If the man saw him waving he ignored it; that or he had his bad eye pointed the wrong way. Dale was clearly on a mission of some importance as he continued on his way.

Finally, after what seemed like an eternity, John found a row of trucks that seemed to be the same vintage as his '70 Ford. Getting close to any of them proved daunting, however, for the snow had drifted up and around each of the hulks. John had to wade through crotch-deep snow, and after checking out four or five, he finally came upon one that looked familiar. His spirits rose and his breathing sped up.

He peered through a broken window and noticed the truck had the same wheel as his—too much the same. It too was cracked. He moved on to the next one—cracked again. He was beginning to wonder at the futility of it all. Did every 1970 Ford truck left in the world have a broken steering wheel? Suddenly he spotted a black truck a short distance away that looked to be in pretty decent shape. He waded to it.

I'll be damned! The steering wheel is in one piece! There were no visible cracks around the rim. It was his for the taking. But first he had to get inside the truck, remove the nut, and pull the wheel. John tested the door—not surprisingly, it was jammed, and the window was rolled up. He tried the passenger side. It wouldn't open either. After looking around to make sure Dale couldn't hear or see what he was about to do, he broke the glass with the wrench. He looked around again as the glass shattered and settled on the torn seat fabric inside. Dale was nowhere to be seen, and he had not seen anyone else on the property since he'd left the office.

He was nervous and jumpy and realized that his hands were trembling, and it had little to do with the cold. He took a deep breath and started wiggling through the broken window. Even though he had put on the warmer clothing, he was still cold.

He was having trouble getting through the window—his bulky coat kept getting stuck. As he pulled his left leg through, he felt a tug—then a tearing sound. "Damn! There go my pants!"

John finally pulled himself through and sat behind the wheel. He was breathing hard. The worn fabric of the seat cushion was cold and barely held back the springs beneath. He took the wrench from his coat pocket, placed it on the nut, and turned the tool. He assumed a left-hand thread was probable, and pulled at the wrench as hard as he could. The nut didn't budge. He decided it must be a reverse thread, so he put his feet on the dashboard for leverage and tried turning the wrench in the opposite direction. The nut finally started to move—just a bit. *What do you know? This might work out after all.* But there was no further movement.

John looked closely at the rusted nut. In the fading light, he saw a cotter pin, which he knew had to be driven out. It would require a pair of pliers, or a screwdriver, or a hammer, or all of the above. *Crap! Now I have to go all the way back to the office.* He looked around for Dale, hoping that the strange man would now reappear—with a much-needed set of tools in his tractor.

John could easily have given up at this point and knew he probably should have but the same stubborn streak that ruled his entire life wouldn't allow him to quit. He crawled out the window and started back down the road. The wind had stopped blowing entirely, and the sun had begun to set. His pace quickened as he strode through the gloaming. The silence of the junkyard, broken only by the occasional barking of dogs in the distance, alarmed him. His own ragged breath echoed in his ears. He felt that time was slipping away. He had come so far, but the fading light might bring an end to his quest after all.

John glanced over his shoulder, feeling as if someone else was close by watching him, but he saw no one. More ghosts, he thought, as he passed the large Anson's Dairy truck. As he drew abreast of the old, high, cube van, John swore he heard someone whispering and swiveled to look. Nothing.

Suddenly, a snow devil popped up fifty yards from John and spun toward him. Caught in the swirl of snow, he closed his eyes and ducked. The miniature whirlwind passed by and skipped over to the side of the dairy truck where it lingered briefly—just long enough to lift a large, yellowed piece of aged paint from the side wall. The paint scrap fell away—carried aloft by the retreating wind, revealing additional lettering. But John had turned away from the truck.

He kept moving, his nerves on edge. He found himself trembling and knew it wasn't entirely due to the cold evening air settling over the snowy fields. He continued toward the office, bothered by the feeling that someone watched his every move.

John reached the office and opened the door. The heat struck him once again—a suffocating closeness infused with rank odors. Rather than warming him in his winter gear, the sudden change only reinforced how cold it was outside. His face burned.

Ray was still behind the counter reading his paper. John said, "Looks like I need some more tools."

Ray folded the paper and glowered. "Now what?"

"Probably a screw driver and a pair of pliers."

16

"I'll have to charge you extra, you know."

"Yeah, well, whatever. I found the wheel and should have it off in a couple of minutes." He couldn't resist one last sarcastic comment. "You don't need another credit card, do you?"

The snide comment was never acknowledged, except by a slight tightening of Ray's hard eyes. He handed over the tools. "We close the gates at 6:00 P.M. Make sure you're back by then."

It was 5:30. The search had taken a lot longer than he thought. John thought he might still have enough time to return to the truck, remove the offending nut, and bring the steering wheel back to the office. He left with the additional tools and caught a glimpse of Dale coming back toward the office—the forklift was empty.

Must be ready to close up. I'd better hurry. After a ten-minute walk back up the hill, John reached the black truck and crawled inside, being careful not to snag his clothing again.

There was very little light now, and John could barely see the cotter key. He pulled out the pliers and bent the key legs straight. Next, he took the screwdriver and tried to pound the key back through the hole in the nut. He almost had the pin out when he heard a motor. He raised his head and watched Dale drive over the hill on the forklift to the west. He could just barely see the machine in the darkening distance as it passed over the crest. Something strangely familiar captured his gaze. Just as the last rays of daylight touched the forklift, John noticed that the vehicle Dale was carrying was dark blue, but gave no further thought to its significance.

John turned back to the job at hand, and finally the cotter key popped free. Now the nut was unimpeded, and in a matter of seconds he had unscrewed it and began tugging at the steering wheel. With some effort, he managed to free it. He climbed back out through the window and took off in the direction of the office, steering wheel and rented tools tucked under one arm.

It was pitch dark on his repeat trip. The howling of the dogs became louder and more plaintive. John shivered as he thought of how unpleasant it would be to confront any of the four-legged protectors of the property. He lit another cigarette to calm his nerves, picked up his pace, and glanced at his watch. It was 5:45 P.M. He hurried down the hill.

As he approached the office building, the lights suddenly went out. A door closed. *What the hell?*

A truck engine came to life with a loud roar. John recalled seeing one other truck parked out front when he arrived. Must have been Ray's. He couldn't see around the building but heard the driver gun the engine as the truck pulled away. It passed into view beyond the buildings, and John could see that it was the same truck he had seen earlier. *What's going on? They must know I'm still here!* He retraced his steps to the rear door.

Earlier misgivings and trepidation of the past hour were now replaced by a real concern. He reached the office door, and tried turning the knob. The door was locked. He pounded on it, expecting someone to respond. Nothing. He didn't hear anything other than the incessant barking of the dogs.

He ran around the side of the building again until he reached a fence. It was at least twelve feet high, topped with two strands of concertina wire, and for the first time John noticed the sign warning that the fence was electric. John had dealt with concertina in the service and knew full well what it could do to a man's skin. He probably could have managed barbed wire, but he wasn't going to mess with an electric fence. "Now what the hell do I do?" His frosty breath blew away without answer.

The barking seemed louder. John shouted, "Hey! Is anybody there? I'm locked in!" Silence—except for the barking of the dogs He shouted again, "Hey! Let me out of here!"

John peered around the corner of the office through the fence, looking for his truck, but he couldn't see it. It was not in

18

sight. His mind raced. Nothing made any sense. Then he remembered Dale—the forklift and the flash of dark blue the last time he passed him. *Was that my Explorer that Dale was hauling away?* John was trembling now, and it was all he could do to keep his teeth from chattering.

It was a bad dream. What were these guys up to? Maybe it was their idea of a joke. Lock the guy in for a few minutes, scare the shit out of him, and then have a few yuks with the boys down at the local 3.2 joint. Bunch of goddamned, stupid rednecks!

"You bastards! I'm locked in!" He willed himself to remain calm. John felt there was a logical explanation for what was happening. He waited.

He stood still, hoping, expecting to hear the sound of his Explorer at any moment. He felt as if he had dropped into some bizarre void. What if Ray and Dale didn't return? How long before someone found him? He thought back to how he came to be in the salvage yard in the first place.

His last stop that afternoon had been at Jerry's Supply in Annandale. The owner, Jerry Stubblefield, had given him directions, and John said that he "might" stop at the French Creek yard, but only if time permitted. He remembered from his chat with Jerry that he was leaving after work to visit relatives in South Dakota, that it had been fortunate that John had come that day as he would be gone for a few days.

John tried to calculate the odds of anyone finding him. He realized that no one would begin to know where to look. He stood confused and dazed by the realization that he might have to spend the night in the junk yard.

And then a new, horrible thought hit him. *Oh, shit! The dogs!* They wouldn't really turn them loose, would they?

❖ 2 ❖

JOHN DECIDED THERE MUST BE another way out of the salvage yard. Perhaps to the west, beyond the KEEP OUT signs. One thing he knew for certain: he couldn't survive the night in the February cold. His only hope was to find some other way out of the junkyard and find some shelter. His first priority, he believed, had to be escape.

He headed back up the hill in the same direction as before, but this time, he would go west. He still carried the steering wheel, but compared to surviving the night, it just didn't seem as important. He dropped it in the snow. Darkness was total now. While it was only 6:00 P.M. or so, the sun set very early in February in Minnesota, and the clouded sky had turned inky. The whiteness of the snow improved visibility only somewhat. Were it not for the snow, John wouldn't have been able to see more than ten feet. He followed the plowed trails through the derelict autos, stumbling now and again.

The dogs sounded much closer than before. He shivered uncontrollably. If the dogs caught him, his only protection would be the tools he carried and perhaps his pocketknife. The discarded steering wheel—the very object that brought him to this evil place in the first place—now lay half-buried in the snow. With the idea of weapons in mind, he returned the few paces to it and picked it up. If nothing else, when he got out of there, it would make for great storytelling. An image of him showing off his restored truck and telling the tale of acquiring the steering wheel flashed through his head.

The dogs barked again, and all extraneous thoughts evaporated. They were definitely getting closer. John was accustomed to large dogs, and he respected them, but didn't fear them—until that moment. It sounded as if there were at least three or four in the compound. If they had been turned loose to roam the property as he feared, he needed to find a safe place to hide. His mind surged as he struggled to think of where to go and what to do.

He looked around for some high tree, but the junkyard had none at all. *Someplace high, though.* He quickly backtracked and headed for the tallest truck he had seen—the dairy truck. It was a cube van—ten to twelve feet tall—and unlike everything else in the yard, it wasn't nearly as decayed or corroded. Somehow, the old truck had fought against time and, for the most part, survived, its ravages and degradation.

If I can get inside, or better yet on top of it, then maybe the dogs can't reach me. It was his best shot. Apart from the sheer protective size of the truck, there seemed to be something else that drew John to it. He felt its presence as oddly comforting, as if it represented safety and security in a sea of cold steel.

John ran as fast as he could through the snow, starting to panic. The dogs' barking had just risen a notch, as if they had caught his scent. His breath came in short gasps as he plowed through the drifts, his progress slowed by the deep snow. It was like trying to run in chest-deep water.

Just as John reached the truck he saw the silhouettes of at least three huge dogs tearing over the hill from the west. They

21

were coming directly for him, and fast. He lost sight of them as they vanished behind rows of wrecks, but the barking intensified to the high yips of excitement.

John scrambled around the side of the dairy truck, paused briefly, just long enough to note that both windows were missing, which made a refuge inside the truck impossible, and jumped on to the hood of the truck. He clambered over the cracked windshield and heaved himself up to the rusty roof. As soon as he reached the top of the van, the first dog braked at the door below.

John immediately recognized his pursuer to be a Doberman Pincher. This one showed John all of his teeth and growled and snarled with a vengeance. *He's probably the chaser*, John thought. The other two appeared moments later. Rottweilers—and they were massive. Their heads were as big as garbage bags.

John knew he didn't stand a chance against the three dogs if their real intent was as ominous as their snarls and barks. They surrounded the truck, leaping to gain a foothold on the hood. He could hear the snapping of teeth along with scraping sounds of teeth and claws on metal as the animals gnashed at pieces of the truck and tried to claw up its sides in their eagerness to reach him.

Fortunately, the dogs couldn't find a way onto the truck. They slipped and fell back to the trampled ground below every time it looked like they might reach the hood. Their claws scraping on the rusted metal was as terrifying as their hideous shrieks. All three kept up an incessant, blood-chilling scream of pure fury.

John stood on top of the old truck—safe for the moment at least. He silently cursed himself for his single-minded stupidity. Had he given up his foolish quest much earlier, he knew he'd be safely home by now. Instead, his safety was in jeopardy, and he had no idea why.

Slowly the dogs quieted. They continued to prowl down below, looking for any opportunity to gain purchase on the truck, but they were clearly losing interest. As time passed, John felt oddly comforted by the old milk truck's solidity and precarious security. His heart rate and breathing—a wild thumping and gasping just moments before—slowed.

For the time being John was safe, but as the evening wore on he grew increasingly cold. He wondered if anyone would come looking for the dogs—or for him. He shook violently—a combination of fear and cold—and it restricted his ability to move or think with any degree of clarity. He felt that he could almost smell the metallic scent of coldness that surrounded him. He lost track of time. He had no idea how long the dogs would continue to circle the truck, or if at any moment one of them would find a way to jump or climb up to his perch. If that happened, John's fate would be sealed, and he knew it.

The dogs gave up and started to wander by 8:30 P.M. John was numb by then. It was twenty degrees, and he was unsure how much longer he could stay on top of the truck exposed to the wind and cold. He might have escaped the dogs, but he could still die out there.

Suddenly he was startled by the sound of engines in the distance. The noise seemed a sharp contrast to the barking of the dogs. He looked west and noticed lights moving back and forth.

Circumstances had forced John into believing that Ray and Dale had stolen his truck, and he was pretty sure the dogs were meant to kill him. And now he was defenseless, trapped in their private compound. As far as he knew, his only means of escape was to attempt climbing the twelve-foot electric fence. Not much of an option.

All John knew at this point was that he was cold, hungry, thirsty and very frightened. He was out of his element, probably outnumbered, and without any sort of legitimate weapon except his pocketknife. On top of that, the dogs clearly were not leaving. After lifting their legs on adjacent trucks, they had settled in below him. They kept an eye on him, though, and barked when he moved. John had few options at the moment. All he could do was to sit it out, try to keep warm and hope for a miracle.

He sat down. The rusted metal on the top of the truck felt strangely warm. He took off his glove and laid his palm down on the rusted steel. Not warm exactly, but not cold either. Weird.

John lifted his hand and noticed that a half dozen flakes of rust clung to his skin. He held his hand close to his face and stared at the dark pieces of decay as they were revealed to him in the dim, cloud-shielded moonlight. Something about this particular truck seemed different from the rest of the wrecks.

Rather than wiping away the few rusted flakes, he put his hand in his pocket and left them to rest against the soft fabric of his inner pocket. He withdrew his hand.

John thought of his wife, Debbie, and his two daughters, Sarah and Melissa. He wondered if they had started calling around, looking for him. John had never been very diligent about phoning home over the years. He was not the sort to routinely call home when on the road. Debbie seldom worried. His behavior and habits were those of a responsible and reliable man.

She must have called someone by now, though, he thought. *It's 9:00 at night! I should have been home hours ago. Who would she call? The police? Her father? But where the hell would they start looking?* The problem remained—Debbie wouldn't have any idea where John had gone. All she knew from their brief conversation that morning was that he was heading out west to call on customers.

John knew "west" might have meant anything within a 200-mile radius of the Twin cities—St. Cloud, Willmar, Marshall, Mankato, Windom, Glenwood—just about anyplace within his sales territory.

Debbie was familiar with his business, but only in a general sort of way. Her interests were more family oriented, and she had never been very involved in his work. She was aware, however, that the product lines he sold were concentrated in the industrial and construction areas, and his typical customer distributed these products to various contractors and industries. She also knew he had hundreds of customers scattered throughout the state, so he could have spent the day calling on any of approximately fifty businesses.

John began losing all hope of discovery and rescue. Only God and presumably the salvage yard owners had any knowledge of his current predicament. He was on his own. Somehow he had to harness the determination that drove him to find the yard in the first place and channel that energy into finding a way to escape.

All at once John heard a loud whistle carried on the chill breeze. His reverie shattered. All his senses came alive as he strained to understand what the whistle meant.

He glanced down at the dogs and watched as they immediately took off in the direction of the whistle—west, toward the lights moving in the distance. He was puzzled by their sudden departure. The thought of what the dogs might have done to him made his skin tense. John's imagination painted a gruesome, graphic picture of his bloody, torn body turning cold and stiff on the frozen ground. He shook his head to rid himself of the image.

John listened intently to see if perhaps it was some sort of trick. The dogs could suddenly return—unseen, unheard. He fought to calm himself and chose to stay where he was for the time being. When he was positive the dogs were locked up, he'd hike over the hill to see if there was a way out.

The moon crept out from behind the clouds. It would provide John with additional light for his trek through the trashed vehicles, but only when he felt safe enough to leave the relative comfort of the dairy truck.

Sitting on top the truck was taking its toll on his body. He was stiff and sore from all the walking, climbing, and running. He stood up to stretch his back and tried to get warm by swinging his arms and jumping up and down. If the dogs were still prowling around, they'd notice the movement and return. If they didn't come back, he'd have one indication it was safe to climb down.

Not only was he cold and stiff, his stomach growled with pangs of hunger. Slowly, blood returned to his extremities, and he began to feel a little better. He felt relatively safe and comforted on top of the truck—somehow attached to it. It was as if the large, broken-down vehicle had saved his life—which it had.

John decided it was time to make his move—he had to at least make the attempt. Just before, with great reluctance, he left the relative safety of the truck, he realized true freedom and safety was much closer than he had thought. He didn't have to deal with his captors! All he had to do was head back to the office, bust in a window, and call for help on their phone. Then he could simply walk out the front door! He'd head back down the road—he'd run into someone sooner or later. It made perfect sense. Suddenly, John's mood turned from despondent to hopeful.

John climbed down from the top of the truck. With a plan for rescue formulated, it seemed important to bring the steering wheel with him. He stood close to the side of the truck for a few minutes, reluctant to leave its security. He still wasn't convinced the dogs weren't lurking someplace, just waiting to sink their teeth into him. He looked around for a full minute, straining to hear them. But it wasn't the dogs that drew his attention. *There's something else here. Someone or some thing . . . ?* He couldn't put his finger on the feeling nor account for anything to cause the sensation of another presence near him. Maybe he had just been so frightened, threat lingered in his mind.

It was deathly quiet, except for the faint sound of engines off in the distance. Certain of an unexplained presence, he reached out and touched the side of the truck one last time and then stepped into the piled snow. John was frightened—eyes wide open, he scanned the landscape. Finally, unable to linger any longer, with great fear and trepidation, he left his safe refuge, hoping he had made the right choice.

He slowly walked down the road toward the office building, looking back over his shoulder with every other step and straining to see between the rusted hulks of autos. He came up over the last rise, and once again he noticed the lights moving around on his left. *God, I hope they're too busy doing whatever the hell they're doing to worry about me.* He picked up his pace and jogged down the hill, certain that freedom and safety lay only minutes away.

As he approached the building, he noticed with frustration that there was another chain link fence surrounding the backside of the office building. *Shit! I didn't see that before.* The gate he passed through earlier was now locked. *What the hell?*

He stopped and looked up at the fence. It was only eight feet high or so, and there wasn't any barbed wire on top.

He threw the steering wheel over the fence and started climbing, sticking his fingers through the chain links and pulling himself up. His boots were too big to gain any kind of secure toe-hold, so he had to depend on his fingers, hands, and arms to do most of the work. It was slow and exhausting, but finally he reached the top. He paused there, looked around and dropped to the other side.

John had a sudden premonition that something was terribly wrong. *I'm forgetting something . . . doesn't feel right.* He didn't know what it was, but it scared him.

He stood in place and listened intently for some sound of impending danger. Hearing nothing, he picked up the wheel and crept toward the building. He stopped once more, looking around and focusing on the shadows near the building. He saw nothing, but he couldn't shake the feeling someone was near.

John reached the office building and stood beneath one of the windows, then he reached in his coat for the box-end wrench, planning to smash the glass and find the phone.

Just as his arm started forward to strike the glass, John understood that his misgivings had been well-founded. He heard the low, menacing growl of a large dog. There apparently were more dogs than those he had seen earlier. The growl turned to a loud snarl. A blur of movement flashed near the door. The dark shadow launched, and John felt helpless.

As the moon came out from beneath a cloud, John could clearly see the dog. He knew he had no chance to escape. His only choice was to stand his ground and defend himself. He covered his face and throat with his jacketed forearm and prepared for the dog's attack.

The dog was on him in an instant. In one quick motion, almost without thinking, John swung the steering wheel at the dog's head. He heard a loud CRACK, and the dog dropped as if it had been shot. The animal quivered and lay still.

John was breathing hard. His heart pounded, his ears roared, and adrenaline flowed freely through his veins. It became quiet. The only sound was his heavy breathing.

After he calmed down, he realized what he had done. He knew he had been very lucky. *If I hadn't taken that wheel with me, I'd be dead meat by now!* After the adrenaline wore off; he didn't feel quite so brave. He looked down at the steering wheel still in his hand and realized that it now looked no different from the one at home. The blow had cracked the wheel in two. Now useless, he dropped it into the snow.

John took a deep breath and considered his options. He turned his attention to his original mission—bust out the glass, get inside and call the police. That accomplished, he would head out the front door and down the road. More than anything in the world, John wanted to leave the salvage yard and find his way to safety.

He swung the wrench at the glass. It shattered. Then, for the third time that horrible night, he heard the dreaded sound of a dog growling, this time from within the building. John was over the edge of rational fear by this point. He was terrified! He had no idea whether the animal inside was chained up or free to roam at will. One thing was certain: John had neither the will nor the energy to fight another dog.

He backed away slowly—toward the fence—retraced his footsteps, climbed back up and over, and dropped to the other side. John's heart sank. What moments ago had seemed like certain freedom was replaced with a morbid sense of failure. He was still trapped. He could envision no way out. His once hopeful spirit was shattered. Tears of defeat and sorrow filled his tired eyes.

He felt absolutely defeated, and a deep sadness settled over him. He had done everything he could, but the yard was sealed off. The fence surely surrounded the entire property, and he knew he couldn't negotiate the barbed wire. He was going nowhere, at least for the present. A dark blanket of depression settled over him like a cold, damp, fog.

He wandered back up the road to the crest of the first hill— no longer hurrying—and leaned against a battered, rusted '81 Dodge pickup. The old wreck looked like John felt—defeated and forgotten. His nightmare wasn't over. He feared it was just a matter of time before he froze to death or someone caught him. They'd either shoot him straight away or turn him over to the dogs. He had never felt so alone and frightened in his entire life. Tears flowed with no shame.

Leaning against the Dodge, John collected himself and reached for his cigarettes—only one left. "The condemned man's last smoke," he muttered. He lit the cigarette and inhaled deeply. As the nicotine found its way into his bloodstream, John thought again of his wife and two girls. Melissa was only sixteen, Sarah thirteen. What would become of them? Who would take care of the business? His partner couldn't run it by himself. Had he told Debbie he wanted to be cremated? Did he have enough life insurance to provide for them? Morbid thoughts filled his head as cold seeped ever deeper into his body.

Any hope of escape was forgotten. He no longer cared about what was really going on in the salvage yard. Instead he berated himself and accepted defeat.

He thought of his parents. His father had disappeared when he was twelve. He was never heard from again. His mother had died at barely sixty. John was only forty-two, but suddenly he felt eighty years old. Fatigue and defeat oozed from every pore. It was almost as if he were dead already. He felt his death was imminent.

The two hunting incidents that nearly took his life paled in comparison to what he now faced. The first time, he had capsized in a duck-boat; laden with heavy clothing and alone in the middle of a lake in water that had already frozen over at least once, he was lucky to have survived. The second time, a few years later, he and a friend had been caught out in a blizzard. John knew he had been fortunate in both instances, but also realized that he'd never given up, never felt like either situation was hopeless. Now he wondered why he was giving up.

In the first incident, he had clung to the boat in the freezing water until help arrived; a fisherman returning to shore picked him up. The second time, he and his friend and their two dogs had hunkered down in the bulrushes for the night, waiting for the storm to subside. They were cold and scared, but all survived— only because they refused to give in.

Then he remembered a third instance way back during his stint in the Army. He knew that of all the times his life had been in danger, that was the one time he could have easily given up. He had been a second lieutenant in command of a tank that caught fire while being refueled. He thought he'd be cooked like a piece of sausage. He suffered fairly severe burns on his arms, but had managed to crawl to safety, grab the fire extinguisher, and put out the flames before the tank exploded. Two other soldiers trapped inside the tank managed to escape with his help as well. Both suffered burns more severe than his, but they survived.

"What am I quitting for?" he said out loud. The sound of his angry voice echoed through the derelict cars and trucks. "Why should this be it? This is bullshit! I don't want Debbie to have to take care of the girls herself."

What finally shook him out of his morbid reverie was the thought of Debbie remarrying. They had met in college, and even though their courtship had been somewhat stormy, they had stayed together for two years, parted, reconnected, and eventually married. He loved her deeply—she and the two girls were the reasons for his very existence. He reached into his back pocket and pulled out his wallet. With half-frozen fingers, he removed a picture of his family. The half-light of the moon provided just enough illumination to see the photograph. He stared at his wife's image for the longest time and thought back to the time many years before when he first saw her in college.

It was 1972, and John was a sophomore at the University of Minnesota, Duluth. He first noticed Debbie in an English class they both attended. She sat across the small amphitheater from him, and he couldn't take his eyes off her. He thought she was beautiful—tall, athletic, with blonde hair that fell softly over one side of her face. John was struck by her obvious self-confidence. She carried herself as if she knew exactly where life would take her.

He was barely getting by in college, maintaining enough of a grade-point average to stay in school but aimlessly floating from one party to the next. He drank too much, and the few times he saw Debbie at any of the numerous parties, he was usually drunk. After a couple of months, he finally got up the courage to approach her.

Fortunately, he was sober at the time. He managed to slip in beside her. "Hi, I'm John!" That was as clever and cute as he could manage.

Debbie looked at him and replied, "Yes, I know."

John felt as if he had blown the whole thing with his weak overture, and with one last attempt at conversation, he asked, "What's your name?"

She smiled as if enjoying John's discomfort. She let him sweat for a bit, and finally said, "Debbie."

He felt stupid at his inability to say anything clever. Not a young man brimming with self-confidence, John's small amount of self-assurance rapidly evaporated. Like a balloon with a slow leak, he wilted under Debbie's playful stare. Normally, the girls John partied with drank freely, and conversations were seldom a problem. Debbie was different, however, and even with only a few words spoken between them, John sensed that she was special. When he began to calm, he found that he was strangely at ease in her company. He decided to say nothing further, and instead turned away to watch other couples dancing to one of the Beach Boys' current tunes.

After a few moments, just when John felt like any further conversation was hopeless, she said, "Why did you get yourself kicked off the hockey team?"

Shocked that she knew anything at all about him, John felt her question cut right through him. He'd grown up loving hockey. For many years, it was all he'd cared about. Once he started playing for UMD in his freshman year, however, something changed. He knew the problem—it was simple: too much freedom, too much beer. Maybe it was a desire to lose himself in all the parties and just hang out with his buddies. He knew the answer to her question, and, strangely for him, he replied truthfully. "The coach caught me drinking—twice—and gave me the boot."

"How did you feel about that?" Debbie asked.

32

This time, John didn't hesitate. "Didn't care much. All my friends were having a great time partying, and I guess I wanted to do the same thing. Besides, I really wasn't that good anymore. College hockey is a lot different from high school."

Debbie stepped closer. "That's too bad. I heard you were pretty good." She paused. "So, what do you do now besides party all the time? I don't see you in class too often."

John remembered losing confidence right about then. This was a new and exciting experience for him. His heart started pounding. The very fact that this gorgeous, intelligent, sensitive girl even noticed his presence in class was more than he could have hoped for. "I guess I do probably party quite a bit."

For the rest of that night, they stayed together. They danced a few times, drank a few beers, but John sensed he had to be careful not to get drunk with her. At the same time, he didn't feel as if he needed to.

That was the beginning of their courtship. From that point forward, John was never with any other girl besides Debbie. She turned out to be everything he had been looking for—someone who actually cared about his feelings, his hopes, and his future.

At first they didn't actually date. John was too shy for that. Instead, he went out of his way to appear coincidentally at some function he knew Debbie would attend. In time, with her help, he grew bolder, less reliant on bottled courage, and they began to date.

Debbie was a freshman. She was an outstanding student, maintained a 3.6 grade point average and hoped someday to become an attorney like her father. With her help, John slowly began to spend more time on his studies and less time partying. Over the following two years, they were inseparable. John often wondered what she saw in him, and finally asked her about it.

"I was curious. But more than that, I didn't believe everything I heard about you. I thought there had to be something more," Debbie said.

"What do you mean?" John asked.

"I mean, no one could be that . . . hopeless. You went around with this, 'I don't give a shit' attitude, and I wasn't buying it. Besides, the first time I saw you in English class, I thought you were really cute." She leaned over and kissed him.

He was embarrassed, so he decided to change the subject. "By the way, why the interest in hockey?"

"Because I used to play as a kid. I was pretty good, too!"

"Come on, really? Where?" John asked.

"At a pond near our house. I used to play with my brother Teddy and all his friends. I never had hockey skates, but it didn't matter. I could skate faster than most of the boys."

John was impressed. "What happened if you got checked?"

"That didn't happen too often. My brother saw to that. If any new boy on the pond got too rough, Teddy would pounce on him, and that took care of the rough stuff. I loved hockey—always wished they'd had girls' hockey when I was in high school."

"That'll never happen. Too rough. It'd be something, though, wouldn't it? A girls' hockey team? Wonder if they'd allow checking?"

"I don't know. Certain parts of our body shouldn't ever be, you know . . . knocked around."

"Oh yeah? Like what?"

"Like that," Debbie said, and put his hand on her breast.

"Yeah, I suppose. Girls'd maybe have to wear boob protectors—like guys wear cups."

They laughed and kissed, but before long Debbie withdrew from his embrace.

"What's wrong?" John asked.

"Oh, I'm sorry. I started to think about my brother."

"You've never really talked much about him."

"He was killed in Vietnam. He was a pilot on a helicopter gunship. It happened during my junior year in high school. That was the worst year of my life, John. We were very close."

"I'm really sorry, Deb. How long was he over there?"

"It was his first flight. He'd only been in the country one week." Debbie's voice trembled. "I'll never forget coming home from school and seeing that green car parked out front. I was so into myself back then. I never really thought much about the war—about the danger Teddy might be in. I walked in the house and saw both my parents crying, and then I knew. My father was so angry. I don't think he'll ever get over it. He had great hopes for Teddy's future. So did my mom. He was a really neat guy, John. You two would have liked each other."

John didn't know what more he could say. He had little experience consoling others. Up until that point, the war hadn't touched him, but the reality of what he would someday face hit him hard. Once he was out of school, he knew he could be drafted. But like most serious things John had encountered in his young life, he decided not to worry until he had to. "I suppose I'm going to have enlist after school."

"Can't you get a deferment? I don't want to lose you, too."

"I don't think so, Deb. I heard that some guys are running away to Canada, but I don't think I could do that. I could never come back. If I did, they'd throw me in jail. Maybe I could join the National Guard. That's only for six months, and I don't think those guys wind up in Vietnam."

"Find out for me, John—please? You'll be graduating soon. Besides, what if they have a waiting list?"

"I'll find out." But of course, he didn't look into the Guard until he had to—when he had no other choice. He'd been content to finish school, spend all his time with Debbie and dream about their future.

John knew he was fortunate to have found Debbie, and he did everything he could to make certain he never disappointed her. Ultimately, other than a few trips away from campus with his buddies, he was with her constantly. He even stopped drinking.

35

He still gambled on occasion, though, and discovered to his amazement that because of his affection for Debbie, he didn't miss any of his former life. They were inseparable, and as time went on, they began sleeping together. John had never made love before. He'd had sex a few times—usually half-crocked—so he remembered little about it, but he had never experienced the real feeling of warmth and tenderness he felt with Debbie.

Debbie had very little experience in sexual matters. She was a virgin, and when they finally decided to consummate their love for each other, neither had any regrets. They shared everything—that was the beauty of their relationship. Once they were sleeping together, no subject was taboo. During his senior year, John remembered asking Debbie a particularly difficult and personal question. "How come you never had sex before me?"

It was a question that wasn't totally out of line, given the depth of their feelings for each other. "I guess I was saving myself for you," she said, laughing at the same time.

"Yeah, I'm sure. Really? How come?" John asked.

She didn't respond at once, but carefully considered her answer before continuing. "I dated quite a bit, but I think my mother influenced my behavior to a great extent." She smiled, remembering some of the boys she dated. "Actually, none of the boys I went out with were all that great."

"Why not?"

"I don't know. They were different from you. The girls at St. Kate's mostly dated the boys from St. Michael's across the street. They had been well coached before we saw any of them. They were all perfect gentlemen, and at least until Mathew came along, no one ever tried too hard."

"Mathew?"

"We dated in my senior year. Pretty serious, actually, but until prom night, we just kissed a lot."

"What happened?"

"Well, he was good looking, I guess. Captain of the football team, good student, and all that, but something never felt right. You know how important honesty is to me? Well, I was never too sure about him. He tried to get me drunk on prom night, and you know me, John—a couple of beers and I'm looped. We went to the dance, and then left early. We drove in his father's Cadillac to some spot he had picked out, and parked." The tone of her voice sounded restrained—she had a hard time finishing.

John leaned over, touched her cheek, and turned her head so he could see her eyes. "What happened, Deb?"

She was close to tears, as if the memory of that night was too painful. She decided to get it all out. "I thought I knew him, but I was wrong. We kissed, and he started feeling my breasts. That was okay, but then he started to get too rough. I know he was excited. I'm afraid I was pretty drunk by then. It was all kind of hazy. He pulled down the straps of my dress, and started kissing my boobs. I remember opening my eyes and staring at him. He had the strangest look on his face—like he had just conquered something."

Debbie continued. "Then he stuck his hand under my dress and started rubbing me. He kept telling me how much he 'loved' me, and I knew it was all a bunch of crap. It was kind of funny, now that I think of it. He was slobbering all over me, and then he took my hand and put it on his crotch. I told him I didn't want to do that, but he wouldn't stop."

Her voiced changed, and John knew it was a very painful memory for her. "You don't have to tell me any more if you don't feel like it," he said, hugging her closely.

"No, I want to. I think it's probably good for me to remember. It just makes what we have that much more special."

She reached into her purse, pulled out some tissues, blew her nose, and continued. "He was moaning and groaning and I'm sure he thought we were going to . . . you know, go all the way.

37

Finally, I had to push him away. I pulled up my dress straps and told him I wanted to go home."

Debbie struggled but managed to say, "All of a sudden, his face turned red, and he shouted at me—called me a bitch. He said I was nothing but a prick teaser. And then he said something like he should have listened to his friends when they said I was a cold fish. He started the car and swore at me all the way home. I felt so bad, John. I don't think I ever did anything to lead him on. Honest!"

"I believe you, Debbie. It wasn't your fault. The guy was an asshole, period. I know his type—cocky, loves to brag about all the girls he's had. Two-faced, kind of like Eddie Haskel on *Leave It to Beaver*, you know?"

He did his best to console her. She was too good a person to be treated that way, and John was angry at the guy for putting her through that. It was at that exact moment that he knew he wanted to spend the rest of his life with her. The simple act of sharing that very emotional, significant event in her life meant a great deal to him.

John felt bad for her, and for the longest time that night, they just held each other without saying a word. He still wondered about their relationship—they were so different—and yet, it must have been that very difference that made everything work.

Their lovemaking was ardent, emotional, and terribly exciting—for both of them. Beyond the sex though, they had plenty of other common interests, and just enjoyed each other's company. They shared a deep-seated respect for each other's feelings and interests. And until the day they split up in John's senior year, their time together was idyllic.

❖ ● ❖

John felt a deep, gut-wrenching sadness as he realized he might never see his family again. He took one last look at the photo, gently put it back into the flap, and stuck the wallet in his pocket. The pain of remembering what he stood to lose jarred him back to the present.

The very real possibility that everything they had worked so hard to attain could come to an end was too much to bear. This was John's dark, emotional abyss. The despair he felt led to more tears streaming down his frigid cheeks. His heart was breaking. He had come so far, had found the woman he wanted to spend his life with, lost her once, and found her again. Together they'd created the only real family he cared about. He was immobilized by sorrow at the thought of losing them all.

He thought again of what Debbie would do without him. Eventually, she would remarry, he thought. She could never stand being alone, and the girls would need a father. That thought seemed to flame a tiny spark of motivation deep in his soul. The image of his wife with another man was not something John had ever worried about. Now, however, the possibility of Debbie remarrying was very real. He didn't like what he now felt, and it seemed to stir something deep inside his gut.

Without being aware of it, John had a new ally. The sorrow he had been feeling was replaced with a sharp resolve. He wasn't going to give up that easily. The thought of Debbie with another man was untenable.

Suddenly, he came to life. He had to find a way out of there, no matter what it took. Feeling sorry for himself wouldn't help. He needed to get out of that hellhole of a auto graveyard and find his way home.

John's cigarette was dead—as cold and lifeless as he had felt just moments before. He tossed the butt and looked west. The lights moving in the distance had diminished. He looked at his watch. It was 11:00 P.M.

He stretched his muscles, flexed his fingers, and trudged off through the snow in search of he knew not what. Headed west, towards an uncertain destination, he moved tentatively—fearful that at any moment the dogs would leap from the darkness. He silently prayed for strength and guidance from his God . . . to see him safely home.

❖ 3 ❖

JOHN CHOSE HIS PATH CAREFULLY. Staying close to the larger vehicles in case the dogs appeared, he slid from one rusted hulk to another. He passed by the KEEP OUT signs conspicuously posted along his chosen route. John knew he couldn't stay out in the frigid night much longer without risking the very real possibility of hypothermia and death. Having failed to find a safe exit from the salvage yard through the office, he had no choice but to investigate a possible escape in the direction of the lights he had seen. If people were present—and if they weren't the men who had imprisoned him—perhaps he could enlist their aid. At the very least, regardless of what the activity portended, there had to be another way out of the property.

John summoned all the courage he could muster and plotted a course through the decrepit autos and trucks toward what he hoped was his ultimate freedom. His breath hung heavily in the still air just ahead of his face. He was hungry, ravenous in fact, but beyond a need for food, beyond the much more pressing need to get warm before he froze to death, he craved escape from his unknown captors.

John finally crested a small hill and spotted a large metal building in the distance. Light poured from its few small windows and a yard light, and the sound of engines and machines came from inside as well as outside the building. That yellow light looked so warm. John's heart soared—finally, people he could perhaps depend on to give him food, shelter, and affect his return trip home. It took effort to force his numbed brain to understand that he had not left the compound of the junkyard; chances were better than good that the people down there had anything but his best interests at heart.

His walk through the graveyard had been nerve-wracking. As if threading through a minefield, he wound his way around the dead vehicles, selecting a route that would provide cover and immediate safety on any of the larger trucks—just in case he ran into the dogs. His worried about the whereabouts of the three animals, but, if he didn't get warm soon, the cold would kill him faster than the dogs could.

John froze. The barking of dogs came from around the other side of the metal building. He had no idea if they were penned or still free to come for him. For a moment an image of the three dogs racing toward him filled his mind. Every shadow seemed to move in his direction. His heart pounded, and he crouched in the snow, terrified to move.

Cold crept up his pant legs. His toes had numbed some time before. He shivered. He looked longingly at the warmth of the yellow light, knowing that, if the dogs were down there, he could not count on aid. Going down there likely meant he would be walking into a trap. He wasn't quite sure what they were doing so late on a February night, but he pretty well figured it wasn't legal. *Worry about what they're doing later, John,* he told himself fiercely. *Get the hell out of this cold—now!*

Slowly he picked his way down the last slope, the cold pushing at him while his terror held him back. He heard all kinds of activity as he neared the barn, most of the sounds metallic, sharp and loud. The small windows that glowed with yellow warmth were frosted over and provided little help determining how many men were inside. He listened to the sound of a large machine on the far side of the building as it clanged and groaned. John couldn't identify what it was and didn't waste much time in that pursuit. He focused on the front of the building.

From what he hoped was a hidden spot near the hulk of some large SUV, he peeked into the lighted yard. He saw a covered semi trailer backed up to a loading dock on the north end of the building but little else. He moved in closer.

Directly in front of him stood his Explorer. Parked a short distance away between the Explorer and the building was the large forklift. The gate stood open just beyond it. His heart pounded—escape was now a real possibility. Freedom seemed to be just a short distance away.

He pulled off one glove with his teeth and felt in his pockets, panic rising before his cold hands closed around his keys. Relieved, he extracted them. *If I can sneak over to my truck without being seen, get inside and start it up, I can escape through the gate.* He looked around. The forklift would provide a certain measure of protection from anyone looking in his direction, so with a little luck, he had a chance at escape.

This would be his only opportunity. He knew with certainty that he couldn't fight anyone as stiff and cold as he was. He couldn't even run if they set the dogs on him. His only hope was stealth. He stood quietly for a few more minutes, screwing his courage, then glanced at his watch. It was nearly midnight.

The dogs worried him the most. He feared they lurked just around the corner of the building. If they saw him, he was done; if they smelled him, he was also finished. He fought the impulse to run and hide and hope he could withstand the cold for the night. He told himself that was a fool's hope. He knew he must proceed but do so slowly—staying behind the cover of the forklift—and then cross the exposed ground to his truck. If someone happened to be outside, John felt it important to act as if he belonged there—that he was just another worker. He would only run if he had to.

He looked up at the moon and waited for it to emerge from behind a cloud, and then scanned the surrounding landscape one last time. He gazed toward the far south end of the large barn and saw the outline of another chain link fence. He could not see any movement.

He checked the wind. The slight breeze came from the west. He would be downwind from the dogs if they were inside the building, but if they were outside roaming around, he could still be in serious trouble. He considered his only apparent option. Walk about forty yards—in the open.

As if he teetered on the edge of a cliff, John feared having to take the first step. He stood glued to a packed spot in the snow, too afraid to move—too afraid not to.

Inside the pole barn, Ray finally tracked down one of his two cousins. "Huge, did you take care of that body yet?"

Huge didn't respond.

Ray tried again, louder. "Huge, you fat shit! Did you dump the guy in the crusher like you're supposed to?"

Huge's given name was Hugh. He earned his nickname after he single-handedly picked up the back end of a Volkswagen in high school. At the sound of Ray's angry voice, the big man stopped and turned around. Whenever Ray shouted, that usually meant he was pissed off about something. Huge, a behemoth of a man at six-foot-four and three hundred five pounds, was blessed with size and strength but little else. Unattractive by almost any standard, he was painfully slow, both physically and mentally.

Huge's responsibilities were intentionally limited. His job included caring for the dogs, siphoning gas from vehicles, and disposing of damaging evidence in the big crusher outside. Huge and his brother Mikey were the family enforcers, but because of their intimidating presence and Ray's well-earned reputation, the pair seldom had to physically hurt anyone.

On this particular night, Huge was suffering from serious stomach trouble. His normal diet consisted of Big Macs, Whoppers, Hostess Twinkies, Snowballs, and anything else he could find that had high fat content. He was not particularly discriminating, either. Unfortunately, that morning he had stopped at the Chat and Chew Café for breakfast and had eaten a large quantity of rank, homemade sausage. As a result, he had spent the evening close to the toilet.

"Huge! Did you hear me?" Ray asked again.

"Yeah. Not yet, Ray," Huge finally replied.

"Why the hell not?"

Huge lacked sufficient mental acuity to think things through very clearly. He had a very short attention span, and his intelligence quotient would have tested alarmingly low. He was content just to eat everything in sight and let others do his thinking for him. But he hated it when Ray was pissed off at him.

Huge didn't know what else to say. "I got the shits, Ray!"

"I don't give a damn if your bowels are tied in a knot! Go take care of the body. Move your fat ass! Now!"

Huge shuffled off, head bowed.

Huge's gastric condition had given John an enormous opportunity. Because Huge managed the dogs, after he had installed the two at the office, he normally would have followed the sound of the three in the field to its bloody conclusion, but, on his return trip to the office to place two other dogs, he'd nearly crapped his pants. Moving as fast as his bulk would allow, he hurried into the john and deposited a large portion of the bad sausage.

He then decided he couldn't leave the safety of the toilet. Rather than drive out and retrieve the dogs and the body, he had whistled them in. Huge headed toward the open door to address his oversight from earlier in the evening.

As Huge left the building, he ran into his brother who stood just outside on the landing at the top of half a dozen metal steps. His back was to Huge, and his head was bent toward the ground. "Whatcha doing, Mikey?" Huge asked his older brother.

John heard shouting from inside the building, though he could distinguish none of the words. He felt he was running out of time and was pressing his luck by hesitating further. He was still reluctant to move, however. Once he committed, there would be no turning back. *What if the car won't start? Come on, John! It's now or never!* He stepped from the darkness into the light, fully exposed. Too late, he realized he should have waited a fraction of a second longer.

Mikey stood just outside the door on the loading dock. He was in the process of relieving himself in the cold night air. Reluctant to follow his over-sized brother in the only toilet on the premises, Mikey chose to pee from the outside landing.

Mikey was born with a few more brains than his younger brother, but years of boxing had sacrificed too many of them, spoiling whatever mental advantage he once had. He was a punch-drunk prize fighter with a bashed-in nose and cauliflower ears. He couldn't smell very well, but whenever his brother used the toilet, even he was repulsed by the lingering odors.

Huge approached his brother from the rear and paused.

46

At that moment, John started walking toward his truck, keys gripped tightly in hand. Fortunately, the Explorer was parked just outside the barn. Initially, he could keep the forklift between himself and the door of the barn. Once he cleared the lift, however, he was in the open. His heart raced. Certain he had been spotted, it took tremendous restraint to keep from running. Head bowed to avoid recognition, he slowly proceeded. Each step seemed to take hours.

John was within ten paces of his truck. He glanced toward the doorway. Mikey looked directly at him. John froze. As if wet concrete had been poured over his head and promptly hardened, he stood immobile.

His fingers shook. He stumbled and almost fell down. *I'm not going to make it! I messed up!* Out in the open and exposed, he knew the man in the doorway had to see him. *There's no turning back now*, he thought.

John couldn't breath. Fear seized every muscle in his body, and he felt weak. Like an infant lacking coordination, John could not separate the keys. *I should have had the right one ready*, he told himself fiercely. Finally, he managed to find the ignition key. He opened the door, climbed in and started the engine.

Mikey had indeed noticed a figure walking across the yard. He assumed it was one of the crew and returned his gaze to the yellow stains below the stairs, and continued to piss. He aimed his stream into the snow and attempted to write his entire name before his bladder emptied. He lost sight of the man in the yard.

Huge tried to squeeze his substantial bulk past Mikey on the way out the door, bumping his brother in the process.

As a result, Mikey cast part of the urine stream onto his foot just as he was finishing up a rather shaky looking Y. At that moment the engine of the Explorer roared to life.

"Goddammit, Huge! I just pissed on my foot, thanks to you."

By the time the boys got over their squabble and realized what was happening, John sped past them in the blue Explorer. The two brothers stood and watched as the truck passed. Mikey thought it might have been Dale or one of the others. Huge simply blinked and stared.

Huge peered over his shoulder at the rapidly departing truck. "Who's that?"

"Dale or somebody," Mikey replied. He shook, casually put everything back in place, zipped up his pants, and watched as John headed for the gate.

John put the truck in gear and hit the gas. Dust and gravel spewed from beneath the tires as he raced past the two brothers. He glanced over his shoulder to see their reaction. He thought he'd heard one of them yell, but he couldn't be sure.

John hadn't switched on the headlights. He headed for the gate somewhere ahead in the darkness. He felt a sudden rush of adrenaline. The gate was still open.

He was euphoric—excited to finally be leaving this nightmare behind. He floored the truck and headed down the gravel road. He still hadn't turned on the lights, had no idea what might lie ahead. He didn't care. Freedom was his at last.

Many years earlier, the French Creek Salvage Yard had been a reputable business, and its original owner, Morris Johnson was proud of what he had built. Now, however, the property was nothing more than a blight on the surrounding countryside. Some thought the place was haunted. In many ways, it was.

A Christian man, Morris always had a kind word for everyone and believed wayward souls deserved a second chance. He was a credit to the community and provided a needed service for his neighbors. It wasn't until Arthur Steckel came along that everything changed—and not for the better.

Art needed work and recognized an opportunity when one presented itself. Aware of Old Morris' charitable nature, Art walked into the old man's office one day.

"What can I do for you, young fellow?" Morris asked.

"Lookin' for work."

"What can you do?"

"Just about anything you need. Pretty good with engines."

Morris looked at the man carefully, and then said, "What have you been doing?"

Art had done his homework, so he spoke the truth. "Just got out of jail."

"That so? What'd you do?" the old man asked.

"Got into a fight."

"Why?"

"Don't rightly remember. I was drunk." This answer was far from the truth. In fact, Art had needlessly kicked a man in the face and almost killed him. It was not the act of a drunken man—it was vicious and cowardly.

Morris saw little need to press the matter. He did need help, so he hired Art to strip parts. It wasn't too long before Art made his move. He knew Morris had no living relatives—his wife had passed away a few years earlier. Without family to inherit the business, Art convinced the old man to write him into his will. The ink had barely dried when Art devised a plan to take over the business.

Less than six months later, he was ready. He beckoned the old man out to the crusher. "I got to show you something."

Morris followed him through the yard to the large pole barn on the west side of the property. "What is it?"

"Don't know for sure. Something's wrong with the crusher plate."

The crusher was a large, hydraulic machine that converted scrap vehicles into cubes of iron. Art had convinced the old man to spend the money for the machine a few months back.

Art leaned over the pit, turned and looked up at the plate on the bottom of the crusher. "See? Look here!"

Morris followed Art's lead, but as he leaned over and turned to look up at the plate, Art suddenly lifted the old man's legs, tumbling Morris into the pit. Then he reached for the power switch, turned the machine on, hit the START button, and slowly walked back to the edge. He peered into the pit, smiling at his benefactor. Morris couldn't move. His spine had broken in the fall. All he could do was stare wide eyed at the descending plate that would soon crush the life out of him. Resigned to his fate, the old man realized for the first time that his generosity had been misplaced. He knew the end was at hand and called up to his killer, "I forgive you, Arthur!"

"Go to hell, Morris!" Art said and watched the crusher continue its relentless descent.

The old man disappeared. Morris Johnson was fused into a mangled rectangle of iron, formerly a 1962 Chevrolet Impala coupe.

No one witnessed the murder of Morris Johnson. According to Art, as he later described the accident to the authorities, "Old Morris must have had one of his fainting spells and fell into the pit." No one ever questioned Art any further. He became the new owner of the yard, and from that day forward, nothing was ever the same in French Creek.

Art immediately fired all the existing help and brought in certain family members that could be trusted to keep their mouths shut. He then converted what once was a proud fixture of the community into an illegal chop shop. Local residents spoke of the transformation only in hushed tones, and it wasn't long before they all realized that to question Art's methods was unwise.

Those who spoke out received threatening phone calls or experienced mysterious fires on their property late at night. Vocal, nosy residents soon learned to keep their mouths shut or move. Art created his own gang of car thieves and thugs. He was in control and shunned almost all legitimate business.

After a while he grew even bolder and more confident and, by pure happenstance, discovered how to expand his evil trade. No longer satisfied with merely stealing cars from around the county, he realized that, occasionally, other opportunities were presented that he couldn't ignore.

One day about a year after Morris was brutally murdered, a milk truck drove in and stopped in front of the office. Art looked out the front window, and noticed that the Swanson's Dairy truck parked in front was new—it appeared to have very few miles on it.

The driver entered the office. "Say, where am I anyway? This is a new route for me, and somehow I got turned around—been driving around in circles for the last hour. I'm trying to get to Cokato."

Art figured the truck had to be worth at least twenty thousand dollars, and if the driver was lost, then no one knew where he was. *Shit, them chillers and coolers alone must be worth thousands,* Art thought.

He told the driver to come into the back room. "I'll show you on a map where you are."

As the unfortunate driver leaned over the desk, Art struck him on the head with a heavy spud wrench. He cleaned out the man's pockets and kept the small amount of cash he found. He discovered a gold pocket watch with W.S.R.—TWENTY YEARS inscribed on the back.

The dairy driver became the second sorry soul to be dumped into the bowels of the crusher. It was presumed by his employer and the police that the driver had stolen the truck and sold it in another state. His family clung to a faint hope that he'd turn up one day and explain everything, but in time they came to believe that he had abandoned them. No evidence ever turned up that led the authorities to French Creek or anywhere else.

Art quickly stripped the truck of its most valuable parts and stashed it far out on the property where no one would ever spot it. He quickly applied a coat of cheap paint to cover up the letters printed on the side and went about his business.

The unfortunate milkman marked the genesis of a nefarious tradition that over the years would claim additional souls who happened to wander into the junkyard. When Art passed away, his two sons, Ray and Dale took over the business. The old man had taught them well. Two rotten seeds sprouted and flourished— determined to eclipse the depravity of their progenitor.

❖ 4 ❖

B ACK INSIDE THE LARGE POLE BARN, Ray Steckel moved from
one car to another. He observed everything—nothing that
occurred in the building missed his watchful eye.

"Larry, did anyone siphon the gas out of the Explorer yet?"
Ray shouted.

"Yep!" Larry shouted back. "Already done. I think Huge
took care of it, Ray."

"Dale, how we coming on the parts?" Ray asked.

Dale backed out of a new BMW he was working on and
turned to face his brother. "Just about done. Should be another
hour or so."

"Good. I wanna be outta of here no later than 1:00 A.M.
Where're those two chowderheads, anyway?" Ray asked, looking
around the interior of the pole barn for his cousins.

Dale had already returned to work and missed hearing
Ray's question. The barn reverberated with the sound of over-
grinders and cutting torches.

Ray was a stickler for details. "Larry, don't forget to pull
our plates off!" he shouted.

Ray was proud of what he had created. The business he "inherited" from Art was transformed into a real money-making operation. Cars of great value were stolen from the Twin Cities by Ray's crew and, one by one, they were driven back to French Creek to be stripped of their valuable parts. The skeletal remains were then hauled to the massive crusher outside to be formed into unidentifiable hunks of iron.

Ray's system seemed to be without flaw. It proved to be so lucrative that he seldom was tempted to stray from the established routine. John L. Rule's untimely visit was one of only a handful of recent hijackings that sometimes tempted the Steckels.

Once a week the crew left French Creek at sunset and headed for the Twin Cities. Once in town, they went to work. The mother car cruised around looking for valuable cars parked out of the way in unobtrusive locations. Once their target was selected, two men jumped out. One broke into the auto with a picking tool and started the car. False license plates were immediately installed on top of the original plates by the other team member for the trip west to French Creek. As the stolen vehicles were quickly driven out of town, the police seldom had a chance to track them down. Most owners didn't miss their cars until morning. The remaining members continued on until all but the chauffeur was left to drive himself back.

It was a foolproof plan. Cops would be hard pressed to figure out what was happening in time to stop them.

Once safely back in French Creek, the stolen vehicles were brought to the barn, where they were stripped of the most valuable, readily salable parts. This included the engine, stereo or CD, tires and wheel covers, leather seats, and anything else easily removed within an allotted one-hour time frame. The Steckels had refined their craft to a fine art. The massive crusher took care of the remaining evidence.

Ray looked around for his two cousins. He couldn't see either one—that always made him nervous. *Those two couldn't butter a piece of bread if they both had shovels,* he thought. He lit a cigarette and pondered how smoothly his operation ran. After being rendered nothing more than a block of steel, the cubes were loaded onto a flatbed trailer for the trip back to the Twin Cities. Complete turnaround time from theft to French Creek to delivery at the scrap yard was always less than twenty-four hours.

The stripped parts were loaded into a covered semi-trailer, and before dawn the truck was on the road to a parts wholesaler out west that never asked questions. The Steckels could easily strip and dispose of no fewer than three to four vehicles in a single night.

What old Arthur had set in motion continued to flourish. Profits from the business mounted, and with very little overhead and zero taxes paid, the current head of the family had become quite wealthy. Ray was proud of what he created, gave little or no credit to his father, and often boasted to his brother about how, "the old man should have hung around a little longer—I'd a shown him how to make some real dough!"

Mikey went back inside and strolled over to where Ray shouted instructions. Huge remained outside. He stopped, not quite remembering what he had been sent to do. Something about the dogs and a body. Oh, yes. The big man smiled broadly and belched. He was proud that he remembered. He stopped again. The dogs were back in the kennel. Half of his assigned task was already completed. He had only to go find the body and dispose of it. Huge was certain he had ample time to finish the unpleasant chore before his bowels stirred once more. The intervals between toilet visits had lengthened quite a bit.

Huge possessed a face and head that was quite unforgettable. His lips were non-existent—nothing more than two lines that met on both ends. His nose was bulbous, an easy target for boys to slug when he had been younger—at least those boys that could outrun Huge, which included ninety-nine percent of his tormentors. Like many children from the Steckel breeding line, Huge's teeth had been badly neglected. When he smiled, the color displayed was best described as swampy green. Because of the enormous quantity of sweets he consumed along with the lack of regular dental hygiene, Huge constantly suffered from horrific toothaches. These, of course, never dented his appetite.

His forehead was prominent—perched like a rocky outcropping over closely set, too small, brown eyes. His hair had never been professionally cut. As a child, his domineering mother took care of that chore once a month, hacking it off with dull scissors.

Once his mother died, his older brother Mikey inherited their mother's scissors. The style of cut remained unchanged. His hair color matched his eyes—muddy brown. The top of his head was as flat as the underside of a baking pan. Tufts of bristly hair poked out in all directions. With ears too small for the head they were born to, Huge retained an unchanging image from childhood on—that of an oversized Stan Laurel.

Huge disliked having to deal with death in any form, but since childhood, he had learned always to follow directions, especially Ray's directions. Thinking for himself always led to trouble for the amiable giant. He kept his task in mind and ambled slowly toward his truck.

"Hurry up you guys! We're behind schedule!" Ray shouted inside, and Huge ambled faster for a couple of paces.

"Hey, Ray, where d'ya think Dale was going in such a hurry?" Mikey inquired as he strolled past.

"What're you talking about?" This came out as a snarl.

Mikey blinked. "I dunno. I just saw Dale drive off in a big hurry in that fella's Explorer."

Ray gave that quick thought. "That couldn't have been Dale, you dumb ass! Dale's out by the crusher."

"I just figgered it had to be Dale," Mikey said, and shuffled back to his work-station.

Ray looked around the barn. He removed his cap and scratched his head. He paced and considered what he had just heard. Something was wrong. Unlike his two dim-witted cousins, Ray had been endowed with sufficient intelligence to keep his business running smoothly. He knew Dale wouldn't have left for home without telling him first.

Ray shouted to be heard above the racket of air tools and grinders. "Mikey! We got a problem! I think the city fella jest grabbed his truck and left! You and Huge take the truck and follow him while I round up Dale. Get on his tail, and let me know where you are on the CB."

Mikey dropped the cutting torch and ran out to catch his brother before he left. "Huge! Hold on a minute!" Mikey yelled, as he raced toward his brother's truck just as it started up. He clumped over the irregular, yellow piss stains in the snow, obliterating what he earlier had proudly created and put even more urine on his boots. He opened the passenger door, climbed inside, and quickly explained what had happened.

Huge, confused, asked his brother to repeat himself.

"That wasn't Dale that just left, you idiot! It was the city guy. Jesus, Huge, didn't you go out and get the dogs like you're supposed to?"

Huge now realized he had messed things up, and Ray would surely take it out on him. As Mikey settled into the Dodge Power Wagon, the larger brother said, "I had the shits, Mikey. I couldn't leave. I was going to go later."

"Well, you screwed up royally if the guy just got away. If he reaches town, we're in big trouble. Get this piece of shit moving! We have to catch up to him!"

Huge put the truck in gear and headed for the gate. Mikey turned on the CB and awaited word from Ray.

Huge was quiet as he tried to recall how he had screwed things up. Everyone seemed to be angry with him. He had a terrible headache, his teeth hurt, and he was suddenly hungry. He thought long and hard for a full five minutes. Large droplets of sweat formed on Huge's forehead. His already ruddy complexion turned many different shades of red and pink and purple. If the city fella got away, Ray would be more than pissed and take it out on him.

Huge didn't fear corporal punishment—physical pain was not something a man like Huge ever worried too much about—he was more concerned about losing his allowance. No money to buy Twinkies or M&M's or Snowballs or Double Whoppers or nothing. That truly frightened the big, simple man.

John knew he had been spotted as he left the property. He wasted no time putting some distance between himself and the junkyard if anyone decided to follow. Once freed, he no longer cared about who the men were nor what they were up to. There would be time enough for the police to sort it all out later. He tore down the dark gravel road. John wanted to get as far away as possible, warm up with the heater blasting and only then think about notifying the police.

The Explorer fishtailed from one side of the road to the other. John eased off on the gas pedal. The last thing he wanted now was to slip off the road and get stuck in a ditch. He hoped to find any road that would lead him south. He knew he'd have to run into the main east-west road, Highway 12. Reluctantly, he turned on the headlights and peered through the frosty windshield.

Once I head south, I'm sure I'll run into Cokato. Then I'll be safe and can call the cops—and Debbie. He sensed his first real feeling of escape and relished the idea of bringing down the gang of thugs at French Creek. Even the little bit that John knew about the activities taking place at French Creek had to be conveyed to the police, and as soon as he found a safe haven he'd contact them.

All at once, for the first time in many hours, John felt a real sense of euphoria. He had successfully escaped. Soon he'd be home again. He reveled in the blast of heat enveloping his chilled body.

Three miles behind him, Mikey and Huge followed. They knew they had to catch John before he reached the next intersection. The little gravel roads they had passed so far just wandered, and with so few of the farms round about inhabited, John would find little assistance. But the paved road at the next intersection led either to Highway 55 or south to Highway 12. Towns and people could help him escape. Chances were he'd head south but maybe he'd turn right in an attempt to fool them. Both men knew that if they guessed wrong, it could spell the end of everything.

Mikey sat up straight and turned to his brother. "Huge, did you at least drain the gas from the Explorer?"

Huge thought for a moment before answering. He tried to remember, but too much had happened. He was confused. Finally he replied cheerily, "Yeah, I'm pretty sure I did, Mikey. Why?"

"Because, you dumb ass, then he doesn't have any gas! That means he can't get very far, right?"

Just as Huge was about to reply, the CB radio crackled to life. It would be Ray or Dale asking where they were.

John's luck held. He reached the intersection of County Road 14 and, without slowing down, turned left, tires screaming in protest. He pressed hard on the gas pedal. *That's it! I'm home free!* The tarmac was clear and gave him new confidence so he kept the SUV floored. He desperately wanted to put as much distance between himself and French Creek as he possibly could. If he got stopped by the Highway Patrol for speeding, so much the better.

John glanced down at the dashboard and noted that he was traveling at eighty-five miles per hour. He'd be in Cokato in no time. However, he also noticed that the needle on the gas gauge was below empty—well into the red zone. *What the hell? I had the damn thing filled!* His heart fluttered.

His sense of euphoria vanished like the blown snow billowing behind the speeding truck. On foot in the dark, strange countryside, he might not have the strength to reach the main highway. And, if he were being followed as he feared, he could easily be tracked down and caught. He breathed heavily and gripped the wheel tightly, his joy giving way to dread.

The once-blessed, life-sustaining heat inside the cab became stifling. Sweat beaded and dripped down his face. If the truck died, all he could do was run into one of the adjoining fields and hide until daybreak. Then he'd just have to take his chances in the daylight. Again his mind ran to the dogs.

Ray was on the CB. "Breaker 19! Razor calling Mike-Man."

"Mike-Man here. Go ahead."

"Switch to the alternate channel," Ray instructed. They had a pre-determined, private channel selected for just such occasions.

"Where you at?" Ray asked quickly after the switch.

"Just approaching the intersection of County Road 14, but we don't know which way he went"

"You guys turn north, and we'll go south. if you spot the truck, give me a call."

"Roger! Mike-Man out"

Ray promptly got back on the radio. "Mikey, did Huge drain the gas on that truck like he was supposed to?"

"Yeah, I think so. He says he's pretty sure he did. That's his job, and he's pretty good about that."

"Bullshit! He couldn't remember when he ate last, much less if he drained the gas."

Mikey tried to defend his brother. "I know, but he always makes sure he empties out the gas in them cars that come in. He tried real hard to remember, Ray, and he's sure he did it."

"I don't trust that fat turd, Mikey. If he didn't drain the tank, the guy could drive all the way to Minneapolis—then we'll never catch him. Get off the radio, now."

Ray was silent as they approached the intersection. He gave the wheel a violent twist to the left, and the truck lurched to one side. "Goddammit, Dale, if that pile of goo messed up twice in one night, I swear I'll kill him!" He reached for the CB once more.

John was just a few miles from Cokato, and the truck had not yet run out of gas. The station he had stopped at earlier in the day was on the east end of town. He didn't think his chances were too great that the station would be still open at that late hour, but it was his only hope.

As he approached town, John noted very few lights. He glided to the Highway 12 intersection, the main drag through town, and looked to his right. Lights were on at Herb's Garage. *Sonofabitch! Finally, my luck is changing!*

John turned the corner and pressed the gas pedal, but there was no response. The SUV lurched, coughed and grew silent. The truck coasted and slowed, and, as he neared the station, John wrenched the wheel to the left. Without the power steering, it took effort to turn the big truck.

With just enough momentum, he slipped up next to the gas pumps, stopped, turned off the ignition and hopped out. He ran to the station door, grabbed the door knob and turned it. The door opened, and with a gasp of relief, John stumbled inside. The station was open; someone was in the small building after all.

Herb left his desk as John entered. "Hey, I remember you," he offered. "You came in earlier today looking for directions to French Creek. You ever find it?"

Breathlessly, John answered in rapid-fire sentences. "Yeah. Damn near got killed. Barely escaped. Guys are a bunch of thieves and murderers. Need to use your phone, quick. Gotta call the police."

"I can't believe that," Herb said, his gentle smile dimpling his stubbled cheeks. "I've known the Steckels all my life. You sure you got the right place?"

"Positive! They tried to kill me with their dogs, then they stole my truck. Where the hell is the phone?"

"Take a deep breath, young fella. Tell ya what. You try to calm down, and I'll call the sheriff for you. Have a seat." Herb pointed at the chair in front of his desk and picked up the receiver.

John knew he was shaking and gratefully did as the old man asked. As he settled into the small folding chair, Herb dialed.

"Hello, Elroy? It's Herb. Yeah, I know it's late. Say, a young fellow is sitting here claiming the Steckels tried to kill him and stole his truck. That's right. He's here now. You want to talk to him? Hang on." Herb held out the receiver to John. "Here you go. You tell the sheriff your whole story."

"Hello? What? No, I'm not kidding. Those assholes out at French Creek locked me in and turned the dogs loose." John paused and sat up straight as he listened to the sheriff. "No, I haven't been drinking, and yes I'm sure it was intentional. I think they chased me into town. You think I made all this up? Send someone over here before they find me again! Yeah, right." John held the receiver out to Herb. "Here, he wants to talk to you. Hurry up, please. I need to call my wife." He settled back in the chair and took a deep breath.

Herb turned away, spoke briefly to the sheriff, and then hung up. John stood, walked quickly around the desk, and picked up the phone once more. Herb stepped aside as he began dialing. John sat down, waiting for Debbie to answer.

After a few rings, his wife answered, "Hello?"

"Debbie! It's me!" John shouted.

"John? Where are you? What happened? I've been calling all over looking for you. I've been worried sick! Are you all right?"

The words quickly tumbled from John's mouth. "I'm in Cokato, Sweetheart, and I'm okay. I don't have time to explain it all to you now. I was almost killed by a bunch of guys at a place called French Cr—" THUMP!

From someplace far away, John heard a roar. White, flashing lights appeared behind his eyelids. His head hurt only briefly before he passed out.

❖ 5 ❖

HERB PUT DOWN THE HEAVY METAL WASTEBASKET. It had served its purpose, ending the phone call well before John could reveal much information. John fell across the desk. Herb stood behind him, poised to strike again if necessary, but there was no need for any further blows. John was out cold. Herb picked up the receiver and replaced it. The garage owner reached for the CB mike.

"Razor? You copy?"

"Go ahead," Ray replied.

"You were right. That guy drifted in here. Right after I turned the lights on, he came barging through the door."

"Where's he at now?"

"You better come over, and I'll show you."

"Roger. Be there in five. Did he make any phone calls?"

Herb paused, uncertain how to answer. "He insisted on calling the police. I called the sheriff for him." Herb purposely neglected to tell his cousin about the second call. He knew he'd have to answer too many angry questions if he did.

"Good job, cousin. I owe you big time for this."

Herb was not a violent man, but he knew enough to protect the family interests. He couldn't allow John to escape. More than once, Herb had alerted his cousin to a particular traveler looking for the salvage yard. If the poor soul was lost, from the Cities, and drove an expensive vehicle, Herb's job was to alert Ray. He never asked any questions.

At one time, Herb had attempted to sever all ties with Ray, but threats to his wife convinced Herb he had better continue to do as he was told. He glanced down at John. He was sorry for what he had done but rationalized his act simply: he didn't owe anything to the stranger and he had to protect Margie.

Herb dragged John's body out into one of the service bays. He didn't want anyone passing by on the street to notice what was going on inside. He gently laid John's head down on the concrete and, once again, thought about Ray. Years ago he had witnessed the severe and unnecessary beating Ray administered to a man outside a local tavern. Ray beat the man almost to death—and felt no remorse for doing so. As a matter of fact, he had a look of pleasure on his face when he was finished. Herb shuddered at the memory.

Subsequently called as a witness at Ray's trial, Herb perjured himself. Ray had threatened to harm Margie if he didn't lie. Didn't matter, though. Six other witnesses testified that Ray had "inflicted extreme and unusual punishment" on the poor man. Ray went to prison. Once released, Herb played along and looked the other way. His health, more importantly Margie's, depended on keeping quiet.

Herb waited for Ray in his office. He closed his eyes and breathed heavily. A slight tremor that began at the tip of one forefinger quaked noticeably, then moved up his wrist and arm. He quickly shook the arm to rid himself of the telltale shiver.

The Rule home stood in stark contrast to rest of the dark, snow-covered neighborhood in the small town of Wayzata. Unlike the other houses on the block, light poured from every window, as if the residents were expecting guests.

Inside, a frightened and concerned Deborah Rule replaced the phone in the cradle, standing on unsteady legs. She was trembling, her face ashen. She struggled to make sense of the few brief words she'd heard from her husband. It was very late; she was alone with her two daughters, and her husband was in some kind of trouble. She stared at the phone in disbelief.

Her conversation with John had been cut short. He had been in mid-sentence when she heard an abrupt, unidentified sound. Then the line went dead. A moment before, she had felt relief and elation. John was apparently safe and would be returning home soon. Now her concern had multiplied.

She waited a few minutes, hoping against hope that John would call back, that there had been some glitch in the phone system. Time passed without a return call. Clearly something else had happened.

She called her father for help and advice: "Daddy? I know it's late, but I'm worried. John called a moment ago, said he was safe and started to tell me where he was. Then we were cut off, and the phone went dead."

"Did he tell you where he was or what he had been doing?"

"Kind of. He was talking really fast. I had a hard time understanding him, but he said something about almost being killed, and that he was in . . . Mankato, I think, but he was all right."

Mac Davis was an attorney; specifically, he practiced criminal law. A widower, Mac lived alone with his dog, Charlie. Ever since his wife's untimely death a few years earlier, he had thrown himself into his work to ease the pain of her loss. His only remaining family consisted of his daughter, Deborah, John, and two lovely granddaughters.

Mac knew John had had a drinking problem. The only time he'd attempted to talk to him about it had been an abysmal failure. As a result, Mac didn't completely trust his son-in-law—not yet, anyway. Confronting John about his problem had just put more distance between them. He now feared that John's mysterious absence was another of his periodic drinking binges. He'd return home when he was ready—not before. On the other hand, if he was off drinking someplace, he probably wouldn't have called.

Mac's training and experience in interrogation promptly took over. "Debbie, try to remember exactly what he said. Take your time."

Debbie paused to collect herself, sitting down on the edge of the sofa. "I'm really scared, Daddy. I'm certain he said he'd almost been killed by some guys. He said he was in a town that sounded like Mankato, but now I'm not sure exactly if he said Mankato. He said something else . . . something . . . 'French.' There was more to it, I'm sure, but right then we were cut off."

Mac took a moment to digest her words. Out of habit, be began making notes on a yellow legal pad. "How long has he been gone?"

"He left home this morning . . . yesterday really, I guess. All he said was he'd be gone all day making sales calls. I think he said he was heading west, but I'm not too sure about that. I was getting the girls off to school. He did say he'd be home for dinner, though. He couldn't have intended to go too far."

Mac decided it was time to notify the police. "You stay there with the kids. I'll call the police, and then come right over. Why don't you call your friend Maggie to come over and stay with you?"

"That's a good idea, Daddy."

"Don't worry, we'll find him!" Mac tried to sound hopeful, but his concern mounted with each passing minute.

He hung up the phone and headed for the shower. He decided he'd spend the rest of the night at his daughter's house, so he might as well dress for the day. After his shower, he took Charlie for a short walk to relieve the dog's bladder, all the while silently reviewing what Debbie had told him. He tried to think of who he knew that could help him.

He ran down a list of people in law enforcement. The police wouldn't get on the case for forty-eight hours—standard procedure. He had to find someone who could cut through the red tape, someone to look into the matter as soon as possible. At once he thought he knew just the person who could help. "Come on, Charlie, let's go."

He returned back to the house and put in a call to a friend in the county attorney's office. Just as he feared, his friend confirmed what he already knew.

"They won't do anything for two days, Mac." Jack said.

"I know. I'm looking for a favor, old friend. Just see what you can find out for me. I'm going over to Debbie's house. She's pretty upset. I'll call you back later."

"I'll see what I can do for you."

Satisfied that something positive was now being done to locate John, Mac summoned Charlie, locked the house, and climbed into his Suburban for the short drive to his daughter's house.

Both he and Debbie's family lived in the small village of Wayzata, a fairly affluent community on the shores of Lake Minnetonka. He and his wife, Barbara, had lived there for many years and raised their family in the very same house he was now leaving.

Years later, Debbie and John built a home nearby to be close to the only family either of them had. As Mac drove the short distance to Debbie's, he still had the same nagging concern about John's drinking problem. He had been sober for two years, had a

68

few slips—but not lately. But John always did his drinking away from home, and that fit this situation.

Mac was pensive—duly concerned about his daughter and her family. He considered that maybe John had concocted this absurd story to cover up another drunken binge. Seemed unlikely and out of character, but even so, Mac remembered the last time John slipped, and how it had caused Debbie a great deal of pain and suffering. He resigned himself to having to question his daughter further about his son-in-law's drinking.

It was 3:00 A.M. when Mac pulled into his daughter's driveway. Debbie peered out and waited at the door for her father. She immediately hugged Mac tightly. Charlie silently entered alongside his master and settled down in a familiar place, underneath the kitchen table where normally he was certain to pick up a few scraps of food. Debbie had done her best to restrain her emotions since John's call, but now she could contain herself no longer.

Mac let her cry for a few minutes and led her into the kitchen. "Sweetheart, we need to talk. Are you going to be okay?"

"I'm sorry, Daddy, but I really am worried about John. Something in his voice terrified me!"

"I know, Honey, but we need to figure out what to do next." Mac's tone was consoling and patient. "Tell me again exactly what he said."

Debbie recounted her brief conversation with John one more time. She was certain he had said "Mankato" followed by "French."

Mac again jotted down what Debbie said, verbatim. He picked up a road map of Minnesota, located Mankato, and noted its relationship to the Twin Cities. "Debbie, did John leave from home, or did he go to the office first?" Mac peered at the map.

"He left from home."

"I have a friend in the county attorney's office. He's going to pull some strings and get the state police involved." Mac recounted the typical forty-eight-hour waiting period. "Deb, I have to ask you a tough question: Are you positive that John has not had a slip in the past two years?"

Debbie paused. She had not even considered the possibility that John might have been drinking. "The fear and relief I heard in his voice was real, Daddy. There wasn't a hint of deception. No, John hasn't touched a drop that I know about. I don't think that's what's happening now."

"I know how you feel about his sobriety, Deb, but we really need to consider the possibility that this could be a bad slip."

Mac considered the possibilities. "Debbie, do you remember what happened after your mom died?"

Debbie looked at her father, a puzzled look on her pale face. "You mean what John did?"

"Yes. Let's talk about that. You know your mother always had the ability to relate to other people's problems, and I gather that Barbara and John had a special relationship. Did John ever tell you about the last conversation he had with your mother?"

Debbie considered her father's question. After silently reliving those painful days, she attempted to answer. "After mom's death, John suffered in silence. He only briefly spoke to me about his last conversation with her. I gathered that in addition to some personal comments, she asked him to stay strong for me and the girls."

She spoke haltingly, trying hard to keep her emotions in check. "Knowing mom, their conversation probably affected John deeply. He told me about it the night he returned home from the hunting trip. She tried to get him to forgive his parents, especially his dad, to bury the past, address his pain and anger and move on. You know, Daddy, nothing Mother ever said was malicious or unfeeling." Debbie wept openly.

Mac laid a comforting arm across her shoulders. "I know that better than anyone, Sweetheart."

Debbie continued. "She had a tremendous ability for saying exactly the right thing at the right time. John just didn't know how to deal with his emotions."

"What happened after . . . after Barbara passed away?"

"After a while, he grew increasingly restless and inattentive. That was when he had his last slip—on the hunting trip."

"You called me after you found out John was up at the camp, drunk and alone. Do you remember that?"

"Yes. You asked me what I wanted you to do."

"And you asked me to drive up and see if he was okay, right?"

"Yes."

"I said I would, but I was afraid the result would be the same as the last time I confronted him about his drinking."

"I remember."

"And, if I had gone, I know what would have happened. Alcoholics are in denial, Sweetheart. Nothing that anyone else says has an impact on them. Other friends of mine who have battled this disease all admit that they have to find the absolute bottom of the pit before they decide to quit." Mac looked at his daughter, knowing his words were harsh, but also knowing she had to hear them and understand what she was dealing with. "I know you were angry with me for not going up there, but believe me, Deb, there was nothing I could have done."

"I know, Daddy. I was so worried about him though." She thought about John's return home a few days later, and how ashamed and apologetic he was.

Mac pressed on. "What finally happened, Deb? What did John tell you when he came home?"

"We talked for the longest time. I think it was the first time I felt like John truly shared his feelings with me—his pain, his anger. And then, he told me about mom's parting words." Debbie dried her eyes. "I believed him then, and I believe in him now,

Daddy. John's in trouble, and it has nothing to do with alcohol. I'm sure of that."

Mac decided that he had to support Debbie's conviction. "I did sense a change in John after that weekend, and if you believe that strongly in his promise, then that's good enough for me. I'm sorry I had to put you through this, Honey."

"That's okay, Daddy. I know you mean well."

Mac decided she could handle another issue related to the same problem. "You remember Jack Stevens? He was here for the Christmas party. He's my friend at the county, and he's well aware of John's drinking problem. I'm concerned that any further investigation into John's disappearance might get bogged down by this drinking issue. The police'll want to know John's history, and Jack would be obliged to provide a background for them."

"Which means, what? That they won't look for him?"

Mac saw the instant panic in his daughter's eyes. He quickly said, "No, but we need to face the facts, Deb. The police are naturally going to be skeptical, and I'm concerned that they might not pursue this as fast as we'd like. We need to try to figure out where he is on our own, just in case the cops drag their feet."

"Us? What can we do?"

"Let's attempt to backtrack John's customer calls yesterday, and see if anyone remembers where he was headed next."

"John's office won't be open for hours."

"I know. Maybe Jack has some news by now." He reached for the phone.

As Mac dialed Jack's number, he kept looking at the French scribbled on the yellow legal pad. Jack answered after two rings.

"Mac here, Jack."

"Hi, Mac. How's Debbie doing?" Jack queried.

"Holding up, but as time passes, it's going to get tougher."

"I know. Here's the deal: The state police have an alert out for John and his truck. Every trooper in Minnesota'll be watching for his Explorer. I've contacted the Mankato police, but so far they report nothing out of the ordinary."

"Jack, remember I told you John mentioned something about a French something when he spoke to Debbie?"

"Yeah. That's got me puzzled. It could be almost anything."

"How do we research anything with that name in the Mankato area?" Mac wondered aloud.

"Someone'll have to access our database at the capital and come up with a list of possibilities. I'll get that started right now. Meanwhile, give Debbie my best. Tell her we are doing everything we can to find John."

"Thanks, Jack. You're a good friend. I appreciate all you're doing."

"It's nothing you haven't done for me, Mac. I'll talk to you later."

Mac hung up the phone and filled Debbie in on the conversation. It was now almost 5:00 A.M. The dawn of the cold, dreary February day would not appear for another two hours. Father and daughter sat in the quiet living room, each enveloped in private thoughts, each worried and helpless to do anything about the situation. They had to wait. As uncomfortable as that was, they each settled into the waiting with determination to remain strong.

At quarter to seven, Debbie decided to make breakfast for her father. She needed to stay busy but had no appetite herself. She already had gone over every possible explanation for her husband's disappearance more than once. Each time, she came up against the same blank wall. None of it made any sense. Yesterday morning had been entirely normal. John's behavior and demeanor were light and playful. He even suggested a quick return to bed before he left! Debbie smiled at the memory.

Then the smile left her face, replaced with worry. The girls would be waking up soon. She would to have to tell them what was going on.

As if her father read her mind, he asked, "Debbie, what have you told the girls?"

At that moment both daughters entered the kitchen, sleepy eyed and immediately surprised by Mac's presence.

"Grampa? What are you doing here?" Melissa asked, crossing the room to give her grandfather a warm hug and kiss. Sarah followed, hugging Mac around the neck. Charlie rose from beneath the table, tail wagging furiously. "Hi, Charlie!" Melissa said, bending down to give her friend a pat on the head.

Mac kissed each of his granddaughters in greeting, then caught Debbie's eye to see if she would okay his giving the explanation. She returned a slight nod. "Your mom called me because she's worried about your dad. He didn't return home last night. We know he is okay because he called, and we should hear from him again, shortly." Mac did not feel it was necessary to enlighten the girls any further.

"So, where is dad?" Melissa asked.

Debbie took over. "Your father called me last night to tell me he was all right, but we got disconnected. Something wrong with the phone, I guess."

The bacon sizzled, and Debbie turned back to the stove.

Both girls looked somewhat concerned, but they went upstairs to dress for school. Mac busied himself pouring over his notes as he ate breakfast. He thought about what Debbie had said and realized they knew nothing more than they had earlier that night. "When is Maggie coming over, Sweetheart?"

Debbie seemed to draw herself up from dark thoughts. "Um . . . soon, I think." She looked at the clock. "In a little while, after she gets her kids off to school."

Mac decided it was time to find out everything he could about John L. Rule. "Deb, I remember only snatches about what happened to John's parents? Didn't his father leave home under, well . . . suspicious circumstances?"

Debbie stopped, turned and wiped her hands on her apron. "His father left home when John was a small boy, eleven or twelve, I think he said. Just disappeared one day along with the company truck he drove."

"Really. No one ever heard from him again?"

Debbie frowned, and then sat down across from her father. "No. John didn't like talking about him much. I don't think John ever forgave him for abandoning him and his mother like that. His father's company thought he stole the truck and took off for places unknown."

"Strange. His name was William or Wallace or something?"

"Um . . . no. Walter. Walter S. Rule."

Mac's curiosity was aroused. "What did he do for a living?"

"He had a route of some kind. Let's see . . . what was it? Oh, I can't remember. John said he had just been given a promotion along with a gold watch. A week later he took off in a new company truck. Everyone else, including the police, thought he stole the truck and sold it someplace, but John and his mother never believed that. At least, his mother didn't."

"Why not?"

Debbie paused, trying to remember the emotion of John's telling. "John said that he and his father were together all the time. Did lots of things together. I could see the love in his face when he talked about the early years. It sounded like they had been very close."

"What did John believe happened?" Mac asked.

"In time he came to believe that his father did indeed abandon him and his mother. He's still full of anger and resentment over the whole thing, although, like I said, he seldom speaks about his father. Oh, I remember! He was a milkman—or maybe a mailman. I don't know, Daddy. What does it matter now?"

"Probably nothing," Mac said. He scribbled on his yellow pad. Father left home. New truck. Milkman? Mailman? Never returned. Son. ditto. ditto. What's the connection? But—John called home! Similarity ends. Interesting, but . . . He scratched his head. Dead end.

"I remember his mother died shortly after you two were married."

"Just six months afterwards. Daddy? What are you thinking? What could this have to do with John's parents?"

"Nothing, Sweetheart . . . You know me, always the nosy one. I'm just trying to find out as much as I can to try and get a handle on where he might be. You know, all of that would be quite a bit for a young boy to handle. It's amazing that John didn't have more problems with all that in his past."

Debbie sat down on one of the kitchen chairs, her eyes misting. "I know, Daddy. That's why I'm so proud of all he's accomplished . . . and I just know that whatever's happening to him now is not of his doing."

Melissa returned to the kitchen. Unlike her younger sister, she knew there was more to her father's story than she had been told. She stood next to her grandfather and laid her hand on his shoulder. "What's really going on, Grampa?"

She peered over his shoulder at his notes. Mac had underscored some of the key words and phrases, and Melissa stared at these now. Aware of his granddaughter's gaze, Mac covered up the last few comments. "Why don't you have breakfast with me, Sweetie?"

"Okay, but you didn't answer my question, Grampa. And what do those notes mean?" Melissa gave her grandfather a very serious look.

Mac glanced at Debbie, eyebrows raised. She nodded. "Sweetheart, we still think your father is safe, but we just don't know where he is, or what happened to him." That said, Mac and Debbie filled Melissa in on all that John told Debbie, though they both tried to keep their concerns out of the discussion.

Sarah came down and the four of them finished their breakfast in silence. Melissa had a late-start morning and returned to her room, but Sarah ran for the bus when it lumbered up the drive.

With the girls gone Mac and Debbie again tried to make sense of John's short, alarming phone call. The words "tried to kill me," had a chilling effect on them both. They spent the next hour working and reworking the words Debbie thought she'd heard, desperate to find some clue as to John's whereabouts. As one, they were all hopeful, but each secretly imagined the worst.

❖ 6 ❖

EARLY IN THE EVENING OF JOHN'S ESCAPE from the salvage yard, the Minneapolis Police Department—robbery and burglary division—were tracking a stolen car. For months, the police had been baffled by the continuing theft of expensive automobiles in the Twin Cities. A sting operation was their only hope of catching the perpetrators. Normal sources had turned up little information about who was responsible, so they decided to set out bait in an attempt to end the spate of thefts. Convinced that the gang responsible had to be local, they concluded a shop had been established somewhere close by. The stolen autos vanished immediately. It was assumed they were stripped of the valuable parts for sale out of state. An operation of such size and scope should have been common knowledge on the street—but it was not.

For the past few weeks, the police had parked a late model BMW on a side street near downtown Minneapolis. The cops monitored their bait with round-the-clock stakeouts. If the thieves plucked the car, it was hoped that the trail would lead to a chop shop somewhere in the vicinity. Unfortunately, the BMW attracted other small-time thieves as well. Employing crude but effective methods, the non-targeted miscreants slowed the police by trying to steal the car. After a couple of insignificant arrests, the cops finally had their first serious nibble.

"I think we've got a live one tonight, Frank."

"Yeah, I see 'em." Four cops, two in two separate unmarked cars, watched as two men got out of a van and approached the BMW. Instead of police radios that crooks could monitor, they used walkie-talkies to communicate.

With little more than a pause one man opened the locked car with a flat-bladed tool, while the other had stooped next to the rear license plate. He ran around to the front license, then hopped into the passenger side of the van. The car engine started up, and the car took off.

Frank said. "Better get on the horn and let Reasons know what's going on. These guys look like pros."

"There they go. Do we follow the Beemer or the van?"

"You follow the BMW, and we'll tail the truck."

Steve and his partner followed the BMW. They stayed well back, just close enough to maintain sight of a tiny, intense beam of light from one taillight. An old trick employed first by the FBI, a small hole was drilled in the red plastic. The sharp beam of light could then be seen and followed from greater distances at night.

Frank picked up the radio to call Detective Sam Reasons, the officer in charge of the operation.

After a brief conversation with his associate, Reasons hung up the phone and put on his coat. "Finally!"

He had just notified the state patrol that they were following the BMW. It appeared the perpetrators were heading west, away from Minneapolis. He left the house and climbed into an unmarked car parked in front. He drove to his partner's house, stopped and honked the horn. Immediately, the door opened. Rick came out and jumped in the car.

"Maybe we'll get lucky tonight, Rick."

"Let's hope so. This is the first serious break we've had on this case in months. Where are they headed?"

"Last report had them going west on Highway 12. You know, that beam idea works great in clear air, but if our guy pulls off on a dirt road, or if it starts snowing, our guys'll lose sight of it."

Sam turned on the siren, put the red light on top, and sped off into the night. "I want to be there before someone screws up this operation."

Reasons was right to be concerned—the chase dissolved almost immediately. The BMW turned off the main highway some distance from town.

"We lost 'em, Sam. Now what?" Steve reported.

"What the hell happened?"

"Hell's bells, I don't know. Either he spotted us or we missed a turn. Lot of dust and stuff flying around on these dirt roads, Sam."

"Where are you?" Reasons inquired.

"Geez, we don't know. Out in the boondocks, that's where."

Detective Reasons was irate. "Dammit it to hell! That guy's got to be close to wherever the hell he was headed!" Sam asked the state patrol to notify him of any suspected repair shop in the area. Before long, the dispatcher replied. "Reasons? There's a salvage yard near French Creek. Could be that's your target."

"Steve, meet us at the French Creek Salvage Yard. I think our boy is headed there."

"Directions?"

"Just go north on 77. I'm waiting for more specifics." He replaced the mike and addressed his partner. "Have you heard what I heard?"

"About the yard?"

"Yep. Apparently it's been under suspicion for years, but so far, it's all rumor. Nothing's ever stuck. That has to be the place!" Reasons picked up the radio. "Steve, you there?"

After a moment, the detective responded. "Ten-four."

"Any word on the van?"

"Roger. Frank lost it coming out of downtown. Could've turned on 394. It's probably headed in the same direction."

"Nuts! Where the hell are we, Rick?"

"Take it easy, Sam. You'll bust a gasket! We just passed through Montrose."

"Jeez, we must be seventy-five miles from town. We're out in goat country, for Christ's sake!"

It was almost 10:30 P.M. "Where are those directions, Rick?"

All at once the voice of the patrol's dispatcher came over the radio: "Reasons? Do you copy?"

"Ten four!"

"The French Creek Salvage Yard is on County Road 34. Two miles west of State Highway 77, and about five miles east of 14."

Reasons palmed the mike. "Where are we right now?"

Rick looked at a map and discovered they'd just passed 77. "Turn around, Sam. We missed the road."

Sam hit the breaks. The car skidded, and he spun the wheel. He stepped on the gas and turned off as instructed. "Now where?"

"Stay on this until we see County 34, then take a left."

Before long they were traveling ninety miles an hour. "Just as Sam started to speak, Rick spotted the sign. "Hold it! There it is!"

Reasons slammed on the brakes. The unmarked car skidded and headed for a deep ditch. Reasons fought the wheel and managed to avoid disaster.

"Damn! That was close."

"No shit, Schmidt! I'd rather not spend the night in the ditch, Sam."

Reasons backed up, reversed direction for the second time, drove back, and turned on County 34. "Now how far?"

"Don't know. The guy didn't say."

Sam kept driving, slower than before. They were on a gravel road, and it was partially covered with snow. "Jesus H. Christ! Doesn't anyone live around here?"

"Sure is desolate. Not a light anywhere. Wonder why all the farms are deserted?" Rick picked up the handset and notified the other patrol cars involved in the chase to converge on the salvage yard. "No sirens, no lights," he said.

"We have to be close," Reasons said. "We're going to have to rely on moonlight, Rick. I don't want to scare these guys off before we have a plan worked out." They crested a steep hill at a high rate of speed and then braked for one last time. The salvage yard spread out before them. They skidded to a stop at the same point that John had earlier that day.

The other patrol cars were already parked in front. Sam and his partner looked over the moonlit landscape. They couldn't believe what they sere seeing. "Holy mackerel! Take a look at all that! This has to be the place, Rick. Looks too quiet though. We must've lost over an hour trying to find this. That Beemer could be in a hundred pieces by now."

By the time the cops gathered in front of the French Creek Salvage Yard, John was driving west—away from his captors.

Ray Steckel was just leaving the west gate to join the chase, when his CB crackled to life. "Breaker 19, Razor—you got your ears on?"

"Go ahead."

"Switch to the alternate, Razor."

"Who's calling?"

"Sentinel."

Ray switched to the alternate frequency. "Roger, Sentinel. What's up?"

"You've got problems tonight—big ones!" Sentinel said.

"I already have enough trouble for one night. Now what?"

"Don't know all the details. Seems the state police and some city cops had a sting operation set up to catch your boys. They lost sight of the car but figured out it had to be headed for a junkyard—yours."

"What are they doing, and where are they?" Ray asked, now alarmed and more than a little irritated at the way the night was unfolding.

"Setting up shop outside your front gate, just waiting for some movement inside, I guess."

"Shit! Okay. Anything else?"

Ray listened intently as his informant passed additional information. "Keep me posted if they start sniffing around the west side."

"You got it." Sentinel signed off.

John was a prisoner once again, and this time Ray Steckel would take charge to insure he didn't slip from their grasp a second time. Ray and Dale pulled in to Herb's Garage. "We got to get this asshole out of here—fast. I need to find out what happened," Ray said to his brother. They left the truck and went inside the service station.

Herb was sitting at his desk when the Steckels entered, but he jumped up from his chair, looking nervous. Ray got right to the point. "Herb, what'd this guy say to you?"

Herb shrugged. "He just said he ran into a bunch of guys that were trying to kill him, Ray." Herb's voice faltered. Always on edge when his cousin was present, Herb's voice slipped to a slight whine. "That's all he said. Then he asked to use the phone."

Ray eyed his cousin closely. "Made just the one call, right?"

Herb was frightened, sweating in the overheated shop. "Yep. Soon as he turned his back, I clobbered him!"

Ray watched as Herb removed his cap and ran nervous hands through his grey hair. *He's lying—the jerk looks like a headache with hair!* Convinced that Herb would stick to his story anyway, he let the subject drop. "Where'd you stash him?"

"He's in the back, Ray. I tied him up just in case he woke up before you got here."

"Did you gag him?"

"No. Jeez, I forgot, Ray. I'll go take care of that right now." Herb ran from the office.

After Herb left, Ray told his brother his plan. "We got to get this guy out of here. His truck too. I'm gonna have the two idiots load him in the semi and take him out to Herman's. That way we get rid of *all* the evidence."

"How they gonna do that?" Dale asked.

"Don't you worry your little pea-brain any more than you have to. I got it all figured out. I'll tell 'em what to do when it's time. I'm gonna unload all the stolen parts at Herman's."

"Will Herman take 'em?"

"He's done it before. Besides, he won't have any choice in the matter. Anyway, if he doesn't cooperate, he knows I have someone who'll beat the daylights out of him—and that half-wit kid of his too!" Ray moved away from the front window and faced his brother. "Quit looking at me that way, will ya? That goofy eyeball of yours gives me the willies!"

Dale turned his head away. "Aw, Ray, you know I can't help it!"

"You could control the damned thing if you wanted to."

"I can't. It kind'a goes where it wants to."

"The old man always said you looked like a Studebaker with one headlight! He wasn't too far wrong." Ray enjoyed berating his brother.

"Get on the radio and have Huge and Mikey go back to the shop. Tell them to load the semi with the parts and meet us at the roadside park east of town. And tell 'em to hurry up. If the cops show, they should call me on the CB before they say anything. Got it?"

"Yeah, I guess so." Dale turned away, shoulders slumped. "Wait a minute. One more thing. Make sure they clean up the shop. I don't want any evidence laying around."

Dale headed out to his truck. Ray turned out the office lights and went out to get John's Explorer. He pumped a few gallons of gas in the empty tank and drove it around to the rear. Back inside, he walked over to the still form of John L. Rule. He rolled him over with his foot, and looked down. "How the hell did you away from the dogs?" he said to the still form. "You're not very big. Don't look too tough. Must'a jumped up on something or hid inside one a them bigger trucks. Well, you sure got your teat in a wringer this time didn't you, boy!" Ray said as he removed John's wallet.

"John L. Rule. Wayzata." Ray removed the picture of Debbie and the girls. "Nice looking skirt you got there, Johnny. Too bad you won't be pokin' her no more." Ray chuckled. "Herb, get over here and help me move this guy."

Herb joined his cousin, and together they hauled John's limp body out to the Explorer. "Boy! You must've whacked him good, Herb. Guy looks deader than a mackerel." He closed the tailgate and peered in at John. "Well, asshole, you won't be causing me any more trouble."

Ray turned to face Herb. "Go home and keep your mouth shut!"

"You can count on me, Ray." Herb closed up the station, knowing his night's work was done, and headed home. He cast a regretful look at John, then hurried home, thoughts of Margie and of protecting her foremost in his mind.

Ray drove the Explorer behind his brother to the designated rendezvous. The town and highway were both nearly deserted.

The semi had been loaded with the stolen parts. The last of the cars were crushed and placed on the flatbed. Huge and Mikey replaced two steel planks inside the semi and closed it up.

Larry was in charge of the flatbed. Once loaded with the cubes of steel, he would drive to Minneapolis. He was to phone Ray at home before he left the steel wholesaler for the return trip.

In a hurry to vacate the building, Larry had bumped the BMW with the forklift. The two rear plates, the bogus plate and the original, fell off. Larry missed seeing them in his haste to finish and, as one, they slid across the floor and settled beneath the welding tanks. The brothers shut down the crusher, finished loading Larry's flatbed, turned out the lights, locked the doors, and drove the semi away. All evidence of the night's activities had been removed. The building and gate were locked. The shop had been swept clean.

Just as Huge and Mikey left the premises, Detective Reasons decided to break into the main office on the east side of the sprawling property. One of the troopers took his night stick and broke out the window in the front door. As the trooper reached through the broken glass to unlatch the door, the remaining Doberman grabbed the cop's wrist. The trooper screamed and reached for his sidearm. He pointed it at the dog and pulled the trigger. A second shriek filled the night air. The shot struck the dog on the shoulder. Distracted, the dog loosened his grip on the cop's arm.

Relieved that he was free from the animal's jaws, the trooper staggered back and collapsed to the ground. Shaking and in a great deal of pain, he stared at his bloody arm.

Detective Reasons approached the broken window. He played the flashlight beam back and forth inside the office, looking for the wounded dog. He caught a brief glimpse of the animal as he limped away. He pointed both his service revolver and flashlight at the retreating form of the dog, waited for it to turn, aimed for its chest, and pulled the trigger. The impact knocked the dog across the room. It landed against the parts counter and collapsed to the floor. When Reasons was certain the dog was down for good, he signaled the all clear.

The police entered the office in force. Weapons drawn, alert for any additional canine presence, they searched the building. Outside, behind the building, they found another dog, dead from an apparent blow to the head. They noted the broken window in the rear, and wondered who might have attempted to enter the building that same night, and why.

Somehow this just doesn't fit, Reasons concluded. *This night's getting stranger by the minute.* "Place's empty. No sign of any recent activity. Rick, you find anything in the other buildings?"

"Nope. Nothin', Sam. None of these buildings are big enough to strip a bunch of stolen cars. Must be the wrong place."

"I don't think so. None of this makes any sense, though. Why the broken window? Where the hell did the BMW go?"

Sam walked around the property. He glanced west, over the hill, and noted lights moving in the distance. Then he realized his mistake. *They strip the cars somewhere else—away from the main office! Of course! They wouldn't risk discovery by peeling cars around here.*

"Rick! Quick, get a couple of cars headed down the road. I think there's another entrance—more buildings."

He took one more look around the interior of the dingy office, shut the door and followed the others. As he climbed into the squad car, Reasons berated himself for being so stupid. *I must be getting old. Too many years on the job. Hell, not too long ago, I could have rounded up these clowns by myself.* Angered at his own stupidity, he watched the lights disappear in the distance. *Shit, if we blow this I'm going to have some serious explaining to do.*

Huge and Mikey were the last to leave. They drove the semi down the gravel road toward Cokato. They were well out of sight as the first police cars reached the west entrance.

Rick shot the lock off the gate. He and the other cops entered the property, weapons drawn. Rick decided to wait for Reasons. Two of the troopers walked around the back of the building.

By the time Detective Reasons reached the scene, Huge and Mikey had turned south on 14 on their way to the roadside park to hook up with Ray and Dale.

Sam and the others entered the building, weapons drawn. They flipped a bank of switches and a grid of florescent lamps illuminated the shop. Reasons took a quick look around and realized that he still had a problem.

There was no evidence of the stolen BMW. He'd made an illegal search. He looked around the interior—nothing incriminating in view. "Take two cars and drive down the gravel road," Reasons instructed. "See if you can catch whoever just left—stop everyone you see. I don't care if it's the pastor coming home from choir practice!"

The troopers sped off, sirens blaring and lights flashing. Detective Reasons continued to search through the pole barn. He was in too deep now to leave empty handed. The place just felt right to Reasons; the place even smelled illegal to the alert detective. He needed more than a strong feeling, however, before he could build a case against the perpetrators. Thus far, all illegal activity was alleged.

Sam was short two men, as the unfortunate trooper who had the run-in with the Doberman had to be driven to Litchfield to have his arm treated. "Rick, take the rest of the guys and go over this place as carefully as you can. Look for anything incriminating. There has to be something here they missed."

The air was heavy with the acrid smell of burnt carbide and fumes from acetylene torches. *I know what they were doing—but I need evidence!* Reasons poked around the interior, anxious to discover proof of his suspicions.

The cops spent the next hour going over the pole barn, crusher, and adjacent property with great care. All incriminating evidence seemed to have been removed. Everything appeared to be as it should be—a legitimate country salvage yard. Reasons knew better, but he had to prove it.

He had an idea, however. "Rick, was the county sheriff notified?" Out of common courtesy, local law enforcement was kept current on the activities of visiting officials.

"I think he just pulled up outside."

Reasons had it in his head to hear what the sheriff knew about the French Creek Salvage Yard and the man who owned it.

Rick returned. "This is Sheriff Elroy Nichols," and introduced him.

Reasons wasted little time with pleasantries. "Sheriff, what can you tell me about this place?"

"Hmmm. Not much, I'm afraid. Ray and Dale Steckel own it. Inherited it from their daddy years ago. Never had any complaints, if that's what you want to know." Nichols fidgeted with his hat.

Sam studied the man carefully. An older guy approaching sixty, Reasons thought. He sensed an unexplainable antagonism from the man, as if he resented their intrusion. "How long have you been sheriff, Elroy?"

"Going on twenty years, I guess."

Elroy Nichols was a slender man. His face was deeply lined with red, blotchy spots covering both cheeks and nose. His upper lip looked like the side of a hill after a heavy rain—rippled with eroded cuts.

"And in all that time, you've never had cause to suspect that this bunch might be dirty?"

"Nope."

Sam's instincts told him that all was not what it appeared to be. He continued to quiz the sheriff, who became more and more evasive. Sam looked directly at the man. He studied his eyes, noted a nervous tick on his cheek, and decided the constable knew more than he let on.

"What about complaints from the local citizens?"

"Nope. Nothing in all the years I've been sheriff."

"You mean that in twenty years you've never had a single complaint about this place? Or, about the Steckels? That's hard to believe, 'cause I know these guys are dirty! I can almost smell what's been going on here, and I've only been here for an hour!"

Nichols didn't respond all at once. He took his time, choosing his words carefully. "All I can tell you is what I know to be the truth, Detective."

Reasons considered the man's answer and decided that any further inquiry was useless. "Excuse us for a minute, Sheriff?" Sam requested, and pulled Rick off to the side. "This guy's either scared, involved somehow, or both. Keep your eye on him—and don't let him get away."

"Okay, Sam."

The troopers returned from their pursuit. "Didn't see anything, Detective. Sorry."

"Keep driving around. Go into Cokato. See if anything looks out of the ordinary. You might spot the BMW. Stop anyone you see, ask for IDs and start asking questions about this place. We'll look around here for a while longer."

90

Ray pulled in next to the semi and sat for a moment observing Dale and his cousins prepare for loading. Ray was in trouble, and he knew it. He had covered his tracks well up to this point, but he had to dispose of the body in the back of the Explorer—quickly. For the first time since taking over the salvage yard from his father, he had a genuine concern for his personal safety. He feared being sent back to Stillwater more than anything else in the world.

Ray's previous experience with prison life had left him with more than just a facial scar. On the first day of his incarceration, Ray quickly discovered that he was surrounded by other bullies who were bigger and tougher than he. The first and last time he'd stood up to one of the other inmates caused Ray to rethink his relative position in the penal pecking order. A man had asked for Ray's weekly cigarette allowance, and in a typically bold but foolish response, Ray had said, "Go screw yourself!"

Ray quickly learned what tough really meant. Not only did the other inmate have friends, they decided that they needed a new playmate. Ray was summarily raped and beaten. In a final act of brutality, his cheek was sliced open with a sharpened table knife.

The prison doctor, not known for his cosmetic surgical skills, put twelve very large sutures in Ray's cheek. He would forever carry the crescent shaped mark on his face—the signal to the prison population that Ray was available for the perverted pleasures of one and all. Since he had received the scar, he never knew another peaceful moment in Stillwater prison.

Once free, Ray never told anyone what had happened to him, not even his brother, Dale. But eventually, stories about the scar circulated, and most of those in Ray's family knew the true origin and meaning of the scarlet cut.

The experience left its mark on Ray in more ways than one. Every time he looked in the mirror, he was reminded of the pain and humiliation he'd suffered at the hands of the other inmates. That experience turned a bad man into an evil man. Few people ever questioned Ray about the scar on his cheek; at least they never asked about it twice. Ray hated the memory of what he had endured, and the scar was a constant reminder that he would never, ever return to prison.

As Ray thought through the meaning of what had occurred that night, he grew desperate. The idea of more prison time fueled that desperation like gasoline. His two idiot cousins had messed up— big time. He knew he should get rid of them once and for all, but he resisted that temptation. Over the years, they both had provided certain value to the operation—mostly muscle. They didn't cost Ray much and, beyond all else, both were loyal. Huge, in particular, was tolerated because he was Ray's personal whipping boy.

Ray resented the big man's strength and took every opportunity to prove he was superior in spite of his small stature. Ray relished berating Huge for his stupidity. Occasionally, his cruelty took the form of physically striking the larger man, a coward's act for sure, as Huge would never lift a finger to defend himself against Ray.

Huge became Ray's perpetual ego boost—a constant reminder that size wasn't everything. Now, the gang's leader reached a decision. With some reluctance, he would have to send Huge and Mikey away with the semi. *I've got to get that guy and his truck out of here. If the cops start asking questions, one of those two boobs will talk—sure as hell!*

Ray left the Explorer. "Huge, you and Mikey load this guy and his truck into the back of the semi."

Huge immediately pulled out the ramps, and Mikey drove the Explorer into the trailer.

Ray reached into his pants and pulled out his watch. "It's getting late—move it! Dale, check his pockets again."

"Hold it, you guys. We got to search him before you lock the doors."

"While you're at it, make sure he's tied good and tight, and the gag's in place," Ray said, satisfied that he had thought of every last detail.

John heard voices and struggled to make sense of what had happened. His head throbbed with every breath. He couldn't think clearly and wasn't certain if he was awake or not, but soon realized that by some miracle he was still alive.

He listened to the sound of voices somewhere outside and tried to move. But, he was tied—hands and feet bound—so that he could hardly move, hardly breath. As his senses returned, he tasted oil or grease. He wanted to vomit but willed himself not to. Suddenly the door opened, and the dome light came on.

The sudden illumination added to his discomfort. He closed his eyes, feigning unconsciousness. Hands groped his body. Fingers reached into his front pockets. He sensed his pocket knife and cigarette lighter being removed. His spirits sank. He heard the sound of the shovel being removed from the back of his truck.

Apparently satisfied, John's unseen captor left him alone. The dome light went out as the door closed. John opened his eyes and raised his head. Moonlight filtered through cracks in the trailer doors. Once again, voices came from outside the truck. He thought he could hear three or four guys. John was terrified—

helpless. *Please, God, I don't want to die—not like this.* His entire body shook as he lay awaiting his fate.

❖ ● ❖

Ray gave instructions to Huge and Mikey. "Take the trailer out to Herman's in Milbank. I'll call him and tell him you're coming. Before you stop at Herman's, you're gonna have to get rid of this guy—and his truck. There's an old quarry outside of Milbank—it's abandoned. Dump him there. Don't let anyone see you. Now make sure you stop there *before* you go to Herman's."

"How do we . . . ?" Mikey started to ask.

"Shut up! It's west of town, easy to find. Look for a sign that says Simonet Granite Works. Here, I'll show you on the map."

Ray unfolded a state map of South Dakota and scribbled directions. "It's full of water, and it's deep. The truck'll sink and we'll be rid of him. When you're finished, go on to Herman's and unload the parts. Don't let Herman give you any shit and don't mention the Explorer! He has to take *all* the parts. After you unload, come on back home. Understood?"

"You gonna toss a perfectly good truck without strippin' it?" Mikey asked.

"That's what I said. Don't think too hard, okay? Just do as you're told. Moron." Ray coughed and spit in disgust.

"Leave him in the back end, dump his ass in the quarry, and unload the semi at Herman's! How many fuckin' times do I have to explain this to you? Then bring the semi back home." Ray still worried about whether or not Huge and his brother could carry out his plan, but he didn't have a choice. Intimidating them might make them get it right. "Now, get your fat asses moving!"

Mikey and Huge were silent. Neither would question Ray again. They had messed things up, and Ray was pissed. The two large brothers prepared to leave.

"Hold it a minute!" Ray said. "Here's $500.00 for expenses. You don't get a cent more. You should reach Milbank by 8:30 A.M., or thereabouts. Call me before you leave there, just in case there's a change of plans. Oh, yeah, and don't stop for *anything* except gas. I mean it!" Ray said in a threatening tone. "I don't want anyone poking around that truck asking questions, clear?"

"For sure, Ray. You can count on us! Let's go, Huge. We got a lot of drivin' to do."

At that moment, Huge was more concerned about his empty stomach. $500.00 could buy a lot of food for the big man. He quickly lost track of the real purpose of their trip. Now that his diarrhea had passed, it was time to eat again. Ray's admonition fell on at least one pair of deaf ears. Fortunately for both of them, Mikey had responded as if he understood.

They climbed into the truck, Mikey behind the wheel. Ray waited until they pulled out on Highway 12. Milbank, South Dakota was a small prairie town about 200 miles west of Cokato. Huge and Mikey would continue west to Ortonville, pass through Litchfield, Willmar, and Benson, before crossing Big Stone Lake into Milbank. The trip should take about three hours, with perhaps one stop for gas. The roads were clear, and there would be little traffic that early in the day. By any measure, it was an easy drive.

As the semi's taillights disappeared, Ray and Dale climbed into their truck and headed home. Ray believed his plan would work as long as Huge and Mikey followed directions.

Dale broke the silence. "You think Herman will play along?"

"He'd better if he knows what's good for him."

Herman Fogelman, one of the Steckels' cousins, had moved to Milbank years earlier. He had grown tired of Ray's illegal activities, and, after the birth of his son, Barry, a Downs child, Herman's interests had changed. He was devoted to his son and believed it was best if he moved on. He escaped to set up a similar, but honest business away from his cousin Ray.

95

Ray had permitted Herman to leave only because it suited his purpose to do so. His cousin's business became a convenient place to dispose of certain stolen parts. Herman was forced to cooperate. For the present, Ray was only concerned about getting rid of the police. With the semi gone, he began to relax. If the police wanted to talk to him or Dale, it'd be best if they were at home.

"You sure the Explorer won't be found, Ray?" Dale flinched as he completed the sentence. He seldom questioned his brother's decisions and immediately regretted opening his mouth.

Ray's head snapped around. He glared at his brother. "That quarry pit is three hundred feet deep! What do you think? So long as those two dummies do like their told. If they screw this up, I swear to God I'll personally cut their balls off and shove 'em down their throats!"

Ray dropped Dale off at his house, and headed home. He was confident that he had taken care of the one messy detail that might have been his downfall. Satisfied, he smiled, lit a cigarette and sped toward home. *Think I'll roll the old lady over when I get home and give her a tumble.* His smile broadened at the thought.

❖ 7 ❖

A T THE VERY MOMENT RAY REACHED HOME, Detective Reasons and his partner were scouring the pole barn, carefully searching for clues. Because of the still-pungent odor of smoke from welding rods and abrasive wheels, Reasons knew the shop had just recently been evacuated. Maybe they had been pressed hard enough to clear out to have left something behind.

"We must have just missed them," Reasons said to no one in particular. "Rick, make sure you search outside, and I'll keep looking around here."

Sam wandered over to the forklift and noted that its engine was still warm. *Place sure is clean—too clean!* They had already been through the building once, and now probed with much greater care. Their mission was clear: find some telltale piece of evidence, no matter how small, that linked the gang to the stolen BMW.

"I want you guys to look at everything! Let me know about anything you find, no matter how insignificant it seems."

One of the troopers strolled past two welding tanks. He stumbled over a loose piece of metal and kicked it away. Reasons turned toward the sound, startled and instantly alert. He spotted the trooper, then fixed his gaze on the welding tanks.

"What the hell was that?"

The trooper stopped. "Dunno."

"Well, find out."

The trooper returned to the tanks, bent over, stuck his hand underneath, and pulled out the two license plates. He brought them over and handed both to Sam.

Reasons extracted a piece of paper from his pocket. He quickly compared the numbers on the license plates to the numbers scribbled on the paper. "Bingo! We've got 'em! One of these is our BMW plate! Go out and bring Rick back in, will you?"

Sam sighed and ran his hand through his hair. "Sometimes it pays to be lucky. Now we're legal!" He could explain away the discovery of the plate any way he chose to, and no one would question him. His suspicions were justified at last.

Sheriff Nichols observed Reasons' discovery, and started to fidget. He swayed from side to side and, in spite of the cold air, began to sweat.

While Reasons and his partner went out to their car to begin the process of obtaining warrants and tracking down the owner or owners of the shop, Sheriff Nichols slipped unobtrusively into a small office. "Sentinel" had one more call to make.

Ray had just finished with his wife and smugly lit up an Old Gold filter. He inhaled deeply and recounted the day's events—not to his wife, of course. He tried to recall any detail that he might have missed that could spell trouble. He could think of nothing. He snuffed the butt and lay on his side.

Just as he was dozing off, the phone rang. He woke with a start, heart pounding. He reached over and picked up the handset.

"Yeah, this is Ray."

"Ray, it's Nichols. We've got trouble. That detective got into the pole barn and found a license plate that matched the BMW they were following." Nichols paused, waiting for Ray's reaction.

Ray was immediately alert to the danger he now faced. His mind raced. "Shit!" he responded. "What're they doing now?"

"Calling for warrants, trying to find out who owns the yard. Once they have the names their going to come looking for you, Dale, and the others."

"All right, stay close to 'em—and, damn it, keep your mouth shut! If you say anything at all, your ass is grass, and you know what I mean!"

Ray hung up the phone and began dressing. "Sonofabitch! I knew I couldn't trust those numbskulls to clean the place up! Once they started digging, they'll find a lot more than just a license plate. Nichols can't help me now. Got to get the boys together and get the hell out of here!" He knew with certainty that somebody would talk if pressure were applied. It was time for Ray and his gang to disappear. Fortunately, he had long since formulated a contingency plan to be used in this precise circumstance.

He picked up the phone and called his brother. "Tell the boys to pack a bag for a long vacation. Don't tell 'em where we're going. Have them meet behind Herb's Garage." Ray paused. He mentally identified everyone in the gang and assessed the probability that they would follow him out of town. "Call Herb. Have him meet us there, too. I'll pick you up in fifteen minutes."

Ray finished dressing and hurriedly packed a bag. He wouldn't tell his wife where he was going, of course. She served few purposes, and he had just finished utilizing one of them. He had little concern for what might become of her or his daughter.

He rushed to the basement, unlocked the wall safe and withdrew a small fortune in cash he had accumulated. Ray had an innate distrust of all banks and preferred to keep his money where he could put his hands on it. He stuffed nearly $950,000 into a black, nylon bag, grabbed two pistols with extra ammunition, picked up his travel bag, and left the house.

Ray considered what he had to do next. He knew Herb couldn't be trusted. He'd never leave without his wife. He considered Nichols. He was with the cops but knew Ray would kill him if he talked. He climbed into his truck and raced to his brother's.

❖ ● ❖

Huge and Mikey had been driving west on Highway 12 for a couple of hours. Huge had already run out of his supply of sweet, greasy food. His stomach rumbled, and he was uncomfortable. He had to fuel his immense furnace—soon.

They approached the town of Ortonville, the last Minnesota town before they would cross the border into South Dakota.

"Mikey, let's stop for breakfast, okay?"

"Jesus, Huge! You ever think of anything else but food?"

"Sometimes I think about trains. And sometimes I think about big trucks." Huge was fascinated by anything big and noisy: trains, trucks, and big tractors. He never wondered about much else. Even girls had never been of much interest. As a matter of fact, Huge had never had sex. He had kissed girls a couple of times on a dare from his brother but found it kind of funny. He didn't like having a girl's tongue in his mouth. For the most part, he just liked to watch big machines, drive trucks and eat.

"I could eat, I guess," Mikey said. "We'll stop in Ortonville."

❖ ● ❖

It was 7:30 A.M. John had been in the back of the truck for over two hours. A lack of food, frigid temperatures, and inability to move had sapped his strength. He hovered between periods of consciousness and deep, troubled sleep. He woke, shivering violently from fear and cold. His teeth chattered. He was as terrified as a helpless animal caught in a leg-hold trap. His only chance for escape had been thwarted.

More than ever, John desired freedom and escape. He had been in life-threatening situations before . . . hunting accidents, the tank fire . . . but he always had some control in each instance, something he could do for himself. Now, he was at someone else's mercy. He didn't think he dared hope for much. He feared he would die without a fight. He was very tired, his head hurt, and he was growing weak from hunger. He did what he could to keep blood flowing by rocking back and forth. His eyes closed, and he drifted off once more.

Because of his capture, John had plenty of time to consider certain behavior patterns that clearly led to the trouble he was in. When he awoke once more, he realized that if he didn't do something, he'd bring the same pain and suffering to Debbie and the kids as his father had brought to him and his mother. *I'll just disappear, and they'll think I abandoned them—just like dad. No one will ever know what happened!*

He was close to tears. Bile rose and settled in the back of his throat. He lifted his head and looked around. There was nothing to see, nothing to help him get loose. All he could do was wait for his captors to end his suffering.

John shook his head to clear the cobwebs. *No! It can't end like this! I got myself into this mess through my own stupid compulsion—the same sick behavior that has haunted me all my life. Think! You still have your mind—use it! I don't want to die like this—not without a fight.*

As the truck bumped along the highway, John looked around the dimly lit interior. He had no weapon, no way to untie his bindings, and the longer he remained where he was, the colder he would be. Soon, his limbs would be numb—frostbitten and

101

useless. He was being transported out of the area to some un-known destination. He knew when the truck stopped that would probably be when they'd kill him. He had to do something—any-thing.

John had managed to work the gag loose an hour into the trip by rubbing against a tool box. He could breathe easier with the gag removed. Now, as the early morning light began to filter into the trailer, John understood that he was entirely on his own. The two men had decided to move him to some other location. But, he didn't know why. He concluded that something must have hap-pened back at French Creek. Was it the cops? Were they on to them? His heart raced with the thought that perhaps someone might track the truck and discover him before it was too late. *No, I can't depend on that. It's up to me.*

Sooner or later the truck would reach its destination, and if he hadn't frozen to death by then, they would finish the job! He looked around the interior of the Explorer for something he could use to cut his bindings.

All of a sudden, the truck came to a halt. He heard noises out-side. Someone on a loud speaker was talking rapid-fire. John tried to hold his breath and halt his chattering teeth. He listened closely.

Huge and Mikey had arrived in Ortonville. As they approached the outskirts of town, they noticed an auction taking place at a local farm equipment dealer. "Mikey, look! Tractors! Lots of 'em!" Huge exclaimed. He turned to his brother; a wide smile broke across his face.

Mikey glanced out the window. He didn't share Huge's pas-sion for all things large and noisy, but they needed a break and had to fill the truck with gas. "Okay, let's stop. There's a Country Kitchen next door. We'll eat there."

Mikey pulled the big rig into the parking lot adjacent to both the dealership and restaurant, and stopped. "We better check on the guy in back."

They piled out of the cab and walked to the rear of the trailer. Mikey climbed in, walked to the back of the Explorer and peered in the window. All he could see was John's inert form, lying in a fetal position pretty much where they had left him three hours earlier. Mikey climbed back down and locked the doors.

As the doors closed, Huge asked, "Mikey, can we watch the auction before we eat?"

"No. We're going to eat, gas up, and get the hell out of here."

John suddenly realized that this might be his only chance at escape. If he could get his hands loose, untie his feet, yell and scream, someone might hear. He panicked at the thought of missing perhaps his only opportunity to get loose.

Then he felt the oval FORD plate pressing against his butt. Yes! He had forgotten about the plate he had pocketed at the salvage yard!

Cushioned by the handkerchief in his rear pocket, the metal plate had escaped detection. He turned over on his stomach. Numbed, frozen fingers failed to cooperate. He worked furiously to reach into his pocket. Without feeling, he could only guess where his fingers were. The numbness infuriated him. *Come on, dammit! Work! Please?*

He relaxed and decided he had to get circulation started first, get blood flowing to his fingertips. Rolling back onto his side, he began flexing the fingers of both hands. He sat up and propped his back against the rear seat. After five or ten minutes of manipulation, he began to feel sensation return to some of the digits. He slid down and turned over. Then he heard a small voice outside the semi.

"Daddy! It's an eighteen-wheeler!" a small boy exclaimed.

John couldn't hear a reply, but he thought that if he could hear the boy, then perhaps the child could hear him "Help! Help! I'm in here!" John shouted.

He paused and listened intently, hoping, praying for a response. There was no answer. His voice was hoarse, raspy from hours without liquid. He feared he couldn't shout loud enough to be heard.

"Please! Somebody help me!"

The small boy did hear John's shouts but was puzzled about where they were coming from. He was only six years old and thought someone was playing a game of some sort—kind of like the funny man at Donny's birthday party who had a talking doll in his lap. He stepped closer to the truck and listened as his father moved further away. Sure enough, the sounds were coming from inside the truck.

"Daddy, Daddy! The truck can talk!" the little boy exclaimed.

John heard the boy's words. His heart soared. He was giddy with excitement. He yelled again. "Please! If you can hear me, I'm trapped inside the truck. I need help!" His throat was raw. The words tumbled from his parched lips.

The boy's father was in a hurry. He had driven in from the country to attend the auction. He was focused on a seven-year-old Bobcat skid-steer loader and had no time for his son's foolishness. He stood some distance away from the truck. After too many years riding a noisy tractor, his hearing was less than perfect. He heard nothing but his son's voice.

"Tommy! Come here, now!"

Once again, John heard the boy's voice. "Daddy! The truck can talk!"

That was the last John heard from the boy.

Tommy's father gave the boy a stern look that said, "Get your ass over here now—or else!"

The boy ran to his father but looked back over his shoulder at the talking truck.

John continued to yell. This time there was no response. The faint voice of the auctioneer was the only audible sound. John's heart sank. His stomach was in knots. In spite of the cold, he broke into a sweat. His brief hope of escape had vanished as quickly as it had appeared. He was even weaker than before. *I need to get loose before they come back—I just have to.* Once again, with fingers half-frozen, he reached for his back pocket.

Huge and Mikey finished their breakfast, wandered out of the restaurant and sauntered past the auction. Huge barged ahead and led his brother over to the crowd gathered around the auctioneer. Between them, they still had almost $500.

Mikey was anxious to leave but all of a sudden his interest was peeked. He stopped and glanced at one of the items left to be sold.

The brothers had lost sight of their primary mission. The delay bought precious minutes for John.

The two large strangers stood in the crowd. Mikey's eyes focused on the next item to be offered: a John Deere garden tractor. He stood tall and watched the small, green machine as it was wheeled up to the platform. This was exactly what he wanted. He had no idea how much the tractor might sell for, but knew there was room for it in the truck. In addition to the money Ray gave them, Mikey had two hundred dollars of his own to spend. He edged to the front, prepared to bid.

Huge had little interest in the small tractor. It wasn't big enough. Still, he enjoyed the singsong voice of the auctioneer. While his brother concentrated on the lawn tractor, Huge wandered over to look at some of the bigger items yet to be sold.

As the bidding for Mikey's John Deere got under way, John finally regained some feeling in his fingers. He touched the FORD plate in his pocket. Very carefully, he pinched it between his middle three fingers and slowly drew it out. It was still fairly dark inside the trailer, but John didn't really need to see to know what had to be done next. If only the edge were sharp enough.

John's heart sank. He fingered the edges and realized that not only was the plate too dull, but it was rusty as well. This was going to take a while. He began sawing at the twine. He had no idea what Huge and Mikey were up to, but he guessed they were close to their final destination.

John worked feverishly at the bindings. The effort kept him warm but depleted what little energy he had left. He paused every few minutes to rest and catch his breath. He breathed deeply—knowing he must stay calm. His heart raced and fingers trembled. He continued to rub the metal plate against the unyielding twine.

Because of the way his hands had been bound, the top hand, his right, was the only one he could use. He tried to pace himself but was frantic to free himself as soon as possible. He stopped to rest his aching shoulder and hand. Progress was slow, and John had no idea how much he had left to cut. Too tired to continue, he slumped on his side. Strength diminished, he couldn't proceed.

Mikey remained focused on the John Deere tractor. The auctioneer was asking for a bid of $300.

"Do I hear three hundred?"

Mikey raised his hand, and the auctioneer acknowledged his bid.

"I've got three hundred! Now, how about three fifty?"

Mikey's bid remained. He was the current high bidder. He grew excited. His eyes widened as he created a picture of himself riding the small tractor.

Huge paid little attention. He drooled over a large skid loader due up as the next item to be sold.

The auctioneer asked for a bid of $350. "Any last bids? Three fifty? Nope? Okay, going once, twice . . ."

Mikey pictured himself crawling up and down his yard on the green mower.

Suddenly a man standing a few feet away with a small boy at his side raised his hand. Mikey looked sharply at his competitor. He nudged his brother, who had returned to his side. "Huge, how much money you got?"

Huge slowly turned. "Huh?"

"Quick! How much money you got?" Mikey repeated. He grew increasingly angry and frustrated.

Just as Huge answered, the auctioneer intoned, "I've got $400. Do I hear $450? Going once, going twice . . ."

"Why?" Huge asked.

"'Cause I want to be sure I got enough to raise the bid. Now how much, quick!"

Huge reached into his overalls and pulled out a battered wallet. He slowly opened it and peered inside. He slowly counted out loud: "Ten, fifteen, sixteen, nineteen, no, seventeen, let's see now, hmm . . . twenty-two dollars, Mikey."

Just as Mikey raised his hand for one last bid, the auctioneer called out, "Sold for $400.00 to the man with the little boy!"

Mikey's hand dropped. He cursed under his breath. "Aw, crap! Goddamned skinny turd just cost me my riding mower!"

"What'd you say, Mikey?"

"Nothing, forget it. Let's get the hell out of here."

"What about your mower?" Huge looked puzzled but only for a second. The skid loader was being driven into the auction circle. His eyes lit up as he imagined himself steering the red and white Bobcat.

"Come on," Mikey repeated. "We've got to get gas and hit the road!"

"Can't we see who gets the Bobcat?" Huge entreated.

"No, now move it!"

The brothers worked their way out of the crowd and headed for their truck. They climbed inside. Mikey started the engine. "Should probably check on the guy one more time—aw, piss on it!" He pulled into the gas station, stopped the engine, and climbed out. Huge remained in the truck, munching on a bag of chips.

John listened as the two men returned to the truck, heard the engine start, and waited as the truck drove a short distance. The truck stopped. He heard the door slam. He was tempted to yell for help once more, but knew the driver would hear him as well. He remained quiet, terrified, waiting to see what would happen next.

He could barely detect a repeated ding, ding, ding. *Must be getting gas.* This gave John hope. *Means we still have a ways to go.* He started back in on the twine. He couldn't feel much but hoped that he was at least halfway through the bindings.

He was exhausted. He willed his fingers to move. He knew he had to keep working, but his strength was leaving him. He paused once more. His ears ached. An unbearable growl filled his head. He had trouble breathing. John hyperventilated and couldn't stop. The plate slipped from his fingers. He panicked as he groped for it.

John heard one of the men yell, "Should we check on the Explorer?"

Another voice responded, "Nah, it's okay. Besides, we're late as it is. Ray'll be pissed off if we don't get to Milbank in time."

John was elated. He still had time. Slowly, his breathing returned to normal. Now he knew where they were going! Milbank, South Dakota. But why? What the hell was in Milbank? John had been to this small border town a few times before but only on his way further west. He figured they must be in Ortonville. He still had time! He began working his fingers again and then felt something wet and sticky. Blood! The twine was cutting his skin! He didn't have time to worry about how deep the cuts might be. He fumbled in a desperate attempt to locate the metal plate.

His left hand brushed the tool. Cautiously, John transferred the plate from his left hand to his right. Because of the blood, it was slippery and difficult to hold on to. John had very little energy left, but he forced himself to saw and rub against the twine.

What little hope he had earlier disappeared as the large truck came to life and roared down the highway. John's bloody fingers were useless. He was drained—emotionally and physically. He was desperate now. He fingered the plate and twisted it around—then it was gone. He lost his grip for the second time. He had no feeling left in his bloody fingers. He settled into the thin carpet pile and sobbed, knowing his fate was sealed.
"No, no, no . . . Debbie, I'm sorry . . ."

❖ 8 ❖

REASONS RETURNED FROM HIS CAR with the John Doe warrants. Now he could track down everyone involved, but he still required the help of the recalcitrant local sheriff. Aware that he would probably run into additional resistance, he mentally prepared to deal with the elderly constable.

Sam approached Sheriff Nichols. "Nichols! You said that two brothers, Ray and Dale Steckel, own this place?"

Elroy Nichols felt as if the air had been sucked from his lungs. If the Minneapolis police discovered his involvement in the operation, he'd be in serious trouble.

Reluctantly he responded. "Yeah, that's right. Ray and Dale Steckel." The tone of his shaky reply didn't fool Reasons.

"Do you think you know where they might live?"

Nichols paused. "No, not for sure."

"Well, how the hell do we find out?" Reasons studied the nervous man closely. The tick was more pronounced. He had a strong feeling the man knew the owners, perhaps was on their payroll. Reasons waited, remembering a saying his mentor had taught him years earlier: he who speaks first—loses!

The sheriff grew increasingly uncomfortable under Reasons's scrutiny. Promptly he blurted, "I guess I could call the office . . . and, uh . . . have the dispatcher look up their addresses."

"Well, why don't you just do that!" Reasons responded sarcastically. As Nichols left to go to his car, Reasons had another thought. "While you're at it, find out about any known associates." His suspicions of Sheriff Nichols increased with each passing minute.

Sheriff Nichols was in trouble, and he knew it. In spite of the twenty-five-degree temperature, he began to sweat. He knew exactly who was involved with Ray and Dale. It would be information that any legitimate, reasonably intelligent, local cop would know. Nichols knew he had to play along with Reasons and hope that if he provided the requested names, it wouldn't get him in trouble with Ray.

Nichols stalled. He placed a call to his dispatcher then returned to the shop. "Guess there's seven in all, including Ray and Dale." He gave the names and addresses to the detective and anxiously hoped he had extricated himself from further suspicion.

Reasons filled out the warrants and instructed the troopers to split up and find the names listed while he and Rick headed for Ray's house. Sheriff Nichols turned to leave. "Hold on there, Nichols! Follow us to this Ray Steckel's house, will you?"

As Reasons walked out to their car something nagged at him. *Something's wrong. This was too easy. I'm forgetting . . . something. What?*

They drove to Ray's house. When just a few houses away, Rick doused the lights. Nichols, following closely, did the same. They parked and silently exited the car. Reasons strode back to the sheriff's car. "Stay here, Nichols. Keep your eyes open."

Reasons and his partner approached the house. "Go around back, Rick," whispered Reasons. "I'll knock in two minutes." Sam waited the allotted time then knocked on the Steckels' door. There

111

was no answer. He knocked again. After a moment or two, the porch light came on.

Before long, the curtain over the window parted and a dowdy, beaten-down woman of undetermined age peered out at the detective.

"What do you want?" she shouted.

"Police! Open up! We have a warrant for Ray Steckel."

She opened the door. "He's not here."

"Where is he?"

"Dunno. He was gone when I woke up," the sad-faced woman replied.

Sam noted she hadn't bothered to ask why they wanted her husband. "I need to come in and search the house." He flashed the warrant. Rick returned to the front of the house, and together the two cops entered.

They searched the house and returned to the front hall. "Looks like your husband left in a hurry, Mrs. Steckel. Do you have any idea where he might have gone?"

"He don't tell me nothin'! I got no idea. Try his brother's house or the salvage yard." By this time, a sleepy-eyed young girl that looked to be about fifteen joined her mother. "This here's my daughter, Raylene."

It was clear to Reasons that this frail, woeful woman had no idea where her husband had gone. In time she might be convinced to talk about his activities, but for now she was of no help. Ray's wife refused to look directly at the detective. Instead she studied her worn slippers. Reasons knew she was scared—not of him—but of her husband. Given the opportunity and assurance of safety, she might talk, but he doubted it.

"If your husband returns before we catch up to him, tell him the Minneapolis Police Department has a warrant for his arrest. If he runs, he'll only make things more difficult, Mrs. Steckel."

"I'll tell him, but he don't listen to no one—least of all, me."

Sam and Rick left. They sat in the car and contacted the other cops. They quickly discovered that their counterparts had met with the same result trying to find other gang members. Everyone on their list had suddenly disappeared.

"Let's meet back at the salvage yard and decide what to do next." Sam said. He waved at Sheriff Nichols to follow.

When they reached the pole barn for the second time that night and after a head count and tally, Reasons realized that something still didn't fit. He left the crowd of cops and once again took a walk around the shop, looking for some clue as to where the Steckels might have gone.

He went back outside and walked around the building. It was cold, but fortunately the wind was down. The moon had slipped behind a bank of clouds. The stillness belied all that had transpired that night. Reasons shivered and pulled up his collar against the frigid night air. He came to the large crusher on the south side of the building and stopped. That didn't trigger the scrap of information that teased at his mind, so he continued around the east side. As he turned the corner, the quietness of a moment earlier ended. Spotted by a trio of large dogs, the noise coming from their pen was not only deafening, but frightening as well. Reasons jumped back and his hand went to his automatic before he saw the fence.

A mean-looking Doberman and two Rottweilers snarled and bared snow-white teeth as he edged past. Reasons was glad they were locked up.

Reasons stopped, turned, and looked back to the east. *That other dog! Back at the office, someone else other than the Steckels had been here. Who? Where'd he go?* He now knew there had to be more to the events of that night than simply chasing down a bunch of thieves. Something else had transpired, and he felt certain he knew who could give him the answers he sought.

Reasons continued his search then returned to the relative warmth of the shop. As he strode to the assembled cops, he asked, "What the hell is that big machine outside for?"

One of the troopers responded, "It's for crushing cars. When they get done strippin' 'em down, the remaining chassis is crushed into a small cube."

"What happens to the cube?" Reasons asked.

"Sold to a scrap yard and ultimately melted back down into usable steel."

"Where's the nearest scrap yard?"

"Probably back in the Cities," the cop replied.

Reasons stared at the cop, eyes open in sudden awareness. He knew what had been bothering him. If the mashed up blocks of steel weren't there, they had to be somewhere. "Damn! Rick, we missed something. They crushed the cars tonight and shipped them off someplace. Get on the horn. Get all the license plate numbers and descriptions for every car or truck owned by the salvage yard, including Ray and Dale Steckel's personal vehicles. Do the same for all the other names on your list."

"You got it," Rick responded.

"Sheriff, do you have any idea where these guys went?"

"No. Sorry." Nichols actually didn't know for sure. Ray hadn't shared that bit of information with him. He was more concerned about his own future—specifically the additional knowledge he possessed about the kidnapped salesman from the Cities. Theft was one thing, but kidnapping and murder were crimes Nichols wanted no part of. Ray's Sentinel was filled with despair, and it was apparent from one glance at his ashen face.

Sam still felt that not only was Sheriff Nichols being less than cooperative, he was convinced the man knew a lot more about what was going on around the area. "Let's find out if there are any other family members around who might give us some information. You know any one else related to these Steckels, Sheriff?"

114

Elroy Nichols stood silently as Reasons and the others headed for the telephone.

As Reasons and the other officers manned the phones, the Steckels gathered in the back of Herb's Garage on the main street of Cokato. Ray's jumpy cousin Herb did his best to avoid any further involvement. He watched Ray pace back and forth around the cold garage bay.

Ray was upset. His plans had been disrupted, and he blamed everyone but himself. He stopped pacing and stared hard at Herb. He had to leave the area immediately, but he wondered about Herb. He couldn't be trusted, and Ray knew Herb would never leave his wife.

Ray had one other minor detail to deal with. "Dale, remind me to call Larry later on. We have to catch him before he leaves the scrap yard. Don't want him coming back here. He'll have to meet us at Herman's in Milbank. Oh, yeah. Leave a message at Herman's to have those two big boobs stay right there until we call again later. Don't let on to Herman what we're up to—don't want him getting suspicious."

"For sure, Ray."

"We have to ditch all our trucks and find something else to drive."

"What about that new Ford van outside, Ray?" Herb offered. "I can tell the cops it was stolen. It's a custom job, built for a large family. You guys can travel to Milbank in style."

"Good idea, Herby. Dale, tell Jimbo and Willy to take whatever they need from their trucks. Then take the trucks down to the lake and ditch 'em."

"Sure, Ray. Come on, you guys, let's get moving." Dale left with the other two gang members.

"Come here a minute, will ya, Herb?" Ray stood blocking the doorway. "Herb, you and I need to chat a bit." He stepped toward the trembling garage owner, draped one arm over his shoulder, and steered him deeper into the service bay. "Sure you don't want to come with us out to Herman's?"

"I c-c-can't, Ray. You know I c-c-can't leave Margie in her condition." Herb hadn't stuttered since high school. Ray's arm felt heavy on his back. He tried to shrug it off, but Ray gripped him tightly.

Herb's wife had multiple sclerosis and required constant attention. Herb doted on her and did everything he could to make her life as bearable as possible. He would never leave her to fend for herself. She knew nothing of his participation in the salvage yard operation. As far as she knew, Herb ran a clean business.

"Yeah, I know ya can't leave her. Too bad. Thought I'd ask anyway." They strolled close to one of the hydraulic hoists, a Chevy Cavalier parked on top. "You going to be okay, Herb?" Ray asked his cousin, as he pulled him close and squeezed his shoulder tightly.

"Yeah, I got some money saved, and . . . you-you know . . . you don't have to worry about me saying n-n-nothin' to no one, Ray. You know my word's as good as gold!" He knew Ray—knew what he was capable of. Anyone who had ever crossed Ray Steckel ultimately lived to regret it.

Herb smelled garlic. The strong odor oozed from his cousin's skin. He trembled, refused to be nudged any closer to the lift. He wanted to plead but couldn't. Words caught in his throat. He looked into Ray's coal-black eyes and shuddered. He was shaking visibly and didn't know what to do.

All at once, the garage owner's bladder released, and he felt his own piss running down the inside of his trousers. Herb was embarrassed. He stopped shaking, took a deep breath, and silently prayed.

116

"I know, Herb." Ray picked up a three-foot length of pipe leaning against the brick wall and swung it at the back of Herb's legs.

The garage owner crumpled. Ray dropped the pipe and dragged the old man over to the hydraulic lift. "I just can't take a chance, Herb. Sorry."

Herb was conscious but had no feeling below the waist. He was helpless. Ray, with one arm around Herb's shoulders, ran his head flush into the steel piston supporting the car lift. Herb never resisted.

He crumpled like a pop can stomped flat by a heavy boot and fell beneath the lift. Dazed but aware that Ray was about to kill him, he looked up with tears in his eyes. He knew the end was near. His last thoughts would be for his wife, Margie.

Ray watched as Herb crumpled on the filthy, cement floor. His eyes turned to the ramp directly above Herb's body. He stuck out one foot and rolled Herb over so he was lying on his back. Then he twisted away, and as he walked past the control box, shifted it to release.

Ray left the service area. The sound of his cousin's moaning echoed through the cold bay. Ray flexed his neck as if to loosen a bothersome knot and walked out.

The lift slowly dropped. Herb watched it approach, then closed his eyes. The ramp slowly crushed the life from Herb's body. The sharp edges of the metal ramp nearly severed his body in half. He jerked and screamed. Both eyes almost left their sockets. He threw his arms outward in agony as the relentless pressure of the hydraulic lift drove the life from his body.

With one final burst of adrenaline, he reached out and scrabbled his fingers on the filthy floor, now pooling with his own blood. A brief smile played across his bluing lips as he completed one grisly, terminal act of retribution.

Ray returned to the office. "Dale, pile everything into that Ford van outside, and let's get out of here."

Dale and the others knew better than to question Ray about Herb. If Herb hadn't returned with Ray, then he had been disposed of, another loose end taken care of by their leader.

Herb's accident would slow the cops. Ray knew his wife would never talk, and besides, she had no idea where they were going. Ray smiled, confident there was nothing left that would lead the cops to Milbank.

It was 5:00 in the morning by the time the Steckel gang piled into the van. Ray felt he was one step ahead of the police—again. Boiling with confidence, he was already planning exactly how he would take over Herman's business in Milbank and modify it with his personal stamp.

Ray slid behind the wheel and addressed the other men. "When the time's right, after a year or so when the dust settles here in French Creek, we can slowly move our families out to Milbank. Until then, we'll all just have to hunt up some of the local skirts out there. After all, a guy's gotta have some fun after a hard day's work, right boys?"

"Yeah, for sure, Ray," Dale responded.

Ray chuckled as he sped into the night. "Besides, South Dakota has titty bars! This'll be like a vacation away from our old ladies."

❖　●　❖

Things were definitely looking up for Ray Steckel. He would do whatever it took to avoid being caught, no matter who got in the way. Under no circumstance would he go back to prison. One filthy hand left the steering wheel and, unconsciously, he reached up and ran his fingers across the crimson scar on his cheek. Tracing its outline, he swore once again. "Bastards!"

"Whatcha' say, Ray?" Dale asked.

"Nothin'. Settle back, boys. I'll drive for a while. You guys relax and think about them titty bars! Dale, don't fall asleep. I need you to make sure I stay on the road."

"Sure, Ray." Dale looked straight ahead, but his errant left eye rotated toward his brother.

As the Steckel gang raced to Milbank, back in the Twin Cities, Jack Stevens had drawn a blank. There was no information forthcoming about John L. Rule. No one had seen him, he hadn't been arrested, and hospitals in the area reported no one that fit his description. John had vanished.

Jack was puzzled. He felt as if he had missed something—some clue as to John's whereabouts, but he couldn't put his finger on what it might be.

"Damn, I don't want to make this call." He had to report the lack of news to his friend, Mac Davis; he could no longer put off making the call.

Reluctantly, Stevens phoned Mac and conveyed what little information they had. "Still can't figure out what French indicates, Mac. We've checked our database looking for any business in the area beginning with that word, and we've sent patrol cars to each location, but nothing turned up."

"Well, we're all stumped on that one, Jack. I appreciate everything that's been done." Mac said.

"We'll keep looking. Tell Debbie to keep her hopes up. We'll find out where John is. We still believe there could be some rational explanation for his disappearance that doesn't include foul play, but we'll continue to explore every avenue."

"Thanks. Call me when you have something." Mac hung up the phone, disappointed but determined to continue his own investigation.

He picked up the phone and dialed John's office. "Is Pat in yet?" He waited while John's partner came to the phone. He quickly introduced himself and explained what had happened. He added, "Pat, where did John say he was going yesterday?"

"He cancelled all his appointments in town, and said he was going to make calls out west, Mac."

"You sure he said he was going west? Not south?"

"Positive."

"Can you give me the names of any customers in his territory he might have visited yesterday?" Mac asked. "Oh, and one more thing—does the word French mean anything to you? Could it be some business John calls on?"

"No to the last question, Mac. Don't know what French has to do with John. Hang on a minute." After a few minutes, he came back on the line. "John most likely would have stopped in Annandale, Kimball, Montrose, Glenwood, and maybe Buffalo."

"What about Mankato?"

"Mankato? Why?"

"Well, that's where he told Debbie he was calling from."

"He wouldn't have been in Mankato. That's too far south. He always covered Mankato on his way to Sioux Falls. Something doesn't fit here." There was silence on the other end of the phone. "Mac you still there?"

"Yes, sorry. None of this makes any sense. Debbie's certain John said he was calling from Mankato."

"Maybe so, but if he was, he was 100 miles from where he was supposed to be. He's very diligent about setting up calls beforehand, and if his plan was to travel to the cities he'd outlined, that's where he probably drove to."

"Pat, do me a favor. Call all the customers you think John might have visited out west. See if you can find who he actually saw. We might be able to piece together why he might have gone to Mankato. Try to get a time line for each stop, up until his last stop. Then call me back here at John's house. Until we find him, I'm staying with Debbie. Okay?"

"Certainly, Mac. Give Debbie a hug for me and tell her not to worry. I'll talk to you soon. Goodbye."

"Thanks, Pat. Talk to you later."

Mac hung up the phone and went into the kitchen. His mind raced. Debbie's friend Maggie had arrived, so Mac felt comfortable leaving his daughter in her care for a while.

He went out to his car, opened the glove box, and withdrew a state map of Minnesota. He had a feeling something was terribly wrong with their search. He needed to check something out. Pat was fairly certain that John had no intention of traveling anywhere near Mankato. If that was so, then why did John mention it? Mac slammed the car door shut. Maybe it wasn't Mankato . . . maybe Debbie . . . ?

Mac was excited and angry with himself at the same time. He ran back into the house, settled in the chair in the kitchen and spread out the map.

Charlie sensed his master's growing excitement, rose from beneath the table, put his head on Mac's lap and licked the back of his warm hand. The dog's tail beat steadily against the table leg. "I may be onto something, Charlie old boy!"

Huge and Mikey were back on the road, headed for Milbank. Huge's hunger had been sated, and, at least for the moment, he stopped thinking about his stomach.

Mikey drove in silence, still upset about the turn of events at the auction. The air inside the semi was foul. Neither man seemed to notice. A combination of body odor, accumulated trash and debris, strengthened by the blast of heat from the truck's blower filled the small space. Mikey stared ahead as he shifted gears, bringing the big truck up to speed.

Outside, the barren, chisel-plowed fields, wind-blown with little or no cover, held small drifts of blackened snow. The crop land stretched for miles in every direction, looking more like a great black sea with a slight, frothy chop.

The landscape lacked definition—distances were deceiving. No living thing could be seen. Pheasants, song birds, jack rabbits, even the predators were all hunkered down somewhere within the thick hedgerows that crisscrossed the area. Motorists on Highway 12 traveling at modest speeds provided the only dynamic relief from the monotony of the winter-stilled landscape.

Huge and Mikey remained silent. Before long, the larger brother would once again give in to the call of his bottomless stomach, but for now he sat quietly, wondering why his brother was so pissed off.

❖ ● ❖

The jarring movement of the semi jolted John back into action. After a brief rest and flexing of his fingers, he successfully retrieved the metal plate and resumed sawing at his bindings. The repeated twisting and flexing caused the twine to cut even deeper into his flesh, and blood flowed freely. His wrists hurt, but he thought he was making progress. He was growing weaker with every passing mile, however, and time was running out. He needed food and something to drink, but first he had to get loose!

❖ ● ❖

After half an hour of driving, Huge could remain silent no longer. He complained of being hungry again. "I shoulda bought some snacks, Mikey. Now we probably have to stop again."

"Bullshit! You heard what Ray said." Mikey was still angry at his brother. He really wanted that tractor.

Huge implored his brother one more time. "I need to eat, Mikey! Please?"

What a fat slob! Mikey mused, refusing to answer his brother.

"Can we stop soon, Mikey?"

"No! We're late. We got to keep going. Suck on your thumb for a while!"

"Aw, don't be like that, Mikey." Huge could be persistent when he was motivated, and nothing motivated the big man more than hunger. Food, the idea of food, the actual eating of food consumed much of what Huge thought about when awake. He was not about to give up. "I got an idea, Mikey . . ."

John couldn't hear any of the brother's conversation, but he knew he was running out of time. He continued working on freeing himself as the trailer moved ever closer to its final destination. Based on his experience traveling the area, John estimated that, if their last stop had been Ortonville, they were no more than an hour from Milbank. He had to set himself free, at once.

As he continued working on the twine, he thought ahead to what he would do once his hands and feet were free. Maybe he could crawl into the front seat of his truck, start the engine, and attempt to smash the rear doors of the trailer open. At sixty miles an hour, though, then what? Certainly he'd lose control, roll over, and they'd come back and get him. He'd just have to wait until the truck stopped, then make a move of some sort. But even then, if he waited until they opened the doors, he couldn't just drive out the back without some sort of ramp. Besides, if they were armed, they'd start shooting! No, there had to be some other way.

Until he had a plan, the smartest thing he could do would be start the truck, turn the heat on, and wait for the right opportunity. As he summoned every ounce of energy left in his body to cut the twine, he recalled having left two Milky Way bars in the glove box.

The candy bars as well as his thermos of cold coffee gave him a new focus. His arms, shoulders, and neck ached with the effort, but he pressed on. Blood dripped steadily and made each stroke of the plate feel like wasted effort. He had no idea whether he was making progress or simply cutting into his own flesh.

❖ ● ❖

The large truck chugged along Highway 12. Road signs advertising various businesses in Milbank were more frequent. Huge studied each with increasing interest, particularly the signs proclaiming delicious varieties of fatty food. Before long, they would cross the Red River at Big Stone Lake. From that point, Milbank was only fifteen miles away.

When the two brothers arrived in Milbank, they'd have to find the quarry. Neither of them had ever been to the small prairie town, and one or the other of them had managed to misplace the map Ray have given them.

"You had the map, Huge. What the hell'd you do with it?"

"Dunno . . . thought I put it in my jacket." Huge fumbled around, pulling candy wrappers from his pockets and dropping them on the vinyl truck seat. Mikey opened the window and the wrappers flew in every direction. He swatted at a large Charleston Chew wrap that smacked him in the forehead.

"Goddammit, Huge! Where's that damn map?"

Huge lost track of things easily, and as far as he was concerned, the map never existed. He took a quick look around the interior of the cab and gave up. "Maybe Ray forgot to give it to us, Mikey."

"You stupid ass! Shit, Huge, now we got to stop again and buy a map! Ray circled Herman's address, the name of the quarry, and the road to the quarry, but I don't remember what it was, do you? No, of course you don't! Christ, you hardly know your own name."

Huge answered his brother's question routinely. "No." Cheerfully he asked, "If we stop, I need to use the bathroom, Mikey! And, what about getting some snacks?"

"You always got to take a crap, Huge. How do we find Herman's location? Why am I asking you? Might as well be asking this steering wheel."

"Dunno. I s'pose we ask somebody."

"You s'pose? Talking to you is like talking to a rock." He was at a loss as to what to do next and had once again accepted full responsibility for their predicament.

John couldn't continue. He was exhausted. He relaxed his grip, and the rusted, bloody Ford oval slipped from his numbed fingers and lay beneath his hands. He was spent and realized that all his efforts had been futile.

A cloud of depression settled on his head like a choking, black yard bag. *It's hopeless.* Without thinking, John tried to stretch and flex his wrists. He heard, then felt something snap. The final strand of twine separated. His arms flopped to his sides, useless, but freed of their bindings.

Jubilant but still disbelieving, he rolled onto his back, raised his head, and stared at each limb in turn. *I'll be damned! I did it.* He tried to flex his shoulders first, slowly regaining circulation and movement that eventually traveled down each arm. Before long he was rubbing his bloody hands and wrists. He took a close look at the deep cuts and realized that while each wrist had bled steadily, there was no major damage. All he saw was a lot of reddened skin and a few shallow tears.

Stretching to loosen tired and cramped muscles, he slowly climbed over the seats to the front of the Explorer. As he settled into the driver's seat, he noticed a map on the floor. Before reaching to retrieve it, however, he decided he had to risk not only detection by his captives, but suffocation as well.

He turned the key and started the engine, hoping that someone had put some gas in the truck in order to drive it into the semi. He hoped the old trailer had some ventilation. He cranked the heat up to max, opened the glove box, and withdrew the candy bars. He opened one, took a large bite, and savored the melting chocolate. As the first hint of warmth from the engine began to fill the space, he leaned over and picked up the map.

Scribbled across the top of the map was the name, "Herman's Auto Parts, Milbank, So. Dakota," with an address, "1244 west Hwy 12." He then read, "Simonet Granite Works— quarry, watch for sign on 12 west of town."

John was puzzled. Why stop at a quarry? Who's Herman? He finished the first candy bar, opened the sealed thermos, and drank deeply. The cold, dark coffee combined with sugar from the candy supplied much-needed energy and warmth.

He still had no idea what the plan for him was, so it was useless to worry about it until he knew for sure. He was fairly certain, however, that the instructions for locating the granite quarry somehow involved him. Whatever the plan, he now knew that his first, and perhaps only, opportunity for escape would occur at the granite works.

As the heat built up inside the Explorer, John finished the second candy bar. His body was run down. The sudden warmth surging through his body raised his spirits but also left him feeling terribly sleepy. He fought to stay awake. He shook each arm, rotated his neck, thought of pleasant memories. Then his eyes grew heavy and, even though he fought to control them, they closed. . . .

John thought about how good a hot bath would feel right then! He slept and dreamt of bathing—just like he and Debbie used to do in their first house. That wonderful old tub they had was big enough for both of them. The girls had been very young back then, four and seven years old. He envisioned Debbie covered with suds—they were in the tub together. It felt so good, so warm! The kids were downstairs watching TV. The phone rang. He and Debbie heard small footsteps. It was one of the girls running to answer the phone. Debbie was smiling as they both listened. "Hello? Oh, Hi, Mr. Munson." Melissa said to their friend, Nick Munson. "No, Daddy's in the bathtub." John laughed. "Stop laughing, John. Wait! I can hear Melissa again. "No, she's in the tub with him!" Debbie's face turned red as she giggled and covered her mouth. The dream faded. John wanted to stay in the tub. He mumbled, tossing his head from side to side.

"No, don't go! Please, Debbie, stay?" Her vision became cloudy. John struggled to recapture the dream, the image of his wife. God, so beautiful . . . fair skin . . . tan, long legs. Delicate fingers. Always smiling . . . full lips . . . bright, white teeth . . . Debbie was everything he ever wanted. *No, please come back . . .*

John was jarred awake by a jolt from the semi as it hit a bump in the road. His heart pounded. Shaking his head and blinking awake, he willed his brain to catch up with what his widened eyes took in. He quickly came alert. He shook his head and tried to think about how long he might have been asleep. John feared he wasted precious minutes. The heat in the small space was stifling. Breathing faster, eyes wide with fright, he twisted the knob on the heater to low. He was having trouble breathing and started to hyperventilate.

John turned the engine off and stepped out. His legs were very weak, and he had to lean against the truck for support. He pitched forward until his breathing returned to normal. The swaying of the trailer made standing difficult, but slowly he felt his muscles respond, and he walked carefully back and forth down the length of the trailer.

Noting the car parts stored in the nose of the trailer, John quickly concluded that after he had been disposed of, the parts were to be delivered someplace close to Milbank. He stepped closer and gazed at the pile of parts. Must have been in a hurry, he observed. The various pieces were loosely stacked; they jostled with every bump in the road.

John turned, then stopped. He returned to the pile and began sorting through it looking for something—anything—that would serve as a weapon. He fixed on a short, heavy piece of metal that appeared to be a shaft of some sort. Stepping carefully on an engine block, he reached up and tugged at the desired object. Just as he pulled it free from the tangled mess, the trailer lurched. A heavier manifold nestled on top loosened and tumbled off the pile. John leaped aside as the hundred-pound missile headed his way. With a loud CRACK, it landed on the worn planks and dug into the frayed wood. All at once, the truck slowed and braked.

John grabbed the bar and quickly shuffled back to the Explorer. He waited for the inevitable.

"What the hell was that?" Mikey shouted.

Huge turned, cranked down his side window, and stuck his head out. "Dunno. Must've hit somethin' in the road. Probably someone's tailpipe."

Mikey glanced in the side mirror. "Don't see nothin' in the road. Maybe we should stop and open up the back."

"Maybe. It probably was somethin' back there, but if one of them engines slipped or somethin' it ain't goin' no place."

"Yeah, I guess." Mikey shifted gears and stepped on the gas.

John waited and waited for the truck to stop. He wasn't sure what he would do, but he knew if they opened the doors now, they'd smell the fumes, and he'd have to take some sort of action. He sat tense, his hand fidgeting on the door handle. He raised his other arm and hefted the metal bar, readying himself to attack his captors if he needed to. He felt he could at least take one of the men out with the heavy weapon.

When the semi didn't stop, John relaxed. After a bit, he started stretching his arms and jumping up and down. Once his head cleared and circulation returned, he slid back into the Explorer, started up the engine, and settled back to wait. Alert and strangely refreshed, John studied his few options. He willed positive thoughts and began devising a plan that might effect his ultimate, final escape.

❖ 9 ❖

Debbie answered the phone on the second ring.

"Hi, Debbie. It's Pat. How are you holding up?"

"I'm okay, Pat. It's the girls I'm worried about now. They think something terrible has happened to John, and it's hard to convince them that he's probably safe someplace."

"I know. But we're all praying for you guys, so hang in there, okay?"

"I will, Pat, and thanks. Do you want to talk to Dad?"

"Please."

"Just a minute, he's right here."

"Hello, Pat. What did you find out?" Mac inquired.

"Well, something sure doesn't fit. John made all of his calls in the towns I mentioned. Here's a recap for you. Got a pencil handy?"

"Yes, go ahead."

"He stopped at Severs Construction Supply in Buffalo at 9:00 a.m., Modern Equipment in Montrose at 11:00 a.m., Industrial Supply in Glenwood at 1:00 p.m., Newman Wholesale in Annandale at 2:00 p.m., and his last stop was Jerry's Supply in Kimball at 3:00 p.m."

130

"Did any on his customers mention whether he discussed going someplace other than home when he was through?"

"Nope. The secretary at the Kimball place thinks she overheard John and Jerry talking about something to do with parts for a pickup truck, but she was pretty vague. Unfortunately, Jerry left town for a few days. He's visiting some relatives in Yankton, South Dakota. He's out of touch."

"Damn! Now I'm really puzzled. Mankato just doesn't fit, does it?"

"No, it sure doesn't."

"I've been studying a state map. Mankato seems to be too far away from where he was supposed to be."

"I pried the phone number of Jerry's relatives from his secretary. I'll try to reach him for more information."

"That's great, Pat. Thanks. Call me when you have something."

"You bet! Talk to you later."

Mac had read through the entire index of Minnesota cities listed on the state map, looking for any town that ended in ATO. If John was in a big hurry, Debbie might not have heard him correctly. He looked at a short list of names:

Plato—fifty miles west of Minneapolis, near Glencoe—Possible?

Loretto—no, wrong pronunciation.

Cokato—on Highway 12, seventy-five miles west of Minneapolis—Possible?

Albinato—near Duluth, wrong direction

Mac stared at the list, then looked at the map. Only Cokato and Plato seem to be in the right area. Both relatively close to the towns on Pat's list. *Cokato's closer to his customers.* He shoved the list aside and picked up the map once more.

Mac looked at the index again searching for any city or notable landmark listed that began with the word French. He found nothing. He knew, of course, from years of representing clients scattered all over the state that many of the smaller towns didn't even have a state listing—too small. Many were unincorporated villages that over time, because of population loss, became nothing more than whistle stops on the way to someplace else.

Mac's tired, aging eyes could hardly read the names of some of the small towns on the map, even with his reading glasses. Debbie and her friend, Maggie, were in the kitchen with him. "Debbie, do you have a magnifying glass?"

"I think so. I'll be right back." She left the kitchen.

She returned shortly and handed her father the optic. Mac looked at the area in and around Plato. Spotting nothing resembling French he moved up to Cokato.

Melissa entered the kitchen and stood next to her grandfather. She looked at his notes silently, twisting one of the many long curls that fell across her cheeks. "Can I help?"

"Hmmm? Oh, thanks, Sweetheart, but we're kind of at a dead end here." Mac continued his search.

"Don't bother your Grandpa, Melissa. Besides, you need to get ready for school," Debbie said. "Your bus will be here any time."

Melissa attention remained fixed on Mac's notes. The curl she was working on became knotted. Angrily, she gave the lock one last tug and left the kitchen.

"Dammit it to hell! Where did he go?" Mac pushed back from the table and tossed the magnifying glass down. It landed with a THUD! Charlie jumped up and stuck his head between Mac's knees. "Sorry, old boy. Didn't mean to scare you."

"You okay, Dad?"

"Just frustrated. Think I'll take Charlie for a walk and clear my head. Back in a bit." Mac stood, put on his coat, whistled for Charlie, and left the warmth of the kitchen.

Debbie and Maggie chatted about the girls, about school, about nothing really. Anything at all was better than dwelling on

132

John's fate. Debbie only half-listened to her friend, who knew full well she had lost Debbie's attention. She prattled on anyway.

"So, David came home with this puppy! Can you stand it? Never even discussed it with me, of course. 'Course, by the time the kids saw it, it was too late. He knew that would happen too, the stinker."

"Huh? Oh, a puppy? How cute!"

Mac returned just as Melissa bounded down the stairs. Ready for school, she was on a singular mission. She was determined to help her grandpa. She rushed into the kitchen and stood directly in front of the large man she cared for deeply.

"Grampa, could Daddy have been talking about French Creek?"

Mac stared at his granddaughter. Thick eyebrows raised—mouth wide open.

He took three quick steps, sat back down in his chair, and picked up the glass. It hovered in mid-air, highlighting streaks of red, blue, and yellow. He stared at the illuminated images that resembled the multi-colored veins on the backs of his hands.

Finally, after what seemed forever to the young girl, Mac turned his head and looked at Melissa. He stared at his granddaughter. After a moment, he carefully asked, "What did you just say, Sweetheart?"

Unsure of herself, Melissa repeated, "Was Daddy maybe talking about French Creek?"

"Why, Melissa?"

"My friend Joanie has a cabin out at French Creek; I mean her parents do. I think it was on French Lake. I went out there last summer and spent a few days with them. I remember stopping in Cokato for lunch."

Mac stared at Melissa in disbelief. "Good Lord! Of course! That makes perfect sense. Your Dad must have been referring to French Creek!"

Mac picked up the magnifying glass and held it over the map. He moved it slowly over the town of Cokato and inched it northward and a bit east. There it was: French Creek! Mac studied the tiny red letters, barely legible on his map. "Located on County Road 34," Mac said out loud.

Just to the north of the tiny village was the body of water Melissa had visited and for which the town had been named. It was only a few miles north of Cokato, not far from John's last stop in Kimball.

"Debbie, come here! I think Melissa figured out where John is!"

Debbie rushed to her father's side, her heart pounding. Sure enough, after he pointed out both Cokato and French Creek to her, both names fit perfectly. "John said he was in *Cokato*, not *Mankato*, and had been almost killed by some people at a place called French Creek! That has to be it, Daddy! Quick, call Jack!"

Maggie stood up from the kitchen table, stepped close to her friend, and put her arm around Debbie as Mac reached for the phone. After a few minutes, Jack came on the line.

"Jack, it's Mac. I've got some news. We think John was referring to Cokato, not Mankato. Also, there's a small town nearby by the name of French Creek. It's very close to the last stop he made in Kimball." Mac waited for a reply from the attorney. "Jack, are you there?"

"Yes, sorry. Hang on a minute, I want to check on something."

Mac could hear shuffling of papers in the background, as he waited for Stevens to return to the phone.

"Son of a bitch!" Stevens exclaimed.

"What is it, Jack?" Mac asked.

"How could I be so stupid! About an hour ago, I had to sign a number of John Doe warrants to be issued in and around guess where?" Stevens said.

"French Creek, or Cokato, or both . . . ?" Mac replied, his mind racing ahead of what his friend was relaying.

"You got it, Mac. I never made the connection. Now that I'm looking at the documents a little more closely, it's starting to make sense."

"So tell me what the John Does are for."

"Well, the Minneapolis Police Department had a sting operation going yesterday. To make a long story short, they tracked a stolen car out to a junkyard in French Creek."

"How does their sting operation relate to John's disappearance?" Mac asked. "How is John involved in a ring of car thieves?" Mac glanced at his daughter and granddaughter and winced. He raised his hand and waved it back and forth. He didn't want either of them alarmed more than necessary.

"Well, I don't know yet," Jack said. "We're not sure that he is. Maybe he stumbled into this situation purely by accident. Details are sketchy, as they're just now attempting to round up the entire group."

"What can we do?"

"Sit tight. I have a call out to speak to the detective in charge of the investigation, Sam Reasons. Know him?"

"Only by reputation. I guess maybe we've met a few times. Used to be in homicide, didn't he?"

"Yup. Transferred over to burglary a few years ago."

"A good cop—been on the force for about as long as I've been practicing law." Mac remembered running into Reasons a number of times over the years. Predictably, Sam would appear as a witness for the prosecution, and Mac would have to cross-examine the cop.

"Yeah, that's Sam. Anyway, I should be talking to him shortly, and we'll find out how John fits in. I'll call you soon, Mac."

"Thanks a million, Jack." He turned to Melissa and smiled broadly. "If you hadn't come up with the solution, Sweetheart, we

135

could still be wondering where your Dad went. At least now we know, thanks to you. What do you remember about the town and the area?"

"Not much, Grandpa. French Creek wasn't much of a town—just a little grocery store with a couple of gas pumps. I remember a little white church on a hill just down the road, and an old junkyard about a mile away. That's about it. I do remember there weren't many houses around—just a bunch of deserted farms. We spent most of our time at the lake."

He looked at his notes one more time. John's partner had mentioned a conversation between John and Jerry Stubblefield about auto parts. Mac felt there was a connection somehow.

Mac repeated for Debbie and Melissa most of what Jack had told him. They hugged one another. Debbie was overcome with gratitude and now believed that soon John would be home. She too worried about the stolen car ring and how John was connected, but she kept her thoughts to herself.

John and the girls were her entire life. She needed him, and the thought of his dying, of being gone forever, was too much for her to bear. At least for now, she had hope of his safe return—certainly more hope than earlier that morning. Thanks to her father and Melissa, they now knew for certain where John had been, and might still be.

"Debbie, I need to run home and take care of a few things. I need to clear my calendar for the day and feed Charlie. If Jack calls back, have him call me at home. I should be back here in thirty minutes or so. Will you be all right?"

"Sure, Daddy. Maggie's here. We'll be fine."

"Okay. I'll see you in a bit. Melissa, you were a big help. Don't worry, we'll find your dad, I promise." Mac put on his coat, called Charlie, and left.

Melissa left for school a few minutes later. Debbie looked at Maggie. "I don't want the girls to worry any more than they have to. Maybe going to school and keeping up a normal routine will help take their minds off of all this."

"I think you're right, Sweetie." Maggie sat down and poured another cup of coffee. "Do you want to go lie down for a while, get a little rest?"

"Not now. Maybe later. I couldn't sleep now. I can't stop thoughts about . . ."

With Debbie sinking into the kitchen chair on the verge of tears, Maggie thought her friend needed some distraction. "You know, we've known each since grade school, have kids in the same class in school for three years now, been in PTA meetings together, stood side by side at bake sales, but I've never really heard how you and John met. I mean, I know you met in college, but you've never shared all the details with me. When we were at St. Kate's, I was certain you'd wind up marrying someone like Matt."

Debbie considered her friend's question, especially her last comment. "You mean you don't think John and I are suited for each other?"

Maggie quickly backtracked. "To a T. Now. I just meant that you and I used to dream about the perfect husband, remember?"

"Yes . . . and are you saying that John never fit into that mold?" Debbie said.

"Well, he really doesn't, you know. You wanted someone artistic, someone . . . who spoke in a British accent. John is a lot of good things, but he's neither of those. Look, I'm not being critical, but you know . . ."

"It's okay, Maggie. I get your point."

"So, how did you two meet?"

"Well, you remember John was a sophomore when we met my freshman year. I first noticed him in an English class we were both taking. I thought he was really cute in a rugged sort of way, so I asked some sophomore girls about him."

"And?"

Debbie smiled at the memory. "John L. had a reputation as . . . kind of a loser. Barely making grades, partying all the time, drinking too much, and I later discovered that he liked to gamble."

"Really? I didn't know that."

"Yes. You're right, I guess; on the surface we didn't have too much in common and he wasn't my dream image of a husband. But I was sick and tired of all the phonies I used to date—guys who spouted poetry without being the least bit artistic. One thing John wasn't, was phony. He went to North High. His parents didn't have much money, and about all he had going for him was hockey. He was apparently very good, but got himself kicked off the team the year we met."

"For what?"

"Drinking. John just couldn't pass up a party—or a beer. He lost interest in hockey, and I think he only stayed in college to avoid the draft."

"I knew about the drinking problem."

"Yeah. Everyone did. We used to see each other at parties, and finally he got up enough nerve to approach me. He didn't know what to say at first, all stumbling and awkward." Debbie laughed. "I remember not making things very easy for him, either. At first, I was probably more curious about him than anything. After I got to know him, though, I realized he was very intelligent, that all he needed was some direction, some motivation."

"And knowing how much you like a challenge . . ."

Debbie pursed her lips and looked down at her coffee. "Maybe. But beyond the curiosity factor, he was fun to be with, and I sensed that in spite of his reputation and all the stories, he was, uh . . . looking for something or somebody more meaningful. You know, Maggie, we never even kissed until our sixth or seventh date!"

"Really? How nineteenth century. 'Course, that doesn't surprise me. You were the only one of all of us that went to college still a virgin." Maggie smiled at her friend and sensed their conversation was helping keep Debbie's mind off of the current situation. "Did he quit drinking?"

"Yes, at least I thought so. Every so often he'd slip off with his buddies and get drunk, but that was rare."

"If everything was so perfect, why'd you split up?"

"It was his senior year. He got a call from his mother that his grandmother died, and that he should return home for the funeral. His grandmother helped raise him, and they were very close. He used to go and stay with her when he was a boy. Apparently, his father was a drunk, at least until the year before he took off and abandoned them."

"His father abandoned him and his mother?"

"When John was twelve, I think. His dad just didn't come home one day. The company he worked for accused him of stealing their truck. They tried to get his mom to pay for it for a while, too. Then let it go.

"Anyway, John was devastated by his grandmother's death. I had never seen him like that. He came to me and asked to borrow 200 dollars to buy a suit for the funeral. Of course, I gave it to him without even thinking about it. He left, and three days later we split up!" The sadness of that memory caused Debbie to choke on the last few words.

Maggie reached for her arm. "Debbie? I'm sorry, Sweetie. You don't have to tell me any more if you don't want to."

Debbie stood and walked over to the counter. She leaned against it a long moment, then reached for a tissue, wiped her eyes, and returned to her seat. "That's okay. I don't mind." She paused before continuing. "It turned out that John did attend the funeral, but not the wake. He never bought the suit, either. Instead, he went and got drunk, and wound up in a poker game in St. Paul."

"Oh, no."

"I guess he was playing with a pretty rough crowd. He accused somebody of cheating, so they took him outside and beat him up. When he finally returned to Duluth, his nose was broken, his eye was swollen shut, and he looked like hell."

"What'd you say to him?"

"He finally admitted that he lost the money, and I just decided that anyone who used his grandmother's death as an excuse to drink and gamble was incurable. It broke my heart, Maggie, but I told him I couldn't continue."

"I never knew any of that, Deb. I'm so sorry. What'd you do then?"

"I dated another boy, David, for the next year or so, but it was never the same as when I was with John. David and I had no future together, but we decided to give it a chance just in case."

"What did John do then?"

"To his credit, he graduated that year and joined the National Guard. A unit from Eveleth needed an officer, so John volunteered for OCS and spent nine months in the Army."

"Did you see him during that time?"

"No. We sent very impersonal letters back and forth, and never spoke. I could tell from his letters, though, that he was unhappy. He was almost killed, by the way, when a tank caught on fire. John rescued two other guys, and was burned in the process."

"Is that how he got those scars on his arms?"

Debbie nodded. "He was very lucky, but the other two men were even luckier that John pulled them out. They would surely have died. Anyway, David and I eventually split up, and when John heard about it, he came home from Colorado . . . and the rest is history, as they say."

"What was he doing in Colorado?"

"Skiing! Or so he said. Actually, I think it was another of those lost periods. He had no reason to come home, at least until he heard about me, I guess."

"I'm curious. Why didn't he go to his grandmother's wake?"

Debbie stood and stretched. She walked over to the counter again and leaned back, arms folded. "John told me that when he was a young boy, his grandmother gave him a St. Christopher's medal for a confirmation present. You know, Maggie, John always was very superstitious. He believed in good luck charms—lucky numbers, that sort of thing. Still does, actually. That medal was supposedly lucky for him. When she died, he thought that she, in spite of the St. Christopher's medal, had abandoned him, much like his father had."

"Boy, he was a mess, wasn't he?"

"He told me that he walked up to her casket, took the medal from around his neck, and placed it over her hands. He just could not deal with her death, so he ran out of the church and went and got drunk. That's how he used to handle pain."

Maggie was interested in pursuing this latest revelation about her friend's husband, almost to the point of forgetting that she was trying to distract Debbie. "How far did this good luck fetish go?"

"Pretty far. It still affects almost everything he does. He's very obsessive about creating good fortune. Sometimes I get irritated by it all, but for the most part it's pretty harmless." Debbie stopped and looked down at Maggie. She knew she was talking out of school about her husband, but Maggie was her best friend and they had always shared everything with each other.

"Good Lord! He's sure had a lot to deal with," Maggie offered. "But I suppose, of all his excesses, the superstitious part is probably the least harmful."

"I guess. Sometimes he drives me crazy with some of it though."

"Like what?"

"Oh, I don't know. He gets a bug for something, and nothing will deter him from getting it. And then, once he has it, he forgets about it and moves on to something else. He collects things, too."

"What do you mean?"

"Well, I know it sounds weird, but for some reason he always buys more than one of something—it can be anything."

"Like what?"

"Hats, shoes, ties—you name it, and John has lots of 'em!"

"Sounds like it's all part of the same behavior pattern, doesn't it?"

Debbie sat down and rested her chin on her hands. "Do you know the saying, 'Step on a crack, break your mother's back'?"

Maggie completed the sentence. 'Step on a line, break your mother's spine'? Yes, we used to say that as kids."

"Well, to this day, John will not intentionally step on a crack in the sidewalk."

"You're kidding, right?"

"Nope. I'm serious. I think it's funny, and am used to it, along with most of his other fetishes. But he grew up believing this stuff, thanks to his mother and grandmother, I think, and he's never been able to shake it."

"Wow!"

"Yeah. And all of that was what attracted me to him in the first place. I told you he was different from all the rest, didn't I?" At that moment, the phone rang. Debbie jumped, raced to the far end of the kitchen, and picked up the handset. Her heart was pounding, fully expecting to hear John's voice on the other end. "Hello?"

"Hi! Deb. Did anybody call?" It was her father.

"No, Daddy. It's been pretty quiet."

"Okay. Listen, this is going to take me a while longer. Then I'll be back over. Are you all right?"

"Yes. Maggie is still here. I'm fine, Daddy. I think I'll go up and lie down for a bit, though."

"That's a good idea, Honey. I'll be over later."

Debbie hung up the phone and turned to her friend. "Do you mind if I go upstairs for a while, Maggie?"

"Not at all. I've got some calls to make, so you go on up. I'll be right here if you need me."

Debbie gave her friend a big hug. "Thanks. You're a dear friend." She kissed her cheek and left the room.

Debbie climbed the stairs and entered their bedroom. At once, she noticed John's slippers and bathrobe. She picked up his hairbrush and idly ran it through her own long hair. She sat down on the bed and lay back for just a moment. As she did, she quietly cried and thought about all the years she and John had been together; they'd seldom been apart, except for that year after his graduation.

She wondered why it was that at moments of stress a person was driven to reflect back on her life. Maybe it was the idea of having no future memories together like the ones they already had. Losing her brother, Teddy, and her mother had been almost more than she could stand. *Please, God! Let John return home soon! Please watch over him and keep him safe!* She drifted into a worried sleep, her silent prayer tossed out in desperation.

Debbie sat up and looked around. She'd been dreaming, and while she couldn't clearly remember what she had been dreaming about, caught between that fuzzy state of not quite awake and not quite asleep, she knew the dreams hadn't been pleasant. Then she knew what had caused her to awaken: downstairs, the doorbell rang for the second time. Maggie would answer it.

Debbie didn't want to return to the unpleasant dreams, so she stood up, straightened the bed, and glanced into the mirror above the dresser she shared with John. She stared at her reflection. The face reflected back at her was sad, older than the one a day earlier.

She sighed, left the dresser, and passed by the bed on the way to the door. She stopped and shuddered. Gripped by a fear she'd not felt since her mother died, Debbie had a brief premonition of something dark and evil. Her entire body shook. She wrapped her arms tightly around herself and looked again at the bed she and her husband shared. She walked to it and reached down, running her hands over John's pillow.

She shook her head. "Stop it, Deborah! Don't give up on him!" She couldn't imagine life without him. "Hurry home, John L.!" She said, and left the room.

❖ 10 ❖

HUGE AND MIKEY REACHED the outskirts of Milbank. All of the food Huge had been eating along the way worked through his system. Loud farts, one after another, echoed through the confined space.

"Jesus, Huge! Cut it out, will ya! God, that's awful! You sure you didn't crap your pants?"

"Can't help it, Mikey. My belly hurts. You remember what Grandma used to say don't ya?"

"No, I don't remember what Grandma used to say." Mikey rolled down his window and leaned out.

"Sure ya do. 'Member she used to fart all the time. And then she'd say, let's see . . . hmmm how'd that go?"

"What a dumbass," Mikey muttered.

"Oh yeah, I remember. 'It's better to bear the shame than bear the pain!'" Huge laughed at the memory. "What's 'bear' mean, Mikey?"

"I dunno. Shut up for a while, will ya? Both your ass and your mouth!"

"I'm going to have to go pretty quick!"

"Too bad. Squeeze those fat buns together. You're just going to have to wait until we get rid of this guy. We're late enough already."

"How we gonna find the quarry without the map?" Huge asked.

"Got me. But, what the hell, a quarry's a quarry. Let's just find one and dump him in it." His brother replied.

"Okay. But let's keep it a secret from Ray. Okay, Mikey? I don't want him to get mad at me again."

They drove through Milbank and continued west. Both men forgot all about buying another map. After covering ten miles or so, Huge noticed a sign on the left that said Clearwater Granite Works—Quarry.

"This must be it, Mikey. It says Quarry."

Mikey grunted an unintelligible reply. He wanted to be rid of their cargo and then find Herman's.

Mikey turned left at the sign. It was 10:30 in the morning, and they were late. The big truck rumbled over the gravel road. Built from small pieces of granite, the road was rough and unsettled. Without smaller binder rock to hold the bed in place, sharp pieces of granite flew from the truck's tires. Mikey had to slow down to keep the truck on the road.

Like all the granite mines in the area, the Clearwater produced a high grade of stone. Used for building construction, counter tops, and decorative artwork, the purplish, brown-and-blue-streaked marble could be polished to a brilliant sheen. The most lucrative and demanding market for the stone was for headstones and monuments. Granite mined from the Milbank quarries was trucked all over the country to be carved, etched, and inscribed as grave markers.

The road wound south for a few miles. The constant bounce of the poorly suspended truck added to Huge's discomfort. He continued farting—one loud blast after another with each jolt.

Finally, much to Mikey's relief, the road abruptly ended.

There were a number of buildings ahead of them, various pieces of machinery parked nearby, and a short distance away was the open pit of the granite deposit. Mikey looked around with his head out the window. "No one around. Place looks abandoned, all right." He pulled the semi up to the edge of the cliff.

The Clearwater Granite Works was a working mine, a fairly new dig in the area, shut down for the winter. Consequently the depth of the pit was only seventy-five feet. Abandoned pits that had run their course, like the Simonet Mine, typically were three hundred feet deep. Water quickly filled up the abandoned quarries, forming very deep, sterile, man-made lakes.

The Clearwater Quarry only held only thirty or forty feet of water in the bottom. Large pumps turned on in the spring would rapidly empty the unwanted water, and mining could once again begin. At the open-pit mining operation, the granite was excavated from veins along the sides, loaded into large dump trucks, and driven back up to the top along a winding, switchback road.

John knew they were close to their destination. When Mikey turned off Highway 12 onto the Clearwater Quarry road, he shut off the engine of the Explorer and crawled back into the rear.

His body temperature had returned to a point where he felt strong enough to effect some sort of escape if the opportunity presented itself. He lay down with the iron bar tucked under his stomach. The truck bounced and rocked over the gravel road.

Huge and Mikey climbed down from the cab and approached the edge of the quarry. They crept close and peeked over the side.

"There's a road snaking down to the bottom," Mikey said. "We got to move over a bit, though."

"Why?"

"There's a ledge down there, stupid. The truck could get hung up." An outcropping of granite lay directly below them. Mikey looked to his right, west. "Over there. That's where we're going." The road from the bottom began directly below the point Mikey pointed to, but the cliffs were steep enough for a direct descent to the ice below.

"Lake's frozen," Huge said. "Wonder how thick the ice is?"

"Who cares? Even if it's a couple feet, the weight of that truck will bust right through. By tomorrow it'll freeze over and no one will ever know what happened."

They climbed back into the cab, started the semi, and headed to the designated drop-off point.

John was puzzled by all the stops and starts. He heard the brother's brief conversation, but the words were carried away by the incessant prairie wind before he could understand what they were talking about. He thought about starting up the truck to be ready for his escape. He knew that might be his only chance.

John didn't move. He feared that his captors might have guns. If they thought he was still tied up, maybe they wouldn't have them out.

He didn't know what to do. He sat up and thought over the few options available to him. As frightened as he had been up to this point, his fear leapt to a new level now. This would be the moment of truth.

Mikey halted the semi one last time. "Let's get this over with." He pulled the parking brake and reached under the seat, withdrawing a large, black Colt .45.

Huge's eyes widened when he glimpsed the weapon. "What'cha need that for, Mikey."

Mikey knew of Huge's horrible fear of guns. When they were small boys, Ray had surprised them both by dumping out a sack of unwanted puppies and shooting all five in the head as they stood and watched. Ray smiled with every tug on the trigger. "Don't know. Might need it."

Mikey climbed from the cab and stuck the pistol down the front of his jeans. "Come on, Huge. It won't bite!"

Huge sat unmoving. "I don't want to. Put it back, okay Mikey?"

"Shut up your babbling and get out. Now!"

Huge did as he was told. He walked back to the rear, opened the back doors, and pulled out the ramps.

Mikey walked up the ramps into the trailer. He looked in the rear window, noticed that John was motionless. Face down, hands tied, he wasn't moving. Mikey concluded that the man in back probably froze to death, which was just as well.

Mikey opened the door to the Explorer, climbed in and started the engine. Because of his inability to smell as a normal person might, he never noticed the strong smell of exhaust that filled the interior of the trailer. For the past thirty minutes, Mikey's nostrils had been burdened with the persistent ill wind from Huge and the pungent odor emanating from abundant pig farms they had passed along the way.

John felt the Explorer begin to move as Mikey backed it down the ramps. He didn't dare look up for fear he would be noticed. He remained still as Mikey turned the truck around and edged it nearer the quarry. He heard the front door open. The engine continued to run quietly. After a few moments, John felt, then heard a loud roar as the engine was revved up. The truck jerked forward. John was thrown to the very rear and slammed against the tailgate.

Mikey left the engine running, and got out. He stood and looked around, carefully surveying the landscape to see if anyone was watching. Satisfied that they were alone, he bent over, picked up a piece of granite, reached inside the Explorer, pulled the parking brake, and wedged the rock against the gas pedal. He slowly eased himself out of the truck.

Mikey took one last look around, saw that Huge was clear of the Explorer, leaned in, released the brake, then put the gear shift into DRIVE and quickly jumped away from the truck. The blue Explorer shot straight ahead for about fifteen feet, its engine roaring loudly. Then it nosed over the drop and disappeared from view.

The two brothers stepped to the edge and watched it plummet to the ice below, a fall of forty feet. They heard the crash of the truck as it broke through the ice. The Explorer quickly settled into the frigid lake. Within thirty seconds, it had vanished from their view.

"There. Now let's get the hell out of here," Mikey commanded.

Their job now complete, they hurried back to the semi, turned the truck around, and headed back the way they came. Their next stop—Herman's. Fortunately, they now knew where to go, as they had passed by the junkyard on their way out of town.

At least one of the two remembered where they were going. "Where to now, Mikey?" Huge asked.

Mikey looked at his brother as he replaced the pistol beneath the seat. "Did you forget already, Huge?"

"Forget what, Mikey?"

"That we have to drop the parts off at Herman's before we can go home." Mikey felt a bit more accommodating now that they had completed the first, most difficult part of their mission.

"Oh yeah! I guess I forgot. Can we stop and get something to eat on the way?"

"We'll see." They were late, and they had to get the truck unloaded. In a matter of thirty or forty minutes, they would be sitting with Herman while his boys unloaded the back of the truck. Mikey smiled, satisfied that their loss of the map would go undetected by their short-tempered cousin. As far as Ray would know, everything went off without a hitch.

John never had a chance to put anything into play and the iron bar did him no good. The truck was airborne. He watched the cloudy sky rotate and blend into the jagged sidewalls of the quarry. Surprisingly calm, he waited for what seemed an eternity for the jarring crash that would snuff the life from his tired body.

He waited and waited. The roar of the engine slackened to a quiet idle as the piece of granite slipped from the pedal. John had no idea how far the truck would fall. *God, please let this be quick!* Blood pounded through his veins; his entire body ached. He tensed, sensing the impact. *Our Father, who art in heaven . . .*

Detective Reasons hung up the phone. His conversation with Jack Stevens left him perplexed. The attorney had just spent five minutes describing the disappearance of John L. Rule. The man's involvement in the French Creek mess made no sense at all. How did Jack's missing person fit in? They had seen no evidence that anyone other than the Steckel clan had been around there lately. Stevens had said he was certain, however, that somehow, this Rule had wandered in to the junkyard late yesterday and had not been heard from since.

Reasons felt as if he had missed something. Somehow the Steckels had to have caught Rule on their property and were either holding him captive or worse, had already killed him.

As he turned to join his partner, he stopped. He suddenly remembered the broken window. That had to be it! "I'll be damned! Rule managed to escape at least once . . . but then what?" Either way, this investigation had just gotten a lot more complicated. Kidnapping was a capital offense, and Sam was certain that some other governmental agency was going to become involved in the case. The feds probably. He'd be asked to back off of the investigation. Reasons had wanted to nail these assholes himself.

Sam approached his partner. "Rick, there's apparently a new wrinkle to this case." He filled in his partner on what he had just heard. They instructed the troopers to keep their eyes open for John's blue Explorer, and for the third time that morning, searched the shop and surrounding area for any sign that John had been there. Reasons wondered whether this bunch routinely included murder as part of their activity.

After completing their search, Reasons addressed the assembled cops again. "Spread out and start questioning the neighbors. I want to know if anyone had knowledge of what has been going on here. Find out if anyone is more willing to talk now that the Steckels have apparently fled. Let me know as soon as you hear anything."

The troopers left Sam and Rick alone with Sheriff Nichols.

"Rick, make sure when the crime boys get here that they pull prints from that broken glass over at the other building."

"I'll take care of it, Sam."

❖ ● ❖

Elroy Nichols took all of this in. He remained silent as the cops went about their work. He watched as they systematically tracked down the vehicles belonging to gang members.

"Rick, where was that truck found?" Reasons asked.

Rick pulled out his notebook. "Behind a place called Herb's Garage in Cokato."

"All right, that's where we're headed. Sheriff, I want you to follow us there."

On the drive back to Cokato, Sam told Rick of his suspicions about Sheriff Nichols. "Keep your eye on him. If he's involved, he might bolt before we can nail him."

"If he is involved, I wonder how long this operation has been going on?"

"My guess is that with his protection, quite a while." At that moment, their radio interrupted their conversation. "Reasons here. Go ahead."

It was Sam's superior, Captain Swenson. "Sam, you need to know that the Hennepin County Attorney's office, along with the state police, have come up with a disturbing sidebar to your investigation."

"I have a hunch I know what you're about to tell me, but go ahead, Captain."

"For a number of years, apparently, a series of missing persons reports have been filed with the state police, all roughly in the area around French Creek. According to the county attorney, they suspect that a certain missing person is involved with your case—the name is John L. Rule."

"Yes, I'm aware of that, Captain. Jack Stevens called earlier and filled me in. I couldn't figure out how this guy became involved, but based on what you just told me, I guess there's a disturbing pattern here. Anything else, Captain?"

"None of the cases has ever been solved, nor have any bodies ever been recovered. At one point, the sheriff in the adjoining county pointed a finger at this Ray Steckel, but he had no proof. That sheriff is now deceased—and his files were destroyed."

"Hmmm. Looks like this poor Rule fellow gets added to the list?"

"Yeah, I guess. His family is very concerned, but I'm afraid that if he stumbled into something out there, that bunch would get rid of him rather quickly from the sound of it."

"I agree. It doesn't look too good. At least we know what we're up against. I'll keep you posted, Captain, if anything turns up. By the way, when I spoke with Jack, he said this Rule fellow was Mac Davis' son in law?"

"Yep! So let's do all we can to track him down—at least as long as we're left on the case. I fully expect that the FBI will be stepping in soon, but we still need to complete our original investigation."

"I understand, Captain. Talk to you later."

Reasons and his partner pulled into Herb's Garage. Already present was one of the troopers. He was speaking to a man outside the building. Sam and Rick got out and approached the two men.

"Detective, this gentlemen came to pick up his van this morning, and not only is the garage closed, but his van isn't here," the trooper said.

"Did you call the garage owner?" Reasons asked.

"Not yet."

"Well, see what you can find out while I speak to this gentleman."

Reasons began questioning the man, away from the others. He soon learned that not only was the customer eager to reclaim his van, but when he heard about the investigation of the Steckels, he willingly offered additional information to help Sam build a case.

The trooper returned to Reason's side. "Detective? I spoke with Herb's wife. Herb left home unexpectedly very early this morning after receiving a phone call. She hasn't seen him since. She didn't know where he was going and couldn't tell me who called, but she assumed he was coming to the shop."

"Thanks. Rick! Jimmy the lock and let's look inside. Excuse me, sir. Would you wait here for a moment, please?" Reasons said to the chatty witness.

Reasons waited while Rick broke the lock. This case was getting more and more intriguing to him. He wondered how many people were involved. If this Herb fellow was in on it, then they had to find him as well. The next item on his list was to see if he could break down Sheriff Nichols.

Rick had the door open quickly and they all went inside, including Sheriff Nichols. After scanning the office, they went back to the two service bays. There was no evidence of the customer's white van.

They moved on to the last bay, and there, lying beneath one of the hydraulic lifts, was what was left of Herb's body. A pool of blood surrounded his crushed, lifeless form. The lift, with a car still sitting on the two ramps, had nearly sliced him in two.

They moved closer. Sam thought about how slowly and painfully the poor guy must have died. Reasons took in the scene. "Made to look like an accident, I'll bet." He walked over to the control on the wall. "This lever has to be thrown into the DOWN position, which is exactly where it's at. Whoever did this forgot to move the lever back to UP."

Sam walked back to Herb's lifeless form. "The lift didn't fail, and it didn't knock this guy down, but it did crush him to death. The top of his head is all bashed in." Reasons now knew that he was dealing with a deadly, ruthless bunch, and that anybody who got in their way was expendable. He bent over and stared intently at the pool of blood.

"Rick, come here a minute!"

"What is it, Sam?"

"Look at this," Sam said, pointing to the dark red stain. "What else do you see besides the blood?"

Rick looked closely. After a few seconds he turned to look at his partner, eyebrows raised. "What the hell is that? Looks like . . . letters."

"Looks like our poor friend here left us a message. He suffered a great deal before he died and apparently used the last of his strength to scribble H E R M A N." Reasons turned and addressed the sheriff. "Nichols, come over here."

Sheriff Nichols did as he was told. He approached Herb's body and looked down. His face blanched and he took a step back. Reasons indicated the marks in the blood. "Any idea what that means Sheriff?"

Sheriff Elroy Nichols knew that coupled with what the owner of the van had told them, Herb's death could be tied to him easily. He was an accessory to murder! He quickly ran through his available options and realized he had only one choice: to tell them everything he knew that wouldn't tie him to murder. He needed to cut a deal. "Yes, I'm afraid I do," Nichols said quietly.

"You'd better talk to me, Sheriff. Now!"

After Reasons read him his rights, Sheriff Elroy Nichols proceeded to tell Reasons about Herman's place, and promptly stated that he'd had, "Nothing to do with killing Herb or anyone else!"

"I think you and I had better have a little chat, Sheriff. Let's go into the office. Rick, seal this off for the Crime Bureau, and then come into the office. Let's go, Nichols."

As he closed the door behind them, Reasons looked at the sheriff and spoke quietly. "I'll need your sidearm, Sheriff." The sheriff surrendered his weapon, and the two men sat down in Herb's office.

Sheriff Nichols looked at Reasons, his face a ghostly white, eyes empty, hands folded in his lap. "I suppose you want to know how I'm involved?"

"That would be a good place to start. Tell me how deep you're in this mess, and for how long."

Nichols made his move. "If I tell you everything I know. Can we make a deal of some sort?"

"You know better than that! You're a cop, or at least you pretend to be one. I don't have that authority, but if you cooperate, it'll go in my report, and I'll ask the county attorney to be lenient."

Nichols studied Reasons's eyes for a moment, then his shoulders slumped in resignation. "Where do you want me to start?"

"Start at the beginning, and tell me about events you have direct knowledge of." He quickly stood up. "Hang on a minute." He walked to the door. "Rick! Come in here and bring the tape recorder from the car!"

Sam returned to his seat behind the desk. Before long his partner came through the door with the recorder. Sam looked up. "The sheriff has decided that it would be in his best interest to cooperate with us."

He turned to Nichols. "Okay, tell me about the Steckels. How does their operation work?"

"They steal cars from the Cities, strip them down, sell the parts out of state, and crush what's left. Been doin' it for years."

"How many years? When did it start?"

"Long time ago. Ray and Dale are brothers. They inherited the business from their old man, Art. After Arthur got out of prison a number of years ago, he went to work for the original owner, Morris Johnson. Art was a slick one. Managed to get on the good side of the old man. Then get himself written into his will. A few months later, old Morris . . . had an accident. Then Art was the new owner."

Reasons perked up. "What kind of accident?"

157

"Slipped and fell into the crusher—at least that's the story Art told. Became part of a block of scrap iron."

"So this accident may not have been an accident at all?"

"I didn't say that, and I wasn't involved back then."

"Okay, we'll let that go for now. So Art takes over and does what?"

"Well, he turned a legitimate salvage yard into a chop shop. He and his relatives started stealing cars, stripping them, and selling the parts."

"Is that all they did? We have reason to believe that over the years, a number of innocent people mysteriously disappeared out there. Know anything about that?"

Nichols didn't answer right away. He knew this was dangerous ground for him, and he had to answer very carefully. "Rumors was all I ever heard. I knew nothing about any killings—or anything like that."

Sam cocked an eyebrow at him. "I didn't say anything about killings. I just said mysterious disappearances. What rumors did you hear?"

Nichols didn't want to continue. He was in over his head and knew it. He was sweating, and his left leg kept a steady beat, alternating from toes to heel. He looked over Sam's head, then down at his boots. "I heard that once in a while, old Art would take it upon himself to steal expensive cars and trucks from . . . certain customers that wandered in."

"What happened to the customers?" Reasons asked.

Nichols panicked. "Don't know for sure. Word was the dogs took care of them at night—then maybe they got put in the crusher. I don't know. No one ever knew for sure, 'cause no one ever talked about it. Art was a mean sonofabitch and would have killed anyone who talked."

Reasons wondered just how many of those poor souls met their end out on that property. He shuddered to think of what

158

those dogs could do. "How about Ray and Dale? How did they get control, and did the operation change when they took over?"

"The old man died, and the two brothers took over—actually, Ray took over. If anything, the operation became even more active. Ray was the spittin' image of his old man, meaner if that's possible. Word was that if old Art hadn't died, Ray would have killed him and taken over the business. After Ray got out of prison, he was never the same. Before, he was just a mean bully—afterwards, he was evil!"

"What do you mean? What happened?"

"Well, some guy wandered into town a few years back and told this story to another fellow in a bar. Turns out the guy was in prison same time as Ray. He got in some trouble, and I had to throw him in jail overnight. Gave him his one phone call, and the next morning Ray shows up and posts bail. Unusual for Ray to spend money on anybody but himself. Anyway, the story goes that on Ray's first day in prison, Ray gets crossways with some bad-ass and refuses to give the guy his cigarettes. Ray thought he was pretty tough, but he wasn't tough enough."

"What'd he get sent away for?"

"Manslaughter. Damned near killed some poor drunk with a piece of pipe. They was fighting, and Ray was losing, so he picks up this length of pipe and bashes the guy's skull in. Poor slob was a vegetable after Ray got done with him. Old Herb out there witnessed it. Said Ray would have killed the guy if he hadn't been pulled off."

"Go on."

"The tough guy in prison and his buddies beat Ray up and did God knows what all to him. When they got done with him, they carved that mark on his cheek."

"What mark?"

"That's right, you ain't seen him yet, have you? There's a C on his right cheek. Everyone in prison knew what it meant.

Anytime anybody wanted a piece of Ray, he was theirs for the taking. He was powerless. He was marked and without any friends. This went on for a while until Ray got a new cell mate—then everything changed."

"Why?"

"Well, you know how prisons are run on favors—everyone owes someone else one thing or another. I guess Ray's new mate was pretty bad-ass hisself. Ray promised him something, 'cause the next thing anyone knew, Ray's problems ended. The guy that cut him up was found in the latrine with his throat cut."

"Hmmm. I'd venture a guess that old Ray came out a pretty pissed-off guy," Sam volunteered.

"Got that right! No one ever messed with him after that. And no one in their right mind ever asked him about that scar—including me. Ray by hisself wasn't that tough unless he figgered out an unfair advantage. But he always kept his bigger cousins, Huge and Mikey, around for muscle. Everybody was afraid of those guys—they did exactly what Ray told them to do."

"Whatever happened to the cell mate?"

"Don't know." Nichols said.

"So Ray expanded the operation. Send a crew to the Cities, drive the stolens out to French Creek, strip 'em down, and turn what's left into a steel ice cube. Now, how does this Herman fit in?"

"Herman Fogelman is Ray's cousin. Never cottoned to Ray's way of doin' things. Decided to move away with his family and start a legit operation. Picked Milbank, South Dakota, for some damned reason. Never did completely understand why Ray let him go. Wasn't like Ray to let any of the gang get out. Only thing I can figure is that Ray knew Herman would keep his mouth shut—probably threatened his family. Besides, if Ray ever wanted to move some parts other than in the Cities, he could always get Herman to take 'em."

"What about the poor guy out in the shop, Herb?"

"Herb was also a family member. He wasn't real active, and didn't really like what Ray did, but he was afraid for his wife Margie, so he played along. I don't know for sure, but I think Herb sent certain strays out to Ray if they were driving a spendy vehicle or were looking for directions to the place. I never wanted to know exactly."

Reasons paused before continuing. On a roll, he decided to milk Nichols for everything. "Sheriff, it appears that we also have a missing person involved here. A John L. Rule. It seems as if he may have stumbled into the salvage yard on an innocent errand, and now he's disappeared. Any idea what Ray would have done with him?"

Nichols knew precisely what Ray would have done, but had to be careful. "Now, look, I told you I had no part in that kind of stuff. And I'm only guessing, mind you, but probably they would have locked him in the yard and let the dogs loose."

"And once the dogs did their dirty work, then what?"

"Well, I guess old Huge'd pick the guy up and haul him to the crusher—what's left of him anyway. Then they'd strip his car and, you know, crush it."

"I see. So how would you explain a dead dog behind the main office and the broken window?"

"Don't know. Just a guess, mind you, but maybe he managed to escape from the dogs, tried to break out through the office, and ran into the other dog. I really don't know—honest."

"If he did manage to escape and the Steckels caught him a second time, what would they have done with him?"

"Jeez, I don't know!" The old man was close to tears. He realized that his former life was over and that soon he would be behind bars for the rest of his life. "I told you, my part in the operation was just to keep nosy people away—keep the cops at bay when they came sniffin' around—put up a roadblock for Ray's operation. I never got involved in any of that other crap!"

FRENCH CREEK

Reasons pressed him further. "I understand that, Sheriff, but take a guess: What do you think they would do with him?"

"If they were in a hurry and didn't want to leave any evidence around here, well . . . maybe they took him with them. I don't know. I'm tired. Can I call my wife?"

"You'll get a call from lock-up. I suggest you save it for a good lawyer—you're going to need one."

"What do you mean?"

"I mean that in spite of all your denials, I'll bet you've been up to your neck in this thing, and at some point you could have—make that, should have—blown the whistle. Because of your silence, innocent people are probably dead, and frankly I hope they lock you away for good."

"But . . . but you promised! You said that if I cooperated, you'd put in a good word for me!"

"Yeah, well, that was before I heard your slimy story. Sue me." Reasons sat up straight and leaned across the desk. His sparkling blue eyes fixed on Nichols' mouth. "You wear dentures, don't you?"

Nichols flinched. "Yeah . . . Why?"

"Oh, I was just thinking . . . I'm sure all those guys that carved up your cousin's cheek are probably all dead by now, but I'll bet there's a new bunch that'll be tickled pink to see you coming down the hall. Get him out of here, Rick, before I puke!"

Reasons was pretty sure they we're too late to help Rule, but he sure wanted to catch up to the scar-faced character, Ray Steckel. Sam watched Rick handcuff the sheriff and lead him out.

Reasons considered his next course of action. He knew with certainty that he'd be told to back off the case. He hated the idea of handing the case over to the feds. *Those guys move so slow—if Rule happened to still be alive, they'd probably be too late.*

Rick returned to the garage office. "One of the troopers is taking the sheriff in. What's next?"

162

"Ever hear the story about the blue jay, Rick?"

"No."

"My grandfather told me once that the reason you never see blue jays on Fridays is 'cause that's the day they all take sticks down to Satan. They tell old Satan about all the gossip in the world—then return to earth on Saturday. Saturdays are when the jays sing and chirp the loudest—'cause their so happy to be back on earth. Our little sheriff just sang his heart out and gave us everything we needed—and it's not even Saturday! Question now is, what are we going to do with this information?"

"Well, don't you think the feds will take over?"

"I guess . . . still, I'd like to take a crack at finding out what happened to this Rule fellow." Reasons stood and stretched. "I'm tired. Guess we'd better report to the captain."

❖ 11 ❖

Ray, Dale, and the rest of the Steckel gang reached the outskirts of Milbank. They had made good time; conversation on the trip had been minimal. Ray was preoccupied with working out the details for taking over Herman's business. He lit another Old Gold. The interior of the van filled with smoke. Ray gazed out the window looking for something, anything on the barren plain that might alter how he felt about relocating in the Milbank area. Seeing nothing but dirt and fence rows, he felt it was a depressing, sterile environment.

Dale opened his window. "You say somethin', Ray?"

"You just keep that one good eye on the road. If I want you for somethin', I'll holler!" Ray's mind was thinking ahead to what he had to do. He felt he had just the plan that would put him and his family back in business. He sat up straight and crushed the butt in an already stuffed ashtray. All his senses were alert. He was calculating his next move. He felt alive and energized for the first time since they left French Creek.

"I love it when a plan comes together!"

"What'd you say, Ray?" Dale asked.

Ray looked at his brother. He was smiling, and slapped Dale on the shoulder. "I said I just love it when a plan comes together! By tonight, we'll be set up in a new business, have a thick steak someplace, and see if we can't get laid! Whatcha think of that, boys?" He glanced around the interior of the van, looking for an enthusiastic response.

"Sounds great, Ray," Dale said. "You gonna tell us what your plan is?"

"In good time little brother. Don't you worry your pea brain about it. Old Ray's got everything under control, as always." He took a deep breath and slid down against the bench, then snorted—loudly. "Phew! What the hell is that? You do something in your pants, little brother?"

Dale inhaled. "That's pig stink, Ray. Don't'cha remember all the pig farms out here?"

"Oh, yeah. Been a while since I was out this way. Forgot about that rotten smell. Who the hell would ever want to be a pig farmer, anyway?"

The odor caused Ray to think of his father. He seldom thought of him, and certainly never felt any warmth toward the old man. *Taught me well, the old bastard.* He always said thinking of what used to be was a sign of weakness—always be thinking ahead, instead! *Yeah, well I'm doin' that very thing right now. Table's set. All I got to do is put the frostin' on the cake and then it's party time!*

His mood changed as a flood of memories intruded. *Never quite had to kill you, you piece of shit! But I would have, sooner or later. That bum ticker of yours gave out just in time—otherwise I'd've finished you off myself!*

Ray sat up and shook his head. He lit another cigarette and told the others about his plans—most of them. With a new set of rules, fear and intimidation as his allies, Ray would soon be back in business. He was excited by what the future had to offer. He had his money, the boys were there with him, and with his wife and daughter back in Cokato, he could do anything he damn well pleased!

"Dale, you remember where Herman's is?" Ray asked his brother.

"Yeah, it's just a few miles up the road on 12."

John was still alive. He had been fortunate in more ways than one. Had he not moved to the back of his truck when Huge and Mikey stopped at the edge of the quarry, and instead remained in the front seat, he probably would have been killed instantly when the truck hit the ice.

The impact lifted John and threw him against the roof of the vehicle. The blow knocked the wind from his lungs. He collapsed in a crumpled heap as the Explorer slowly slipped through the thin ice.

He was barely conscious now—gasping for a breath that would not come. His chest heaved, ached from the force of the collision with the ice and water. He shook his head and, as he struggled to breathe, took a quick survey of his condition.

I'm still alive—nothing's broken. Then he heard it: the sound of water rushing over the truck. *Shit! I don't have long. This thing is going to fill . . . how deep? God, my chest hurts so much!*

The truck slowly settled into the man-made lake. John had no idea where he was. He remembered the word scribbled on the map: Quarry? He scrambled to the rear window and pushed as hard as he could—nothing happened. He pounded bloodied fists against the cold glass. Too much pressure . . . have to wait . . .

The truck settled on the solid bottom of the lake. Inside, water was rapidly displacing the available air. The Explorer's engine had long since quit. The only sound John heard was the terrifying bubbling and gurgling as the frigid water found openings in the chassis. He was numb with fear. His entire body ached. His heart raced.

It was completely dark. John couldn't see two feet. Within seconds the cold water struck his already frigid limbs. He gasped. His lungs locked from the incredible shock, John fought to release them. Nothing happened.

The water covered his body. Only his head and neck were left in the open, in a small pocket of air formed on the roof of the Explorer.

John fought to retain control of his brain—his next move was critical, and he knew it. Terror filled his heart! From his previous experiences duck hunting, John knew exactly what the cold water would do to his body. He had two previous encounters with near-drowning.

John recalled a friend's description of a similar experience while ice fishing on Leech Lake. His brother was trapped inside a car that broke through thin spring ice. He never escaped. It was later determined that instead of slowly opening a window or door after water had filled the interior, he apparently had attempted to push the door open all at once. It wouldn't budge. He panicked and drowned. Water pressure outside has to equal the pressure on the inside.

John floated from back to front and tested the electric door locks. *Nothing . . . windows don't work either!* The electrical system had shorted out. There wasn't much air left, and John's limbs felt dead.

The truck was now almost completely filled. The only sound to be heard was his teeth clicking. The roar of water eased. John could barely move his limbs from the cold. *I have to break out a window . . . where's that iron bar?*

John returned to the rear and, without thinking, dove to retrieve his heavy weapon. He groped and finally felt the slim shape. He had to grab the metal with both hands to hold it. He straightened up until his head contacted the roof. He opened his mouth and gasped for more air.

The only remaining air was quickly vanishing. John tilted his head back for one last, desperate breath. He opened his mouth and sucked long and hard. The interior was full—the pressure equalized.

As the water finally covered his face, he began kicking and pounding at the rear window. His fingers had no feeling. The bar slipped from his grip after the first weak blow.

John braced against the heavy file boxes behind the rear seat. He kicked at the glass with both feet.

He was running out of time. He had to close his eyes. The frigid water stung. White specks dotted the blackness behind his eyelids.

John experienced a pain unlike anything he had ever felt before—it was his lungs. His heart would soon stop, but his brain would continue to function for a short while. Soon, there would be no more pain. From someplace far away, he slowly recited: *Lord is my shepherd; I shall not want . . .*

With one last kick, the window broke loose. John moved in slow motion, his body shutting down from the early stages of hypothermia. It took all his remaining strength just to slip through the opening. He was losing consciousness as he drifted upward, his green down jacket helping to provide buoyancy.

He was unaware that he had escaped. Time ran out. He opened his mouth, and the frigid water entered the cavity. Without restriction, without conscious effort, the killing water flowed down to his starved lungs.

At that instant, his head broke the surface of the water. He coughed repeatedly, rejecting the icy water. Fresh air filled his mouth and nostrils. His eyes opened briefly. He sputtered. Bile rose in his throat. He was only barely aware of what he was doing as he drew in the life-giving oxygen in short, staccato-like gasps. Reflexively, he began treading water. His lungs filled with air; his head cleared.

John's body still suffered from extreme cold, however. He was drowsy and nearly unconscious. Fortunately, when he finally found the surface of the lake, he was only a short distance from shore. Only partially consciousness now, he tried to paddle. He floated shoreward—mouth and nostrils barely above the water's surface. He bumped against and parted chunks of ice as he moved closer to the bank.

Once his small store of energy was used up, his body temperature fell rapidly. Somewhere in the recesses of his brain, he knew he had to get up. *Can't stay here . . . move . . . crawl.* Sleep and inactivity meant certain death. He felt clumsy, confused, and very weak as he clawed his way across the rocky shore.

He began the climb to the top on his hands and knees. *Move . . . don't stop . . . got to keep going . . .* Up the winding trail, he stopped to catch his breath after traveling six or seven feet. John was delirious. He lived a nightmare, a bad dream. *That's all it is . . . wake up soon . . . have to get home . . . Debbie . . . there . . . there she is!*

It took John twenty minutes to reach the flats above. He had nothing left. Now, the battered, half-frozen salesman had a new enemy—hypothermia, and that enemy was easily beating him. He was very confused and mumbled a jumble of words that made no sense. "Too tired. Where'd she go? Dammit, I know I have to . . . what? Okay, I will. Hurts . . . knees hurt. Help me . . . help me . . . please . . . God . . ."

John swayed on all fours like a newborn colt after taking its first, shaky steps. He raised his aching head and, through a foggy mist, looked around. There was nothing to see but emptiness. He fell to the hard ground and lay motionless.

His core body temperature was now at a dangerously low level, but he no longer could help himself. Soon his internal organs would shut down. He would slip into a deep coma and die. He had no strength left and lay like a discarded, worn out rag doll on the barren plain.

A lifeless, half-frozen, sodden heap. The end was near.

❖　●　❖

Huge, Mikey, and Larry were inside Herman's when Ray and the others pulled in. Ray noticed the semi backed up to the loading dock. "What the hell? That trailer should have been emptied hours ago. Park in front, Dale."

They parked the van in front of the old, wooden building and entered the office.

Herman and his son Barry were behind the parts counter. Huge, Mikey, and Larry were perched on stools sitting across from them, munching from bags full of Whoppers and fries.

"Hey! Herman. How ya doing?" Ray could be silky smooth when he wanted to convey a sense of ease and friendliness.

"Hi, Ray . . ." The surprise in Herman's voice was unmistakable. He was not taken in by Ray's smarmy tone. "I'm okay." He looked at the assembled mass and silently counted heads. I see you brought everyone with you. How come?"

Herman glanced nervously from Ray to Dale to the others and back again to Ray.

Herman not only never liked Ray very much, he never trusted him either. He had tolerated doing business with him only to keep peace in the family. And he feared retribution if he ever crossed the man. The distance separating Milbank from Cokato was sufficient, however, to insure that their paths seldom crossed. Now, however, what was supposed to have been a simple trailer unloading seemed to be something more. He didn't like it.

Ray smiled and considered his response. "Do you remember when I told you about that debt you owed?"

The small room seemed to close in on Herman. Numerous pairs of eyes focused on him. He felt his armpits leak, and he wiped his upper lip. "What are you talking about, Ray? I don't owe you any money, do I?"

Ray leaned close. The scar was a deep red, like some sort of pulsating beacon. "I'm not talking about money, Herman."

Herman's mind sped ahead, then backed up. He searched for answers. "What do you mean then? Why are you and the rest of the guys here?"

Ray put his arm around Herman's shoulder. "Let's go into your office, and I'll explain the facts of life to you. Dale? Why don't you take Barry out and show him our new van? Fill in Huge and Mikey about our new venture."

Herman was fully alert now. "No! Barry, you come back into the office with me." He cast a worried look in his son's direction.

Barry turned, scratching his head. He loved trucks and vans. "No. Please let me go, Daddy?" Barry said.

Dale and Larry escorted him out the door. Barry smiled. A happy eighteen-year old with Down's Syndrome, Barry was friendly to everyone and trusted all.

Herman was helpless to stop them. Barry was beaming. Herman looked like he had just seen death. He trembled and resisted Ray's prod. He held back. Spittle ran from one corner of his mouth. He truly feared for his son's life. "Let Barry stay here, Ray. He'll be afraid if I'm not with him," Herman pleaded.

"Don't worry, cousin. Dale and the boys will take good care of him. Come on!" He was fast losing patience with the Milbank junkyard owner. "Let's go into your office and have that chat."

Herman's bookkeeper observed all of this with a total lack of interest. Hired years before because of his own checkered past, the accountant knew how to keep quiet about Herman's occasional illegal activities. He turned back to his journal entries as Ray guided Herman into the back office and closed the door.

171

The door slammed shut. Ray walked over and sat down behind Herman's desk. He put his feet up and quickly got down to business. "Herman, you're going to sell me your business." He smiled, showing Herman a full set of yellowed teeth.

"What the hell you talking about, Ray?"

"Just what I said. You're going to sell me the business for $50,000. It's a fair offer—not top dollar, but what the hell, we're family. Right, Herman?" Ray chuckled.

"You're crazy. In the first place, I don't want to sell, and in the second place, it's worth ten times that amount!" Herman was sweating heavily now. His voice shook. "Forget it, Ray!"

Ray enjoyed the moment. It was time to play his trump card. "I don't think so. I thought you might be a little hesitant, so just to be sure you'd cooperate, Dale took Barry for a little ride. He's okay for now, but you know, a kid that stupid could easily have an accident." Ray looked down at his fingernails, as if by looking he could somehow remove the grease and dirt beneath. He waited for Herman's response.

Herman was speechless—he knew Ray was serious. Herman was terrified for the safety of his only son. He collapsed into one of the armchairs, face folded in his hands. "Why, Ray? Why are you doing this to me?" Herman was sobbing now, envisioning his helpless son being bludgeoned to death by Dale or one of the big goons.

"Nothing personal, cousin. Had a small problem back at French Creek and had to leave town. Now we need a new operation, and your little business is perfect. We'll be up and running again in no time."

Herman knew it was hopeless to plead or argue. Ten minutes earlier, Herman had a business, a family, and a future—albeit only semi-legitimate, but he still had successfully put his past behind him. Now everything was gone. He knew he had to give Ray what he wanted.

Herman stood and faced his antagonist. A slight man, Herman hated violence, hated deception, and he had always avoided confrontations. He clenched his fists, half-tempted to leap across the desk. He resisted the angry urge. "All right, but what's my assurance you won't kill Barry and me anyway after I sign the papers?"

Ray turned loose all the charm and assuring conviction he possessed. "Herman, I may be a lot of things, but once I give my word, you can go to the bank on it! Trust me. I don't need to hurt you. Once you sign the business over to me and collect your money, you and your family are free to leave. Know this though: If you ever, ever tell anyone about this, I'll find you, wherever you are, and make your last days on earth a living hell!" Ray's black eyes conveyed the real meaning of his last words.

Herman knew this was true. In order for Ray to succeed him in Milbank, there had to be some legitimacy to his taking over the business. If he just disappeared, questions would be asked, especially if Ray and his bunch ran the business. He knew he had no choice but to agree to Ray's proposal.

Herman unclenched his fists. His lower lip quivered. "I'll have my bookkeeper draw up the bill of sale. He's a notary, so it'll be legal." Herman felt as depressed and alone as no other time in his life.

"Atta boy, cousin! You made the right decision. Dale will be back with that idiot son of yours in fifteen minutes. All I have to do is wave to him, and the boy's safe. Get the bookkeeper started on the papers." Ray rose from the desk, crossed the room, and patted Herman on the shoulder as he walked past.

Herman remained motionless for a few moments, slumped in the chair. He knew what must be done. He figured that if he were a braver man, he would go over to the desk, open the drawer, take out the pistol, and shoot Ray. Instead, he decided to agree to Ray's terms and hope that Ray made a mistake. He sighed, slowly rose from the chair, looked around the office one last time, and went out to explain what he needed to the bookkeeper.

Ray walked over to Huge and Mikey. He shifted gears quickly. "Everything go all right with the Explorer?"

"Yeah, Ray. Went like clockwork," Mikey responded. He was nervous and tried to hide it.

"That so, Huge?" Ray asked the bigger man.

With his mouth full of food, Huge replied, "Yef! We did it just like you said!" Pieces of the burger, cheese, and all, flew from between his lips. Most of it landed on Ray's shirt.

Ray looked down at the gob of mush that clung to the front of his shirt. Casually, he flicked the mess off with his middle finger. An additional grease stain remained on the already soiled blue shirt. Ray slowly raised his head and quietly asked, "Is that right? What time did you get here, Mikey?"

"Oh, a while ago, Ray." Mikey was really nervous, and wanted nothing more than to keep Ray from getting angry, but he didn't know what to say.

"Well if that's so, how come they were still unloading the truck when we got here?" Ray's voice raised an octave and had an ominous tone. He was clearly pissed off.

Ray stood quietly cleaning his fingernails with a toothpick while Mikey and Huge glanced at each other.

Mikey tried to change the subject. "So, what's next Ray?"

Ray wasn't buying any of Mikey's cock-and-bull-story. "You didn't answer my question! What the hell happened? Tell me, now—or else!"

Both had seen Ray angry all too often. Eyes downcast, they stared at their muddy boots. Guilt surrounded the two big men like a thick, wool blanket. Neither brother responded.

"One last chance! Mikey? What happened?"

Mikey couldn't stand it. He promptly blurted out, "We was late cause . . . we stopped at an auction in Ortonville!" He was surprised at how quickly he came up with an answer that might get both off the hook.

"Okay. What else?" Ray asked. "There's more to this, isn't there? I repeat, what else did you guys do?"

Huge bravely answered, "That's it. Honest, Ray!"

Ray was silent for a long time. He studied his two weak-minded cousins. "What about the business at the quarry? Any problems there?"

Both had agreed that there simply was no reason for Ray to know about losing the map. "No. Honest, that's all." He still couldn't look directly at Ray, however.

"All right—for now. You better not be bullshitting me. You know I hate surprises." Ray decided not to push it. If they somehow bungled dumping the truck in the quarry, they either wouldn't admit it or he would find out later. Right now, he needed to finish with Herman and get everyone settled in a motel. *They'll tell me—sooner or later.*

Dale and Larry returned to the shop and parked out front with Barry. Ray left his two cowering cousins, stepped to the front window, waved, and sauntered back into the office. It had gone smoother than he had expected. They would be up and running in no time. He was very pleased with himself.

Huge and Mikey looked at each other. Mikey winked, and both relaxed. They had admitted to the lessor of two mistakes and gotten away with it. Besides, they still had expense money left over. Ray hadn't asked for the remainder.

Dale brought Barry back into the office. Herman had been anxiously waiting for the safe return of his son and came out to meet them. He hugged his son, took his pudgy hand, and led him back into his office with Ray and the bookkeeper, closing the door. Herman's life had suddenly taken a turn for the worse.

Reasons and his team completed their questioning of as many residents of Cokato and French Creek as would speak with them. Apart from information provided by the van owner, no one offered anything further about the Steckels. *Probably scared to death of that bunch*, Reasons surmised. After so many years of fear and retribution, he couldn't blame them.

Most of what he now knew either came from Sheriff Nichols or what he had managed to piece together himself. The state crime bureau was called in to take over the murder scene at Herb's Garage, and Reasons was certain that the FBI would be on the missing person's case shortly.

The list of missing persons had grown to at least seventeen unaccounted-for individuals who had disappeared over the past several years. In fact, many of the missing persons' reports dated back thirty years or more.

Reasons was deep in thought. *I feel sorry for all the families involved . . . sure would like to catch those bastards!* He hated to give up now. Besides, they still didn't know about John L. Rule. The death of the service station owner was no accident, even though it had been set up to appear that way. Reasons would give anything to catch up to the gang. He was positive they had headed for Milbank.

Reasons knew that it was unlikely that he would be permitted to pursue the case out of state. If they took Rule with them, that was kidnapping and sure as hell, the FBI would be called in, and he'd be out of the picture. Then an idea occurred to him.

He called his precinct and asked to speak to Captain Swenson. Before long, his superior picked up the phone. "Hi, Sam! Anything new?"

"Yeah, Nichols spilled his guts. He was supposed to look the other way at the stolen car operation in return for a monthly stipend. He swears he knew nothing about any of the missing persons, including John L. Rule."

176

"Do you believe him?"

"No, but it really doesn't matter. He's been part of the gang for a number of years and is guilty of just about every crime you can think of. I do think he told me everything he knew, though. He's looking to cut a deal with the prosecutor, but I won't go to bat for the bastard. Hope they lock him up and toss the key."

"What else?"

"Herb, the service station owner, was clearly murdered. Made to look like an accident—car hoist came down and almost cut him in two. He managed to scribble the name Herman with his own blood before he died. Nichols thinks Herman is Ray Steckel's cousin—Herman Fogelman of Milbank, South Dakota."

"What's his connection, then?"

"Not sure, but we think Steckel and the others are headed there to hide out. Hopefully, they didn't have time to snuff Rule before they left. He might still be alive—probably not for long, though."

"Well, that cuts it. It's a matter for the feds now."

Sam decided to take his shot. "Captain, we're going to have to track them down quickly if there's any hope for Rule." Sam chose to make his move. "I'd like to stay on the case, Captain—head out to Milbank and see if I can be of help."

"No chance—not our jurisdiction. You and Rick finish up there and return home. The state crime boys'll take over."

Something about the Rule situation didn't feel right to Reasons. Besides, the feds would take forever to set up shop out there. He could be in Milbank by nightfall, and if Rule was still alive—well, he might get lucky. "Captain, do I still have any vacation time left?"

Captain Swenson knew Reasons well—had, in fact, known him for twenty-six years. He wasn't surprised by the detective's request. "Don't do it, Sam. You have no authority in South Dakota. Let the feds handle it."

"I know, Captain, but I'm kinda tired—need a little break. This case wore me out. Rick can finish up out here. I think I should take a couple of days off."

Captain Swenson knew it was hopeless to argue. Reasons had made up his mind—he was going to see this thing through to the end. "All right! You've got a few days coming. If you somehow wind up in South Dakota on your vacation, remember you have no authority out there. I don't want to get a call from the feds complaining about your getting in their way, understood?"

"Yes, sir. I understand."

"Very well. Good luck, Sam. Stay in touch."

"Thanks, Captain. I'll keep you posted." Reasons hung up the phone and went looking for his partner. He knew he could hook a ride back to the Twin Cities with one of the troopers and leave the squad car with Rick. He planned to visit Mac Davis and his daughter. He needed a physical description and a picture of Rule. He hoped he could get to South Dakota in time to be of some use to the man. He feared that he might be the only hope Rule had left—if he was still alive.

❖ 12 ❖

SAM REASONS CLIMBED OUT of the trooper's car. "Thanks for the lift."

"Glad to help. Have a nice vacation," the trooper said with a knowing smile.

Reasons walked into the Minneapolis Police Headquarters and marched straight for Captain Swenson's office.

"Come on in, Sam." Swenson said in reply to Sam's knock. "Anything new to report?"

"Nope. Still no sign of that guy Rule," Sam replied. "How about you? What have you heard?"

"Feds were notified. They'll be on scene sometime tonight. What's your plan? Although I'm not too sure I want to know."

"I'm going home to change clothes, pack a bag, and then I think I'll pay a visit to Rule's wife. Like to get a picture and description of her husband if I can."

"Okay, but remember what I said: You're on vacation as far as this precinct is concerned. Help the government boys if you can, but stay out of their way. I mean it, Sam. I don't want to hear anything about your messing around in their investigation."

"I hear you, Captain, and thanks." Sam went to sign out, but before leaving, he put in a call to the county attorney's office. He needed to find out if Jack Stevens had come up with anything more on all the missing persons out at French Lake. It could be that Rule's tracks led elsewhere. He would need all the help he could get if he was to find the missing salesman.

❖ ● ❖

Debbie agonized over the whereabouts of her husband. Maggie stayed with her, but no amount of distraction could keep Debbie from fearing the worst. It was all she could do to help her put her worst fears aside and stay positive.

Debbie and her father had been in constant contact with her father's friend, Jack Stevens. They now knew that John had intended to drive to this French Creek Salvage Yard. Why? She just knew how fixated John was about getting that steering wheel for that old truck. It was all he'd talked about all weekend. He couldn't let it go—like everything else he did. A one track mind.

"He could be injured someplace, Maggie. Or—kidnapped. Maybe he's delirious and wandering around in a daze, or, or . . . God forbid . . ."

"Don't say it, Honey! You have to stay positive. You told me John's a survivor. Please, don't give up hope," Maggie said.

"You're right, Maggie. I don't want the girls to see me like this." Debbie blew her nose and straightened her blouse. She took a deep breath and smiled weakly at her friend. "I'm okay. Just needed to vent a little, I guess."

"You don't have to apologize, Deb. Lord knows, you have every right to let loose. That's why I'm here."

"Thanks, Maggie. You're a dear friend."

Mac, much like his daughter, was also losing hope. He knew the likelihood of John turning up alive was fading fast. If he was taken away someplace, he was a liability as long as he was still alive.

Debbie noticed the sad look on her father's face. She walked over and laid an arm over his shoulders. "Daddy, are you all right?"

Mac was still caught up in morbid thoughts. Too many lost cases. Too much sorrow. "Huh? Oh, sorry, Sweetheart. Afraid I was letting myself slip into the past just a bit."

"What were you thinking about?" Debbie sat down and faced her father. Maggie left the kitchen.

"You know, after your mother died, on top of Teddy's death . . . it was tough to keep going." As the words tumbled out, he felt his eyes tear. A single tear slipped from each misty eye and ran down his cheeks. "It's been difficult . . . you know . . . to keep going the past few years . . . to remain positive about much of anything. Don't seem to have much enthusiasm. I miss your mother terribly, Sweetheart."

"Oh, Daddy. I know you do. So do I." She took three quick steps and threw both arms around him. He cried for a long time, silently weeping in his daughter's arms.

After a while, Mac straightened and blew his nose. "Thankfully, you and the girls live close by—otherwise I don't know what I would have done. I guess John's situation brought all this back to the surface. I'm sorry, Honey. I don't mean to sound like the grim reaper."

Together, Jack and Mac had calculated the odds of John's still being alive. There simply was no reason for that gang of thieves to allow him to live. John represented the threat of discovery and capture. Mac couldn't allow his daughter to know what he suspected about her husband.

"I'm all right, Deb. How about a cup of tea?"

It was late afternoon, and as he sipped the warm drink he wondered what Detective Reasons would tell them. The detective had phoned earlier and asked if he could stop by.

181

The doorbell rang. Charlie rose from his spot beneath the kitchen table and ran to the door, barking shrilly. Mac rose wearily from his chair and went to greet Reasons.

"Sam! Long time no see," Mac said as he opened the door.

Reasons stood in the doorway, dressed casually in jeans, a parka, and a blue Minnesota Twins cap. "Hi, Mac. Nice to see you again. Wish we could be meeting under, uh . . . happier circumstances, though." Sam spotted Debbie in the background.

"Yeah, I know. I appreciate your taking the time to stop by. Come on in." As Reasons entered and began removing his parka, Debbie advanced and stood in the hallway.

Sam was struck by Debbie's simple beauty. She wore little or no make-up, and the strain of the recent events showed on her face. In spite of this she was still a beautiful woman, Sam observed.

"Sam, I'd like you to meet my daughter, Debbie. Honey, this is Detective Sam Reasons."

"Hello, Debbie. It's nice to meet you. I'm sorry about your husband, but rest assured, we are doing everything we can to find him." Reasons realized his words of encouragement probably sounded hollow and forced, but she needed to hear something hopeful.

"It's nice to meet you too, Sam. Thank you for all your help," Debbie replied. "Why don't we go into the kitchen?"

Sam could hear the TV in the family room, and he followed Debbie and her father into the kitchen. He brought Debbie and her father up to date on everything he knew that pertained to John. "The FBI has taken over the case, and they're setting up shop in Milbank. You know that's out of our jurisdiction, but I've decided to go out there anyway. I've seen the federal government in action before. Sometimes they can take forever to move on a case, and I just feel like time in this instance is, well— critical."

Mac's bushy eyebrows rose a full inch. "Sam, you don't have any authority out there."

"Yeah, I know. Got a little vacation time coming so I thought I'd, uh . . . go west."

"Your boss okay with this?"

"Sort of. He's looking the other way."

"Thank you, Detective. I feel better already." Debbie's gratitude was obvious.

"Debbie, can you give me a description of what your husband was wearing, and perhaps a recent picture?"

Debbie went through what John had been wearing that previous morning as if she had already given it much thought. "I'll get a picture for you; excuse me," Debbie said, and left the room.

Sam leaned across the table and lowered his voice. "I think you know what we're faced with, don't you Mac?"

"I know, Sam. I appreciate your going to all this effort for us. We'll just have to stay positive."

Debbie returned and handed the detective a picture of her husband.

Sam studied the photo for a few minutes. Average looking, prematurely graying hair, athletic, nose busted a few times. Otherwise pretty ordinary. "Can you tell me anything else?"

"No, except for the birthmark on the back of his neck—and the scars on his arms . . ." She stopped in mid-sentence. She couldn't continue. She raised one hand to her mouth, and tears streamed down her cheeks. She couldn't continue. She covered her face with both hands, sobbing uncontrollably.

Sam retreated to the doorway. He hadn't meant to upset these people any more than necessary. He gazed down at his feet, unsure of how to proceed.

At that moment, Melissa entered the kitchen. "Mommy? What's wrong? Is it Daddy?"

Mac rose from his chair and went to his granddaughter. "Melissa Honey, this is Detective Reasons. He's going to help find your Dad for us."

Debbie promptly collected herself and wiped away the tears that streaked her red cheeks.

"Hi, Melissa." Reasons stepped across the kitchen to shake the girl's hand.

"Hello." She walked to her mother's side and put both arms around her.

"Melissa, we're doing everything we can to locate your father," said Sam. This was precisely why he had wanted out of homicide. Too much pain, too much heartache. *That last kidnapping case took nine months to solve.* He shuddered at the memory of the final outcome. Burglary and theft had no real victims—normally. He'd do his best to find the young girl's father, but . . .

Mac broke the silence. "Sam, I'd like to go with you." Mac seldom acted impulsively.

Reasons wasn't prepared for Mac's offer. It took a moment for the detective to respond. He scratched his head and coughed to buy time. "I don't know about that, Mac. Remember, I'm only going out there on unofficial business. I can't guarantee your safety."

Mac was prepared for an argument. "Look, it's a long drive out there, and you haven't had any sleep. At least I can keep you company. Besides, the TV says a storm is coming, and I've got a four-wheel-drive Suburban. I'll stay out of your way, Sam, honest. It would mean a lot to Debbie and me if you let me tag along."

Reasons pondered Mac's suggestion. The thought of driving his Plymouth alone all the way to South Dakota didn't sound too appealing. The prospect of a snowstorm made it less so.

He and Mac could hardly be described as friends—their only connections had been official business in the courts—but he respected the man, liked his honesty, and felt he could be trusted to remain at arm's length. Mac's specialty was criminal law and his reputation in the Twin Cities was above reproach. On more than one occasion, he and Sam had been on opposite sides of a courtroom, but that was all part of the business.

"I guess I could use the company. I really haven't had much sleep lately. We have to get moving though, especially if there's a storm coming. One last thing, Debbie. What is John's full name?

"John L. Rule."

"What's the L stand for?"

Debbie chuckled. "It doesn't stand for anything. His father named him John L. after some boxer he idolized. What was his name, Daddy?"

Mac was distracted thinking about what he'd need for the trip with Reasons. "Hmmm? What, Honey?"

"What's the name of that boxer John was named after? I never remember."

"Sullivan. John L. Sullivan."

"That's right. I Guess John's dad was quite a boxing nut. So his first name is actually John L."

"Interesting. Okay, that should do it. You ready, Mac?"

Mac was more than ready. "You bet! Debbie, will Maggie stay with you and the girls?"

"I'm sure she will, Daddy."

Mac turned back to Sam and said, "I only live a few blocks away from here. I'll need a few minutes to change and pack a bag. Then we can leave." Mac rose to put on his coat.

"What about Charlie, Daddy?"

"I'll take him with me. He's no problem. Goes with me everywhere else. He'll be fine." Actually, the dog was his constant companion. A combination border collie and golden retriever, ever since his wife's death, Charlie had become more than just a pet. Charlie was his pal, and their relationship was special.

"That dog hunt, Mac?"

"You bet! He's a terrific bird dog. Has an unbelievable nose and with that border collie blood, he can run all day. He's just as comfortable in the back of my truck as anyplace else. Don't worry, Sam. He'll stay out of the way."

Reasons patted the dog and shrugged. "Fine with me."

Mac moved closer to his daughter. "I'll call you when we get to Milbank, Sweetheart. If Jack Stevens calls with any news, tell him where I've gone. I'll call him in the morning. You'll be okay?"

Caught up in the emotion of the day, Mac felt tears form in each eye. He couldn't speak. His heart ached for the pain he knew Debbie felt. He held on a moment longer until he regained his composure and gave her one last hug.

Mac's show of emotion wasn't lost on his daughter. "We'll be fine, Daddy." She gently placed her hands on either side of his head, stared into each shining eye in turn, and wiped away his tears. She stood on tiptoes and kissed his cheek. "You be careful, promise?"

Mac cleared his throat. "Yep. I will." He quickly turned and headed for the door. "Charlie! Let's go, boy."

"Don't forget your medicine, Dad," Debbie commanded. She gave him another kiss and zipped up his jacket. She leaned close, and whispered, "I love you, Daddy. Please bring John home safe."

Mac looked intently at his daughter. She represented all that was left of his life. "I love you too, Sweetheart."

Debbie gave her father one last hug and turned to Reasons. "Goodbye, Sam, and thanks again for all you're doing." She smiled. "And . . . watch out for Dad. He can be rather stubborn at times!"

"Your father's welcome company. We'll get along just fine." Reasons headed for the door. "I'll follow you to your house, Mac."

Mac and Sam went to their cars. Charlie jumped through the open door of Mac's Suburban and settled in the front seat. Mac silently wondered if they would ever find his son-in-law—dead or alive.

As Mac and Sam were leaving Debbie and the girls, the Milbank police chief, Harold Karnowski, hung up the phone. "Doggone it! That's all we need—the FBI!"

Harold had been chief for thirteen years. Aside from occasional family disputes and infrequent petty crimes, he relished the quietness of his town. He rose from his desk, walked to the small window, and looked across the street. A few pedestrians strolled down the main avenue. Peaceful, just the way I like it. Chief Karnowski hitched his wide belt to just below his generous belly and took three steps toward the door.

His dispatcher, Karl Butts, whose desk sat just outside the chief's office, had, as always, overheard his chief's conversation. The FBI was launching an investigation into a bunch of car thieves from Minnesota. That meant more work for Karl, and he knew the chief wouldn't be too happy with outsiders coming into his town.

Chief Karnowski stopped in front of Karl's desk. "Dammit! This case has nothin' to do with the citizens of Milbank. What the hell am I supposed to do about it, anyway, Karl?"

"Cripes, I dunno, Chief," Karl replied.

The chief had been instructed to wait until the field agents arrived from Sioux Falls. "Said they'd be looking into the activities of Herman Fogelman. Him and a bunch of guys from . . . let's see . . . oh, yeah . . . French Creek, Minnesota. You know where French Creek is, Karl?" the chief asked the small man sitting before him.

"Can't say as I do. That where these guys are from?"

"Yep. Supposed to be headed to Herman's Auto Parts for possible sanctuary. You know Herman Fogelman?"

"Nope. Heard of him is all." Karl waited until the chief turned away, jabbed his little finger up his nose, pulled it out and took a quick look at the black chunk clinging to his pinkie. In one swift move, he swiped the booger under his armpit and snorted. Satisfied there were no other objects to be plucked, he looked at his watch. Karl Butts loved picking up whatever gossip and dirt came his way, but he valued the information only as far as he could use it to impress others. He had heard all he needed and didn't want to miss any of his one-hour dinner break.

The FBI had mentioned nothing to Karnowski about John L. Rule. Insufficient evidence could not support a formal charge quite yet, so they refrained from discussing the possible kidnapping.

"I'm to wait for two agents to get here from Sioux Falls," the chief said again. "Hell, with this storm coming in, they'll be lucky to reach Brookings."

"Yeah. Guess we don't need to do nothin' till the morning, eh, Chief?" Karl asked hopefully. He had plans. He didn't want anything getting in the way of his nightly trip to his favorite watering hole. "All the weather forecasts I've heard say this storm is bringin' in lot'sa snow and high winds. It's got the makings of a blizzard."

"If the storm's coming from the southwest the FBI guys will never make it to Milbank tonight. Just as well. Won't have them in my hair until tomorrow, I'll bet," replied the chief.

Karnowski continued. "What the heck is Herman Fogelman doing in this thing, Karl? If he's the guy I'm thinking of, he's a member of my church. Yeah, Fogelman is the guy with the Downs kid. He and his family are good people. Can't imagine the man involved in anything illegal. You just never know, I guess. And why's the FBI interested in a case of car theft? That sounds a little outside their typical involvement."

The chief rubbed the back of his bristly neck and rotated his head. "Aw, who cares? That's their business. Anybody report a white van with Minnesota plates, Karl?"

"No, sir. No reports of any suspicious characters in town, either," Karl added, anticipating the chief's next question.

"Yeah, well sooner or later in a town this size, anyone new will stick out like a sore thumb. Just a matter of time. Keep your ears open. Right now, I got more pressing matters to attend to."

Chief Karnowski was shorthanded, and with the storm hitting that night, he had to make sure he had enough deputies on duty. He doubted anything would happen during the storm. If it was as bad as forecasted, the roads would close, and the town would shut down.

The chief felt no particular urgency to do anything, except get home in time for his favorite TV show. He looked at the clock on the wall and realized he had to get moving. He grabbed his coat and headed for the door.

❖ 13 ❖

RAY STECKEL WASTED NO TIME. He told Herman to fire all his employees. "Including the bookkeeper. Don't need him anymore." Ray was in charge. He would run the operation just as he did at French Creek. He was pleased with himself. By 5:00 P.M. that afternoon, Ray had managed to turn his cousin's world upside down but right his own. Everything was going according to plan.

Herman did as he was told. He knew that if Ray were ever caught, his own past would come back to haunt him. He had to protect Barry. If he served any time in jail, they'd put Barry in a group home someplace. To resist Ray meant certain pain and suffering for his family.

Dejected, Herman left his office with $50,000 in a manila envelope. Barry trotted along with his father, smiling, unaware of all that had taken place.

As he swung the front office door shut, he heard Ray yell out, "Remember what I said, Herman!"

"Yeah, I know," he said quietly. Head bowed, he closed the door and left. He knew exactly what his cousin meant. If anyone asked what happened to his business, he guessed he'd just have to say he retired. He slowly walked away from the shop with Barry in tow.

Herman's Auto Parts & Salvage now belonged to Ray Steckel, and he was in a jubilant mood. It was time to celebrate! Dale had booked rooms for everyone at the Super Eight. They would have to figure out some sort of permanent housing in a few days.

Ray joined the others. He felt good—and it showed. He noticed that Huge had a worried look on his meaty face. "Hey, Huge? What's eatin' at you?"

"Huh? Um . . . just wonderin' who's gonna take care of my dogs now, is all."

"Aw, hell. Someone'll take 'em in. Don't worry about 'em." He stepped closer and laid a dirty hand on one of Huge's broad shoulders. "Say, you know why those dogs of yours are always lickin' their balls?"

"Uh . . . no." Huge replied with a puzzled look.

"It's 'cause they *can!*" Ray could hardly spit out the words, he was laughing so hard. "Get it?" he asked, looking directly at Huge.

"Ahh, yeah. That's a good one, Ray." Huge did not get it.

"Hey! Who's hungry?" Ray asked. "Man, I could eat the ass out of a cow. How 'bout you guys? Don't know what I want the worse: a large steak or a piece of tail! Dale, what's the name of that strip joint you heard about?"

"Uh, let's see. What the hell'd that clerk tell me? Oh, yeah. The Stardust!"

"Do they serve food?"

"Yeah, I guess they got steaks and burgers and stuff."

Ray reached in his pocket and withdrew his watch, checking the time. It was 6:30 P.M. "That's where we're headed, then. We'll have a few drinks, polish off a thick steak, and check out the babes. Who wants to come along?" He picked up his black bag and headed for the door. Ray was in a hurry now. Eager for, food, booze, and sex—in just that order. He felt he deserved a reward.

Mikey spoke first. "Guess Huge and I'll just go to the motel if that's okay, Ray. We're kinda' tired." Mikey worried about Ray. He wanted an opportunity to talk to Huge alone.

"Aw, gee, Mikey. I could sure use a steak." Huge offered.

"We'll get some pizza or somethin' at the motel." Mikey gave his brother a stern look. "You don't like watchin' naked girls, anyway. Should be some movies we can watch on cable, Huge."

"That'd be all right, I guess. Don't need some girl shaking her things in my face. Rather eat pizza."

On any other night, Mikey would have joined Ray. However, he knew that, whenever he drank he talked too much. "Guess that's what we'll do then, Ray . . . just go eat pizza and watch movies."

Ray studied their faces, still not convinced he knew the real truth about their day. Whatever it was, though, it didn't seem to have affected his plans any. "I don't give a shit! If you two clowns want to go back and pull each other's pud, that's your business. Have fun!" He laughed and turned toward the door. "Whoever's coming along, let's go!"

Larry and Dale decided to go with Ray to the Stardust. The gang had already acquired two additional trucks during their short time in Milbank—one from Herman, the other stolen. The plates had been changed so Ray felt confident they'd avoid detection for a day or two until the vehicles could be stripped.

Huge, Mikey, Jimbo, and Willy took the two trucks back to the motel. Mikey pushed Huge ahead of him, anxious to be out of Ray's sight. "Come on, Huge. Let's go."

Ray picked up his moneybag, and left. "Come on, you guys. I need a drink!" Ray smiled and scratched his crotch, then crawled behind the wheel of Herman's truck.

It was dark outside and the snowstorm had hit the area in earnest. Snow was falling at a steady pace and already had created problems for anyone attempting travel. The roads south and west of Milbank were closing rapidly. Just as Chief Karnowski predicted, the two FBI field agents had driven only as far as Brookings.

The agents had received their instructions earlier that day: set up shop in Milbank and wait for the rest of the team to arrive from Minneapolis. There had been no accompanying request for urgency or haste, so they chose not to fight the storm. The kidnapping issue had not been confirmed, and both agents felt that no one's life was in imminent danger. Familiar with late-winter storms on the prairie, the two men were content to hunker down and wait.

When one of these prairie blizzards hit, nothing much moved. A heavy snow accompanied by strong winds made travel impossible. Even the highway department refused to send the plows out until the wind had subsided.

Ranchers and farmers were sometimes stranded for days on end. Drifts as high as twenty feet were common. Only the biggest truck-mounted snow throwers could bust their way through. For all intents and purposes, commerce slowed to a crawl. Only a very few businesses bothered to stay open. Those that did catered to customers intent on enjoying the evening regardless of the weather. The Stardust, located on the edge of the city limits, kept its doors open for anyone looking for such enjoyment.

As Ray and his cousins made their way to the strip joint, Chief Karnowski felt confident in his decision to leave the office. He knew the town would shut down. Everyone would stay home and wait to see what daylight brought. He only needed a couple of men on duty. The chief wanted to be home with his family, and his favorite show, *Hill Street Blues*, started in half an hour. The chief hated to miss that show.

"Karl, call me at home if you need me."

"Okay, Chief. See ya later," Karl replied, happy to see his boss leave.

Sam and Mac left the cities as planned. Their route took them directly through Cokato. Sam decided to stop briefly and check in with Rick. It was late in the day, and Sam wanted to find out if there was any more information about John.

What Mac witnessed at Herb's did nothing to allay his worst fears. As they walked through the door, Mac stopped and looked around. He glanced across the front room to the office in back. All of his senses were alert. *Place has the smell and feel of evil.* He felt uneasy. In spite of the warmth coming from the overhead space heater, Mac felt cold. Mac entered the office and followed Sam out into the service bay.

Reasons stopped and turn to face his companion. "Mac, hold on a minute. I need to fill you in on what happened here."

Mac listened intently as Sam described Herb's grisly death. Mac's face paled. His hands trembled as he peered over Sam's shoulder into the service bay. "Where'd it happen, over there?"

"Yes. You sure you're up to this?"

"I'm okay, Sam. Let's go in."

As the two entered the shop, Mac spotted Rick, who was huddled with the team from the State Crime Bureau. They were already on the scene dusting for fingerprints and searching for additional clues.

Rick looked up. "Sam, what the hell are you doing back here?"

Sam walked in their direction. Mac trailed behind, his eyes glued to the bloody spot on the floor. "Had to pass through here on our way west. Rick, say hello to Mac Davis. Mac is John L. Rule's father-in-law."

Mac shook the cop's hand, but glanced beyond as the exchange was made. He spotted the chalk outline on the floor and shuddered. The little color remaining in his face drained away.

Sam glanced at Mac. "Mac, you all right?"

Mac slumped against the wall. He took a deep breath. "I'm okay, Sam. Just noticed the blood . . . all at once the reality of all this hit me, I guess . . . Was John here?"

"We don't know for sure. You have anything new, Rick?"

"No. Sorry, Sam. They've lifted quite a few prints, but no word yet on whom they belong to. The poor guy we found here left us the only clue. His wife collapsed when she found out what happened. Some relative is staying with her. Poor woman! Apparently she's confined to a wheelchair and depended on her husband for fairly constant care."

Mac listened carefully. He was more convinced than ever that John had been in this place at one time. Suddenly, he experienced a familiar feeling of deep depression and sorrow. *I've been in this place before—maybe not here, exactly, but . . . What am I doing here? I don't know if I can go through all this again!* All of the pain and agony Mac had dealt with from the death of his wife and son came rushing back. It was more than he could bear. He had to get out of there! His heart pounded and he gasped for air.

At that moment, another of the crime team entered the shop from out back. He approached the group. "Lieutenant, we found this in the dumpster." He handed a plastic bag to his boss.

Mac was alert and on edge. He focused on the bag as it changed hands. He watched as the lieutenant stuck a pen inside the plastic and slid a brown wallet out on to the hood of the parked car. He knew right away it was John's.

The lieutenant put on rubber gloves and opened the wallet. He withdrew a driver's license and said, "John L. Rule. Wayzata."

Mac sagged. His knees were weak, and he gagged. Saliva gathered in his mouth. He bent over and took a series of deep breaths.

The police huddled over the wallet. They now knew John had been in the garage. Sam walked over to Mac. "I'm sorry, Mac. But don't give up hope. All this means is that he was here, just as we suspected. They'll have to keep the wallet as evidence. Debbie will get it back later."

After a few more minutes of conversation, Sam decided there was nothing more they could do. "Rick, we're going to take off. I'll see you in a couple of days."

"Okay, Sam. I'm heading back right now. Not much more I can do here."

Sam guided Mac out the door. As he touched his new friend's arm, he felt a softening—Mac's limb drooped in response to the gentle tug. "Let's get going, Mac. Let me drive for a while, okay?"

"Sure. That's fine, I guess." Mac's reply was noticeably understated. His despair was evident in every word and gesture.

Sam felt helpless. He felt sorry for Mac, but he knew it would only get worse. He was starting to have doubts about his decision to allow Mac to come along with him.

Mac let Charlie out of the truck for a quick pee. Then they drove away, continuing their journey west. Mac feared the worst. What little hope he had of finding John alive was slipping away.

As Sam drove off into the gathering darkness, they could see a solid wall of slate-colored clouds forming on the horizon ahead of them. The wind was up as the first of the cloud puffs scudded across the sky. The sun's final orange glow behind the cloud bank vanished very quickly.

Mac was caught up in his own thoughts of what John's death would mean to Debbie and the girls. He didn't think she would be able to handle it. John had some shortcomings, but he was a good husband and father. And most important—Debbie was deeply in love with him. They had survived enough pain and heartache to last any young couple. Mac wanted his daughter and her husband to have a chance to continue their life together.

Mac knew he had to move past the feeling of impending doom. If his fears proved to be correct there'd be plenty of time later to figure out how to tell Debbie. It was a long drive to Milbank. He knew he had to try and stay optimistic or he'd be a wreck by the time the trip was over.

Mac inhaled deeply, stretched, and poured himself a cup of coffee from the thermos. He turned to his new ally, determined to engage the man in a bit of idle conversation. "Want some coffee, Sam?"

"Thanks. Half a cup'll be fine."

As Mac poured the coffee, he decided to ask his friend a question that he'd been meaning to ask since the journey began. "What happened to you, Sam? At one time you were the shining star in the homicide division. All of a sudden, you kind of disappeared, and the next I heard, you were working burglary."

Realizing he was being more than a bit presumptuous in prying into the man's private life, he added, "You don't have to talk about it if you don't feel like it."

"No, that's okay. I don't mind. I guess it was the Peterson case that finally did me in. Do you remember the details?"

"Hmmm. Yes, I think so. Young child kidnapped, raped and mutilated as I recall. Horrible thing! You caught the guy, didn't you?"

"Yeah. Should have killed the bastard when I had the chance! Almost did, too. Good thing my partner came in when he did. The guy pleaded insanity and bought twelve years at the state hospital. He'll be out in two years. A level-three sex offender, and he'll be back on the street!" Sam spit the words out in disgust.

"I think I know where you're going with this, Sam."

The memory of the case never left Reasons. "I just couldn't stand all the pain and suffering anymore, Mac. No offense, but most of those guys get off on some technicality, or because some sharp attorney pleads it out to a lesser charge. The system just wasn't working for me anymore, so I decided to transfer to burglary."

"Why burglary?"

"Victimless crimes and all that shit. Catch the perp, let the prosecutors have a go at him, and after that, I don't give a damn. Burned out, I guess."

"I'm sorry, Sam. I remember the Peterson case well. It was a travesty and I fully understand your frustration."

Mac continued, "You know, most of the time the system works. Some times, unfortunately, things break down, as with the Peterson case. I suppose we just have to hope that when the guy gets out, someone is alert enough to keep track of him and stop him from doing the same thing all over again." Mac knew his response was trite and weak.

"Well, you know how that'll go. The guy'll get out, slip through the cracks because some agency won't have enough manpower to keep track of him, and he'll do the same thing again. If I hadn't quit when I did, I'd of done something stupid, so I thought it best to transfer out. I'm much happier not having to deal with scum like that."

Mac decided to change the subject. "What about your family?"

Reasons looked straight ahead, not responding at first. After a while, he answered. "Kathy and I split up right about then.

She couldn't stand the lack of attention, and wanted out. Never did have any kids, which I guess in retrospect was a good thing. I'd have been a lousy father. Too involved with work, I'm afraid."

"Sorry to hear that, Sam. How long were you married?"

"Ten years."

"Wow, that's a long time. Meet in college?"

"High school. I was a junior and she a senior. Kathy was kind of a groupie. Liked to hang around the jocks. I didn't know that at the time. Not too much experience with girls, I'm afraid." Sam smiled as he recalled their first date.

Mac glanced at his friend and noticed the smile. "What was she like, Sam?"

Sam didn't hesitate. He felt comfortable talking to Mac, and the memory of his early dates with Kathy were fun and exciting. "One of my teammates told me about Kathy. I found out much later that she had been with more than a few of the guys on the team. I didn't care. Finally got enough courage to ask her out."

"So you dated for the next two years?"

"Yep. Two of the best years of my life too. Prior to Kathy, all I cared about was playing whatever sport was in season, but that eventually came to an end. She helped me realize that I needed to think about my future, and try to figure out what I wanted to do."

"And what did want to you do?"

"Well, I always wanted to be a cop, so we figured out that if I joined the Army and became an MP, it would give me the training I needed. That's what I did. Kathy and I married after I graduated, and I joined the Army."

"Where?"

"Spent three years in San Diego as an MP, and she moved out there with me. We had some great times back then, but then something happened, and it was never the same."

Mac wasn't sure he had a right to talk to Sam about his relationship. After all, they really weren't close friends.

Sam offered, "When we found out that Kathy could never have any kids, she changed. She always looked forward to having a family, and somehow finding out about her sterility hurt her deeply. She really had no other interests, and after I got out of the service and started work as a cop, I wasn't around much. We drifted apart."

A noticeable sadness filled the detective's voice. "I think I knew she was fooling around, but our relationship had really broken down, and I didn't care much anymore. So we decided to get divorced."

"I'm sorry, Sam. Do you still see her or hear from her?"

"She died in a car accident a few years after our divorce."

"I'm sorry," Mac said again. "It's really too bad she couldn't have any children."

"Yeah, I guess. I'm not too sure that even with kids the end result wouldn't have been the same, though. I was just too deeply involved in my work. I probably would have been a lousy father."

"I doubt that. I have a hunch you would have found a way to back off from your work and spend time with your kids," Mac said, but he sought another change in subject matter. "So, how is work? Do you ever miss the homicide division?"

Sam shrugged. "Yeah, I guess. Every now and then when a capital case comes along, I get kind of an itch to get involved, but it passes quickly. Burglary is much less demanding. This case is the exception. We've been trying to catch these assholes for years. Never could get a line on who they were. Now we know why."

"Why? What do you mean?"

"They're a ruthless lot, this Steckel bunch. If I get close to them, I'm going to have to be extremely cautious. They've killed before, and I'm certain they won't hesitate to kill again. But what about you, Mac? You've been listening to me for the past thirty minutes or so. Have you thought about retirement? How long are you going to keep practicing?"

"A very good question. I've pared my practice down quite a bit already. I like spending more time with Debbie and the girls, so I'm taking on very few new cases now. I have a few hobbies to keep me busy, and Charlie and I get out bird hunting whenever we can in the fall. I've tried to get John interested, but he doesn't seem to have the patience yet. Someday, maybe." The sudden memory of the real purpose of their odyssey intruded.

And then they were back on the topic both had been avoiding. Like a somber, low-hanging storm cloud, John's disappearance reappeared. Sam made one more attempt at diverting their thoughts, but immediately regretted opening another wound. "What about your wife, Mac? I remember hearing that she passed away a few years ago?"

Mac felt obligated to respond. "Yes. Cancer—after fighting it for almost two years." He stopped and turned away as tears filled both eyes.

"Sorry. You don't have to say anything more. I understand."

"No. That's okay. Sometimes it helps to talk about it." Mac paused. "We were very close. High school sweethearts and all that. Neither of us ever dated anyone but each other. Somehow, we both knew we were meant for each other. I miss her terribly, but I'll always have wonderful memories of our years together."

"What was she like?"

Without hesitation, Mac replied. "She was the kindest, most thoughtful person I have ever known. Totally unselfish—she always put everyone else's interests and problems ahead of her own."

"She sounds like someone I would have enjoyed knowing."

"Ever hear about givers and takers, Sam?"

"Yes, I think so."

"Well, Barbara was the consummate giver. She never once complained of her illness or felt as if God had played some kind of cruel trick on her. I was bitter and resentful, but not Barbara."

"I've met Debbie," Sam said. "Did you have any other kids?"

"We had a son. Teddy. He was killed in Vietnam." Mac replied, quietly.

"Oh, I had no idea! I am so sorry! That goddamned war! What a waste!"

"I agree. It was his first mission. He was a helicopter gunship pilot. His mother and I were very proud of him for enlisting. It was just the sort of thing Teddy would do. Felt it his duty to serve his country and all that. They never recovered his body. Brought his dog tags home, and that was it!"

"Well, I'm really glad you've still got Debbie and the girls. I know it's hard to stay positive about John right now, but keep believing that he's still alive, that we'll find him in time, okay?" He hoped he sounded convincing.

"Thanks, Sam. I'm doing my best."

Both men grew silent. The miles went by. The blackness of the night crept into the Suburban. Charlie snoozed in the back. Sam and Mac prepared for what both feared they would find at the end of their journey.

They made good time until they ran into the storm. They stopped in Willmar for dinner, and as they left the restaurant, the first flakes of snow began to fall. They were still a hundred and twenty-five miles from their destination. The wind had increased steadily for the past hour or so, and both men knew the rest of the trip would be much more difficult.

As they climbed into the Suburban, Mac offered to drive. He had slept briefly. "You must be tired. Besides, I know how this rig handles in the snow." Sam agreed and settled into the passenger seat for a bit of nap. Mac felt a bit better than he had earlier, but couldn't shake the feeling that they were chasing a ghost—John's ghost.

Once they reached Ortonville the snowstorm intensified. Visibility was down to a quarter mile, and their progress slowed.

Fortunately, there were few cars or trucks on the highway. Most other travelers had already pulled off.

Sam and Mac felt they had to reach Milbank that night, so they kept driving. The highway department decided to pull all the snowplows off the roads until the following day; consequently the snow depth on the highway was increasing by the minute.

All of a sudden, out of the darkness ahead, they noticed the flashing lights of a Minnesota State Highway Patrol car. Mac slowed, and finally stopped. A barricade blocked the highway, halting their progress. Mac rolled down his window as the trooper approached. "Shit. Now what?"

"Let me talk to the guy and see if I can convince him to let us through." Sam climbed out of the Suburban, pulled up the hood on his parka, and turned away from the howling wind. He approached the trooper and after a few minutes, both cops climbed into the patrol car.

Mac watched from the warmth of the Suburban. As the highway patrolman checked Sam's identification, Mac concluded that if the patrol had the road blocked, conditions ahead had to be pretty bad. Fortunately, if they were allowed to continue, they only had about thirty miles to go before reaching Milbank.

Sam returned to the truck. As he slid in and removed his hood, Mac noticed the trooper was pulling aside the barricade. He waved them through.

"What the hell did you say to him, Sam?"

"Just told him the truth. He had heard about the case—had been watching for the white van those guys are supposedly driving. He felt that if we wanted to run the risk of getting stuck by going on, that was our business."

Sam neglected to mention that he'd also told the trooper that Mac's son-in-law's life was in jeopardy. "He just decided to look the other way. Did say he didn't want to have to shag us out of a ditch, though."

They drove on into the storm. Three or four inches had already fallen. Driven by thirty mile winds that gusted to forty, drifts formed on the road. They passed infrequent shelter areas of fence lines and small tree stands. Every time they encountered the windbreaks, they discovered the blacktop had collected additional snow.

These stretches were particularly treacherous, as the snow depths in the drifts varied greatly. Mac had the Suburban in four-wheel drive, and with the vehicle's substantial gross weight, they plowed through with relative ease.

"Hope these drifts don't get much deeper, Sam."

"I'm a city guy. What causes these snow piles?"

"Wind blows the snow over these shelter belts or fence rows and dumps down on the other side. If the wind was blowing from our right—from the north—the piles would build up on the lee side. Funny how it works."

The storm would ultimately drop twelve inches on the area, but for now, at least, they could continue driving. Their progress slowed considerably, however, and it took them twice as long as it should have to reach Milbank.

Mac focused on trying to negotiate the treacherous, snow-covered highway. It was a blessing really, as it took his mind off of what they faced in Milbank. He shook his head and focused on the road ahead.

Because Highway 12 was officially closed, they didn't have to worry about oncoming traffic. "Be thankful for small blessings, eh?" Mac said.

"How do you mean, Mac?"

"That we don't have to deal with any other cars. I remember a few years ago I was out here pheasant hunting. Snowing just like this, except the roads were still open. Rained first, then it froze. Like driving on a skating rink. This is piece of cake compared to that."

Mac glanced at the detective and noted the concern in his eyes as he stared into the blinding snow. "Don't worry, Sam. We'll be okay."

Sam tried his best to sound reassured. "I'm counting on you to keep me dry and warm, Mac. Hate to wind up in one of these ditches." An accident at this point in their journey would not only imperil their own lives, but practically demolish any hope of rescuing John.

Sam shifted his attention to planning his next move. When they reached Milbank, he'd have to check in with the local police . . . find out where the FBI was set up. If they've already found John, then he'd help track down the Steckels or turn around and take Mac home. Then he had a sudden, chilling thought: What if the feds couldn't get there because of the storm?

Sam realized that John, if he were still alive, was on his own.

❖ 14 ❖

OTTO STUBBLEFIELD LOOKED DOWN at the newborn calf. Both calf and mother seemed to be doing all right. No matter how hard Otto tried to get all the cows into the pen before they calved, there were always a few that eluded herding and decided to have their babies far from the comfort and safety of the barn. At least this one didn't have any problems. "Probably just shy, eh, momma? First baby an' all."

Otto had spent the last few days canvassing his twelve-hundred-acre ranch, looking for heifers ready to calve and strays.

"There ya go, little feller. I'll come back for you and momma later on when yer stronger." Satisfied he had done all he could for the first-time mother and her calf, the third-generation rancher looped his rope and turned to leave.

Otto's was a working cattle ranch. Unlike many of his neighbors, the old man had resisted giving in to the popular and more profitable trend toward feedlot operations. He watched the young calf struggle to its feet. He couldn't stand having his cattle penned up! This was how his granddad and pop had ranched and if it was good enough for them, it was good enough for Otto. Between the feedlots and the stinky pig farmers, someone had to take a stand. Otto's operation was unique and singular. He grew corn and alfalfa as feed for his cattle, resisted all overtures to modernize, and ran his operation pretty much as he always had.

Satisfied and pleased at having found the struggling mother, Otto looked around. He scanned the landscape. Proud of what he owned, proud of all their work, he knew no better way to live. He and his wife Betty made a decent living—they loved it out there. He didn't see any need to change things now.

Otto loved to ride across the ranch on horseback, though his back sometimes gave him trouble. He hated the noisy, smelly four-wheelers—didn't see a need for them as long as he could ride or drive his jeep. Only on days when the back pain was almost unbearable, did Otto opt for the Jeep instead.

He stood and took in the view to the west toward the unseen ranch house. It had been built of hand-hewn Douglas fir by his grandfather, and he recalled his father describing how Grandpa Stubblefield had stripped and shaped every log all by himself.

Otto twisted to the south and noticed old William, his prize bull, standing alone in the distance. The coal-black animal was old but he could still attend to the ladies just fine. Otto refused to consider artificial insemination. That didn't seem natural to the old rancher. Besides, he knew William would produce nothing but quality.

Otto treasured the Western traditions. He grew up depending on the ranch and its Herefords not just for the income they provided, but also for what they did for his soul. He prided himself as a steward of the land. He was as tough as the hide of one of his steers, but also full of compassion and respect for every living thing.

Otto and Betty were childless. "It was the Good Lord's way!" Betty often said. She had miscarried twice. Finally, concerned for her safety, they stopped trying. It had been hard to accept for a while, but they had each other and the ranch. He'd gotten used to the idea that he had no son to inherit his ranch when he died.

And Otto worried about what would become of the ranch. His property bordered a granite quarry to the east; his east fence line ran along the edge of the open pit. The Clearwater Corporation had been after him to sell out for years. The vein of granite they were currently working ran directly under his fence line and well into his property. But Otto would have none of that. He would sooner die as have any of the company's machines tear up his beloved grassland. *To hell with those bastards*, Otto thought.

As he climbed into his Jeep, something nagged at him. Like an itch that couldn't be scratched away, the old man was bothered, as if he forgot something important. He closed the door and returned to the cow. Maybe she would throw a second one? As he drew near, the mother and newborn trotted away. That wasn't it. Something else. He paused and scoured the landscape.

The wind was down—unusual for that time of year. Still colder than hell, though. Otto drew up the heavy collar of his old coat. It was still no more than thirty degrees, with very little snow cover. Not too bad a day for mid-February. It felt like a change in the weather, though. *Probably snow coming tonight.*

His gray-blue eyes moved slowly over the horizon. Suddenly his gaze fixed on something in the distance—something out of place on the barren plain.

The normally unbroken grassland held an object that didn't belong. As he studied the prairie, he thought it could be one of his cows in trouble, or a coyote feeding on a dead critter, or something else entirely. He returned to the Jeep, opened the door, and withdrew his 30-06. With one practiced motion he removed the cap from the scope and pointed the rifle east, in the direction of the quarry, about a thousand yards away. He focused on a motionless clump that was nothing more than a small pimple that rose above the plain. It was bright green, however. Not a dead animal, not a coyote, certainly not a cow, and besides, it was on the Clearwater side of the fence. Not his problem. *Those lazy quarry employees probably dumped some kind of shit out there.* He thought maybe he ought to call them up and complain about littering the landscape, but he ought to know what they dumped first.

Otto replaced the rifle on the rack, climbed into the Jeep, took one last look at the cow and calf he had just tended, and decided he'd drive down the line for a ways as long as he was headed in that direction. He'd have a quick peek and see what kind of crap they dumped.

As he approached a point directly opposite the green pile, the hair on the back of his neck stood tall. He was beginning to believe it wasn't a pile of garbage, after all.

He stopped, opened the door, stepped out and looked over the hood. He was trembling by now, as he focused on the green object.

He was certain he was looking at the body of a dead man.

The green shape, now a mere 100 yards away, remained motionless. Otto nimbly stepped through four strands of barbed wire and approached the body. With little hesitation, the old man knelt down, reached out, and shook the body. No reaction.

He removed one leather glove, turned the body over, and placed two fingers against the man's cold neck. The skin was stiff and frozen. He couldn't feel a pulse. The man's face was the color of new ice. He put his ear to the man's mouth. After a bit, he pulled back, startled. *I'll be damned! I can hear somethin'!*

The man was alive, but not for long. Otto knew from experience what hypothermia could do to his cows—once down, too heavy to move, they rarely survived.

Otto knew it could be too late to help the man, but he had to try. The old man struggled with John's wet jacket. It was heavy and sodden, so he removed it and tossed it aside. With great effort, he removed his own sheepskin coat and drew it over the man's arms and upper torso. Then Otto raised the man to a sitting position, draped both arms over his own shoulders, and stood up. He took a deep breath and heaved the lifeless body over one shoulder. Even at sixty-eight, through years of hard labor working the ranch, Otto was as fit as any man half his age. He carried John the hundred yards back to the fence. He was breathing heavily by the time he gently laid John down. He climbed back through the fence, dropped to the ground, and pulled John underneath the wire. Then he lifted John one more time, carried him to the Jeep, and placed him in the front seat. He had to get some heat going and warm the man up fast!

He had left the Jeep running, so he reached over and turned the heater on as high as it would go, then covered John with a wool blanket from the back. Otto ran around to the driver's side, climbed in, and put the truck in gear.

As he pulled away from the fence, he reached over and felt John's cheek—it was still icy cold. It would be a miracle if the man survived. Otto gunned the engine and steered the Jeep back across the prairie toward the ranch house. His mind raced as he imagined all sorts of scenarios that might account for the stranger's presence out on the prairie. He had briefly looked back down the cliff and spotted the hole in the ice. "What the hell'd you do, young feller?" *Time enough to figger it all out later; I need to get him home.*

He raced across the flat ground, alert for any bumps or prairie dog holes that could flip the Jeep. His entire attention was focused on getting back to the ranch as quickly as possible.

After a harrowing twenty-minute ride over uneven ground, Otto finally reached the ranch house. He stopped by the front entrance, ran around to the passenger side, and opened the door. He was breathing heavily as he lifted John's half-frozen body out and carried him up the porch steps to the front door. He reached down, turned the knob, and stumbled inside. "Betty! Come here!"

His wife came around the corner and stopped. She stared at her husband and his burden. "What in the world?" She wiped both hands on her apron and rushed over to her husband.

"Quick, Betts, we got to get this guy warmed up. Go upstairs and draw a warm bath," Otto instructed. Laboring under the dead weight of John L. Rule, Otto managed to carry him up the stairs and into the bathroom. He laid him down gently, stood, and straightened his back. "Whew! I'm too old for this!"

Betty had the tub half full. She tested the water. "Where'd you find him, Honey?"

Otto bent back down and began removing John's wet clothing. "Over on the Clearwater property, at the top of the pit. Just happened to spot him as I was finishing up with one of the cows. First thought it was a pile of trash those nincompoops from Clearwater dumped over there."

"What do you think happened?"

"Dunno. City fella from the looks of his clothes. Sure not from around here. Hard to tell what happened. Must have fallen into the pit, or drove in, I guess. He's pretty far gone, Betts. Don't get your hopes up."

The tub filled with warm water, and together the older couple gently placed the man in the bath. Betty began rubbing both his hands and feet. She immediately noticed the burn scars on his arms, but what really caught her eye were the deep cuts left by the twine. Otto saw the cuts also. They knew he had suffered at the hands of others.

John was comatose—barely alive, his body all but shut down. "By all rights, this poor man should be dead. He's ice cold!" Betty said. "Wonder what's keeping him alive?"

"Dunno. Looks to be pretty fit. Kept himself in shape. Don't look too good now, though. He's been through some trouble, for sure. Skin looks like the underside of a gray carp."

The two washed the wounds on John's wrists and tried to warm him with rubbing in the warm water.

"We better call Doc Wilson, Betts. Make sure we're doing the right thing for the man." Otto left his wife with the stranger, and went to the phone in their bedroom. Dialing Dr. Wilson's office, he wondered again, how the stranger had ended up in the quarry. He figured it had to be more than some kind of accident. Not a suicide or that he got too close to the edge of the pit and fell in.

"Hello, this is Otto Stubblefield. Is Doc in?" He was. Otto explained to Doc Wilson everything he knew of John's condition. They spoke for ten minutes.

"Otto, it's very important that you and Betty don't rush the re-warming process. Rapid re-warming will cause the surface blood vessels to enlarge, causing a rush of blood to the extremities. This will deprive the vital internal organs of the required blood necessary to keep functioning. In short—rapid warming will likely kill the man."

"I understand, Doc."

"Notice any other wounds, broken bones, anything like that?" Doc asked Otto.

"Well, looks like some of his toes and fingers are frostbitten. He's got a bump on the back of his head and some deep cuts on one wrist. Looks like he might have been tied up. There's some old scars on his arms—like he was burned at one time. Birthmark on the back of his neck. Nose broken a few times, but that's about it."

"How old would you guess he is?"

Otto stepped to the doorway and glanced in John's direction. "Oh, I'd say late thirties or early forties."

"Okay. I'll be at the hospital. Suppose I better notify Chief Karnowski of your mystery guest. Try to get him here as soon as his temperature rises a bit more. Talk to you later."

"Okay, Doc. Guess we'll just have to watch and see if he improves. Soon as we get his temp up a bit, I'll haul him into the hospital. We'll call before we leave here. Thanks, Doc. See ya later."

Doc Wilson hung up the phone. If the John Doe survived, it would be a busy night at the small hospital. Some young mother would undoubtedly decide to deliver her baby during the storm, or some fool would stick his hand in a snow blower and lose a few fingers. Something else would happen, and they were already short staffed. One of the residents was stuck out west. That left only one intern on duty. But, they had been through such a night before. He sighed heavily and returned to his duties.

Otto replaced the phone and returned to the bathroom. "Doc says we're doing the right thing, Betts. Need to get his core temperature up, but not too fast. Doc didn't think we should take him to the hospital until he warms up. Said it was critical to raise his body temperature slowly."

"Did he give you any idea about whether he thought the poor man would survive?"

"Nope. Too soon to tell. Guess if he doesn't warm up soon his chances don't look good. If he lives and we get him to Doc, they'll immediately begin giving him intravenous fluids—something about glucose and something else. Don't like the looks of his toes and fingers . . . almost look black, don't they?"

Betty winced at the sight of them. "Yes. He must have been out in the cold a long time."

They kept a close watch on John as he lay partially submerged in the warm water. Periodically, Betty took his temperature, but it rose only a few degrees from when she took it initially.

The two kept attending to him, though, rubbing his arms and legs and adding a bit more warm water. John was unresponsive—still in a deep coma.

The elderly couple tried their best to remain optimistic about the fate of their guest. They were doing all they could for the stranger, but sooner or later he would have to be transported to the hospital in town.

The approaching storm posed a bit of a problem, but Otto felt confident that if their guest survived he could get him to town in the Jeep.

"After another thirty minutes in the tub, we're supposed to move him to the bedroom and wrap him in an electric blanket. Doc said that if his body temperature dropped below ninety degrees, he had only a seventy percent chance of living."

Betty's face paled as she listened to her husband. "Well, we just can't let that happen, Otto. This fellow has fought too hard to stay alive." She continued alternately rubbing his fingers and toes. Otto shook his head. "I'll be back in a few minutes, Betts. Want to check on the new calves in the barn." Otto felt that if their stranger died while in their house, Betty would take it very hard. He knew he had to get the man out of the house and on the way to town as soon as possible.

As he opened the front door, he was greeted by a blast of wind that carried a thick veil of snow. Already three or four inches lay on the ground. This was going to be a bad one. Otto ducked into the wind and headed for the barn.

John was comatose, oblivious to everything Otto and Betty were doing to keep him alive. His brain remained active, but not his body. Disjointed, nightmarish thoughts filled his head . . . He was still in the lake—floating to the surface. Reaching the top, he

214

knocked on a door—cold and hard. He realized with terror the door was ice—solid and unmoving. It blocked his access into the sun and air above! Trapped! No way through!

He scraped his nails against the underside of the ice. What's that—blood? It oozed from broken fingernails. John pressed his face against the cold surface. Incredible, cold pain forced him to withdraw. He looked up. Debbie's face appeared. Her blue eyes were smiling. If only he could touch her, let her know he was there.

He tried to call out to her for help, but couldn't utter a sound and drifted back down, down, down to the dark, cold depths below. A barking dog watched his descent. Its teeth were bared, ferocious. John was numb, helpless to hold back the snarling animal. It would tear him to pieces. A bloody stump of an arm floated past.

John looked down at his own two arms. Oh no! He had only one! The stump was his! The dog had already ripped into him, and now it wanted more. John kicked his legs. The dog jumped. Instead of the dog's face, he saw the front end of a truck. It was going to run him over! Swanson's Dairy? He couldn't run fast enough to get away. The face in the windshield was laughing. Who was it? He had seen this person before—where? John fell down. The truck ran him over.

But he was still alive! Debbie stood along the road, waving to him. She was nineteen, just out of school. *God, she's so pretty*. A shadow appeared from behind him, menacing somehow. John tried to shout. Debbie, look out! Nothing came out of his mouth. He couldn't speak. The shadow became a man. Large, ugly, grinning, he put his hand under Debbie's short skirt. She kept smiling. *No! Debbie! Don't let him!*

John swam in the warm water, gaining ground on the two figures. But they weren't swimming! They were walking together down a road. The grotesque man removed Debbie's blouse. Grabbing each breast in turn, he squeezed hard. She cried out in pain. John had to get to her before the ugly man hurt her again. The man had a bright red scar on his face—a half circle that flashed red.

John was naked, vulnerable, helpless. He kept swimming to Debbie, now also naked. She was floating, face up. The hideous man grabbed her face and turned her toward John. *Debbie! Kick! Kick hard! Hurry!* John couldn't reach her.

She slipped loose and glided to him. The ugly man vanished. Debbie drew close. She pulled his face to her chest. He kissed her nipples, then her stomach. Her legs spread, beckoning. They were together, floating, soon coupling. He raised his face to kiss her. She opened her eyes.

John shrank in horror at the visage! It wasn't Debbie! It was the face of another man! He was mesmerized by the man's left eye. It was evil—crooked. It stared at Debbie. Then she disappeared! The queer eye turned back to him. Now it was his turn. John felt himself shrinking—sinking into a whirlpool of ice and blood. The man with the scar was gone. The man with the evil eye was gone. Debbie was gone! He was alone. What had he done?

John fell away—deeper into the frigid water. He was standing—alone, then walking down a sidewalk, stepping on every crack and laughing. Ahead of him a woman was lying face down. Who was it? *Mother? Is that you?*

And there he was again, from the shadows, massive, ugly, menacing. That ugly scar moved. It had lips. It could speak! "You stepped on a crack, kid. Now I have to break your mother's back. See what you did?"

John couldn't move. He was frozen to the pavement. Millions of cracks formed around him. "I'm sorry! I won't do it again! Please don't hurt her!" Too late. *She's in pain. Why? Why? It's all my fault! Mother! I'm sorry! Where's Daddy? Was that Daddy? Why'd he leave?* John was trapped. With cracks in every direction—he was helpless. He froze in place . . . forever.

216

❖ ● ❖

"How's he doin', Betts?"

"A little better, I think. Color came back to most of his fingers. Some of his toes still look pretty bad, though."

"Well, if he lives, wouldn't be the end of the world if he loses a few toes and a finger or two. Hell, I've done just fine with only eight myself." Otto held up his left hand to display the missing digits lost to an axe as a young boy.

"Yes, I know, 'Stub.' You've always been proud of that nickname, haven't you? Kinda' like a badge of courage or some such nonsense. You know, I could'a swore his eyelids flickered a while back—like he was having a bad dream or something."

"Maybe he'll make it after all." Otto leaned down and looked into John's face. He thought some color had returned to the man's face, but Otto still wasn't too optimistic about his chances for recovery. The practical, hard-edged rancher yielded to his many years of experience: he had seen death too many times and believed he was staring at it once more.

Otto blinked and turned away. "Jerry just arrived. You didn't tell me he was coming, Betts."

"Oh, yes, I guess I forgot in all the excitement."

Otto's nephew, Jerry, had driven over from Yankton. Home from the Cities to visit his father, Jerry always offered to help his Uncle Otto whenever he could.

"He's getting a cup of coffee. Better go down and get him started bringing in a few more calves. Think we should move this fella to the bed, yet?"

"Yes, I think he's been in the tub long enough."

Betty pulled the drain plug and with Otto's help, they lifted John out, dried him off, and wrapped him in the electric blanket. Otto picked John up as he had before and carried him to their bed.

217

"Guess I'll go down and get Jerry started. Need to bring in a few more calves that're close to the barn. You be okay?"

"I'll be fine. You go ahead."

When he learned what his uncle had discovered earlier that day, Jerry was amazed the stranger was still alive. "Any idea who he is, Uncle Otto?"

"Nope. Not a clue. City fella, I'd say. Come on. Let's see how many calves we can get in before the snow gets too deep. Gonna have to take the guy to town soon as we're done."

Otto worked his way east of the ranch house and Jerry searched the west sections. After an hour, both returned to the barn with two newborn calves.

"Guess the rest will just have to fend for themselves, Jerry. That snow's too deep now. If you want to bed these down and feed the others, I'll look in on our guest. Come upstairs when you're done."

"Okay, Uncle Otto. See you in a bit."

When Jerry finished, he climbed the two flights of stairs and entered his aunt and uncle's bedroom. "Hi, Aunt Betty!"

"Oh. Hello, Sweetheart!" Betty drew up the blanket so only a portion of John's face was visible. She stood and gave Jerry a big hug.

"Looks like you have your hands full. How's he doing?"

Betty stepped aside as Jerry moved closer to the bed. "Oh, I think a little better. His temperature is up some more and he's got more color in his face."

Jerry stared at the inert form before him. "Who do you think he is?"

"Don't know, Jerry. A tough guy, though. He should probably be dead by now, but he's hanging on. Looks like he's been in trouble before. See the burns and cuts on his arms?"

Jerry leaned down and pulled aside the blanket. He peered at the man's wounds. "What are you going to do with him?"

"Well, Otto will take him to the hospital. Doc says they need to get fluids into him, next thing. How's the weather?"

Jerry paused. He took a long look at the stranger in bed. He shrugged. "Not good. It's snowing hard, and the wind's picking up. If Uncle Otto plans to take this guy to town, he should probably get going soon."

Jerry realized there was little he could do to help his aunt, and went back downstairs. It seemed to him that he had seen the guy someplace before. He sighed.

Betty took John's temperature one more time. Unchanged from ten minutes before. He was still pretty gray—his skin cold to the touch. *He isn't faring well. He needs to be in the hospital. I've done all I can for him.* She sat and prayed for his recovery.

Betty had seen death before. She had miscarried twice. Her mom and dad had died early. Her sister Mary had been crushed by a tractor. Only the man's will to survive would see him through this—that and lots of prayers. She held his hand. Her fingers traced the outline of John's old scars, knowing the man had been through other battles.

As she rubbed John's hands she flinched as one of his fingers twitched. "Yes! That's it, young fella. You keep fighting—don't you give up!"

John couldn't move. Heavy link chain covered his entire body. Something covered his face—tasted like oil. He couldn't see, but he could hear. A pack of wolves approached—they snarled, teeth snapping like castanets. He could feel their hot breath. The animals moved away and waited. For what?

He opened his eyes. The wolves were gone. He was inside a truck—no, it's a tank! "Fire" someone yelled. It was his voice. He was screaming for help, but the words were dead, letters spewing from his lips, silently.

He was going to be burned alive! He pushed at the small round metal door—FORD was scrawled on the front. It was an escape hatch! He stuck his head out. People running everywhere! He fell to the ground and looked back. Someone was trapped inside. More screaming. "He's on fire!" *Who is it? Go back! Hurry! God, it hurts! Someone's on fire! There, on the ground! His shirt . . . his blue shirt is on fire! What's that smell? No, no! His flesh . . . burning . . . who is it? Get his shirt off. Who's that? Someone else . . . smoke coming from his head. Cover his face. Who are you? No! Yes! It's Dad! Is it really you? Don't go . . . please?*

And then the dreams ended. There was nothing left—only darkness.

Otto and Jerry returned from a last trip to the barn. The new calves were doing fine. They leaned into the thirty-mile-per-hour wind. Otto noticed the deepening drifts. "Can't wait any longer, Jerry. If I don't leave soon, I'll never make it to town."

He and his nephew went up to the house. Otto quickly closed the door behind him, before the blowing snow filled the front hallway. Without removing his coat, he rushed upstairs.

"Betty! Get some clothes on our guest!" He entered their bedroom.

Betty turned. Alarm filled her face. "Otto? What's wrong?"

Otto's voice had a hard, serious edge. "No time to waste, Betts. Already eight inches of snow down, and more's coming. We have to get him dressed and loaded in the Jeep. If I don't take off now, it'll be too late!"

Betty looked up. "I don't think he's doing too well, Otto. For a while there he seemed better—a little warmer but still unconscious. He seemed to be dreaming. But then, I don't know . . . something happened. Almost like he took a turn for the worse. He doesn't look good, Otto. What about these cuts on his wrist?"

"Looks like he might have been tied up," Otto said matter of factly. "If so, he must have fought like hell to get loose. Those look pretty deep. Probably better put some dressing on 'em, Betts."

Betty opened up the medicine cabinet to dress John's wounds. "You really think we should move him now?"

Otto promptly replied, "Got no choice. The storm's getting worse. Put some of my clothes on him. I'll put the back seat down in the Jeep and wrap him in a sleeping bag." He leaned down and gave his wife a hug. He knew what she was thinking. "Don't worry, Honey. You've done all you can for him, and I'll get him in to Doc Wilson's in time—I promise!"

Otto went downstairs, grabbed a couple of donuts, and filled his thermos. He then headed for the front door to get the Jeep ready. "Jerry, can you stay with Betty? I don't like her to be alone in a storm, and I'm still kind of worried about those last three cows that haven't dropped yet."

"Sure Uncle Otto. No problem. I'll help you load the guy in the Jeep."

Otto left the house. By the time he was finished, his wife had dressed their guest and wrapped him in blankets. His head was totally covered by the wool fabric. "Keep his head covered, Otto." She watched as Otto and Jerry carried John downstairs.

"I will, Betts. Don't worry."

When they reached the front door, Betty held it open. A blast of snow hit her full in the face. She turned sideways and watched as Otto and Jerry loaded John into the back of the Jeep. The motor was running. Otto had left the heater on high, and warm air filled the interior.

221

As Jerry backed away from the car he again felt something about John was familiar. He had the impression he had seen the man before. He thought hard. As Otto slid into the driver's seat, the dome light came on. Jerry noticed that the blanket had slipped. In the dim light he took a good look at the man's face.

Otto wrapped John in a sleeping bag and supported his head on another blanket. As his door closed, the light went out. He waved at his wife, climbed into the driver's seat, and put the Jeep into gear. Before pulling away, he rolled down his window. "Jerry? I'll call when I get to the hospital."

He drove away slowly, plowing through the piles of snow in the driveway. Jerry Stubblefield watched his uncle drive away. All of a sudden he realized exactly who the man was. *I'll be damned! It's that salesman from Minneapolis—John something or other. He was sitting across from me back in my office just . . . yesterday!* "Uncle Otto! Uncle Otto!" He yelled at the retreating vehicle. "Uncle Otto! I know that man!"

The wind carried Jerry's voice with it. Otto had rolled his window up, and Jerry's shouts went unheard, except by Betty, who remained in the doorway. They watched Otto disappear into the darkness, and then both retreated inside to the warmth of the house. Together, they would spend the next few hours puzzling over just how John L. Rule, a salesman from Minneapolis whom Jerry had visited with the day before, had wound up half-dead on the Clearwater Quarry property.

❖ 15 ❖

J UST AS OTTO DROVE AWAY FROM THE RANCH, Ray, Dale, and
Larry stepped out of the van and into the blizzard. They
leaped over piles of snow and strode into the Stardust
Lounge. Once inside, they paused. Ray shook the snow from his
cap and looked around.

The dimly lit saloon held a smattering of drinkers and
gawkers, most of whom were crowded into the front row beneath a
small stage. "Come on boys, let's get something to eat. I'm
starved." Ray led the way to a small table near the stage.

They took their seats and removed their coats. Music from
four large speakers blared a popular tune. As the three settled into
well-worn, vinyl chairs, they turned their attention to a young red-
head on the large stage.

It was Amateur Night at the Stardust, and the well-
endowed girl was trying her best to win the 100-dollar prize. Ray
was not impressed. "Other than a nice rack, that babe should go
back to the farm and finish milking the cows!" He threw his hand
in her direction, palm out, in disgust.

A scantily clad waitress appeared "What'll it be, fellas?"

"Hi there, Doll. We're hungry. How 'bout three of your best and biggest steaks with all the trimmin's?" Ray ran his eyes up and down the tired-looking waitress. "And for desert we might want to nibble on you, Doll."

"That'll be the day," she muttered. "You guys all want your steaks rare, or what?"

"Yeah! The bloodier the better. Tell yer cook to drag the meat over the fire one time and slap it on a plate."

"You got it. How 'bout drinks?"

The three ordered cocktails, and the waitress left.

"Guy at the motel said we gotta see the star of the show. Said she does somethin' with her titties that's hard to believe," Dale said.

"That so? Good, cause these amateurs just ain't makin' it," Ray replied.

Behind the curtain, in a small, brightly lit dressing room, Darla LeMay, Stardust's featured attraction, was getting ready for the second of three shows she performed each night.

Darla hated her job, hated what she had become, and especially hated the stench that permeated the town. Darla was thirty-two, still pretty by most standards, and had managed to keep her attractive figure in spite of her age. She was a natural blonde with striking blue eyes, full red lips, fair skin, and long, lean legs. Unlike most of the girls she worked with, she had resisted having her breasts enhanced. She hated that look . . . hated the phoniness of it. *My boobs ain't that big, but they still stand up like their supposed to.*

Two of the local amateurs sat at the dressing table, watching Darla dress. Rene, an eighteen-year-old brunette, had dreams of her own. "How'd you get started, Darla?"

224

Darla paused and studied the two youngsters. "Well, I've been doing this for more than ten years. Come from Rapid City. A friend talked me into entering a wet t-shirt contest when I was about your age. Wanted to be a Las Vegas showgirl." She paused and gave a melancholy sigh. "Never happened."

Darla stroked her long blond hair and studied her reflected look from the scarred mirror. "I did win the contest though. I was kinda' embarrassed at first but found out that I really liked all the attention." She smiled at the two young women. "Kinda' like you two, I'll bet. Young enough to be flattered, innocent enough to believe all those men really care about you. I was young, dumb and innocent. Next thing I knew I was traveling all over the Dakotas takin' my clothes off—and getting paid for it!" She tossed the brush, and it slid across the cluttered counter and slammed against a tall can of hair spray.

"What happened to your dream, though?" Rene asked.

She snorted. "Listen, you two. If you think showing off your chest to a bunch of farmers is going to be your ticket to the big time, think again. I'm afraid it ain't going to happen. Just like you, I was proud of my body. But, once I started takin' my clothes off and the Vegas dream faded, well, I figured that if these yokels wanted to pay money to see me naked, what the hell. Before long, I was making more money than I could with some sort of straight job."

"You've kept your shape pretty well for, uh . . . you know what I mean." The young girl blushed.

"That's okay, honey. I know what you mean. I work out—have to make sure all the parts are in order." Darla arched her back, which pushed her breasts out and upward. She laughed and caught her reflection in the mirror. "As a matter of fact, my breasts really aren't my best feature."

Rene arched both, dark brows and asked, "What do you mean, Darla?"

Darla spun sideways. Her butt faced the girls. "A few years ago I was partying with a bunch of teachers from Bismarck. One of them kept watching me and not saying anything. I finally stood in front of him and asked what he was thinking. He asked me to turn around, then said, 'Yep. Just as I surmised, my dear. You are indeed callipygous!'"

Both girls looked at Darla in puzzlement.

Darla wiggled her rear end and giggled at the same time. "'Course at the time I had no idea what the gentleman was talking about—but, I do now. Callipygous means that I have 'beautiful buttocks.'"

The two girls laughed along with Darla. "He was right, Darla," Rene said.

Darla turned back and curtsied. "Thank you, young lady. I think so too."

"Anyway, most of the other girls in this business bought their boobs. Not me. I left mine alone and tried to see if I couldn't sort of . . . uh, expand on what I already had. I just started foolin' around and learned that with enough practice and concentration, I could actually make both nipples harden up whenever I wanted to. Didn't need to be excited or cold—I just focused on each one and before long I had a pretty neat act. Kinda' like mind over matter, if ya know what I mean."

In time, Darla had created a costume and a routine that seemed to appeal to the older crowd. Hers was a little cowgirl show. Her outfit included sexy, frilly chaps, a cowboy hat, a garter belt with white stockings, and a gun belt for two pearl-handled cap pistols. Draped over one of the pistols was a small lariat. More than a simple fixture; Darla could actually twirl the rope quite skillfully. As a young girl she had mastered the art of baton twirling and had won a number of statewide contests. Using the same dexterity and coordination, she could spin and throw the loop with ease.

226

Darla dressed as she chatted with the two girls. She donned a fringed, leather vest, and a short leather skirt. She wore the required g-string beneath the garter belt. Her white gun belt and pearl-handled cap pistols and a fancy pair of high-heeled cowboy boots completed the outfit. She pulled her boots on as the girls watched.

Darla's act was different from what most of the strip joints in the Dakotas offered. She danced to "I Shot the Sheriff" while firing both cap pistols at selected patrons in the audience. In between gun shots, she prowled the stage, lariat twirling, breasts bouncing provocatively.

"The secret to this is ya got to look for the big spenders. Those'll be the guys—usually pretty drunk—tossin' tens and twenties instead of ones and fives. Then I throw my loop over 'em, and they're mine!"

Both young girls perched on their stools, eyes wide, mouths open, as Darla revealed her secrets.

"Look, I know my act is corny, but these Dakota yokels love it. And, of course, it doesn't hurt to have my, ah . . . special talents, either." She finished dressing and faced the two young strippers.

"I cater to the striped whistlers. Know what those are?"

"No," the girls responded in unison.

"Well, these guys all dress alike."

Both girls hesitated. "What do you mean?" Rene asked.

"Well, for those who crave my personal attention, a lap dance is available for a fee. First of all they always ask, 'How much?' Depending on the night, I might say, 'Fifty bucks.' When they hear that, most of these clowns look like they seen a ghost, and whistle. Then they say something like, 'Whew—that's a lot a money!' See, they all wear these stupid, hick bib overalls—you know, the ones with stripes! That's why I call them my striped whistlers!" Darla laughed as the girls finally understood what she meant.

Darla had become adept at singling out the real spenders in the crowd. "Look, either of you two grow up on a ranch or farm?"

"I did," Rene volunteered.

"Well when I'm performing I always watch the crowd. Then, when I spot my guy, it's just like a cuttin' horse goin' to work—you know, the horse prances this way and that, all the while keeping her eyes on the target. I do the same thing. I can pick these goofballs out of a crowd in seconds—the ones with fat wallets!"

Darla decided not to tell the girls about her current dream: that someday some elderly, rich gentleman would stumble in and carry her away. Sometimes she was mistaken, but generally she could spot the ones with too much money and too few brains.

The club manager stuck his head in the door. "Darla! You're up next."

"You girls will have to excuse me while I apply the finishing touches."

Both knew what she meant. They had hoped to find out Darla's real secret. "Can't we watch?" Rene asked.

"Nope. Sorry. This is my trade secret. Don't want one of you goin' home and practicing and then showing up as a younger version of Darla LeMay. Now, scoot. I'm late." Darla hesitated, then said, "Wait a minute, you two!"

The girls turned and came back into the room.

"One more thing, and you can take this for what it's worth. There's plenty of money to be made in this business without hooking . . . you both follow?"

Rene replied, "We know what you mean, Darla. Thanks for the warning."

"I'm serious. Turning tricks will bring you nothing but trouble: cops, disease, beatings, and you'll associate with the scum of the earth. Promise me?"

"We promise," they both said in unison.

"Good! Now get out of here so I can finish getting dressed."

Beneath Darla's leather vest, unlike most of the rest of the girls at the Stardust, she wore nothing but pasties attached to each nipple. Hanging from each was a long tassel, which, when put into motion, could be made to twirl in any direction. As long as the nipples were inert, suction alone kept them in place. Glue wasn't necessary.

Darla was proud of her skill, and she loved the attention evoked every time she performed her unique act. She paused in front of the mirror, applied one last streak of red lipstick on her lower lip, pouted, and smiled. Still not bad for thirty-two! Then it was time to go to work.

❖ ● ❖

Out front, the lights dimmed. Ray, Dale, and Larry had finished eating and were well into their fourth cocktail. The loud music stopped, and a tape recorder began playing a scratchy drum roll.

"And now ladies and gents, let's give a warm, Milbank welcome to our star performer—Miss Darla LeMay!"

Spotlights shone on the curtain. The four loudspeakers blared "I Shot the Sheriff" as Darla swished the purple curtain aside and paraded to the center of the stage.

A restless Ray Steckel shouted, "It's about time!"

Darla heard the loud voice and in no time located Ray. She twirled her lariat, flipped her skirt, and leaned over provocatively so the men at the edge of the stage could get a good look at her cleavage. Her toy cowboy hat was cocked to one side—held in place by a thin, red cord.

She pivoted, leaned down, and raised her taut butt high in the air. Dollar bills were tossed onto the dusty stage. With practiced skill, barely missing a beat, Darla collected each and stuffed them into her gun belt, after all, this was the whole point of her performance.

She continued to twirl, fire her pistols, and entice the crowd for another ten minutes. During this phase of her act, she kept her few articles of clothing on.

Ray stood and walked to the stage. He pulled out a twenty and waved it at her. She saw him coming. She whirled her lariat around Ray's shoulders and stooped so he could place the bill in her belt. Not satisfied with the gun belt, he moved higher and slipped the twenty down the front of her vest. Darla smiled and blew him a kiss.

Ray returned to the others. He leaned his elbows on the table. "She's mine tonight, boys! All ya got to do is wave money at 'em and they melt like butter!"

Darla sensed that the crowd was growing restless. *They're sittin' on their wallets like hens on eggs. Time to show 'em some skin* . . . Besides, she had her pigeon for the night . . . the guy with the red scar . . . ugly as hell, but she didn't care.

Darla turned her back to the small crowd, looked back over her shoulder, and slowly removed her vest. At just the right moment, when the hoots and whistles were the loudest, she spun and put both hands behind her head. Then, she whipped the vest over her head and threw it behind her back. It was time.

Darla continued her slow strip. She removed her skirt, again with her back to the audience. Only the garter belt and the white gun belt with pearl-handled pistols remained in place. She pranced to the edge of the stage and shook her breasts. Regulars in the crowd howled with delight; they knew what she would do next.

As she danced to the music, she slowly began twirling each breast in the same direction. Then, without any apparent effort, her left breast reversed direction. While each long tassel spun with dizzying speed, she flexed her right nipple. Erect and hard as a rock, the nipple broke the suction from the pasty. One lone, multicolored streamer was sent spinning through the smoky, foul-smelling air across the stage to the right.

Like a detached party favor, it sailed up and away. She repeated the move with her other nipple—its tassel flew to the left. Once uncovered, the large, dark, hardened nipples stood out in sharp contrast to the milky whiteness of her breasts. Those patrons hovering near the stage went wild. This was the part she enjoyed the most: the looks on their faces as the pasties flew through the air. Time to rake in the dough.

Ones, fives, and tens flew from eager hands. The stage was littered with money. Darla retrieved it all in time to the music and stuffed it into her g-string. She spun across the stage one more time, stopped, shook her breasts, pulled out the two pistols, and fired both in Ray's direction. She winked, the lights went out, and she left the stage to loud howls of delight.

Ray stood and clapped. Dale hooted like a sick calf. Larry slammed down his drink and simply smiled as if enjoying a secret only he was privy to. Once the applause subsided, they sat down, and Ray beckoned the waitress. She trotted over. "Another round . . . and tell Miss Twinkle Tits I want a private dance. Got it?" He winked and gave her five dollars.

The waitress took the bill "I'll tell her." She looked at Ray long and hard. "By the way, her name is Darla."

Backstage, Darla downed a can of warm soda and removed most of her outfit. She left her boots, stockings and garter belt on. She threw a thin, light-blue, silk half-robe over her upper torso and considered how to play the scar-faced guy in the dirty blue shirt.

The guy looked kind of mean, so she decided she would proceed slowly. Even though the money Darla made was good, her job was not without certain inherent dangers. Darla lived and moved in a world of men from all walks of life. Most were harmless, simply out for the night with their buddies for a few beers and lots of laughs. Not all of them were innocuous, however, and Darla knew all too well just how careful she had to be.

Sidney, Darla's manager, would sometimes accompany her for protection. He also helped collect additional monies owed by customers who could afford after-hours, private sessions.

But tonight, she and the other girls were on their own. Sidney had decided to stay in Fargo for a few days. Turning a trick was frowned on by the club's owners, and Darla had learned long ago the pitfalls that followed girls that did more than take their clothes off.

She drew the line at selling her sexual favors, and she particularly hated the few men she encountered that wanted to rough her up. She had run into a few tough guys before, however, and felt she could identify the troublesome ones before things got too serious. That ornery looking guy with the scar could be one of those. *Don't do anything stupid, Darla!* She wished there were more customers in the bar, however, so she had other options besides the mean-looking guy. She took one last look in the mirror, flipped her blond hair back, and left the small dressing room.

Darla approached the bar. "How's about a rum and coke, Petey?" she asked the bartender. "Oh, and hand me my purse, will ya, Sweetie?"

The bartender reached down and pulled out Darla's purse. She quickly stuffed her earnings for the night inside. She felt a tap on her shoulder and turned.

"You got a live one over there, Darla," the waitress advised, nodding in Ray's direction, her expression deadpan.

Darla looked over her shoulder. Sure enough, the ugly guy that gave her the twenty was looking her way. He looked mean, nasty in fact. She could only roughly judge his age—not that it mattered. Probably fifty or so. Not very big with a large, ugly, half-moon shaped scar on his cheek. Darla's dream was to find some rich old guy in one of the many joints she worked, marry the guy, and spend her golden years enjoying his money. Sooner or later she was certain her striped whistler would appear.

Darla smiled seductively at Ray. "Okay, I'll just finish my drink, first," she said to the other girl. She took a deep breath and downed her rum and coke. Then she straightened and walked over to Ray's table. He was sitting with two other men; one looked like a relative, the other not. The two apparent brothers had the familiar, leering grins she had grown accustomed to over the years. The tall, fair-complected third member of the party reminded her of a ferret. His eyes darted back and forth as if he were expecting his next prey to sit down at his table. Darla shuddered. It had been a slow night because of the weather; this might be her only chance at making decent money.

Ray had wolfed down the biggest steak in the joint, was well on his way to being drunk, and with his black moneybag still at his side, had selected the girl he wanted to bed down. Rather than put his money in Herman's safe, Ray chose to keep the bag of money with him. He planned to buy a new safe, but until then the bag wasn't leaving his side. He watched Darla draw near, wiped his greasy mouth with the crumpled napkin and leered as she approached.

Ray was feeling cocky. He twisted his head to the side and told Dale, "I'm goin' to find out if she's for real. And after a private dance, I'm gonna see if I can hire her for a little party back at the motel. You boys'd like a little private entertainment, wouldn't ya?" He grinned as he watched her walk toward them, eyes focused on her jiggling chest.

Darla stopped directly in front of Ray. Dale stood up. Larry did not. Dale had his good eye on a younger version of Darla, a redhead perched at the bar. He had decided to make his move, but hesitated when Darla approached. After watching her perform, he decided to hang around for a while. He sat back down.

"You want a private dance, uh . . . " She leaned down and read his shirt. ". . . Ray?" Darla placed her too-small cowboy hat on Ray's shaggy, grey/black head. As she did, her foot bumped the black bag on the floor next to his chair. "What's this, Honey? A bag full of money?"

Ray kicked it under the chair. Darla's attempt at humor missed the mark. Ray was not amused.

She tossed his ball cap on the table and twisted his chair away and to one side. She stood in a way that gave him a generous peek down her low-cut robe. She was the experienced temptress setting the bait.

Never one for subtlety, Ray asked, "How much for a private dance?"

Darla leaned closer and whispered, "Fifty bucks! And I'm worth every penny!"

Ray dug into the pocket of his jeans and pulled out a roll of bills. He peeled off two twenties and a ten, and stuck them in the front of her g-string. He leaned back, hands behind his head, looking her entire body over while licking his lips in anticipation. "Tell me something, Blondie, how you do that with your tits? That's the damnedest thing I've ever seen!"

"Mind over matter, Honey." Darla replied. "First of all you've got to have the best equipment!" She arched her back and gave Ray a good look. Her large nipples threatened to break through the thin, blue fabric. With moves designed to tease and titillate, she began her special dance.

First one pale shoulder appeared—then the other. She untied the sash and spread her arms wide. She stepped even closer and put both hands on Ray's shoulders. Her breasts now hung inches from Ray's mouth. Darla moved from side to side and smiled coyly.

Ray reached out to grab one of her breasts.

Darla straightened up. "Uh-uh, big boy! No touching allowed." She leaned forward and whispered, "Bartender will throw us both out—it's against the rules to touch. Sorry." She licked her lips and smiled, showing her perfect, snow-white teeth.

Darla straightened up, shook her shoulders, and caught the robe in one hand. She draped it over Ray's lap and ran her hands down her rib cage, past her hips, and around her back. She was well into her routine; it was time to set the hook.

❖ 16 ❖

WHILE RAY WAS BEING ENTERTAINED by the eager Darla, Otto Stubblefield fought to keep the old Jeep from slipping off the gravel road on the way to the hospital. It was just past 7:00 P.M., and Otto was surprised by the depth of the snow. The ten-minute drive from the ranch house to Highway 12 took forty-five minutes. If he had waited even ten more minutes before leaving, he never would have made it to the highway.

Otto approached the highway and slowed. Even though his bright lights were on, he could hardly see the narrow tracks in front of him. One last drift, then he'd be on the blacktop. He shifted into low and gunned the engine.

The Jeep barreled into the mound of snow, rose three feet off the ground, and with all four wheels spinning, cleared the drift. Otto glanced left and spun the wheel as he skidded onto the snow-covered tarmac.

He craned his neck to check on his passenger. John lay pretty much where he had left him. Snow continued to fall, a steady one to two inches every hour. Whipped by strong winds, their narrow road became impassable behind Otto. He knew he would have to stay in town until roads were plowed. He tried to concentrate on keeping the jeep on the highway.

Otto soon tired. The events of the day were catching up to the old man. He tried to relax his grip on the worn steering wheel, but failed. At least there wasn't any other traffic to worry about.

He had instructed his wife to call Doc Wilson, and let him know he was bringing their patient in and to meet him at the hospital. He had no idea how John was faring but couldn't risk stopping to check on him.

Otto drove as fast as he dared, but the blowing snow made driving more than twenty miles an hour impossible. Otto stared into the falling snow. The huge flakes were mesmerizing, and Otto continually had to refocus beyond the face of the windshield.

Blown by the fierce wind, the snow appeared as one solid blanket of white. Even though he didn't want to, Otto had to stop every ten minutes to clear off the windshield wipers when they caked with ice. The defroster in the old Jeep could hardly keep up with the build-up. A few times he opened the window, leaned out, and, as the wiper made a pass, he'd grab the blade and slap it against the cold glass. The wipers would gather additional ice and slush with maddening speed. He felt he had to be getting close to town, but this was only a guess as the road signs were all obliterated by the heavy snow.

Otto had driven to town thousands of times before over the years, and could sense when he was getting close. All of a sudden, the Jeep skidded!

Otto fought to bring the Jeep under control. The old truck slid from one side of the road to the other. He felt the tires grip and slowed the vehicle down even further. His heart raced and hands shook. He grimaced at a sudden pain in his chest. *Careful Otto. You're too close to blow it now.* Probably way too tense with the storm. He rubbed at his jacket front, hoping the pain would go away. He willed himself to relax, took three deep breaths, and continued his journey.

Finally he detected a few faint lights in the gloaming. He'd reached the outskirts of town. His chest still hurt, and he wondered what that was all about.

He drove past Herman's Auto Parts. Milbank Community Hospital was located in the heart of the city. Travel became easier once he was in town. Buildings sheltered the roads from the relentless wind—drifting was at a minimum. "Just a little bit longer, my friend. Hang in there." Otto said faintly to his unconscious passenger.

Just as Otto entered Milbank, Chief Karnowski settled down in his Lazy-Boy and turned on the twenty-seven-inch Panasonic. He had hurried home to catch *Hill Street Blues*. The TV screen went from black to full color. The chief rubbed his hands. The show was just starting. He cracked open a can of Pabst Blue Ribbon and tossed a handful of peanuts into his mouth. He was oblivious to everything going on in the town he had been elected to serve and protect. Chief Karnowski had his priorities.

When Doc Wilson called the police station to inform the chief about Otto and a half-frozen, unconscious man, he discovered the chief had already gone home. The dispatcher on duty said he would phone the chief at home and let him know of the stranger being brought in by Otto Stubblefield.

In a hurry to take his dinner break, however, and aware it was time for *Hill Street Blues*, Karl Butts decided to leave a note for the temporary dispatcher. Karl was in a hurry. Darla had finished her second show. Maybe tonight she'd give him a look. Karl was permitted an hour for dinner, and he didn't want to waste a minute.

The love-sick dispatcher arrived at the Stardust at the exact moment Ray Steckel was negotiating with Karl's dream girl—the lovely Darla—for something more than a lap dance.

Ray stuck three twenties in Darla's hand. "Come on, Blondie, what's it gonna cost me to touch those things right now?"

Darla didn't answer. Instead she began a slow gyration in front of Ray, swaying from side to side. She glanced at the silent one, the ferret, surprised at his total lack of interest in her.

After a couple of minutes, she turned around and bent over. She looked back up at him through the provocative V of her lean legs. She remained in this position for a full minute, moving her rear end up and down in slow motion. Ray breathed heavily in anticipation and rubbed both hands back and forth across his knees.

He resisted an intense urge to grab her ass. He was having fun playing this little game, but sooner or later, he'd have to have her—one way or another. He hadn't spent all that money just to watch her shake her titties!

Darla continued her well-choreographed dance routine. She sensed at least two of the men watching her every move. Ray was her target, however, and she concentrated on him. If the tall guy wasn't interested, she didn't care. She spun and allowed her breasts to bounce up and down. Her large nipples were fully extended.

Her long hair swished across each hard bud, as if each was performing a private dance of veils. She smiled coyly, and the laugh lines around each eye accentuated the pleasure she felt. *Damn, I'm good! I've got these guys purring like little kittens.*

Ray could hardly restrain himself. His voice quivered with excitement. "Damn, girl! You *are* good!"

He was hooked, just as Darla intended.

"How much for a private party at our motel?" Ray's hardness was barely hidden by Darla's blue robe. He squirmed and adjusted his package. The heat generating from his body intensified the strong smell of Old Spice he had doused himself with earlier that evening.

Darla wrinkled her nose in distaste. She hated that smell! Darla spread her legs and straddled Ray. She toyed with him a bit longer, then gently settled into his lap.

"Four hundred!" Darla whispered. She blew softly into his ear. "In *advance.*"

She looked into his eyes and as she did, shivered without intending to. Darla was suddenly frightened. She didn't like his eyes. There was nothing in there . . . just an icy cold stare, like two pieces of coal. The only thing warm about the guy was his crotch!

For the first time in years, Darla was genuinely afraid. This could be a big mistake! She stood up and lifted one leg over his knees. Normally a pretty good judge of the types of men she routinely encountered, tonight Darla's judgment was being tainted by the storm outside. The manager told her earlier that he might have to close early as the customers were tending to stay home. The smelly man beneath her might be her only chance to score that night.

"You got it, Honey. When you done here?" Ray glanced down at his pocket watch, then back at Darla.

Darla retrieved her robe. She was finished with the lap dance. "I've got another hour here . . . then I'm all yours."

Darla knew she was taking a big risk. She wished for Sidney's presence. Ultimately, Darla decided that Ray's money was as good as the next guy's, and tonight it didn't appear as if there would be a next guy.

She leaned over and brushed his nose one more time with her silky hair. "This will seal the deal, Sugar! See ya after my last show." Darla smiled, ran her fingers along his cheek, briefly lingering at the scar, then tossed her hair back and returned to the bar.

Ray could hardly stand the wait. He slammed back what was left of his whiskey, adjusted his trousers, and looked around for Dale, who'd followed Darla to the bar.

Ray's brother decided it was time to make his move. He hoisted his ample rear end onto a stool. Then he promptly made a play for the young redhead he had been eyeing all evening. "Hey there, toots! What say you and me get together later for some fun?"

The girl glanced at Dale briefly and snorted, "Get lost!"

Dale lacked the few skills his older brother had when it came to women of this sort—namely the not so subtle act of flashing wads of money to get their attention. After years of being rebuffed by women of all types, Dale still had not accepted his fate. He simply was too ugly and uncommunicative.

He nursed a beer—more than a little frustrated.

A man climbed up on the stool next to Dale and began talking to Darla. Within seconds, it was clear that the guy was hitting on Ray's late-night date. Dale listened intently.

"Hi, Darla. How ya doing?"

Karl Butts had set his sights on the blonde stripper when she first started dancing at the Stardust. Unfortunately, just like his neighbor on the adjoining stool, he not only lacked the necessary funds, he was totally unappealing and had little or no tact.

Either Darla chose to ignore Karl's question, or she hadn't heard him the first time. Karl tried again. "Hey, Darla! How's it going tonight?"

Darla felt that the dispatcher was harmless, and brief conversations with the man helped pass the time. "Oh, you know.

Same old, same old, Karl," she replied, taking a sip from her drink. "What's new and exciting in the police business tonight?"

The dispatcher did have big ears and an even bigger mouth. Karl tried hard to impress anyone who would listen, especially Darla. He had always dreamed of becoming a cop but had failed the test three times. The next best thing he could do was pretend.

"It's a dog-eat-dog world, Darla, and today I'm wearing Milk Bone underwear!" He laughed loudly, exposing misshapen, yellow teeth. He'd been waiting for just the right moment to try that line out. He waited for her response.

"That's a good one, Karl," she said, knowing full well that the dumpy dispatcher had stolen the line from a recent *Cheers* episode.

Karl pressed on. "Pretty quiet tonight, Darla, but I did have one strange call. Somebody found a body out at the Clearwater Quarry west of town." Karl paused for effect.

Darla perked up. She faced the rotund man. "That so?"

"Yep. Guy's still alive, but just barely." The dispatcher thought this should arouse Darla's interest.

Not only was Darla anxious to hear more, but Karl's neighbor on the next stool was also interested.

Darla wanted more. "Who found him?"

"Rancher by the name of Stubble . . . something or other. Let's see . . . Oh yeah. Stubblefield. Drove through the blizzard and dumped him off at the hospital. Guy was pretty much goners when the rancher found him. Just about froze solid from what I hear. Doc Wilson is trying to keep him alive." Karl was encouraged by Darla's unusual display of interest.

"What happened to the poor guy?" Darla asked, eager for more information.

"Don't know for sure. Somehow he was soaking wet . . . like he'd been down in that quarry or somethin'." He had her attention and edged closer. He tilted his head for a quick peek down the front of her robe.

Darla smiled. Karl's leering look didn't go unnoticed by the stripper. She let the front of the top fall open just enough to afford Karl a long, long look. "Do they know who he is?"

"Nope. No ID, and not from around here by all accounts. A real mystery, ya know."

Dale had heard enough. He quickly slipped from the barstool and headed over to Ray's table.

As he neared the table, however, he hesitated. He didn't want to tell his brother that Huge and Mikey had once again messed up but knew he had to. He also didn't want to spoil Ray's good humor.

Ray was caught up in telling another dirty joke to Larry, hoping to get a rise out of him. An unrelated member of the gang, Larry was a man that Ray depended on for some of the touchier jobs they sometimes encountered. He seldom smiled, spoke only when spoken to, and gave little evidence of being afraid of Ray— unlike the rest of the gang.

When Ray finished with the punch line, he waited for Larry's reaction. The tall man failed to crack a smile.

"Jesus, Larry. You need to lighten up once in a while." Ray shook his head and promptly looked away. *Sometimes he gets so damn spooky looking.*

In fact, Larry understood the joke but failed to see the humor—so he refrained from laughing. He stared Ray down, a habit he had of visually challenging people—for sport.

Ray noticed Dale approaching. "Get anywhere with the red-head, Dale?" He knew full well that his brother not only did not, but never would.

Dale dodged Ray's insult and sat down heavily. "We got big trouble, Ray." He then proceeded to tell Ray what he had just heard. He leaned across the table and waited for the expected explosion. He didn't have to wait long.

What started out as a relaxed, booze-filled night that promised wild sex and bawdy jokes had suddenly gone sour. Dale knew his brother would be furious, and he was. He watched as the crescent scar turned beet red and seemed to pulse with every breath.

Ray studied his brother's misshapen eyes for a long time. He stared without blinking, bored into his brother until his eyes watered. Finally he blinked. Tears escaped and skidded down each whiskered cheek. A solitary drop lingered on the blazing scar and immediately vanished, as if boiled by the intense heat.

Ray sucked saliva back, swallowed, and stood up. His knees banged into the underside of the table. Cocktail glasses flew in every direction.

Petey, the bartender, looked up. Darla turned toward the noise as well.

Ray made eye contact with Darla, cracked ten knuckles one at a time, and motioned her over.

"I'll take care of it, Petey. It's okay." Darla said, not totally sure she should respond to the angry man's wave. She finished her drink, wrapped her robe securely around her, and strode toward her date.

"Easy, Ray," Larry said. "Take a deep breath and calm down."

Otto finally reached the emergency entrance. He honked the horn and waited. He was exhausted but knew he couldn't dally. Time was critical.

Two orderlies rushed out, pushing a gurney. Together, they loaded John onto the cart and wheeled him inside.

As the orderlies took John away, Otto collapsed into one of the leather chairs in the waiting room. He was anxious for Doc Wilson's report on his charge. He had already decided to stay at the hospital for a while, especially since he really should stay off the unplowed roads.

Doc Wilson and his team immediately undressed their patient, inserted multiple IVs, and began monitoring his vital signs. John's body temperature was still dangerously low, but it had risen from its lowest point of some time before.

The intern recited John's vitals: "Pulse steady, heartbeat weak, and the EEG indicates normal brain wave functions."

"Let's give him a complete going over." Doc ran his hands over John's still form. "Let's see, apart from a few bruises and superficial cuts on one wrist, and . . . oh yes, a nasty bruise on his head, I don't see any other problems. I'd say his frostbitten toes look to be the most serious injury. Couple of fingers are discolored. We can probably save those."

"We'll keep moderate heat on the toes, Doc," the intern said.

Doc Wilson nodded. "That's about all we can do. With any luck, and his will to survive, we should have his core temperature restored within an hour or so. List him as critical. We'll watch the toes. If he survives, we'll probably wind up having to amputate two . . ." he checked the toes again and added, "maybe three, I'd say. That can wait, however."

"Should we move him to intensive care?" the nurse asked.

"Yes. Monitor him and notify me of any change."

John was wrapped in blankets and wheeled out of the emergency room. A lone orderly took him down the hall to a set of elevators.

Otto stood as John passed by.

Doc Wilson walked over to join the rancher. "He's stable, Otto. Pretty much up to him now. We're sending him to ICU. He'll be watched closely. Why don't you get some rest?"

"Thanks, Doc. Think I'll mosey upstairs and wait there."

"Okay. Gotta run, Otto. We're short on staff tonight, and I just saw another patient wheeled in. See ya later."

"Thanks Doc." Otto walked slowly down the hall.

John's fate now depended on his own strength, his will to live, and the warm fluids working their way through his veins.

❖ 17 ❖

RAY STECKEL WAS FURIOUS. A large, blue vein threatened to explode in the middle of his high forehead.

After waving Darla over, Ray waggled a finger under Dale's nose. "I'll cut their nuts off and throw 'em in the first pig pen we pass, I swear to God, Dale!" Gobs of spit flew with each vicious word.

Dale shrank and wished he were back in French Creek.

Larry reached up and laid a large hand on Ray's arm.

Ray sat down. He shook with fury as he digested his brother's words. The scar on his cheek burned. He sat motionless for a full three minutes. Everything had been working out perfectly. Until those two knotheads botched things up. Now he needed another plan.

Darla had crossed the distance from the bar and stopped near their table. Ray reached out and grabbed her arm, snatched his bag, and stood up. "Let's go! We've got business to attend to."

"Hey! Take it easy! I've got one more show to do!"

Ray held her arm and wouldn't let go. The transformation in his face terrified her: a combination of hatred and anger. The

246

ugly crescent-shaped scar on his cheek glowed like an ember—a bright, ugly red. In that brief moment, she felt as if the man clutching her arm were a rabid cur.

Ray leaned close but let go of her arm. His free hand found its way to her butt. He caressed one cheek, wantonly, roughly. "How long will that take?"

Darla forced her voice to calmness. She had long-since learned that pulling away from a man in this mood only intensified the anger. "Well, there ain't too many guys here tonight so I'd guess maybe half an hour or so. Manager said he might close up early, anyway."

Ray considered his options: leave now without Darla and come back later to pick her up, or wait for her last show and take her with them to Herman's. He decided on the latter. If the guy in the hospital was in a coma as reported, he wasn't going anywhere soon.

Ray calmed minutely. "Okay. We'll wait right here. Make it a quick performance, sweetheart. I got plans for us tonight." He spoke sternly, and his breath was sour. It smelled of onions, whiskey, and cigarettes.

Darla eased back, rubbing her reddening arm. "A deal's a deal. You pay me now, and we have a deal—four hundred." Darla held out her hand.

Ray reached in his pocket and peeled off four hundreds. He slipped them into Darla's waiting hand.

"I'll be back here as soon as I can."

I'll be waiting, Ray thought, almost forgetting to smile.

Ray cupped her chin. He looked longingly into her blue eyes and squeezed her face. "You won't be sorry, doll."

Darla grimaced in pain. Ugly thoughts about his intentions made the short blond hairs on her neck stiffen.

Darla shuddered, turned away, and walked toward the stage.

247

Ray watched her retreat, picked up his bag, and returned to their table. Dale and Larry sat down, as did Ray.

"You sure we shouldn't leave now, Ray?" Dale asked.

"She'll be done soon. Besides, the guy in the hospital ain't goin' nowhere. You said he was unconscious, right?"

"That's what I heard."

"Well, when she's done up there, we'll take her with us to Herman's. I'll leave Larry there with her until we return from the hospital. Think you can keep an eye on her for a while, Larry?"

"I dunno, Ray. Seems like we should leave now. What're you planning, anyway?" Larry asked. He was uneasy about the way things had been going. Unlike Dale, he didn't want to return to French Creek, but he hated untidiness in any form.

"Never you mind. I'm gonna fix things myself—once and for all. Then I'm gonna give that little tootsie a night she'll never forget back at the motel."

"Hard-ons ain't got no brains, Ray." he muttered.

Ray turned to him. "What'd you say?" His tone threatened, but immediately he backed off.

"You heard me. Think—use your head, not your johnson." For Larry to speak out against Ray was not out of character, but he seldom did so unless it was in private.

Darla gave a farewell performance that had the small crowd howling with excitement and delight. So she danced, and gyrated, and shook, and fired her pistols and attracted most of the few dollars that were left among the sparse crowd. She smiled tentatively, took one last bow, and headed for the dressing room.

Darla could have still backed out of her deal with Ray, but the money he offered was too important. Had Darla known of Ray's reputation with girls like her, she never would have consented to go with him.

The last time Ray had picked up a girl from one of the strip joints he frequented, the poor woman wound up in the hospital.

248

She'd failed to grant his specific request, and he'd beaten her senseless. She sustained a fractured jawbone and multiple contusions over much of her body. Because of the nature of her business, however, she couldn't press charges against Ray without putting her own freedom in jeopardy. Ray, of course, knew that and had walked away, unscathed.

Darla slid into a pair of tight jeans, a loose sweater, and pulled on an old pair of cowboy boots. She threw a few other articles of underwear in a small, red bag, dabbed her face with make-up, tossed back her hair, and left the dressing room. She stopped at the bar to retrieve her purse from Petey.

"Darla, you aren't leaving with that bunch over there are you?" Petey said, nodding in the direction of the Steckels.

"Don't worry, honey. I'll be all right." She leaned close and kissed his ear. "Besides, I have bills to pay. See ya tomorrow, Petey."

"Be careful, Darla. I mean it. Those guys don't look right."

"Don't worry. I can take care of myself—always have, and always will." She turned and strode toward Ray and the others.

Ray took Darla's arm and escorted her from the Stardust. Dale and Larry trailed close behind.

"Where we goin', Sweetie?" Darla asked.

"I've got a room at the Super Eight, but first we got to drop you and Larry at my office. It's not far from here. Once I'm finished at the hospital, I'll be back."

"Someone hurt?" she asked.

"Friend of ours—broke his leg. Nothing serious."

"That's too bad. I didn't know you guys were from around here. Thought you were from out of town."

"We are, but now we have a new business here, so we'll be living in town." Ray said.

They leaned into the storm and plowed through foot-deep snow to the van. "My truck's over there," Darla said and pointed to her new candy-apple red, Laredo sports utility vehicle. Under usual circumstances, she liked to drive herself, so she could leave when she wanted.

"Nice wheels," Ray said with obvious admiration. "Thought you'd like to come with us, Doll." Ray said.

"I always like to have my own transportation, Sugar. I'll follow you guys, okay?"

"Sure. No problem." Ray figured they'd eventually need the extra vehicle anyway, so he didn't object.

Dale scraped the windshield as Ray climbed into the driver's seat. Once they were loaded, they drove to Herman's. Darla followed closely behind and had little trouble negotiating the snow covered roads, especially since she followed in their tracks.

Ray stopped in front of the junkyard. Darla pulled up next to the van, turned off the engine and lights and got out. She locked the truck and joined Ray in front of the office.

"This your new business? A junkyard?" Darla asked.

"This is it," Ray said. "It's called Herman's Junkyard now, but there's been a recent change of ownership. New name will be Steckels', for me and Dale here. C'mon in, Darla. You can wait here in my office with Larry until we get back. Why don't you keep him entertained while we're gone." Ray peeled off a fifty and gave it to Darla.

Darla glanced at Larry. She didn't want to be alone with the unresponsive man, much less dance for him. "It's been a long day, Sugar. I'm going to need to rest up for all of you boys later, but I'll give ol' Larry here a little taste of what's to follow." She reached over, removed Larry's ball cap, and rumpled his hair.

Larry's expression never changed. He grabbed Darla's hand and said, "Put the hat back!"

Darla was startled by the deep, gruffness of the man's voice. Every syllable held a clear threat of danger. She quickly replaced Larry's hat. His long, blond, wavy locks reformed beneath the hat and flowed over each ear. "Sorry, Sugar. Didn't know you were so shy."

Ray could see that Larry was of the opinion that bringing Darla along had been a mistake. He stepped between Larry and the woman. "Darla, why don't you go into the office while I talk to Larry for a minute. Here, I'll turn on the lights for ya." Ray stepped through the door, flipped the switch, and led Darla into the office. He pointed to the armchair. "Have a seat. We'll be back soon." Ray gave her ass another squeeze and closed the door.

Ray put his arm around Larry and walked to the front door. "Larry, wait here. Relax, enjoy yourself. Everything's going to work out, you'll see. We'll be back with the others in no time. Once I take care of that guy in the hospital, we're home free. See ya later."

Larry glared at the smaller Ray. "You've got too much to lose to make any more mistakes, Ray. Take care of business." He turned toward the office, opened the door and slipped inside.

Dale looked at his brother carefully. He knew that Ray and Larry had a different sort of relationship, and he had seldom heard them speak to one another. What he had just overheard startled him and was puzzling. His brother never allowed anyone to talk back the way Larry just had. "Ray? What's going on?"

"Nothin'. Mind your own business. Let's go."

Once inside the van and on their way, Ray outlined his plan. "We're gonna pick up the two stooges, head for the hospital, and take care of that guy once and for all. If we can't kill him there, then we'll bring him back to Herman's and get rid of him here."

"How we gonna get him out of the hospital without being seen, Ray?"

"I'll figger that out when we git there."

"What about Jimbo and Willy?" Dale turned and aimed his good eye toward his brother.

"They can stay at the motel—don't need 'em. All we need is Huge and Mikey."

"Why? What are ya gonna do?"

"None a yer business."

Ray and Dale drove to the Super Eight. "Keep yer mouth shut, Dale. Let me handle this."

As always, Dale had no idea what his brother was talking about, much less what his plans were. He was the consummate mute; he carried out orders from his brother because he had never known any other way.

They entered the motel and asked the clerk for Huge and Mikey's room number. "Thanks. This the local paper?" Ray asked.

"Yep! Fifty cents a copy," the clerk replied.

Ray paid for the paper and tucked it under his arm. They walked down the hall and knocked on the door. Huge answered. "Hi, Ray. Hi, Dale." Huge had a bag of Doritos in his meaty hand. He held the bag out. "Want some?"

With growing impatience, Ray replied, "No thanks." He pushed Huge aside and stomped into their room. "Mikey! Wake up!"

Huge had been watching reruns of *Mary Tyler Moore*—one of his favorite shows. He had devoured two large pizzas, several bags of chips, candy, and then washed the entire mess down with copious quantities of soda. Nearly sated, Huge was in a better mood than earlier in the day. He stood behind Ray and Dale and farted.

Mikey had scouted the cable channels for a good porn flick when they'd first arrived and settled on one called *Thar She Blows!* Unfortunately, when he set the remote down to go take a whiz, Huge took control of the clicker. Huge promptly started fiddling with the device and found Mary throwing her hat in the air back in Minneapolis. Mikey knew he'd never get his brother to change the channel, so he gave up and fell asleep.

Ray's voice intruded on Mikey's erotic dream. He woke with a start at the sound of Ray's voice. Once he shook out the cobwebs, he stared at Ray and Dale. He hadn't expected to see them until the next morning. Alarmed, Mikey quickly rubbed sleep from his eyes. "Hi, guys. What's up?"

Ray glanced at the larger of the two men. "Turn the god-damned TV off, Huge!" He backed up to the single dresser and perched on the edge. The scar on his cheek shone like a white-hot coal. The blue vein was again distended, like a thick worm gorged with soil.

Ray had the look of a man composed and totally in control. "I want to ask you both a question," he said quietly, "and if you tell me the truth, that'll be the end of it." He crossed his arms. "But if you bullshit me . . . if you give me some cock-and-bull story that you clowns have cooked up, I'll know you're lying." He paused for effect. "You two know me well enough to know that you don't want me pissed off. So just tell me what I want to know and everything will be fine." Ray waited. As he did, his ebony gaze darted from one cousin to the other.

"Gee, Ray. Me and Mikey wouldn't lie to you!" Huge blurt-ed out. He almost choked on a cupcake.

"That right? Tell me again where you dumped that guy in the Explorer."

Mikey swung both legs over the edge of the bed and looked at Ray. "Right where you said we should, Ray." Something bad happened. What? Mikey was scared. He needed to piss. His head was killing him. His earlier dreams of sexual fantasy were long gone.

"And where was that?" Ray asked quietly.

"In the quarry."

"Which one?"

"Uh . . . I forgot the name of it, Ray."

"Was it . . . the Clearwater Granite Works Quarry?"

"Yeah! That's it. Wasn't that it, Huge?" Mikey answered quickly, without thinking.

Huge had a mouthful of gummy bears. He was as nervous as his brother—so he ate. He had heard Ray's tone and realized he and his brother were in trouble. He was sweating profusely.

He looked at Mikey for help. There was no help for Huge. He finally answered his brother's question. "Yup."

Silence filled the room. Both Huge and Mikey looked to Dale for the slightest hint of compassion or understanding. Dale shifted nervously. He knew what his brother intended. He averted their gaze—at least his good eye did. The cocked eye stared between the two and focused on the bedside radio.

"All right," Ray said. "Fair enough. Now tell me exactly what you did and how you did it." Ray had set his trap and both men unwittingly fell into it.

Huge looked at his brother. He was confused. He couldn't remember very clearly what had happened earlier that day. His head pounded. He had no idea what he had done wrong.

Huge and Mikey stared at each other. Mikey finally spoke. "Dumped the truck just like you said. Guy was in the back. Put a stone on the gas pedal. Guy might have already been dead in back. No one saw us. We made sure no one saw us."

He didn't wait for Ray to respond. "Then we closed the doors on the semi and drove to Herman's." Mikey paused and took a deep breath. That was the whole, complete truth.

"You didn't wait to make sure the guy didn't come up?"

The ex-boxer had his first inkling of what might have happened. Sweat ran down his armpits, and he felt a tightening in his gut that made him want to puke. "Why do you ask, Ray?" he asked carefully.

Ray stood to his full height and slowly walked between the twin beds. He hovered over both. His head turned from side to side, watching the two brothers squirm. If either had dared to look up, they would have seen Ray's scar turning a deep shade of purple. "BECAUSE THE GUY IS *STILL* ALIVE!"

"Aw Jeez, Ray. No way! That truck must have dropped a hundred feet or so." Mikey was desperate. Any lie he could grasp might get them off the hook.

Ray backed away, spun around and stepped toward the door. He grabbed the handle, stopped, and twisted to face the brothers. He had all the information he needed. "Doesn't matter now. Somebody found him and brought him to the hospital. He's still alive. We got to get him out of there and finish this once and for all. Get dressed. Meet us out front."

Ray and Dale left the room and went down the hall. Ray stopped at the end and picked up a wall phone. He had one final call to make—to the Milbank Police Department. Ray glanced at the paper he'd brought with him, the *Milbank Plains Dealer*. He cleared his throat as the phone rang on the other end.

The dispatcher on duty, Karl Butts, answered after the first ring. "Police department. How can I help?"

Ray cleared his throat. "Yeah, say, this is Johnson from the, uh . . . *Plains Dealer*. Anything new you can pass on about the fella brought in to the hospital?"

"Who'd you say you were?"

"Johnson. I'm new. Just started this week, and wouldn't you know I'd pull city desk duty on a crappy night like this?"

The dispatcher, satisfied with Ray's answer, was more than happy to talk to the paper. "Yeah, I hear ya. It's pretty ugly outside. How'd you hear about our John Doe, anyway?"

"I'm good, that's how. News travels fast in this town. Any word on who the guy is yet?"

"Nope! No wallet. Nothing to indicate who he is. No one has claimed him yet, and he hasn't spoken a word to anyone. Guess he's still unconscious, far as I know. Rancher by the name of Otto Stubblefield found him out on the prairie. Guy was half froze to death. That's all we know."

"Mind if I quote you on this?"

255

Never one to shrink from self-aggrandizement, Karl was only too eager to comply. "Not at all." he said. "The name's Butts with two T's, first name Karl. That's with a K, by the way."

"Well, thanks there, Karl. Guess we'll go with what we've got. See ya later!"

Now Ray had a plan that would finally tie up the one loose end that might bring him down. As long as he could get to John Doe before anyone identified him, he could get rid of him—for good! All they had to do was slip him out of the hospital. They had to move fast, though.

Down the hall a few doors away, Huge and Mikey were left to ponder their fate. Somehow, they had messed things up once again. "What's going to happen now, Mikey?"

His brother feared the worst, but kept his thoughts from Huge. Their only hope now lay in recapturing their prisoner. "Don't know, Huge. But we'd better stick to our story and help Ray get this guy again."

The two brothers put on their coats and left the room. They met Ray and Dale outside in the snow-covered parking lot.

All four piled into the van. Huge and Mikey remained silent. Ray outlined his plan. "We'll scout the hospital first—then figure out how to either finish the guy right there . . . like he suffocated or somethin' . . . . or take him and kill him later. Any questions? No? If we get him out and no one sees us, we take him back to Herman's. We'll get rid of the guy and the van at the same time. Just like we used to do back home."

Mikey shuddered. Huge stared out the window.

After a short drive through deserted streets, the van pulled up in front of the hospital main entrance. Ray studied the sign out front: CLOSED AFTER 9:00 P.M. EXIT ONLY. PLEASE USE EMERGENCY ROOM ENTRANCE.

Ray reached into his pocket, pulled out his watch, and checked the time. "All right, here's the deal. You guys drop me off at the other entrance then return here. Park and wait. I'll try to slip in without anyone spottin' me, and come back and open the front doors for Dale. Think you can handle that?" he asked, sarcastically.

"Sure, Ray. No problem," Mikey replied.

Mikey climbed into the driver's seat and pulled away from the curb. He drove to the emergency room entrance, let Ray out, and returned to the prearranged parking spot out front.

Ray went inside the first set of doors. He paused and scanned the lobby, hesitated, and bent down to tie his shoe. He kept watching the lobby, finally stood, removed his jacket, and waited for an opportunity to enter unseen.

He wanted to slip in, mix with the small crowd, and go down the hall to the other doors. He pulled his cap down low on his forehead, flipped his jacket up over one shoulder, and stepped through the last set of doors.

The receiving area was crowded. Only one station nurse appeared to be behind the main desk. Just as she got up to attend to something, Ray slipped in, turned his head away and down, and quietly slid past the small group in front of him. He walked down the hall toward the main doors. No one paid any attention to him. He might as well have been invisible.

Ray had one other problem—how to find out where John was in the hospital. He spotted a wall phone at the end of the hall and got an idea. He picked up the handset and dialed the operator. A sleepy voice answered and Ray asked for the number for the emergency room. "Dial 97, Sir."

Ray depressed the cradle and dialed the number. He had an open view back down the hall toward the emergency room. He watched the duty nurse. The phone rang, and Ray was pleased to see that the receiving nurse picked up the phone.

"May I help you?"

"Yeah! How's the guy doing they found out at the quarry?" Ray asked as officiously as possible.

"Who is calling, please?"

"Police department."

"Let's see, now. Latest report has him as stable," the nurse said.

"Where they keeping him?"

"Uh . . . second floor. ICU. Room 248."

Ray tried not to give the nurse time to wonder about his call. "What's the name of the nurse on duty there? I need to get a bit more information from her."

Ray watched the nurse hesitate. Incoming patients stood three deep in front of her desk. She put the phone down and turned to her computer screen. "That's it, Sweetheart. Don't think . . . just answer my question," Ray whispered.

The nurse picked up the phone again. "Margie Albright is on duty. Can I ask who's calling, please?"

Ray was unprepared for the nurse's query. "Yeah, uh . . . it's Butts. Karl Butts."

"Oh. Hi, Karl. Didn't recognize your voice."

"Got a bit of a cold." Ray cleared his throat.

"And how's your mother doing?"

Ray hesitated. "Yeah, she's doin' better. Look, I'm in kinda' hurry. Can you connect me with Nurse Albright, please?"

"Ah, sure."

"Oh, by the way, what room is the patient in again?"

"Two forty-eight. Second floor. Just a minute, please, and I'll connect you."

After a brief pause, Nurse Albright came on the line. "ICU."

Ray forged ahead with yet another charade. "Yes, Nurse Albright, this is receiving. We need you to come down here right away! There's a patient being admitted that specifically asked for you by name. Won't talk to anyone else, and we're swamped down here. Can you get away for a few minutes, please?" Ray tried to sound frantic—urgent.

With obvious concern in her voice, Margie Albright quickly asked, "Who is it?"

"Don't know, Ma'am, but he's been asking for you. I have to go now." Ray quickly hung up.

Ray strode casually to the locked front door. The van was parked outside as expected. Dale stood waiting for Ray to let him in. Ray motioned to Dale, opened the door and quickly let him in. Both men walked to the elevator. Ray noticed his brother fidgeting. "Relax. Nothin' to worry about. Punch the second floor button."

❖ 18 ❖

OTTO STUBBLEFIELD LEFT THE WAITING ROOM on the second floor. He had fallen asleep, and when he awoke, looked in on John. Thanks to Jerry's phone call to Doc Wilson, they now knew who the man was. Because of the rush of patients, however, the doctor had not found time to notify the police. His patients came first, and in due time he would put in a call to the police department.

Now that Otto's charge had a name, John L. Rule's fate became even more important to the old rancher. Otto had become attached to the man he'd rescued from the frigid prairie. He truly cared about his welfare, and prayed for a speedy recovery. He had decided to stay at least until he knew John was out of the woods.

Otto peeked into John's room one last time. He was hungry and decided to find something to eat. John appeared to be resting comfortably, so Otto left him alone and inquired of the nurse whether there had been any change.

"He's responding nicely," Nurse Albright said with a reassuring smile. "His blood pressure's normal, his body temperature's up, his heartbeat's strong, and he's even been mumbling and tossing about. Doc Wilson looked in on him and said it looked like he was past the critical stage. His color has returned, and I'm going to pull the EKG and EEG monitors. We'll probably move him up to the third floor in a couple of hours now that he's stabilized."

"That's good news. Think I'll go down to the canteen for a bite to eat. Can I bring something back for you?"

"No thanks. I'll take my break in a little while."

The phone rang, and Otto waved good-bye to allow the nurse to return to her duties. He took the elevator down to the basement, planning on being gone for no more than twenty minutes.

When they got off the elevator on the second floor, the Steckel brothers turned right and followed the arrows pointing to the Intensive Care Unit. Ray slowed as they approached the visitor's waiting room. It was empty. Now all they had to do was wait until Nurse Albright left.

Ray pulled his brother's arm and dragged him around the corner. They stood in the hall and waited.

"Come on!" Ray whispered, trying to will Nurse Albright to leave her station. "Git off your fat ass and go downstairs!" Ray peeked around the corner and spotted her leaving her station. "She's headed this way! Quick! Over here!"

Ray shoved his brother into the visitors' bathroom. Once safely inside, Ray opened the door a crack and peeked out. Nurse Albright entered Room 248. "She's going into the guy's room," Ray whispered. "Must be going to check on him before leaving the floor."

He let the door close. After a few seconds he opened it again. Nurse Albright stood in front of the elevators, looking up. She paced from one to the other. Finally one arrived, and she stepped inside.

As the doors closed, the brothers walked down the hall and crossed to John's room. There was no one else around.

"Now what, Ray?" Dale asked.

"We don't have much time. I'd like to kill the sonofabitch right here, but we can't take a chance. Better to get him out of here. No body, no evidence. We're going to have to move him. As soon as that bitch nurse finds out my call was a phony, she'll be back up here madder'n a wet hen. We have to be quick about this."

They opened the door to Room 248 and quietly stepped inside.

John was gradually recovering. All of his vital signs had returned to normal. He wasn't totally out of the woods yet, but a short while ago, he had briefly regained consciousness. Out of the coma, he was resting comfortably. The IVs were still in place, but the EKG and EEG sensors had been removed. He lay in the semi-dark, apparently asleep.

As the brothers entered John's room, Ray saw clothes stacked neatly on the table. He walked over to the bed and stood just above John's still form. He clenched both fists, but resisted the urge to end John's life while he had the chance. "You little prick!" he whispered. "You've caused me nothing but trouble!" He pulled a pillow from above John's head and smashed it into his face, but then changed his mind and pulled back.

"Dale, grab his clothes and get him dressed. I'm going to go get a wheel chair." Ray threw the pillow across the room and left.

❖　●　❖

The Milbank Community Hospital contained three floors, as well as a basement. It was seldom full. Tonight, the few doctors, nurses, and orderlies on duty were all busy with emergency room patients, many of them related to the storm—injuries sustained in accidents, frozen fingers and toes, heart trouble from shoveling snow. The duty nurse in ICU, Margie Albright, was left to care for John by herself. Should the need arise, Doctor Wilson could be paged. He was only minutes away.

When Margie left her station to go to the emergency room, she felt fairly secure leaving her patient alone for a few minutes while she went downstairs to see what the problem might be. Her patient was stable. She'd looked in on him and felt comfortable he could be unmonitored for a couple minutes.

She was puzzled about who was asking for her. Worry filled her gentle face as she left John's room. It could be her son or husband, injured somehow in tonight's storm. She left the elevator and hurried down the hall to the emergency room, anxious to find out who'd called her and why.

Ray preferred not having to kill the duty nurse. It would create unwanted scrutiny. He hoped she didn't return to the second floor before they had left with their prisoner. He went back to John's room with a wheel chair. Dale had dressed John as instructed and yanked the needles from his motionless arms. "Okay, Ray. He's ready."

Ray wheeled the chair close to the bed and together they lifted John into it. John's head hung down on his chest. "Prop his head up with a pillow," Ray said. "Stupid jerk looks dead already!"

Just as Dale stepped away, John woke for the second time in the past hour. This time, however, his gaze fell not on Nurse Albright, but instead on the hideous face from one of his nightmares. He blinked once—twice. He closed both eyes. When he looked again, he stared straight into the now familiar, cocked eye of Dale Steckel. Bewildered, frightened, and very weak, John tried to speak.

He couldn't form the words to ask. Nothing but a low gurgling sound came from his lips: "Aaaaaagggh . . ." With his mouth still open, he continued to stare at his antagonists, fear growing geometrically.

"Shut him up!" Ray commanded.

Dale placed a hand over John's mouth.

John couldn't breath, and he pleaded with his eyes. He rolled his head to one side to escape. He recognized familiar smells of grease and oil and wondered if he were dreaming once more. He was still deep in a black hole—the persistent nightmare consuming him. John slumped, closed his eyes in defeat. Dale removed his hand. John was too weak to fight.

They wheeled him out of the room, down the hall to the elevator. A blanket covered his head and body.

"That goddamned nurse better not come back too soon," Ray said.

They stood in front of the two elevators. Ray punched both buttons.

Downstairs, Margie Albright waited for one of the lifts. The door on the left opened. She stepped in and angrily punched two.

Ray noticed that both elevators were ascending. The door on the right opened first. They hustled inside and hit the button. As the doors slid shut, Margie stepped from the second elevator. She glanced to the left toward the other elevator and wondered who had just left.

She stomped down the hall, her heavy, white, orthopedic shoes clacking noisily. "Some fool thinks he's funny down there! How could they play such a cruel trick on me? Scared me to death!" She vowed to find out who was responsible.

She returned to her desk, straightened her uniform and muttered, "I'll find out who the prankster was and give him a piece of my mind!"

❖ ● ❖

The doors opened on the first floor. Ray held out his arm and blocked Dale from exiting. "Hang on. I'll check and see if it's clear." Ray looked around the corner. The hall was empty. He waved to his brother.

They scurried to the main entrance, and Ray held the doors as Dale wheeled John through. In his haste, he slammed the chair into the glass.

"Watch out, you idiot!" Ray said. He glanced back down the hall. At the far end, an old man with his head down shuffled toward them. "Hurry! Someone's coming!"

They cleared the doors and slid down the sidewalk through the snow. As they neared the end of the walk, one of the wheels caught in a particularly wide crack in the concrete, and the chair tipped up on two wheels. John was thrown out of it into the snow. The wheelchair, now empty, lay on its side, a single wheel spinning soundlessly in the darkness. "Quick! Pick him up and get him in the goddamned van!" Ray commanded.

Dale did as he was told. He grabbed John's inert form under both arms and dragged him to the side door of the van. Mikey slid the door open and pulled John inside. They dumped him on the floor—hard.

John's head slammed on the vinyl mat. Dale quickly closed the door. He and his brother climbed into the van, and they all drove off into the night.

John was jolted awake. His mind raced. *Where am I? Who's that?* He struggled to make sense of the events unfolding around him. His head ached, and he felt like vomiting. *Am I dreaming? Is this another dream?*

John opened his eyes. He stared at two sets of legs. Then he remembered. Something about a wheelchair . . . falling. Snow . . .

lots of snow. Everything white . . . a door opened . . . a white door. Had he fallen through a white door?

John heard voices from a long way away. They sounded familiar. He knew these people. He opened his mouth to speak. *Help me!* Nothing passed his lips except his warm breath. He listened again. *I know you! I . . . NO! NO! It can't be! My God, they're all here!* All that actually came out, however, was a moaning.

"Shut him the hell up!" Ray commanded.

Huge stepped on John's trembling form. Mikey covered his mouth with a gloved hand.

Tears flowed steadily. John was in pain. He couldn't breath. He felt a deep, deep despair. Once again, he was a captive. All he could do was remain motionless and wait for their final move. His body shook uncontrollably.

Ray was pleased. His plan to extricate John from the hospital had worked perfectly. No one had seen them, and no one knew where they were going. This time, with him in control, he'd finish the job once and for all! They would never find the guy. Then it's back to the motel to take care of Miss Twinkle Tits.

John was outnumbered, weak, and without hope of escape. As the van drove into the night, John continued to weep, not so much for himself, but for his wife and two daughters.

Otto left the canteen. The cafeteria had been closed, and he had to settle for a very stale ham-and-cheese sandwich, a salad that looked to be four days old, and a can of soda. He passed by the lobby and walked slowly down the hall. Ahead of him, he noticed two figures pushing someone in a wheelchair out the front door. He continued his slow walk, lost in thought.

As he approached the elevators, he thought he heard a shout. He hesitated. Had he turned at that instant, he would have seen a body thrown into a white van. Instead, he punched the elevator button and waited. The elevator appeared, and the doors opened. Before he stepped inside, he glanced to the side. He looked through the front doors out onto the sidewalk.

Otto couldn't be certain, but through the heavy, blowing snow he thought he saw a wheelchair lying on its side—a single wheel still spinning in the darkness. Flashes of light reflected from the rotating spokes. Then the elevator door closed.

Otto exited the lift and walked down the hall to the ICU station. Immediately, he felt that something had changed. He looked for Nurse Albright. The duty nurse was nowhere in sight.

He went directly to John's room and opened the door. The bed was empty, IV tubes hanging limp, the needles dripping fluid on the floor. His heart raced. Alarmed at finding the room empty and disheveled, he turned and ran back to the nurses' station.

Nurse Albright was on the phone. Her voice was full of concern and fear. "I don't know what happened!" she said into the receiver. "I left to go downstairs for a few minutes, and when I returned, he was gone!" She was crying as Otto approached.

Margie turned, seeing Otto. She continued speaking into the receiver, "I told you I didn't see anybody. He just disappeared! I know I shouldn't have, but I had a call from receiving. They said that someone had just been admitted and was asking for me. I had to go down to see who it was, and there was no one to watch the patient for me. Besides, he was resting comfortably." She looked at Otto for sympathy.

"No. When I got downstairs, no one knew anything about it. Yes, I understand. Good-bye." Nurse Albright hung up the phone. She put her face in her hands and sobbed. She felt terrible about leaving her station and now realized that the phone call had been much more than some harmless prank.

Otto went behind the counter and put his arm around the distraught nurse. He had heard enough of the conversation to realize what had happened. Someone wanted John out of the hospital. The guys with the wheelchair! Otto realized he might have been able to stop them had he paid more attention.

He felt great sympathy for the nurse, but at the same time was angry with himself for leaving his post. "Better phone the police, nurse. Tell them someone kidnapped your patient"

Nurse Albright picked up the phone. As she dialed, she blew her nose and took a deep breath. She spoke to the dispatcher, who instructed her to wait for the police to arrive and be certain she didn't touch anything in the room.

Otto decided to wait with her. Maybe he could help. He tried to remember the men pushing the wheel chair. He had not seen their faces, and they had hats and heavy coats on. He felt just as bad about the whole affair as did Nurse Albright. After all, hadn't he been the one to rescue the poor man in the first place? And now, after all they had been through, to have someone snatch him away? Someone had tried to kill him, and now they'd come back to finish what they started out at the quarry. Otto was certain he was right.

Otto and the nurse sat together quietly, both caught up in their own thoughts and waiting for the police to arrive.

Otto was certain that John L. Rule had been dumped into that frozen quarry. He'd survived, only to be recaptured. Someone wanted to get rid of him—bad! Otto was depressed and hated the thought of phoning Betty with the devastating news.

Otto ran his hand over his heart and rubbed across his flannel shirt. His chest pain had returned. He tried to ignore it, but it wouldn't go away. *Stay alert.* The cops were going to have questions, and he had to remember everything he saw. He might be John's only hope. A white van . . . two guys . . . the wheelchair . . .

❖ 19 ❖

KARL HAD BEEN BACK AT WORK for over an hour. The deputy who filled in for him during his break was angry with the dispatcher. He was only supposed to be gone for an hour, and Karl had overstayed his allotted break time.

"Sorry, the storm slowed me down," the dispatcher said.

The deputy knew better. He was well aware of where Karl took his supper breaks. "Yeah, right! Did you finally get laid or not? If you didn't at least get blown after being gone that long, I'll really be pissed!" The deputy had seen Karl in action before. He knew the man to be too cheap and too slimy to ever have much luck with any of the girls at the Stardust.

"That's for me to know and you to find out!" Karl smiled at his clever reply.

Their idle chitchat was cut short by a phone call. It turned out to be Jerry Stubblefield, Otto's nephew. Karl listened with interest. "Balls on a goose!" Karl exclaimed. "Thanks for the info. We'll pass it on to the chief." Karl hung up and addressed the deputy. "Well, now we know. The guy has a name and he's from the Twin Cities."

Karl notified the chief. His response was predictable as far as the dispatcher was concerned. "Yes, sir. I understand. We'll let the FBI deal with it," Karl said.

Chief Karnowski was home for the night. Any further police work could wait until tomorrow. As long as the guy was being taken care of by Doc Wilson, he was in good hands. Besides, if he was unconscious, there was nothing the sheriff could do anyway.

"Okay, Chief, I'll call if anything else pops up. Yep! Yer right. You probably couldn't get outta yer driveway tonight anyway. Yes, sir. See you in the morning."

Karl informed the deputy of the chief's instructions. "We're to stay out of it. Leave the whole mess for the feds." Karl returned to his reading, and the deputy left to patrol the barren streets.

Sam and Mac finally reached the outskirts of Milbank. It had been a harrowing trip, especially the last fifteen miles after they crossed the Big Stone Lake Bridge. Sam knew he never would have made it without Mac and the big Suburban. More than once, they lost traction and fishtailed back and forth over the slippery road.

Only Mac's skill and familiarity with the vehicle kept the truck on the road. If they had slid into a ditch, any hopes of finding John would have been dashed. They were fortunate, and both men breathed easier once the lights of Milbank appeared through the falling snow.

Sam decided they should go directly to the police station for possible word on John's whereabouts. After getting directions from a Holiday Super Station, they drove the three blocks to police headquarters.

Mac became increasingly nervous as they approached their destination. He had been envisioning all sorts of scenarios about his son-in-law's fate—none of them good. Now that they had arrived, he was afraid to face what he felt must be the truth about John. Too much time has passed. The odds of his still being alive were slim. *God, I pray I'm wrong!*

They pulled up in front of the station. Mac noticed only one vehicle parked in front, and it wasn't a patrol car. They went inside.

The only person visible in the station sat behind a low counter. A squat fellow, he had both feet propped up on a desk. A Tiparallo hung from one corner of his mouth. The smell of stale cigar and cigarette smoke permeated the small room. The man behind the desk had his nose stuck in a recent copy of *True Police* but glanced up through a haze of smoke at the two visitors. Sam approached the counter.

The dispatcher straightened up and dropped his feet to the floor. "Yes, sir. Can I help you?"

Sam identified himself and flipped open his badge and ID. "Look, I know I'm out of my jurisdiction, but what can you tell me about the FBI's investigation into the French Creek matter?"

"Not much, I'm afraid. FBI never got here. Holed up in Brookings to wait out the storm. Won't be here till tomorrow—maybe. Pretty bad storm out there"

Sam immediately realized who he was speaking to. "Your chief around?"

"Nope. Snowed in at home. Don't know when he'll be back."

"What'd you say your name was?"

"Butts. Karl Butts."

It appeared as if the little man behind the counter would be his only source of information. "Well, tell me, Karl, what does your chief know about the missing person in this case?" Sam drew Mac to his side. "This is Mac Davis. He's the father-in-law of the kidnapped victim."

Karl yanked the cigar from between his lips. A piece of his lower lip stuck to the plastic tip, and he winced. He pushed back and the chair scraped on the linoleum. He sat erect. "Kidnapped? Who's been kidnapped? We didn't hear nothin' about a kidnapping."

Mac intervened. "You mean to tell me the FBI never mentioned the possibility of a kidnapping?"

"No, sir. If they had, we'd probably have made a connection between the guy Doc Wilson called about—the guy the old rancher found out on the prairie. We just thought the guy got lost or somethin'. I'll be damned! Kidnapped, huh? If that don't take the rag off the bush, as my daddy used to say."

Sam was furious. *Why the hell would the feds not tell the local chief of police about John? Typical! Bastards never share information until and if it suits their purpose.* "So if the FBI isn't here, and they never shared this information with your chief. Then no one is actually working the case. That about it, Karl?"

"Yes, sir. I guess so." Faced with new information from the detective, Karl was excited to be the first to know of the connection between the Steckels and the stranger. "That's about all I can tell you, Detective. But, if the man Otto Stubblefield found is this fella's son-in-law, then he's in good hands with Doc Wilson."

Mac had to sit down. His heart soared when he heard the dispatcher's words. John was alive and in good hands. He felt his eyes fill and quickly wiped away the tears. *Thank you, Lord!*

"What about the Steckels?" Sam asked.

"Been no word about that bunch—no one's seen or heard anything about 'em. We've left Herman Fogelman alone as per the feds' request. Our deputies haven't spotted their van, either. For all we know, they could be headed someplace else. Maybe they're not even here in Milbank."

"Okay, fair enough. We're going to the hospital to check on John. Have you had a recent report on his condition?"

"Yep. When I called earlier I was told the man suffered, uh, what was it? Let's see . . . oh yeah. Hypothermia. He's apparently out of danger though and resting comfortably. Could lose a couple toes, though."

Mac wanted to shout with joy. He stood and approached the counter. His face had relaxed—his laugh lines returned along with a smile. "Do you know if he's awake? Conscious? Does he have any other injuries?"

"No. Sorry. Haven't heard any more. But the hospital's only a few blocks from here." The helpful dispatcher gave them directions to the Milbank Community Hospital and wished them luck.

"Let's go, Mac. Thanks for all your help, Karl. If you speak to your chief, tell him where we'll be, okay?" Sam said. "Mac, do you want to call Debbie from here?"

"I think I'll wait till I see John with my own eyes, Sam. Then I can assure her that he's all right."

"Okay." Sam turned to leave and stopped. "Oh, Karl? One more thing: If the FBI happens to show up, fill them in on my involvement, will you please?"

"You bet! Hope he's all right, sir." The dispatcher was very interested in the case now, even if his boss wasn't. Why did this detective from Minneapolis and the guy's father-in-law drive all this way in a storm? Who kidnapped who? That French Creek gang? The chief sure wasn't too excited about all this, but Karl was! *Holy cow! Bad guys in town, a missing person, the FBI. This is great! Wait 'til I fill Darla in on all this stuff! Then maybe she'll see the light!*

Karl watched the two men leave. He rubbed his hands together and giggled. He opened his drawer and withdrew a small mirror. He reached up and plucked a few long strands of brown hair and wound them around the top of his head, patted each in place and smiled at his reflection. Satisfied and smug as a tabby cat after a bowl of cream that his sparse growth was covering the bald spot, he took a deep drag on his cigar, picked up his magazine, and leaned back with his feet on the counter.

Sam and Mac drove directly to the hospital. Sam hoped for Mac's sake that John was out of danger. Hypothermia was serious. If indeed he was out of danger, he was a very lucky man.

The detective wondered about the events that had led up to John's discovery by the old rancher. How in the world had he wound up out on the prairie in the middle of nowhere? This case was getting stranger by the minute! Sam was convinced that the French Creek bunch was involved. Herman Fogelman, as well.

They found the hospital, parked, and went inside. They were directed to the receiving area. Sam noticed that the nurse he spoke with gave them a funny look, as if she was holding something back.

They took the elevator to the second floor. Mac stepped out first and hurried down the hall. As they approached the nurse's station, it was clear something was wrong.

Sam introduced himself and Mac to the doctor in charge. "How's your patient, Doctor?"

Doc Wilson looked as if he wanted to be anyplace but where he was. He sagged. "I'm sorry. Truly sorry. Mr. Davis, your son-in-law is not here."

Mac listened as Doc Wilson explained the events that led to John's disappearance.

"This can't be happening! How can two men simply march in here and take someone away? Out of ICU even! Didn't anybody notice? This is unbelievable!" Mac stared at the doctor. He had no idea how he would tell Debbie.

"We had no reason to believe your son-in-law was in any further danger, Mr. Davis, and we certainly didn't know people were after him." Doc Wilson refrained from passing blame to Chief Karnowski. In reality, because of the suspicious nature of John's accident, Doc Wilson knew that a deputy should have been stationed at John's door. He chalked it up to the storm. Everyone was shorthanded tonight.

Otto stepped forward and introduced himself to Sam and Mac. "Mr. Davis? I'm Otto Stubblefield. I'm the one who found your son-in-law. I'm sorry for what happened. I hold myself responsible. I was in the waiting room for all but a few minutes. I shouldn't have left." Otto was heartsick.

Mac shook his hand. "It's not your fault, Mister Stubblefield. I'm grateful for all you've done. You saved John's life. What happened here was beyond your control. These are dangerous men. They were determined to take John out, one way or another. You could have been seriously hurt, or even killed, had you tried to intercede. No, if anyone is at fault here, it's the police department, not you." Mac felt sincerely indebted to the old rancher for all he and his wife had done. Now it appeared it would all be for nothing.

"Thanks for trying to ease my conscience, but I do feel a great sense of responsibility. My wife and I sincerely hope you find your son-in-law and bring him home to his wife." Otto struggled with the last few words. His chest hurt again. Otto was in obvious pain. He turned to Doc Wilson and said, "Got a couple of aspirin, Doc?"

The kindly doctor fixed a professional eye on the old man. "You feeling all right, Otto? You missed your last check up, you know. Nurse, get Otto a couple of aspirin, will you?"

"Thanks, Doc."

"Call and schedule another appointment, Otto. Promise?"

"Yes, I will." The old rancher swallowed the tablets and turned back to the two strangers from Minneapolis.

Sam concluded that if the Steckels took John, they must have just left within the past thirty minutes. They had probably passed them on the street without even knowing it. The old cowboy had just missed seeing them when he returned to the second floor, and the wheelchair lying in the snow was used to take him out, just as if a patient was leaving for home. All the pieces to the kidnapping fell into place. *These guys are clever, I'll give 'em that.*

275

Sam reached for the phone on Nurse Albright's desk. "Need to call the police and find out what they are going to do—if anything."

Karl answered at the first ring. "Karl? Detective Reasons here. Yes, we just found out. What did the chief say?" Sam frowned and raised his voice. "What? What the hell does that mean? He has to get involved now! Yes, I'll wait." Sam covered the mouthpiece and told Mac the dispatcher was calling the chief at home.

After a moment or two, Karl came back on the line. "Sorry, Detective. The Chief can't get out of his driveway. Snowed in! Plows won't get him out for another couple of hours or so."

"Oh, for Christ's sake! What kind of operation are you guys running here? I don't give a shit! Where's the other deputy?"

"Only two on tonight 'cause of the storm, and they're both out. We just had word of a bad three-car pile up east of town, and that's where they are. I don't have anyone here to respond."

"Look, time's critical, Mr. Butts. It's clear that these people intend to kill Rule once and for all. Somebody has to do something, and if your fat-assed chief can't or won't help, then I'm going after these guys myself!"

"I don't know if you should pursue this on your own, Detective, lacking authority and jurisdiction, and all," Karl replied.

"Don't lecture me about jurisdiction, you pompous little ass! I won't wait. I want you to give me the address of this Herman Fogelman—now!"

"I could get in trouble for this, Detective."

The entire Milbank Police Department was irritating the hell out of Sam Reasons. He had heard just about enough from Karl Butts. "Listen, Butts, if we wait for your chief, it'll be too late! Now give me the address!" Sam was almost shouting by now.

Sam jotted down the address. "Yes, I've got it. If your chief ever wakes up from his long winter's nap, tell him where I've gone."

Reluctantly, the dispatcher did as he was told. "I'll inform the chief as to your intent, Detective."

"Fine! If any of your crack police force ever does show up, we could probably use some help at this Herman's place. I'll let you know what happens." Sam promptly slammed down the receiver.

"Let's go, Mac. We're wasting valuable time. Nothing more to be done here. We've got to find this Herman fellow and see if John is there."

As they turned to leave, Otto spoke up. "Excuse me, gents. Mind if I tag along? I still feel kind of responsible, and maybe I can help." Otto rubbed his chest as he waited for an answer.

Sam turned and studied the man intently for the first time. Otto's dark brown eyes shone brightly. Sam noted that the old man's eyes were set deep into a face filled with cracks and crevices. But, the man still carried himself well. If he still worked a ranch, he was strong as an ox. To pick John up and carry him off the prairie, meant he still had plenty of life left. *He clearly wants to help . . . maybe he can be useful.*

"Come on along, Otto. We'd be glad to have your help. Who knows what we're going to run into!"

The three men left the hospital and climbed into Mac's Suburban. Otto sat in back and introduced himself to Charlie. He then gave Mac directions to Herman's house.

"Hold it a minute, Mac," Sam said. The reality of what they were about to do suddenly struck the detective as not only foolish, but dangerous as well. Among the three of them, they had only one weapon. If they were going to handle this with no help from the police department, they'd need more than Sam's forty-five.

Sam considered what he was about to do and knew it was a mistake. The advisability of taking Mac and Otto with him, of putting them in harm's way, was irresponsible and foolish. The Steckels were killers as well as car thieves. Sam could end up with more than John's death on his hands if he wasn't careful.

"What's the matter, Sam?" Mac asked.

Reasons didn't know what to do and voiced his concern openly. "First of all, I don't think I can allow you two to put your lives at risk. This is a job for trained law enforcement officers. Problem is, I don't think we can wait." Sam removed his cap and brushed back his hair. He made up his mind. There was no time to waste.

Mac opened his mouth as if to argue, but Sam held up a hand. "On the other hand, I'm going to need help with this. I'm going to let you two come along but only if you agree to follow my orders. I have to have your promises that you'll do exactly as I say." Sam stared at both men, looking for any hint they either wanted out.

"I've come too far and have too much at stake to back out now, Sam. I'm in," Mac said.

"Always could take orders—especially from someone who knew what the hell he was doin'. Don't worry about me, Detective," said Otto. "I ain't in no hurry to get myself killed."

"All right, but we have another problem."

"What?"

Sam explained their lack of firepower, especially if they encountered the gang all together. "I pray we won't need to use any weapons, but we're dealing with some pretty nasty characters."

"Not a problem." Otto offered. "Hang on a minute, I'll be right back." He opened the door and went to his parked, snow-covered Jeep, quickly returning with two additional weapons. One was his 30-06, which he always carried with him to shoot varmints. The other was a Winchester Model 12 shotgun. "Will these do?"

"What do you carry those around for, Otto?" Sam asked.

"Critters that threaten my livestock, plus those damn prairie dogs that dig holes all over the place." He emptied his pockets of ammunition. "Guess we're all set then?"

Sam took one quick look, satisfied that at least they each now had a weapon. "Okay. Good enough, Otto."

Otto returned to the back seat and placed the weapons on the floor in front of him. "Reckon we can go now, Mr. Davis."

Mac turned around and smiled. "You can call me Mac." He put the truck in gear and drove off through a solid wall of heavy snow.

"You know, I don't believe we'll need these weapons with Herman Fogelman," Otto said.

"What do you mean?" Sam asked.

"Well, Herman's a family man—has a handicapped son. Never known him to be violent or dishonest. Far's I know, Herman ain't no criminal."

Sam responded immediately. "I appreciate that, Otto, but he's involved somehow. His name is all over this case, and right now, it's the only lead we have. We have to start someplace and this guy Herman is related to the Steckels. His house is as good a place to start as any."

Sam wondered again just how smart his decision to pursue the Steckel gang really was. He was going after a gang of desperate men who had already demonstrated their willingness to kill. He would be taking two old men who had zero experience in police work. Further, he was no spring chicken himself. "Must be nuts," Sam mumbled.

"What's that, Sam?"

"Nothing, Mac. Just talking to myself, that's all. I tend to do that when I'm jacked up."

Snow continued to fall, although it had lessened in intensity. It was a short fifteen-minute drive to Herman Fogelman's house.

Caught up in the emotion of the night, Mac silently questioned his sanity, as well. Soon to be a retired attorney, he found himself chasing bad guys out on the prairies of South Dakota in the middle of a blizzard. Certainly he trusted Sam's instincts, but the three of them against how many?

Mac was no stranger to guns. He owned a Model 12 just like Otto's, and had hunted birds most of his life. What they were about to undertake, however, was an entirely different matter. Shooting birds was one thing; shooting a human being was something else again.

Mac had been in the service, but served as a lawyer under the judge advocate general. *Not too many opportunities to shoot people in the courtroom,* he thought. But he was caught up in the chase and cared little for his own safety. His primary motivation was to find John and bring him home in one piece.

The short time Mac had spent with Sam had instilled a feeling of confidence in him about the detective. He was certain that Sam was good at his job, and would take great pains not to put himself and Otto in harm's way unless absolutely necessary. He also knew Sam couldn't do the job himself. He needed a show of force. If they could surprise the Steckels . . . well, who knew?

Mac chose not to call Debbie until he knew with absolute certainty about John's safety. She had enough on her mind.

Otto also remained silent during the drive to Herman's. His chest still hurt, and he didn't want Sam or Mac to know. He sat in the back with Charlie. Otto scratched his ears with a free hand, and Charlie leaned into the old rancher's body.

Otto wondered what twist of fate brought the young man to his ranch. He could have easily missed seeing him. God must have had a hand in all this. If so, then let's see this thing through. Otto felt at peace. His heart slowed and the pain subsided. He calmly stroked Charlie and waited.

The snow pounded on the windshield with unrelenting force. The only sound inside the truck was that of the wipers scraping against cold glass. Otto's deep voice broke the brief silence.

"That's Herman's house right up there!"

"Stop here, Mac. Turn out your lights," Sam instructed.

They parked a few houses away. A few lights were on inside. A lone pickup truck was parked out front.

Sam waited and scanned the front of the house. There was no movement. The truck clearly had been parked for some time; it was covered with a heavy layer of snow. Sam couldn't see any other tracks in the snow. Something didn't fit!

"Mac, I want you and Otto to stay here, and be ready to move. If you hear shooting, grab your weapons and move in carefully, okay?"

"We'll be right here, Sam," Mac replied. His voice quaked.

Quietly, Sam got out and closed the doors. As he approached the house, Sam paused, stepped up on the stoop, and then rang the doorbell. He was jumpy and had his gun out. His heart beat rapidly. Every sense was alert to any sound or movement. He waited for something to happen.

Herman's son, Barry, answered the door on the second ring. "Hello. Who are you?" the young man said.

Sam kept his pistol out of sight. "Hi, there. What's your name?" He immediately recognized Herman's mentally challenged son.

"I'm Barry. What's yours?"

"Sam. Is your daddy home, Barry?"

Barry turned and shouted over his shoulder, "Daddy, someone's here!"

Herman appeared at the door and put his arm around his son. "Can I help you?"

Sam studied the man and concluded that he and his son were no threat. He put his pistol away. Sam quickly explained who he was, and why they were there. "We need your help, Mr. Fogelman. Ray Steckel is a dangerous man. He's apparently killed before—more than once. Of course, you probably know more about him than we do."

Blood drained from Herman's face. His lip trembled, and he clung to his son. His worst fears were realized. Ray had finally gone too far. He immediately decided he had had enough. He didn't want to live in fear of Ray for the rest of his life. Whatever penalty he faced for moving a few stolen parts couldn't be that bad. He'd take his medicine like a man and get on with life.

"Ray forced me to sell him the business. He threatened to kill Barry if I didn't cooperate. Ray and his gang appeared without any warning—I had no choice but go along with his plan. You must understand, Detective—I was afraid for my son's life! Ray Steckel is an evil, evil man."

"I believe you, Mr. Fogelman. Can we come inside? We need to figure out where Steckel might have taken John L. Rule."

"Who's 'we'?"

Sam waved at Mac and Otto, directing them to come inside. Once all three were in the house, Sam explained Herman's involvement. "Herman is not the enemy. He was simply another victim of Ray Steckel. He's agreed to help us in any way he can. Isn't that right, Herman?" Sam looked the junk dealer directly in the eye.

"Yes, of course. What else can I tell you?"

They quickly agreed that John more than likely had been taken to the junkyard. Sam left unsaid what he suspected would happen once John reached the yard. "We have no time to waste."

"Don't you think we should call Chief Karnowski?" Herman asked. "Seems to me we should let him handle this."

"I disagree," Sam responded. "What little I know of the man tells me he's going to be reluctant to move fast enough to save John. He'll undoubtedly want to go in with his own deputies, and that'll take too much time. No, we simply have to do this thing ourselves." None but Herman showed any sign of disagreement.

"I dunno, Dectective. Ray's armed, and he'll never give up without a fight."

"Can't help it. John's life hangs in the balance. You can call the chief after we leave and tell him to meet us there. I won't wait for him though. Tell him that."

"Yes, sir. I will."

"Let's go." Sam turned to leave and abruptly stopped. "Wait a minute! Otto, do you know your way around Herman's Junkyard?"

"No, I don't. Only time I was ever in there was to pick up parts. Never been out in the yard."

Sam turned back to face Herman. "Looks like you're going to have to come with us, Mr. Fogelman. We're going to need help figuring out where to go, what the layout is."

Herman considered the invitation. Bravery was not one of his stronger suits. Besides, he had his family to think of. "Oh, I couldn't do that, Detective. You know, what with Barry and all. I can describe the place for you if you like."

"There's no time for that. Your wife can watch your son. Have her call the chief. Get your coat and come with us—right now!" He steered the reluctant, displaced junkyard owner toward the door.

Herman did as he was told. Herman instructed his wife accordingly, gave his son a hug, and walked out the door.

"Daddy, can I go with?" Barry called after his father.

"No, son, you stay here with your mother. I'll see you in a little while."

"Hold it! Do you own a gun?" Sam asked.

"Yes," Herman said. "But I left it in my desk back at the office. Pearl-handled pistol in my desk drawer. Never wanted one around the house. You know, with Barry and all."

"Okay, we'll have to make do. At least we won't be going in there blind."

The four men left Herman's house and climbed into Mac's Suburban. Charlie bounced from one to the other and applied a wet tongue to each. Mac turned the truck around and drove in the direction Herman told him to.

The junkyard owner looked back and saw his son waving furiously. He waved back as the truck disappeared into the falling snow.

❖ 20 ❖

.

L ARRY QUIETLY CLOSED THE DOOR to Herman's office and stepped into the dimly lit room.

Darla had thrown her bag on the desk and was slowly walking around the room, surveying its contents. She sensed Larry's presence and turned with a start when she heard the door click. "Cripes, Sugar. You sure are quiet, aren't you?"

Larry did not answer her, but instead walked over to the stereo and turned on the radio. He spun the dial until he located the local public radio station, which was playing classical music at the time.

"You like that high-brow kinda stuff, eh, Sugar?"

Larry leaned against the wall unit and said sharply, "Don't call me sugar!"

"Wow. Sorry. Okay, then what should I call you?"

"Larry."

Darla felt a wave of fright pass from her toes to her fingers as she heard his dull reply. "Well, Larry, if you and I are supposed to party a little, I'm going to need some better music to dance to than that crap."

Larry didn't respond. Instead he stared directly at Darla.

"I, uh, didn't mean to imply that your taste in music was shitty, or nothin', Suga—uh, Larry. It's just that I have a certain routine . . . well, hell, you seen it. I don't need to explain it to you, I guess."

Darla studied the man closely for the first time. Unlike Ray and Dale, beneath his leather jacket Larry wore a clean, pressed khaki shirt buttoned all the way to his long, sinewy neck. His hands were not only large and strong looking, but clean—closely manicured. The veins stood out prominently on the back of each. His jeans had a crease down each leg. With his narrow waist, wide belt, and broad shoulders, Darla knew at once that the man in front of her was no one to mess with.

"You know, Larry, you're actually quite good looking. Ever do any modeling?" Courageously, she stepped closer until she was only a few paces in front of him. She looked up and noticed his eyes were gray—like old concrete. His nose reminded her of a Roman statue she once saw in a school book. Unlike Ray, Larry smelled of peppermint.

Fear got the better of her. She tossed her blond hair, spun away and sauntered provocatively over to the armchair. She perched on one frayed arm. "Tell me something, Larry. How come you hang with those guys? You aren't like them at all."

Larry had allowed her to approach him without saying a word. He knew what she was up to—sensed her fear of him. He enjoyed watching people squirm in his presence. He was the cat toying with a mouse in a box, and he was relishing the play.

"Ray owes me a favor. I'm hanging around to collect."

"What kind of favor?" Darla was genuinely curious by now.

Larry turned up the music and strolled over to the desk. He sat on the edge facing Darla—his booted feet dangling and swaying back and forth. "I took care of something for him a long time ago." Larry felt secure in telling her more. "We were in prison together—cell mates, actually." He paused to test her reaction.

Darla showed no alarm. "Really? What were you in for? Oh, sorry, that's kind of private, I guess. You don't have to tell me if you don't want to." Darla collapsed into the folds of the chair.

"I don't mind at all. Ray was in on a manslaughter charge. Me, well, let's just say I was unjustly convicted." For the first time all night, Larry smiled showing a line of brilliant, white teeth.

"You should smile more often, Larry, it's quite becoming." She rose, brushed against his legs with her ass, walked behind the desk, and sat down. "So what was the favor you did?"

Larry turned to face her with one leg crooked on top of the desk. "Ray made the mistake of mouthing off to the wrong guy early on. He thought he was tougher than he actually was. The other guy and his friends showed Ray what tough really was. They turned him into their playmate, cut his face to mark their territory like dogs pissing on a bush, and generally made his life a living hell." Larry waited for a response.

Darla's eyes were wide. She wasn't too sure she wanted to hear any more, but curiosity got the best of her. "That scar on his face? They did that?"

"Yes."

"No wonder he's so . . . mean and angry."

"I guess."

"So, what did you do?"

"You don't want to know. Ray's troubles in prison ceased to exist—that's all. Ray promised he'd make me rich if I protected him. He told me about his business, and once I got out, I joined him and his brother. And, here I am."

"Hmmm. You're right. I don't want to know any more. Now, how about our little party?" Darla stood and began to unbutton her jeans. "I'll just have to slip into the bathroom and change, okay? I'd still like some different music, if you wouldn't mind, Larry."

Larry smiled again and waved her back to the chair with a flick of his wrist. "Save your energy, Darla. Unless you've grown something in those jeans in the past couple of hours, I'm not interested."

Darla gasped. "Of course! No wonder you seemed bored tonight." Darla was relieved—she hadn't lost her charms after all. "Sorry, I didn't know. So, you and Ray . . . ?"

"Well, once I moved into his cell, I kinda took Ray under my wings, so to speak. That'll have to be our little secret though, won't it? Ray gets pretty hostile whenever he's reminded of our alone time," Larry said.

"Sure. You bet. I won't say a word. Whatever's between you two is your business, not mine. I've seen guys that like to swing both ways. Wouldn't of guessed it about your friend, though." Darla returned to her seat behind the desk.

"I wouldn't exactly pin that label on Ray, if I were you. Seems like ever since he got out, he's more interested in proving how much of a stud he is to women."

Darla got the point and vowed to keep her mouth shut. In an effort to lighten the conversation, Darla asked, "Who's in the hospital, anyway?"

"What? What did you say?" Larry's sharp tone frightened the stripper.

"Uh, Ray said they were going to the hospital to visit one of your guys who broke his leg or somethin'. Is he the same man the police were trying to identify? The one from the quarry?" Darla immediately regretted her question once she saw the tall man's reaction.

Larry leapt from the desk, raced around behind, and pulled Darla up out of her chair with one hand bunched around the front of her sweater. "How'd you know about the quarry?"

Darla shook with real fear. She could hardly reply. Her head was thrown back, and Larry's fist was choking her. "Please . . . I can't breath!"

Larry loosened his grip—only slightly. "Talk!"

288

"The dispatcher! Karl, the police dispatcher. He came in tonight and told me."

"Shit!" Larry threw Darla back down into the chair—hard. "I knew it!" His mind raced. He looked down at the stripper. He was breathing hard. He knew what he had to do.

"What? What's the matter? Are the police involved?"

"Shut up! Stay put. I'll be right back."

Darla was in serious trouble. Without knowing precisely what Larry intended, she should have kept her mouth shut. The story Larry told her reinforced her earlier doubt about going along with Ray. Now she believed her life might be in danger. She stood and looked around the room for some sort of weapon. *Don't panic! Slow down! There has to be something here!*

She raced around the room looking for any sort of weapon. She hefted a statue of a horse—too heavy. The letter opener! She swept it off the desk and sat back down facing the door.

The opener was dull and small. Darla wasn't sure that it would offer much of a defense. Her lip quivered, and she was close to tears. She opened the desk drawer, and her heart slammed against her throat when she looked down.

John drifted in and out of consciousness. He struggled to maintain a sense of reality.

Huge and Mikey occupied the bench seat in back. John lay face-down on the cold, slushy floor beneath their feet. He didn't move. Had he shown any signs of alertness, one of the two brothers surely would have knocked him out. In John's delicate condition, any further blows to his head would have been life threatening.

Ray had made it clear that if John eluded them again, both Huge and Mikey would suffer the consequences. They would not let John escape. Mikey looked down at their prisoner. "If he moves, squash him, Huge."

"I will, Mikey."

The brothers knew they were on shaky ground with Ray, and they weren't about to take any chances with their cousin's unpredictable moods.

Roads in and around Milbank had become deeply rutted and bumpy. The van lurched and heaved as the group made their way to the junkyard.

The constant jostling shook John awake. He could hear voices around him, some of them familiar, some not. He kept his eyes closed. Try as he might, he struggled to reconstruct the events that had led to his lying on the cold, hard floor of the van.

He vaguely remembered waking up in the hospital and seeing the face of a nurse. But he didn't remember how he had gotten there.

John willed his distorted brain to step further back in time. Of course! The salvage yard . . . the dogs! He had vivid recollections of the French Creek escape and driving to the gas station. After that everything became fuzzy and disconnected.

The voices he heard around him were familiar. *Were these the same guys that . . . that . . . what? What did they do to me? Think, John! Who are they? Try to remember. How many? Three, four? More? They all looked alike . . . scarred, big, ugly and dirty. They smelled. There's one really large man and another with a nose that's been flattened and another with a funny eye. Who's talking? The leader? Guy with the scar? He knew he'd seen them all before.* John struggled to make sense of everything. He listened intently.

It was still snowing heavily, and the roads had become nearly impassable. It took longer than it should have to reach the junkyard. Ray maintained a constant level of meaningless conversation. Huge and Mikey thought that what they heard was simply nervous chatter, that their cousin had a lot on his mind. Most of what he had to say required little or no reply. He was simply killing time.

"I'll tell ya what, you guys. You missed a hell of a show tonight at the Stardust. Ain't that right, Dale?"

At first Dale wasn't too sure what his brother was talking about. Finally he responded. "You mean the blonde in the cowgirl outfit?"

"What'd you think I was talking about, you moron?"

"I dunno."

"Anyway, she did this thing with her tits that was unbelievable. Good lookin' little girl, too. Right Dale?"

"Yep! She was a looker, all right!"

"After she gets her clothes off, she starts shaking those titties around every which way, those goddamned tassels or whatever they were spinning like crazy! Then all of a sudden, she does somethin' with each boob, and those tassels come loose and fly off across the stage! How you think she did that, Dale?"

"Dunno."

"You don't know! Well, I know! She flexed her nipples—made 'em stand straight out like they'd been rubbed with ice! Those tasselly things came loose right when she wanted them to! Damnedest thing I ever seen! Right, Dale?"

Dale turned to face his cousins. He was caught up in reliving the erotic moments at the Stardust. His one good eye twinkled with excitement. The other eye pointed aimlessly beyond. "You shoulda seen it, you guys! She sure was somethin' special," Dale said, now caught up in the retelling.

"No kiddin'?" Mikey said, feigning enthusiasm. "Guess me and Huge shoulda come along." His nerves were frayed. The ex-boxer felt as if he'd better play along. He glanced over at his bigger brother. Huge appeared uninterested.

Ray looked at Dale. "When we reach Herman's place I'm going to let you out to open the gates. Go into the office and tell

Larry to turn the yard lights on. Have the girl wait there. Then bring him out back. We'll drive around and meet you there."

John wondered what all the chatter was about. He tried counting the voices. *The leader . . . guy with the scar . . . other guy with the funny eye, and the two big guys on the seat above me.* He knew the end of his nightmare was close at hand.

John couldn't imagine how he was going to escape this time. He was helpless. His captors could do whatever they pleased with him, and he was powerless to defend himself. He couldn't overcome a total sense of failure. The events of the past twenty-four hours felt like a lifetime. Time had run out. John was lucid enough to understand that he had no hope of rescue.

As they approached the junkyard, they stopped in front of the office. "You guys wait here a minute. I changed my mind. I want to talk to Larry."

Ray left the van and went inside. Larry was waiting for him, the door to the office was closed. "Well, did you have a good time?" Ray asked, knowing he hadn't.

"You dumb sonofabitch!" Larry said.

Ray shrunk from the venom in Larry's voice. "What? What's the matter? We got the guy, right outside in the van!"

"Good for you. And you've now got a stripper in there who knows more than she should, thanks to you." Larry proceeded to fill Ray in.

"Shit! Goddammit, now we have to kill her too!" Ray said. "Okay, here's what we'll do. I'll drive the van out back. Wait ten minutes and bring her out there." He waited for Larry's reaction.

"I'll clean up your mess just like I always do. I'll take care of her. You make sure we have no more witnesses, got it?"

"Right. No problem." Ray stomped out and slammed the door behind him.

❖ ● ❖

Darla heard the door bang shut and jumped. She had found a box of .38 ammunition in another drawer but only had time to load the gun with three bullets before the door opened and Larry returned. She dropped the gun in her lap and slid closer to the edge of the desk.

Ray drove around to the rear, spotted the large crane used to crush wrecks, and headed toward it. Dale got out as instructed. The crane had been purchased along with a ten-ton wrecking ball. When dropped from a height of seventy-five feet, it quickly flattened anything parked beneath it. Markers were set up, obliterated by the new snow, to position each hulk directly beneath the massive iron ball.

Ray stopped beneath the giant crane and turned to face his two cousins in the back seat. "You guys stay here and keep your eyes on our friend here. I want to talk to Dale for a minute." Ray opened the door and left the two brothers alone with John.

Dale and Ray trudged through the deep snow and stopped next to the crane. Ray tugged on Dale's sleeve. "Think you can run this thing?" Ray pointed to the old American Hoist crane. Dale walked over to the crane, opened the door, and peered inside.

"Yeah, I think so. Don't look too tough."

"Good. Get the van parked beneath the ball and then go get the crane started. Take it up, and drop it on the van when I give the signal."

Dale scratched his head, and then asked, "Why, Ray?"

"Never mind. Just do as you're told. Drop the ball when I give the signal!" Ray commanded.

Dale returned to the van, opened the door and climbed in.

"Where we goin', Dale?" Huge asked.

"No place. You guys sit tight."

John felt the van back up then go forward as Dale jockeyed it into position.

Dale was unaware of the markers and had to rely on his own shaky estimate of exactly where to position the van. He parked it as close as he could, climbed out of the van, and walked over to the crane. He looked up at the ball, reasonably satisfied with his parking job.

Huge and Mikey raised from their seats and prepared to leave the van as well. Ray opened the sliding door. "You two stay there for a minute," he yelled. He leaned into the vehicle, pulled on his black bag, and unzipped it. He stared at both brothers as he stuck one hand inside the bag.

The interior light illuminated Ray's face. He paused, enjoying the moment. A thin smile traced a line across his mouth. His eyes were two black holes set off by the crescent-shaped scar that throbbed on his whiskered cheek. His smile broadened into a wide grin. Yellow, decay-ravaged teeth flashed briefly.

Mikey trembled. He had seen that look on Ray's face before.

John heard a door open and close. He waited as his heart raced and his nerve endings tingled. He felt more alert and aware than he had for a long time. He felt a rush of cold air as the sliding door opened. Something bumped against his feet. He heard Ray's voice again.

"You two made one mistake too many!"

Ray withdrew his hand from the bag and displayed a pistol.

Neither man had time to react. He raised the gun, pointed it at Mikey and fired. The bullet struck his forehead. For one brief moment, Mikey stared at Ray in amazement. His eyes never left Ray's face. A small hole in his forehead oozed droplets of blood. He was dead in seconds.

He fell back against the window, his head resting on the top of the seat. The window behind him was covered in blood and brain matter.

At the sound of the gunshot, John flinched. He willed his tired body to melt into the floor along with the chunks of snow that were slowly turning from solid to liquid. His ears ached from the gunshot. He smelled gunpowder.

Ray redirected the weapon toward the larger brother. Huge couldn't understand what was happening. The sight and sound of a gun being fired terrified him. The big man watched his brother slump down in the seat. Blood and gore were everywhere. Huge lost control of his bladder, and he felt the warm piss fill his trousers. He tried in vain to comprehend what was happening.

Ray watched as Huge stiffened against the seat. He was in total control. "Bye-bye, Hugey! Say hello to your dumbshit brother!"

Ray squeezed the trigger.

Huge understood he was about to be hurt by the very thing he was most afraid of in the entire world. "Ray? Please . . . Don't!" He held up both meaty hands as if they could somehow deflect the shot. They did not. The bullet entered his throat, tore through his carotid artery, and plowed its way through the back of his head.

Huge's body slammed back, then pitched forward. He slipped off the seat. His heavy frame landed on top of John with a loud, thump! Blood streamed from his neck.

In the throes of death, Huge gasped for air that would not come. He twitched briefly, shuddered and lay still.

John had tensed as the second shot was fired. He felt something heavy land on top of his legs. He couldn't move. Pinned to the wet floor, John could only wait for the third shot. He shut his eyes, afraid of what he might see. He was fully awake. He didn't want to believe it, but he now knew the truth.

John was trembling. He fought a sudden urge to vomit. Tears escaped and dropped to the filthy, cold vinyl. He was shaking so hard that Huge's dead weight rippled as well. Blood mixed with the slush and flowed around John's cheek. Terrified, he knew that it would soon be over. For the first time in twenty-four hours, John knew what his fate would be.

He tried to move his legs, but they were trapped beneath Huge's body. John was tired of waiting, tired of doing nothing. Adrenaline surged through his veins. He immediately felt as if he had to face his antagonist once and for all. But he couldn't. He was trapped.

Ray backed away. He was still smiling. He stuck the pistol in his jacket. The black bag remained open on the floor near John's feet.

Ray pulled out his watch and checked the time. He wondered what was keeping Larry and the girl. He leaned in and took one quick look at John, then shook his foot. A strong gust of wind blew in and caused him to turn away. He gave the sliding door a slight shove and stepped back.

Ray walked over to the crane. Dale had finally figured out how to start the machine. He opened the door and leaned out.

Ray shouted to be heard above the roar of both the machine and the wind. "Take the ball up and drop it on the van. I want it smashed like an old cow pie. When you're finished, you and Larry pick it up with the forklift and load it on the flatbed. We'll dump it in the quarry tomorrow." He already decided to dispose of Darla and her red SUV in the same manner.

Dale nodded, closed the door, and revved the engine. He put the hoist in gear, and slowly the ball ascended to the top. With Dale's one good eye, he struggled to calculate the direction the iron ball might fall. By his reckoning, the van looked to be directly underneath the ball.

The ten-ton ball reached the top of the crane, seventy-five feet above the ground. Dale looked out the window for a signal from his brother. Ray raised his hand and extended his thumb. Dale released the clutch. He watched the ball leave its mooring, gain speed, and drop to the waiting van.

John was jolted by the concussion of the iron ball. The van shook and rocked. John raised his head and rolled over on one side. His hands were slippery, wet with the blood of the two dead brothers. He shrank back in horror! He was staring into the grotesque death mask of Huge!

Panic took hold. John tried to push himself away. He was pinned by the weight of Huge's body. Fear replaced a feeling of doom, the same feeling he had come to know all to well. He had to get out of the van.

John pushed and twisted until he was facing the sliding door. He tried to lift the dead man from his legs but couldn't gain any leverage. He wiggled and squirmed but nothing happened. *Hurry! Come on, John! Move!* He reached out and pushed Huge's bloody head away. The hideous, mangled face almost looked alive, but John knew the man was dead.

The smell of burnt gun powder mixed with the sweet, metallic odor of blood—the stench was overpowering. "Ahhhhhh!" His loud groan echoed in the small space. He heaved and pushed and struggled to slip free. He had nothing left. He was too weak.

Dale put the crane in gear. He had always had trouble lining things up. Because he had failed to see the markers and was blinded by the falling snow, the ball landed on just the front of the van instead of the middle. It merely crushed the hood and engine. Ray stood next to the crane. He stared in disbelief. "Dale! Dale!"

Dale opened the door and leaned out. "Yeah, I know. I miscalculated is all, Ray." .

"You one eyed-prick! I'll miscalculate your fuckin' head if you miss again. Take it up again and move the crane to the left a bit!"

Dale closed the door and did as he was told. He took the ball back up to the top, and repositioned the crane for a second drop.

❖ 21 ❖

HERMAN FOGELMAN SAT IN THE BACK of Mac's Suburban and considered how his life had changed. On one hand he was pleased that Sam Reasons had tracked Ray all the way from the Cities. At the same time, he wished he could have remained at home with his wife and Barry and let the three men deal with Ray on their own. He was conflicted and nervous.

The drive from his house to the shop seemed to take forever. With each passing block, the junk dealer fretted over what might happen when they finally confronted Ray.

"What are you going to do when you get there?" Herman asked.

Sam was the first to answer. "Don't know for sure. Have to wait and see what they're doing."

"They're probably all going to have guns, you know," Herman said.

"Well, so do we," Mac said.

Herman counted the members of the gang he knew about, then counted again and added the "meanness" factor of Ray. "Yeah, but what if you're outnumbered?"

Otto said, "You know something, Herman? Worrying about all that stuff is kind of like looking up a dead mule's ass! There's no future in it!"

Herman was stunned by the old rancher's blunt retort. He immediately fell silent. Up front, Mac and Sam stole a glance at each other and smiled.

Leave it to Otto to break the tension, Mac thought.

Sam chuckled. *I love that old guy!*

Mac turned off the headlights as he pulled the Suburban close to the front gate. Lights were on in the office. The red Laredo, already coated with snow was parked out front.

"That your Laredo, Herman?"

"Nope, never seen it before."

"I'm going to get close and see if anyone is in there," Sam said. "You guys stay here."

He left the truck and ran to the front of the office. He looked in the window, waited, then returned to the others.

"No one's in there. Herman, is your office directly behind the parts counter?"

"Yes"

"Any windows in there?"

"Only one, around back."

"It looks like they're all out back. Office door's closed, though. Wonder who owns the red Laredo. Herman? Any ideas?"

"Nope. Got no idea."

"There are fresh tracks leading behind the office. What's back there, Herman?"

Herman shrugged. It hurt to know that the place had been his a day ago. "Couple of sheds and the big crane is all. Yard lights are on out there. Normally I keep them off unless we're working late."

"Okay, here's how this is going to work. Herman, you stay here with Charlie. He'll keep you company. If we don't return in, say, fifteen minutes, take the truck and go get the police. Mac, leave the keys with him, okay? By the way, Herman, what's the crane used for?"

"Crushing cars. There's a heavy iron ball that drops and smashes 'em flat. Could never afford one of them fancy crushers like Ray had."

Sam considered the junk dealer's answer. "Okay. Mac, I really can't ask you and Otto to do this, so I want you to stay here for five full minutes. Then, I want you to sneak along the side of the office building and check out that rear window. Stay in the shadows. I'll go first and see what we're up against. As soon as I determine what they're doing, I'll come back to the rear of the office and give you instructions. Any questions?"

"Go ahead, Sam. Otto and I'll wait five minutes then check out the office. Charlie! Stay!" Mac placed his palm in front of the dog's nose. Charlie sat and waited.

The three got out and grabbed their weapons. "Remember, if you have to shoot, do not hesitate. If we're threatened in any way, you must shoot! We might not get a second chance at this. You guys gonna be all right?"

Mac and Otto looked at each other. Neither man had ever killed another human being. They nodded and assured Sam they were prepared to do whatever was necessary.

"Good! Here I go." Sam trudged off, ducking to keep a low profile.

Mac and Otto watched him dissolve into the snowy night. They waited impatiently. Finally Mac could stand it no longer. "Come on, Otto. Let's go."

"I'm right next to you."

Mac tucked the shotgun under one arm as if he were about to enter a cornfield full of waiting pheasant roosters. Otto shouldered the 30-06 and brought up the rear. They followed the only one of the three who had any experience in such matters.

Herman watched as the two men slogged through the deep snow. Charlie pranced with anticipation from the back seat to front. He observed his master apparently walking off in search of game. He stood on the center console with his gray face pressed against the windshield.

Sam followed the tire tracks to the edge of the office. He stuck his head around the corner of the building and saw the white van parked beneath the crane. There was one man standing beside it and another inside the cab of the crane. He paused, calculating his best approach.

The snow appeared to be letting up a bit. Sam glanced up. He heard footsteps behind him and spun around. "Pretty fast five minutes, Mac."

"I know. Sorry."

Mac and Otto took in the scene under the crane. Mac whispered, "Wind's blowing against us so they won't hear us coming. You two continue on around behind the office and check out that window. There are a few old cars parked between the office and the crane; they should provide cover for you. Be careful you're not spotted. I'll go after those two. Remember what I said—don't hesitate! If that guy's armed and raises his weapon—shoot. Ready?"

"Otto? You okay?"

Both men turned to Otto. The old rancher was rubbing his chest. He straightened, looked them firmly and said, "Yep! I'm fine. Let's go!"

Sam stepped away from the building. He darted toward the van and, as he did, he noticed the iron ball dangling high in the air. Mac and Otto slipped away and hugged the office building. They kept to the deep shadows. Mac led, and Otto followed.

Sam crept to within forty yards of the van. He crouched down and crab-walked through the snow. Unlike Mac and Otto, he didn't have anything between himself and the van for cover. He was totally exposed.

He focused on the man standing next to the crane. He saw the glint of the pistol in his hand. Mac was certain he was close enough for a good shot. He looked to his left and saw that Mac and Otto had reached the window and were peering inside.

Sam stood up, pointed his gun at Ray and shouted, "Stop right there! Don't move! Police!"

Ray jumped at the sound of another voice. He turned in Sam's direction. At first he couldn't see anything. He threw up his free hand to shelter his eyes from the bright yard light and finally spotted Sam. Ray never hesitated. He raised his gun, pointed, and fired.

Sam fired at the same instant. The bullets passed in the falling snow.

Dale heard the shots and paused. His foot held the clutch in place. The massive piece of iron swayed in the wind.

John heard the shots outside the van and knew he had to get out. He was terribly weak but was suddenly charged with a rush of strength. He pushed Huge's body off of one leg, then used that leg to shove the big man's body aside. Too weak to stand, he could only crawl to the door on his belly. He brushed aside a black bag, jammed his fingers in the crack between the door and the frame, and slid it open.

John inhaled deeply, rolled out the door, and landed heavily on the ground below. The fall knocked the wind out of him and he lay on his back, stunned. He opened his eyes and stared above him. The rusted, scarred ball of steel was directly over him.

John's eyes widened in horror as he realized what was about to happen. His heart felt as if it were going to burst through his chest.

Sam's bullet reached its target, clipping Ray's ear. "Owww! You sonofabitch!" The lead tore through skin and tissue and continued on. Ray used one hand to cover what remained of his ear. Blood seeped through his fingers. He watched as Sam fell back and lay still. Then he noticed two other men near the office building.

Larry closed the door and reached in his pocket. What Darla saw next made her blood turn to ice.

"Sorry, SUGAR. I'm afraid you know more than you should. My fault, I'm afraid. Never should have let this happen. Too late to go back." Larry flipped open the blade of a wicked-looking deer knife and approached Darla.

Darla stood and pointed the pearl handled pistol at Larry. "Stay away! I'm warning you!" Her voice cracked and the gun wavered in her hands. "I mean it. I'll shoot . . . I know how to use this!"

"Yeah, I noticed your skill with those cap guns back at the Stardust. Sorry, Darla, nice try." He took two more steps and waved the jagged blade back and forth in front of Darla's face.

"Don't, please . . ."

Larry made a sudden move.

Darla pulled the trigger . . . *click!*

Larry had drawn back, but then he laughed. "Guess I was right, eh, Sugar? What? No caps, either?"

Darla screamed at the top of her lungs, "NO! NO! DON'T MAKE ME! PLEASE!" She pulled the trigger once more. Again she heard nothing but a *click!*

Larry was in no hurry. He was enjoying Darla's moment of terror as he flashed the blade toward her exposed throat.

Darla could smell peppermint again. She closed her eyes and pulled the trigger one last time. *Boom!* The .38 bucked.

Larry stopped waving the knife, and the smile faded from his face. The knife slipped from his fingers. As if they were playing a deadly game of mumbly-peg, the knife fell between Darla's boots and stuck point down in the plank floor. It vibrated and stood erect. Larry looked down at his chest. First surprise, then disappointment showed on his unlined face. His khaki shirt turned crimson. The smell of gunpowder filled the room, overpowering the smell of peppermint.

Larry stumbled, grabbed the desk for support, looked at Darla and said, "I'll be damned . . ."

"Otto? Sam's been hit, I think. What'll we do?" Mac was terrified that his friend was dead.

Otto had just reached the office window and had leaned close to see what was going on inside. Just as he did he heard a gunshot from within. Darla stepped aside as Larry took the bullet in the chest. Otto watched the stranger sway then fall back across the desk.

"Oh my God in heaven!" Otto declared.

"What's the matter, Otto?"

"Girl in there just shot a guy!"

Mac joined Otto at the window in time to see Darla race from behind the desk toward the closed door.

Otto turned back to face the yard to see what happened to Sam. "He's moving, Mac. He's crawling around looking for something. Oh, no! That other guy's walking toward him with a gun. Go check on the girl, Mac."

The two men went in opposite directions.

Back in the truck, Herman thought he heard gunshots. Charlie certainly did, for just as Herman opened the door, the dog bolted. Herman fought an impulse to drive off.

Charlie knew that the sound of gunfire meant only one thing—bird hunting. Head high, nose into the wind, he ran to catch up with his master. The small dog bounded through the drifts and headed toward the distant buildings as fast as he could go. As he rounded the corner of the building he spotted a solitary figure firing a gun. He streaked toward what he thought was Mac.

Sam had been hit high in the shoulder. Momentarily stunned, he shook his head and found that he had been thrown onto his back. His gun was no longer in his hand. He raised up on his one good arm, settled on both knees and felt in the snow for his weapon as Ray stepped toward him.

Dale released the clutch for the second time. The ball fell just as before. He was certain of a direct hit this time. He followed the ball's descent, then caught sight of movement next to the van. He watched the door slide open. Someone rolled out onto the ground. The deadly ball landed with an earth-shaking *Wham!*

Again, the ball struck only the front one-third of the van. He thought he had the ball lined up perfectly but failed once more. Dale lost track of John. His focused on engaging the gears and raising the ball for a third time.

Once Ray saw Sam crawling around in the snow, apparently defenseless, he casually moved to finish him off. Blood streamed from his wounded ear, down his neck and inside his jacket. Angered and in pain, Ray raised the pistol and fired again.

Ray was certain he had hit his target. The man collapsed in the snow. He slowly walked over to the still form and raised his gun, aiming at Sam's head. He squeezed down on the trigger. At that exact instant, something slammed into his legs.

Ray fell and lay half buried in the heavy snow. His errant shot kicked up a puff of snow next to Sam's face.

Charlie's instinctive reaction to the sound of gunfire saved Sam's life. The dog barreled into Ray just as he pulled the trigger. After being cooped up in the truck for a number of hours, full of energy, he had run at full speed toward what he thought was his hunting companion. Because of the darkness, the snow, and the wind, Charlie erred. He ran into the wrong man. Ray collapsed like a bowling pin.

Sam was seriously wounded and unable to reach his weapon. He crawled toward the point where he thought his gun had landed, and once again began digging in the snow with his one good arm. Sam scrambled and pawed through the deep snow. Sam had no feeling in his fingers—they were numb, useless.

Ray had the wind knocked out of him when he struck the ground. He still didn't know what had happened, except that something had knocked him off his feet. He looked to see if he had again been shot. He didn't see any wounds so he stood up and staggered toward the van. He was disoriented and dizzy. His entire head hurt from the wound to his ear. He tried to brush the snow and blood from his face and eyes.

When Ray reached the van, he noticed the van door was open. John lay in the snow just outside. And then he froze!

Just inside the van was his black bag. The zipper was open. He quickly glanced at John, then back at the bag.

He had to get his money. Ray looked up. The iron ball neared its apex. He wiped his eyes, took one quick step toward the van, reached for the bag, and yelled at his brother. "No! Stop! Don't drop it!"

Dale was confused. He couldn't see clearly. The roar of the diesel engine muffled the sound of his brother's voice. Ray's plea fell on deaf ears. The ball was at the top of the crane.

Dale nodded his head, satisfied that Ray was signaling for him to drop the ball. "Got the sonofabitch all lined up this time, Ray!" Dale yelled. He glanced from his brother to the ball and eased off the clutch one last time.

John crawled away from the van. He heard more shots from somewhere on the other side of the van. At any moment he expected a bullet to slam into his body. He clawed and crawled through the heavy snow. When his tired body failed to move another inch, he turned over and looked back.

Just as he rolled over, something wet and warm tracked across his half-frozen face. He recognized Charlie. "Is that really you, boy?" John said.

Ray lunged for his bag just as Dale released the clutch. He fell against the step, leaned in, and grabbed the bag of money. He pulled back, stood up, and once again—for a second time—he was knocked off of his feet. Something hit him in the back with tremendous force.

Sam had found his gun. His fingers were numb, but he knew he could at least point and pull the trigger. He crawled after Ray. He had to get close. He would only get one shot. As he drew near, he could see another man lying in the snow. Charlie was next to him. He rose to one knee, aimed at Ray's back, and fired. The bullet drove between Ray's shoulder blades. Sam was certain he had not missed, but he would never know for sure. He immediately collapsed and lost consciousness.

Ray fell beneath the door. He lost his grip on the bag, which lay open on the floor above. His chest hurt. He rolled over and looked up. His face was covered with blood and snow, but he could see well enough to know that his brother had miscalculated again.

Dale thought he had everything lined up correctly. He was certain the deadly orb hung directly over the center of the van. Dale smiled with satisfaction. Ray would be pleased. He finally got it right! He released the clutch one final time and watched the mass of iron fall.

With great satisfaction, Dale tracked its descent with his good eye. The hunk of iron dropped and gathered speed.

Dale lowered his gaze and suddenly realized his mistake. There on the ground below was Ray, his face twisted in pain. His eyes bulged and his mouth opened in a scream, but Dale couldn't hear a thing. All he could do was watch.

Ray screamed and tried to kick his legs, but they never moved. He was paralyzed. His spinal cord had been severed by Sam's bullet. The ball seemed to take forever to reach the ground. Ray had enough time to curse and bemoan his fate. "You bastards!" he shouted.

Helpless to stop the ball's descent, Dale watched as it found its final resting-place squarely on top of his older brother. Ray's head and upper torso disappeared from view. The black bag was thrown to one side, and its contents vanished in the swirling snow.

Dale shut off the machine and sat in stunned silence. He opened the door and tumbled from the cab, his knees gone to jelly.

The concussion from the iron ball shook the ground. John pulled himself up and clung to Charlie. He stared at the scene before him. Charlie's presence reinforced his belief that he had to be still dreaming; there was absolutely no logical explanation for his presence, yet there he was, sitting by his side, licking his face.

Most of the white van was destroyed, mashed into a mangled mess. A huge iron ball, six or seven feet in diameter, lay in front of where he sat. Blood and gore seeped into the snow around the scarred, black ball. Two legs showed from beneath. The rest of Ray Steckel's body lay under tons of steel. A pistol and an empty black bag lay on the ground near the lifeless legs.

John glanced left and stared at the large track crane. Its engine stilled, like some great beast at rest after a feast. The cab door opened and another seemingly familiar face appeared. The man fell, got up and staggered toward the van. John watched with a sense of detachment.

Dale stopped and knelt next to the iron ball. He extended a hand and touched one of his brother's legs. His head was bowed as if in prayer. He didn't move—couldn't move for a long time. Slowly, he rose, picked up the pistol, turned, and faced John. He raised his arm, closed one eye, and pointed the gun directly at John's forehead.

Now I remember! I saw him at the salvage yard—the man driving the forklift! The man in the hospital! The man in my dreams!

308

Dale screamed, "You! You, bastard! You did this! It's all your fault! I'm gonna finish . . ." He pulled the trigger but never completed the sentence.

The gun fired. As the bullet left the barrel, the pistol was sent spinning from Dale's hand. He jerked. The bullet from Otto's 30-06 entered just behind his right ear and passed through his head. A hole the size of a hockey puck blew out Dale's already dead left eye. Brain matter, bone fragments, and blood flew from his face and mixed with the snow.

John was thrown back by the force of the slug. He was numb—beyond cold. Charlie whined and slowly licked his chilled, gray cheeks. The sounds of the dog seemed to be receding as if the dog had moved away. John was only aware of darkness, wind, and scattered flakes of snow that weaved down. Then there was nothing to see, nothing to hear. Not even his dreams held him aloft.

John was spent. He didn't even have time for one last prayer. Everything stopped, and he slipped away . . .

Otto lowered his rifle and walked toward the carnage beneath the crane. When he drew close he knew he was too late. He regretted not reacting sooner than he had. A man lay beneath the giant ball. He quickly recognized John's still form a few feet away. Sam lay motionless in the snow. He was face down a short distance from the van. Mac's dog lay with his head on John's chest. He whined softly.

The snow fell at a slower pace. Otto knelt beside John and felt for a pulse. He looked up, waiting, hoping. Unlike the first time he laid fingers along side John's neck, this time he felt nothing.

Mac had found Darla, safe—huddled in a corner of the front room. She was sobbing hysterically. He knelt, laid a gentle hand on her shoulder. "Are you okay? Are you hurt?"

Darla shrank from his touch. She raised her head and with a great sense of relief and looked into a friendly face. "Y-y-y-yes. I think so."

"Stay here. Don't move."

Mac ran to the back office, took one quick look at the crumpled man on the desk, and immediately surmised him to be dead. The wooden desk was covered with blood. The only sound he heard was a steady drip, drip of crimson liquid as it spattered to the floor.

Mac left the office and returned to the blonde on the floor. He was anxious to find out what was happening outside. "You'll be safe here, young lady. Stay quiet." He patted her sweatered shoulder and left.

Mac tore out of the shop. When he reached the yard in back, he shouted, "Otto! Otto! What about John? What about Sam?"

Otto had left John's still form and hurried over to Sam. When he reached the unconscious detective, he felt for a pulse. His color was good, and even though he was bleeding steadily from a wound in his shoulder, it didn't appear to be life threatening.

Mac skidded to a stop and knelt next to the rancher.

"How is he? How's John?"

"Sam looks like he'll make it," Otto said. He hesitated, not knowing how to tell his new friend about John.

Mac didn't wait to hear more. He ran as fast as he could through the snow to the crushed van. His heart pounded.

Charlie saw his master approaching and bounded forward. Mac stopped dead in his tracks. He stared in horror at the ball covering the torso of a man.

He fell to one knee next to the lifeless pair of legs. His head sank into his chest. He was afraid to investigate further. Charlie left his side and wandered away. Mac felt as if his heart would burst. He stood and called for Charlie. "Charlie! Here, boy!" He looked around and noticed his dog standing over yet another body half-buried in the snow. Charlie whined softly.

Mac rushed over. John's still form was covered with blood. He felt for a pulse, but he couldn't detect any sign of life.

310

John's head was turned to one side. Blood flowed from a deep wound on the side of his head. Mac felt sick. "John, I'm so sorry!" Mac mumbled. He pulled his son-in-law to a sitting position, wrapped his arms around his shoulders, and pulled his head close to his own. He wept for a long time.

Charlie came over and lay down next to both men. He rested his head on John's thigh

Herman left the truck and walked behind the building. He took in the scene before him and decided it was safe to approach. He quickly spotted the sprawled form of Sam with Otto hovering over him. He rushed to his side and knelt down. Sam's eyes were open, staring into the night sky. "Otto? Is he . . . ?"

"No. Badly wounded, but still alive. Same can't be said for the boy, though." Otto nodded over his shoulder toward the crane. The cop from Minneapolis was still alive, but he had lost a considerable amount of blood. Herman looked up and saw Mac near the van, huddled with another fallen man, probably his son-in-law. Herman rose and hurried over. As he drew closer, he see could see massive amounts of blood on the wounded man's face.

Herman knelt and laid a hand on Mac's shoulder. "Mr. Davis, is that your son-in-law?"

"Yes," he sobbed.

"How is he?" Herman asked.

"I don't know. Not good, I'm afraid."

Herman felt for a pulse. The wound on the side of John's head seemed serious. After a very long time, Herman felt he detected a very faint pulse. It was weak and erratic, but it indicated life. "He's still alive! We have to get these two to the hospital!"

Herman stood up. "I'll get the truck!"

"Check on the girl in the office on your way," Otto said.

"What girl?"

"Don't know. She shot some guy in your office, Herman. Go see how she is."

As Otto and Mac waited, one final, fierce blast of wind blew through the junkyard. It was the storm's last breath. It poured between the buildings and created a monstrous whirlwind. The swirl hesitated near the van, lifted and disappeared into the darkness.

Five souls were carried away that night along with the contents of Ray's bag full of money.

The wind died as quickly as it had appeared. There was no further sound except for John's labored breathing and Mac's sobbing. Otherwise, the yard was as still as a graveyard.

Once Herman returned, the three old men loaded John and Sam into the back, gathered Charlie, and prepared to leave.

"You better drive, Herman . . . don't feel too good," Otto mumbled. He was dizzy and experienced chest pain unlike any other before.

Herman slid into the driver's seat, and the Suburban drove away from the gory site through the deep snow.

Darla waited in front of the office. She climbed into her Laredo and followed the Suburban to the hospital.

Some of the money floated back to earth. A hundred dollar bill rested on Ray's lifeless leg for one brief moment, and then spiraled into the darkness. Over nine hundred thousand dollars disappeared that night.

The wind was dead. And so was the Steckel family.

❖ 22 ❖

MAC RAISED HIS SHOTGUN AND FIRED ONCE. He paused, lowered the double barrel, and looked directly into the late-afternoon sun. He was unsure whether he had hit his target.

Two figures away to his left turned at the sound of the shot. Each raised their weapons in response.

Directly in front of Mac, the tall grass parted. A wave formed and sculpted an opening that led directly to the spot where his quarry had dropped. Mac waited. The two figures in the distance never fired. He looked down once more and followed the movement of the tall grass as the wave returned. It was as if a long string had been extended and then reeled back.

Panting heavily, Charlie returned to his side and waited for his master's signal to drop the rooster. Mac let him enjoy his triumph for another few seconds and then gave him the command. "Drop!"

The dead pheasant fell quietly into Mac's outstretched hand. He stood and held the bird in the air proudly for the others to see, placed it in his jacket pocket, and knelt next to his dog. "Good boy, Charlie." He patted the dog on the head.

Otto strolled over to Mac and his retriever, his shotgun cradled in the crook of one arm. It was early October, unusually warm, with a slight breeze blowing from the west. This was the opening of the pheasant hunting season in South Dakota. Thousands of hunters from all over the United States converged on the prairie to partake in the annual fall ritual.

Otto had invited Mac and the others out to hunt as his guests at the ranch.

"Nice shot, Mac," Otto said, as he bent down to give Charlie a friendly pat. "You were sure right about old Charlie, here. He's a hell of a fine bird dog!"

"Thanks. This sure is wonderful bird country. All this prairie grass, corn, and sheltered areas are perfect habitat. Do you leave the corn standing for the birds or doesn't it matter when you cut it?"

"Little of both, I guess. Always figured it wouldn't hurt to leave some of it stand all winter. Normally, we don't cut the corn until we need it."

"You know, the last time I hunted this part if the country, we almost had to stand in line to get access to fields like this. This is a real treat!"

"Like I told you last night, Mac, we don't let many people hunt our land. I worry about the cattle and all. Should be lots more birds out here for you folks to hunt."

At that moment, the two figures in the distance drew near. A fifth member of their party soon joined the group.

"Mac? What the hell? Are you going to shoot all the birds or let the rest of us have a shot now and then?" Sam couldn't resist needling his friend.

"Hey! Charlie works for the guy that hits something—so he stays close to me! Besides, we might starve to death if we have to depend on you!"

"Was he always this way, Debbie?" Sam asked, turning to face the only female in the group.

"No! Just when it comes to bird hunting—too competitive I'm afraid." She smiled warmly at her father.

"If you and I are going to be in business together, you're going to have to learn something about sharing, Mac," Sam continued.

"Okay, if you're going to whine all afternoon, you get the next shot. I really only care about watching Charlie work, anyway." Mac was anxious to cover additional ground before the sun set.

"Debbie, you and John have to keep up with us if you ever want to do any shooting. If you'd quit holding hands and mooning at each other, you'd probably have more opportunities." Otto and Sam looked at each other and smiled.

John and Debbie couldn't seem to get enough of each other. The nightmare that occurred in February was still too fresh, too frightening. John's life had hung in the balance for three days. He was fortunate that the bullet had only carved a deep groove in the side of his skull rather than penetrate it. His memory of the night was distorted, but he was convinced that along with the three old men, Charlie probably had saved his life that night.

John had suffered a terrible amount of abuse during those two days in February, but with the splendid care provided by the hospital staff and his own strong will to live, he had survived. Unfortunately, he had to have three toes amputated—two on his left foot and one on his right. Once out of danger, he was transported to Minneapolis by helicopter, so he could be closer to Debbie and the girls.

The reunion at Methodist Hospital was joyous and tearful. For the next few weeks, Debbie was a constant presence. He spent many subsequent weeks undergoing painful physical therapy, and it was some time before he could return home. The bullet wound had caused a small amount of nerve damage to John's left side, and it would be many months before he regained full use of his limbs. He was finally able to get around with the use of a cane, and eventually returned to work.

The FBI visited John in June. They had a few remaining questions to ask and wanted to tie up a couple loose ends. John and Debbie sat with the agent in their living room.

"Did you have anything else taken from you besides those items you've already described?" The FBI investigator asked. He had with him a yellow envelope.

John was puzzled. "I don't think so. Why?"

The cop reached inside the envelope and pulled out a gold pocket watch. A short chain was attached. He held up the chain and the watch twisted as if in a silent breeze. "We took this from Ray Steckel's pants. We thought it might belong to you."

The reflected light from the afternoon sun struck the watch and flashed across John's face. He squinted. "No, I've never had a pocket . . ."

He paused and stared intently at the watch. "Wait a minute! Let me see that!" John held out his hand. As the watch dropped into John's palm, he felt its weight along with years of guilt and doubt pressing into his skin. The gold felt warm—comforting. He turned it over. On the back were the initials, WSR—Twenty Years.

John couldn't speak. He stared at the watch, then slowly closed his fingers around it. His eyes blurred and tears ran down his face.

Debbie touched his arm. "John? What is it?"

After a moment, John cleared his throat, turned, and faced his wife. "This was my father's, Deb. I remember the night he came home with it—shortly before he disappeared. He was so proud."

Everything made sense then. John's father had drawn him to French Creek—to set the record straight, John came to believe. The Anson's Dairy truck had to have been his father's truck—the new one from Swanson's. He had not abandoned his family as so many had surmised. Like so many others that followed, he was an innocent victim of the evil that permeated French Creek. After thirty years, Walter Rule's good name was restored.

"My dad reached out for me that night, Deb. He drew me to the only truck that would provide a safe refuge from those dogs— his milk truck."

Together, the FBI and John pieced together the path the watch must have followed from John's father.

"That's unbelievable!" Debbie said.

"I know." John cradled the watch and slipped it gently into his pocket.

John returned to the salvage yard one last time that summer. It was a warm day and the sun shone brightly against a pale blue sky. He walked behind the office and up the long road to the rear of the property. He crested the last hill and stopped. He stood and stared at the milk truck.

"I knew it! It was Dad's truck." The letters on the side of the truck were all visible: SWANSON'S DAIRY.

He stepped closer and leaned against the side. The warmth of the metal on his shoulder and arm felt good—comforting. He had come full circle. He now knew where to find his father's headstone.

He turned around, put both hands over the large letters, and leaned his head against the flaked metal "Thanks, Dad!" Tears flowed down his face and disappeared beneath the collar of his blue shirt. Finally he turned away and walked back down the hill.

A dust devil appeared briefly, hesitated as it danced in front of him, then swept past and vanished over the hill.

He never noticed the cracked steering wheel tucked in the weeds.

Sam Reasons's wound was serious, but fortunately, the bullet passed through his shoulder without touching a vital organ. His shoulder blade had been hit, and required multiple operations to rebuild. By the time the October pheasant-hunting trip came around, Sam could get around with ease, and his shoulder was getting stronger each day. While John walked with a limp, Sam could move easily across the fields following Charlie and Mac.

They all spent three wonderful days together that October. Otto and Betty were gracious hosts and seemed genuinely happy to have their company. They hunted fields all over the ranch property, but carefully avoided the area on the east near the Clearwater quarry.

John still suffered recurring nightmares about the events of those two days, but time would put the events behind him. For now he depended on Debbie to get him through his bad dreams. He was happy to be alive.

The FBI ultimately relinquished all claims on Ray's $900,000. Notice was given to the local residents that any money found was the rightful property of the United States Government, but little was ever actually turned in. The FBI recovered $1,970. The bag reportedly contained almost one million dollars in fifty and one-hundred dollar bills.

Christmas came twice to Milbank in 1993. Residents of the area awoke the morning after the storm to find money scattered all over their yards, streets, and fields. Individuals and family groups spent the balance of the winter and spring mobilized for real-life treasure hunts. Sooner of later, almost every able-bodied citizen of Milbank would find one or two bills that had been carried aloft by the storm that night. The pastor of the Congregational Church of Milbank pocketed $350. He rationalized that it was "a gift from the Lord."

Much of the money drifted east of the city and was deposited across the prairie between Milbank and Big Stone Lake. The events of that bloody February night proved to be a boon to the local economy in more ways than one. The following spring and summer, every motel in town was booked solid with visitors from all over the area. Fortune hunters arrived from as far away as Rapid City, Minneapolis, and Omaha, drawn to the sleepy town by stories of money that blew across the plains.

Hundreds and hundreds of tourists spent the summer combing the tall grasslands around Milbank. Local pig farmers that lived in the newly enriched area discovered unexpected windfalls of their own that spring. Scattered among the muddy, stinky feedlots, much of Ray's money drifted down and settled into the foul pig sties. Greenbacks were trampled into the slimy crap by the fattening swine. Some of it undoubtedly was eaten by the pigs. Quite a few fortunate farmers eventually recovered a good deal of it.

No one knew how much of the money was eventually recovered. Some said that maybe half of it was never found. It was believed to be buried in the grass, slowly deteriorating, and probably lost forever.

It was a gorgeous fall day. The colors on the prairie were a striking contrast to what little John remembered from the previous winter. He was not too concerned about shooting pheasants but was content to be with Debbie and the three men who had worked so hard to save his life.

The hunting party drifted apart once more. This time, Sam stayed close to Mac; hoping for a shot at the next bird.

John and Debbie hiked off by themselves, scarcely paying attention to the birds rising in front of them. Instead, they were content to watch Mac and Sam attempt to reward Charlie by bringing down the cackling roosters. They watched as both men fired at the same time. The colorful rooster fell and Charlie ran to retrieve it. Smiling, they could hear the two older men arguing about who actually had downed the bird.

Otto walked with his guests, occasionally firing at escaping birds, but for the most part, he was content, enjoying the day. He felt good about his life and about his new friends, and he relished the opportunity to share his love of the land with people he cared about. The new relationship certainly made his life more interesting.

As the playful arguing continued, John led Debbie over a hill, out of sight of the others. They sat down among the tall switch grass. John turned to his wife, looking at her with a familiar glimmer in his eye. She knew what that look meant. She returned his look with a playful one of her own. "John, we can't!"

He leaned over to kiss her. His hand reached inside her jacket. They kissed just as they had the first time they'd met, and lay down in the tall grass. John unbuttoned her flannel shirt. As he slipped his hand inside they were joined by a third party.

"Charlie!" John and Debbie exclaimed.

Fast on the scent of a rooster, the small dog had stumbled across them and decided to join their fun. Laughing, they hurriedly buttoned their clothing while Charlie tried to lick their faces. Then he began again to look for the pheasant. The magic was temporarily lost, but not forgotten. Later that night they would rekindle that moment interrupted in the tall grass in the privacy of Otto's guest room.

John and Debbie returned to the ranch house alone. Mac, Sam and Otto still had more ground to cover before calling it quits for the day. John parked the Jeep near the sidewalk, got out, and stood for a moment admiring the golden colors of the setting October sun.

After a bit, they turned and headed up the walk, hand in hand. Halfway to the house, John looked down and stopped. He tugged on her arm, pulling her back to him.

"Look!" He said, pointing down. The sidewalk was of uncertain age, and full of cracks of varying widths and depth. John planted both of his feet squarely on top of one of the widest. He gazed at the tops of his dusty, brown boots and smiled.

Debbie looked up at her husband, quizzically. "John? What's wrong?"

John didn't answer her immediately. Instead, he stared at the sidewalk. Finally he straightened up, dug in his pocket, and pulled out his pocket watch. He turned it over and studied the inscription.

Satisfied, he smiled. "Nothing . . . it's okay. Really, Deb. Everything is going to be okay."

He led her up the porch steps. He was no longer afraid.

❖ Epilogue ❖

MAC DECIDED TO GIVE UP HIS PRACTICE THAT SUMMER. Sam Reasons opted for an early out from the force after three months' convalescent leave. The two retirees spent a great deal of time together and both soon realized they needed something more to do. During one of their many conversations they decided to go into business together. They formed a partnership, Davis/Reasons Incorporated, an investigative service. Their first case was a kidnapping that kept them busy for two months.

Herman Fogelman confessed to the police about his involvement with Ray Steckel. Because of his cooperation, his sentence was reduced to six months and then suspended with three years probation. He regained his business and continued living in Milbank with his wife and son. Herman became a deacon in his church and ultimately ran for a vacant seat on the city council. The $50,000 Ray gave him was never reported, and Herman opened a living trust account for Barry. The money would grow substantially over the years. Barry's future care would always be assured.

Chief Karnowski assisted the FBI in arresting Jimbo and Willy at the Super Eight Motel. They surrendered the following day without a fight. The *Milbank Plains Dealer* published a photo the following day of the smiling chief bringing the two criminals out of the motel.

Darla LeMay married one of her striped whistlers. She had a fabulous June wedding that cost her new husband thousands of dollars, but Leon Clearwater could afford it. He was a rich, elderly widower twice her age. Formerly a cattle rancher, Leon had decided to mine his land of the rich vein of granite that lay beneath. He built Darla a 6,000-square-foot home near the quarry. She developed expensive tastes, did much of her shopping in town, and drove a candy-apple red Cadillac convertible. She and Leon wintered in Palm Springs and have become good friends with their neighbors, Otto and Betty Stubblefield. Darla gave her cap pistols away.

Karl Butts was fired by Chief Karnowski for "conduct unbecoming a city employee." He had been observed exposing himself to a participant in the Amateur Night Contest at the Stardust. The young woman reminded him of a younger, larger version of the lovely Darla. The chief kept the whole affair quiet. He assured the owners of the Stardust that their liquor license would be renewed for the next two years without opposition. Karl is currently a security guard at a rendering plant outside of Sioux Falls.

What the Steckels accomplished during all those years without detection was stunning. Their cunning and evil, along with their ability to operate in complete anonymity, shocked the community and the state. Police officials and legislators argued for months about how such a thing could happen. For the present, however, the gang had been brought to justice, and dozens of missing person files closed. The surviving families were not consoled. However, they finally knew what had happened to their loved ones.

Otto and Betty Stubblefield continued to work their ranch. Otto did return to Doc Wilson for that check up and was found to have blocked arteries. Successful bypass surgery gave him a new lease on life. Their new friends from the city would annually visit them during the fall for a few days of pheasant hunting. In turn, whenever Betty felt the need to visit the Mall of America in Minneapolis, they were welcome guests of Mac and Charlie. Over the ensuing years, the Stubblefields grew very close to Mac, Sam, John, Debbie, and the two girls.

Otto never participated in any of the fortune hunting that spring. It just wasn't important to him. Betty did find a hundred-dollar bill in her vegetable garden one day in May, but other than picking up a few more stray bills that turned up on their own, they left the treasure hunting to others.

The French Creek Salvage Yard never re-opened. Its acres of rusted hulks still sit as they have for fifty years. Now the only activity on the property is that provided by woodchucks, raccoons, gophers, and field mice. The wind blows through the deserted grounds and creates disconcerting sounds, as if each broken-down vehicle were a rusted wind instrument. Many local residents believe the property is full of ghosts and has been ever since the day Art Steckel murdered old Morris.

The cracked steering wheel remains where John dropped it, surrounded by thistle, shoots of wild grape, and spindly willow. It remains mute testimony to the events that took place that cold night in February.

The Swanson's Dairy truck is still the tallest, least decayed truck in the entire yard. It sits where it always has—on top of the hill.